EUGENESIS

INCEPTION

PENNSYLVANIA, USA

EUGENESIS

INCEPTION

AJ HOOKS

To my beautiful and loving wife, Annabelle—

Thank you for being the best friend, partner, and companion that one could possibly imagine having for this improbable adventure called life.

Acknowledgments

This novel, as is no doubt the case for most novels, would not have reached final form without the input from which the author has benefited. If you enjoy this book—as I truly hope you do—then it is because the generous and genuinely helpful contributions of several people helped to elevate both the story and its telling. I would like to express my profound thanks in particular to:

Annabelle Hooks, for her helpful and insightful feedback, suggestions, and unwavering encouragement from the very beginning to the very end of writing this book;

Mike Goodkind, whose many years of experience as a writer and editor helped to considerably sharpen plot, prose, and voice in early drafts;

Cindy Larson, whose impressive 'reader's ear' and intuition challenged me to improve character development, believability, and the emotional content of the story;

Professor Ian Hancock (OBE), a world-renowned expert on Romani culture and languages, who kindly reviewed the novel and provided very helpful editorial input to ensure accuracy and authenticity;

The World Roma Federation, including Janos Sztojka and Deny Dobobrov, who similarly reviewed the novel from a cultural perspective and provided very good suggestions to ensure sensitivity and authenticity;

Kira Goodkind, Brigitte Sobry-Chognot, Kurt Ferstl, Tom Carlson, and Dave Clifford, who generously contributed their time to review revised drafts and who all provided helpful feedback that made it's way into this final version.

Finally, I would like to express my immense gratitude to Wild Ink Publishing's Founder/Creative Director Abigail Wild and Lead Editor Laura Wackwitz (Ph.D.) for bringing this novel into their portfolio and bringing their impressive experience to bear in helping to mold and polish it into its final form.

PART I:

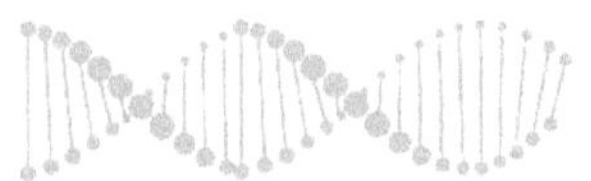

AWAKENING

We are as clouds that veil the midnight moon;

How restlessly they speed, and gleam, and quiver,

Streaking the darkness radiantly!—yet soon

Night closes round, and they are lost for ever:

Or like forgotten lyres, whose dissonant strings

Give various response to each varying blast,

To whose frail frame no second motion brings

One mood or modulation like the last.

We rest.—A dream has power to poison sleep;

We rise.—One wandering thought pollutes the day;

We feel, conceive or reason, laugh or weep;

Embrace fond woe, or cast our cares away:

It is the same!—For, be it joy or sorrow,

The path of its departure still is free:

Man's yesterday may ne'er be like his morrow;

Nought may endure but Mutability.

    —Mutability (Percy Bysshe Shelley)

Chapter 1: April in Paris

Maria stood silently gazing out the window of her small flat on the Rue de la Chaise that Sunday afternoon, alone and nursing a steaming cup of tea with both hands as she watched the rain send the pedestrians below scurrying for cover. Feeling vaguely anxious, she pulled in a deep, deliberate breath and exhaled slowly, coaxing a reluctant calm into her thoughts. She took a tentative sip of tea, then another. Her attention shifted. She studied her diffused reflection in the rain-streaked window, then turned abruptly to walk toward the kitchen, as if to break a spell. The rain continued its muffled patter.

At 5:00 p.m. the phone finally rang. Maria waited until the third ring to pick up. "Hello? Dr. Mendez?"

"Yes. Hello, Maria. Good afternoon. I hope you are well and resting." His deep and unusually accented voice was, as always, warm yet formal.

"Thank you, yes. I'm just having a cup of tea. I hope you're not still stuck in the lab. It's getting late, and the rain is getting heavier. Can I call a taxi for you?"

"No, that won't be necessary. I just finished up, and a car is on the way for me now. But thank you for the offer." The formality in his voice receded slightly. "By the way, Maria, we'll eventually have to agree a date by which you can start calling me Carlos," he said teasingly, as if an uncle to his niece.

"I'll check my calendar Doctor," she replied, knowing he would be amused by the gentle riposte.

"Yes, I'm sure you will." He laughed, knowing she wouldn't. "Well then, let me come to the point. Everything went well again with this retrieval cycle. I was able to confirm that it was a good Metaphase II-stage oocyte suitable for vitrification, and the freezing process has been successful, with no ice crystal formation. So, Dr. Guevara, one more usable egg added to the pool."

"That's wonderful news! Thank you so much. You've been so kind to help me."

"Yes, well… I suppose you were going to carry on with this project of yours one way or another, so we might as well make sure it's done right. Have a lovely evening, Maria, and make sure to get some rest."

"I will. Good evening, Dr. Mendez… I'll see you tomorrow," she said, feeling relieved as she hung up to have escaped the polite tedium of more small talk.

Maria took another sip of her chamomile and honey tea—it always seemed to help with the cramps that followed the retrieval process—and looked at her watch. It was only 5:15 p.m., but it had been a long day. Instead of just the small *merienda* she would normally have around this time, she decided to have an early dinner and try to get to sleep early. Luckily, there were still some leftovers from a dish she had made the previous day. It was *Bacalao a la Vizcaina*—a traditional Basque dish of salted cod fillets and a sauce of red onions, garlic, and a Choricero pepper purée. "A little taste of home should help," she whispered to herself as she spooned the contents into a pan on the stove to warm it up. It was delicious, and she slept deeply that night.

Monday morning was crisp and clear. It was April in Paris, one of those mornings that writers and artists and lovers tend to go on about because they are magical and yet somehow real—a cliché only to those who have never actually experienced one. Maria walked the short distance from her flat to the Sèvres–Babylon Metro Station, which was tucked neatly underneath the Square Boucicaut—a quaint little park with a playground and a carousel with fanciful little neon orange, pink, and yellow cars and trucks for children to ride. She loved living in this neighborhood, even though she could barely afford it. The St-Thomas-d'Aquin quarter of the 7th arrondissment is conveniently situated in the heart of Paris and includes within its boundaries the Musée d'Orsay, with its magnificent collection of Impressionist art and the Hôtel Matignon, the official residence and gardens of the French Prime Minister. It was however the picture-postcard St-Germain quarter, a 10-minute walk to the east in the 6th arrondissment, that she loved the most. St-Germain is the quintessential Paris, packed with charming cafes, chic boutiques, beautiful gardens and squares, fashionable hotels, and even more fashionable people to watch. Ultimately, it was Maria's practical nature that had helped her to finalize (or perhaps rationalize) the decision to take the little flat on the Rue de la Chaise—her door-to-door commute to work never took more than twenty minutes unless the trains were running late.

On this morning, as usual, it had taken Maria only a few minutes to walk from her flat to the Sèvres–Babylone station, her link to Paris' sprawling underground subway system. After an uneventful ride past four stops on Line 12 and exiting the Metro at Pasteur Station, she made her usual stop at the Carisa Paris bakery for a cappuccino and a croissant to go. The campus of the Pasteur Institute was then only a final five-minute walk around the corner from the bakery, and her cappuccino and croissant were, as usual, still warm as she whisked through the gate, looking forward to another day.

Dr. Maria Guevara's initial academic interest had not been in genetic engineering. Her parents, like many parents, had wanted her to be a medical doctor. But during her undergraduate studies at the University of Alicante she had attended a seminar on Genetic Physiology led by the acclaimed microbiologist Professor Francisco Mojica. In the 1990s, Professor Mojica had discovered and later given a name—CRISPR[1]—to the genetic mechanics underlying the revolutionary gene-editing 'tool' (CRISPR-Cas9) that would later be developed by Emmanuelle Charpentier and Jennifer Doudna, winning them a Nobel Prize in 2020. Maria's imagination had been electrified by the implications of the work of this modest and avuncular Professor—the ability to edit genes, the underlying building blocks and blueprint of life itself.

In retrospect, Maria felt that her path in life had followed something of a straight line from that moment in Alicante to her life now in Paris. Another person might have called it fate or destiny, but not Maria—she had long ago decided that she was the one controlling her life and her choices, not some vague supernatural force. After attending Professor Mojica's seminar, Maria changed her undergraduate focus from general biology to microbiology and, after some sustained cajoling, convinced

---

[1] CRISPR – Clustered Regularly Interspaced Short Palindromic Repeats

the professor to be her informal mentor. Mojica was in turn impressed by her work ethic and deep curiosity and eventually took on the responsibility of being her doctoral advisor as she pursued a PhD in Experimental and Applied Biology. Her dissertation on Synthetic Biology had been brilliant and had made it easy for him to then recommend her for a postdoctoral fellowship at the ICGEB (International Centre for Genetic Engineering and Biotechnology) in Trieste, Italy. After three intense years there mostly supporting the research of a senior scientist and doing some teaching on the side, Maria finally landed a position that she had hoped for since her time with Professor Mojica in Alicante—working as a Research Associate at the prestigious Pasteur Institute in Paris. The Institute had been recognized for its world-leading research in biology, diseases, and vaccines since its founding by Louis Pasteur in 1887. The fact that it was where one of her role models—the Nobel laureate Emmanuelle Charpentier—had also done postdoctoral work added a flourish to the sense of achievement she felt when she finally received the news that her application had been accepted. She had arrived.

Maria made her way across the short distance from the campus gate to the lobby of the Institute's sleek François Jacob Center building, swiped her ID badge to enter the elevator, and finally entered her work space on the fourth floor—home to the Synthetic Biology Group of the Institute's Department of Microbiology. After hanging up her overcoat and exchanging morning pleasantries with some of the lab staff, she sat down and took a sip of her cappuccino, powered up her computer, and began nibbling on her croissant. She was not a vain woman, but she was nevertheless conscious of her appearance in a professional setting, and so took the opportunity to briefly check her reflection in the computer screen while she waited to get connected to the network and check her email. Her dark hair was pulled tightly back and woven neatly into a single braid that fell just below her shoulders, and she wore a little makeup to smooth her complexion a bit and add a hint of color to her lips and eyes. Her clothes were what she had come to refer to as her 'work uniform'—pleated trousers with low-heel shoes and a simple but chic blouse. She anyway spent most of the day wearing a lab coat, so there was no point in agonizing over a work wardrobe, except to ensure her clothes were comfortable and just stylish enough to blend in when she had to join her colleagues for the occasional but unavoidable 'team lunch' or evening drinks. Everything was in order—her appearance reflected the practical, professional persona she had carefully cultivated since leaving home for university.

Now fully synchronized to the network, Maria began working through her inbox of emails as she finished off her croissant. Most could be deleted or dispatched with a quick reply and not much thinking required, but one instantly stood out when she saw the subject line.

Private—FSO Inquiry
Chère Dr. Guevara,
Bonjour—this is Remy from the Facilities Security Office (FSO). I am writing to arrange an appointment with you to check in on your facilities access arrangements, as we noticed from your badge access records that you have occasionally needed to come into the Institute on weekends or after hours. Please let me know a day and time that would be convenient for us to meet. Cordialement, Remy Boucher

She stared at the screen for a moment, casually glanced behind her to ensure nobody was looking in her direction, and then slowly and deliberately read the message several times over again before replying.

RE: Private—FSO Inquiry
Good Morning Remy,
I am a little busy this week and will be working from home Friday on a symposium paper. Next Monday around 11am would be a good time.
Thank You,
Maria

A corresponding network calendar invitation arrived in Maria's inbox a minute later, which she accepted. She then leaned back in her chair, closed her eyes, and tried to gather her thoughts for what seemed like only a few moments. When she opened her eyes again though, she was startled by the reflected image of Dr. Carlos Mendez on her computer screen, standing behind her. She swiveled her chair around and stood up, pointing to the screen, and whispered "Did they contact you as well?" She had switched to Spanish—a mother tongue to both of them.

"Good morning, Maria. Yes, I received a similar email from them. Perhaps we should find someplace quiet to talk?" Mendez had also switched to Spanish, and his voice was low and calming, clearly deliberately so. But his gray eyes, flat and expressionless, remained focused on the computer screen. Maria assumed this was just another manifestation of his default formal demeanor and simply nodded in agreement.

They walked to a small conference room on the other side of the lab area, closed the door, and sat across from each other with notepads in front of them and pens in hand. It looked like a normal meeting. After a brief silence, Maria spoke first. "How much do you think they know?"

"I don't know, Maria. Have you mentioned anything to anyone?"

"No, absolutely not."

Mendez sat quietly, looking intently at her, and then leaned slightly forward, clasping his hands in front of him. "Good. First, I'm afraid we'll need to put our little project on hold for now."

"Of course."

"Next, we'll need to align our stories before talking to the security people. Any ideas?"

Maria paused for a while, staring at her blank notepad and then finally responded, "I'm sorry… I'm afraid I can't think of anything right at this moment. Maybe we can each try to come up with some ideas over the next few days and then compare notes to finalize something? I'm working from home on Friday on a paper for an upcoming symposium—we can talk then."

"Okay, yes… *buena idea*. Let's do that, Maria. In the meantime, we should make things appear normal. I understand some of the postdocs and associates in the department are going out to some kind of jazz club on Thursday evening to celebrate someone's birthday? It might be good if you join them, for appearances sake."

"Yes, it's for Gerard Durand's birthday. Will you be joining as well?"

Mendez smiled broadly and stood up, signaling that the meeting was coming to an end. "My dear Maria, I would love to, but I really don't want to be that sad lone *viejo* clumsily trying to socialize with a group of people half his age. It would anyway be quite out of character for me. We can talk on Friday."

Maria laughed and walked with him to the elevator.

≈

Maria had met Mendez not long after beginning work at the Pasteur Institute. He was a research physician at the Pasteur Institute Medical Center, where he specialized in infectious and tropical diseases, and she had come into his clinic for a check-up and to see if she needed to update her vaccinations ahead of a technical conference that she was attending at the Pasteur Institute branch in Ho Chi Minh City. Established in 1891, it was the first of the Institute's global network of branches and affiliates located outside of France, and Maria was especially looking forward to seeing the clinical and research work being conducted there on malaria.

Their friendship had developed quickly, given their common mother tongue, love of good food, and what turned out to be a shared deep interest in genetics. She had been surprised and a little flattered by his enthusiastic interest in her Basque heritage and culture, but also relieved when it became clear that she was not going to have to deflect any awkward romantic overtures from this older man. She was in turn endlessly entertained by his stories of growing up, studying, and working in Argentina and Brazil. He would occasionally ask her why such an eligible and attractive young woman was not yet married and planning a family, or at least actively screening suitors, and she would deflect with her usual story about being too busy and focused on her work. But as their friendship grew, she felt comfortable sharing more.

Maria did indeed want to be a mother… eventually. It was just that she wasn't sure when or if she would find the right partner. Most men her age either bored her, were intimidated by her, or both. And the suitable older ones were mostly already married and just looking for an occasional tryst. Maria had confided to Mendez that she desperately wanted to start freezing her eggs to ensure she would have a chance to have a healthy child. She had mixed feelings about it initially, given her traditional upbringing, but her independent nature had ultimately driven her to the decision. The only thing holding her back now was that she couldn't quite afford one of the private fertility clinics in Paris. Mendez had listened, sympathetically, and without judgement. It was only when she mentioned that she was planning to try to get help at one of the Public Assistance Hospitals in Paris that he had interrupted.

"I'm not sure that is the best option. Let me help you, Maria."

"Dr. Mendez, I wouldn't feel comfortable taking money from you. I'm not sure when I would be able to pay it back."

"That's not what I meant, Maria," he had said, his voice quieted and suggestive.

Maria had been perplexed by his response. "I'm afraid I don't understand," she had said, her eyes searching his.

"The resources and equipment at the Institute's medical center are substantial and first-rate, and given the work that I am doing, I essentially have unrestricted access. The inventory management systems that are in place for non-hazardous substances and equipment are anyway not terribly sophisticated. I can manage them. Let me help you, Maria," he had said again, "to make sure things are done right." And then she understood, and they began.

A few months before the first retrieval of her eggs, they had concocted a cover story, whereby Maria would become a familiar face at his clinic by coming regularly to 'help Dr. Mendez with analysis and management of his research samples because some of the data would also be useful for her research.' They would often deliberately stay into the evening and come in on weekends to establish a visible pattern. The egg retrieval process itself took no more than 30 minutes but needed to be done in Mendez's clinic, as it required a light intravenous sedation. Maria's quiet but increasingly ubiquitous presence around Mendez had the desired paradoxical effect over time—rendering her unremarkable and essentially invisible to the other clinic staff.

Maria knew that setting up a treatment protocol and getting hold of the requisite fertility medications would not be difficult for Mendez. But she had been genuinely surprised when he was able to so quickly secure (from an outside source, in order to avoid using equipment registered in the Institute's inventory) the exact type of liquid nitrogen chamber that would be needed for freezing and storing the retrieved eggs. He had mentioned only something about an old friend in Argentina who specialized in fertility treatment, and who had helped him 'make arrangements' through a German scientific and medical equipment supplier. The chamber had fit neatly into a utility closet in his office, which, conveniently, he could lock whenever he was away. And so, over time, a collection of Dr. Maria Guevara's eggs was accumulated in Dr. Carlos Mendez's office closet, frozen to -196 degrees Celsius in a bath of liquid nitrogen.

The headlining jazz quartet was in top form on Thursday evening. The piano, double bass, and drum players were all exceptional, but it was the trumpet player that teased and ravished and transported the audience. They had to be good of course—this was Le Bal Blomet after all, among the oldest jazz clubs in Europe. In its early years, Le Bal Blomet had been graced by the likes of Joséphine Baker, Maurice Chevalier, Simone de Beauvoir, F. Scott Fitzgerald, Jean-Paul Sartre, and Ernest Hemingway. The interior had been through an extensive four-year renovation and reopened in 2017, and tonight—more than a decade later—Dr. Maria Guevara joined the long list of patrons that now spanned more than a hundred years, all the way back to 1924.

The group from the Institute had pushed together several tables in order to sit together and were already well into their wine and hors d'oeuvres when Maria arrived. She recognized Gerard Durand—the young postdoc in their department being feted for his birthday—seated in the middle of the table with his glass raised as he received a round of toasts just as she approached the group. They all smiled and waved as she took a seat. The waiter worked his way over to pour her a glass of wine, while the trumpet player poured out a homage to Chet Baker's aching version of 'Almost Blue' that seemed to somehow suspend time and collapse the space in the room.

A few minutes later, a familiar woman appeared and pulled up a chair next to Maria. She was a compact but vivacious presence and looked around smiling warmly to everyone at the table. Without missing a beat she sat down with emphasis, a drink in hand and still flashing a cheerful smile. "I'm so glad you came, Maria!" It was Brigitte, a departmental colleague of Maria's who had also become something of a friend.

"Hi Brigitte… me too. Anyway, I think I needed a night out after all the extra work I've been doing on my research paper. And I was hoping you'd be here so I would have someone to talk to."

"Is that the project that you mentioned Dr. Mendez at the Medical Center is helping you with? He's something of a legend in his field I heard—what's it like to work with him?"

"Well, he's sort of acting as an advisor and a sounding board, but it's kind of unofficial, if you know what I mean."

"Sure, sure, I understand," Brigitte replied, nodding emphatically and putting her finger to her lips.

"Anyway, he's nice, but very formal," Maria continued. "I guess it's a generational thing. It sometimes feels like I'm back in graduate school, and he's my professor. But he's been very helpful, which I appreciate, and it's kind of nice to have someone to speak Spanish with once in a while."

"I know how you feel. I once had a brief assignment at the Pasteur Institute facility in Korea… It was such a fascinating place, but there were times I just really wanted to go out and spend an evening speaking French with someone. Speaking of going out, are you still seeing that *beau gosse* banker?"

Maria laughed and shook her head, "You mean Éric? No. That was months ago. He was indeed good looking—even more so with his clothes off," she added, *sotto voce*. "But he was absolutely self-absorbed… including in bed. I think he was just too used to women pursuing him. And I like someone who can make me laugh and sometimes make me look at things differently. With Éric, once you got over the initial hypnosis from his looks, he just turned out to be kind of boring and… *bourgeois*. Is that the right word?"

Brigitte almost snorted with laughter as she lifted her glass for comic effect.

"Status chasers… the corporate simulacrums of manhood. Yes. Oh, I've definitely met that type before."

"So, are you seeing anyone, Brigitte?"

"Well, I met this lovely young Italian man from Sicily. He plays classical cello and got selected for some kind of orchestra exchange program in Paris. But he's very intense and sometimes emotional, which is fine in small doses… maybe on the weekends, but I don't think he's long-term relationship material." They both giggled a bit and then Brigitte continued, "Tell me, Maria, are you still enjoying living in Paris?"

"Yes, it feels so open and free here. I mean, I love my parents of course… my father actually influenced me in a lot of ways, like introducing me to jazz with his record collection and taking me to see different places in Europe. And sometimes I do miss the familiarity of the traditions I grew up around, but I also felt a little confined by them and having to pay lip-service to what felt to me like old superstitions, like worrying about which things might be ritually 'unclean.' Here I can just be who I want to be and focus on my work—does that make sense?"

"Completely. I grew up with cows in the farm country in the northeast. My parents were good people, but very old-fashioned. I couldn't wait to get out and come to Paris before I ended up milking cows and making babies for the rest of my life. I guess maybe that's why we seem to understand each other. I do miss the fresh food from the local farms though."

"By the way, Brigitte, let me know if your Italian 'acquaintance' has any eligible friends. I'm starting to feel like a spinster, eating at home alone every night and going to cafes by myself."

Brigitte laughed and replied, "Will do. What's your type anyway?"

"Funny, intelligent, maybe a little mysterious—"

"*And?*" Brigitte interrupted.

"Well, tall, dark and handsome of course. And with strong, capable hands… like the bass player up there," Maria replied, throwing a mischievous glance towards the stage. Brigitte turned to the stage and then looked back grinning and nodding emphatically, and then they toasted one another and emptied their glasses.

By 11:00 p.m., the wine and music and laughter with colleagues had dissipated Maria's anxiety about the inquiry from the Institute's security office enough that she was willing to try and dance to a swing number with Gerard, who was suddenly intent on doing some dancing on his birthday, no doubt fueled by the absinthe he had been dared into drinking. They were both enthusiastic, if a bit clumsy, on the dance floor and so were regaled with raucous cheers from the now well-lubricated audience as they zig-zagged back through the crowd to their table, where their colleagues all shouted "Bravo!"—clearly entertained by the spectacle of two young scientists trying to swing dance.

Just as Maria was sitting down, the waiter appeared again and moved to refill her wine glass. "Thank you," she said reflexively, barely acknowledging his presence.

"You're welcome, mademoiselle," he said as he turned to walk away.

Maria smiled, amused by his use of the old-fashioned title for an unmarried woman, and watched as his tall, blonde figure disappeared back into the back of the club. "He clearly is not from Paris," she thought to herself as she took the glass and offered another toast to Gerard before taking a drink.

≈

Maria finally woke late Friday morning; it was dark outside. She fumbled around in her bathroom cabinet for some aspirin and splashed cold water on her face. She was glad she had decided to work from home. After freshening up, the need for a strong coffee was the first thing that came to her mind, so she headed into the kitchen. But before she made it to the espresso machine on the far counter, she noticed there was one of those yellow sticky notes on the kitchen table with writing on it.

Bonjour Maria,

I hope you're feeling better this morning. You may not remember everything from last night, but I had to bring you home. I think you maybe had a little too much to drink, so I wanted to make sure you got back safely. Call me if you need anything. Don't worry, everything turned out ok—it was such a fun night!
Prends Soin,
Brigitte

Maria suddenly realized she couldn't remember anything about the previous night beyond returning to her table after dancing. It seemed a little odd to her, as she didn't think she had been drinking that heavily, but Brigitte's note was reassuring so she shrugged her shoulders and started the coffee machine. She then tapped out a brief text message to Brigitte to thank her and let her know she was doing fine.

She was looking forward now to spending some time editing her symposium paper—it was just the distraction she needed. When her coffee had finished brewing, she poured out a cup, sat down at the little dining table adjacent to her kitchen, and powered up her laptop. She knew the title of her paper—'Experimental Protocols for Field-Testing Heritable Genome Editing for Control of Insect-Borne Diseases'—

might raise a few eyebrows, even though to her it seemed just the usual anodyne way scientists tended to write when publishing results or theories for peer review. Heritable genome editing meant permanently altering the genome of an organism in a way that would carry the changes through to its offspring and future generations. Some viewed it as an exciting frontier of genetic engineering, with the promise of eradicating (or controlling) vector-borne diseases like malaria and hereditary genetic disorders like sickle-cell anemia. Others saw it as crossing a dangerous line with unforeseen and uncontrollable consequences. The genie in the bottle or Pandora's Box, depending on your point of view.[2] In any event, she had been elated when Dr. Mendez had shared some of his mosquito samples and data sets with her, and had also acted as an encouraging sounding board as she developed her ideas. The project the paper would describe was a protocol for conducting experiments on introducing a permanent edit into the genomes of a sample population of mosquitoes—a so-called 'gene drive'—but outside the laboratory and in the field.

Just as she had finished editing the abstract of her paper, Maria's phone rang. The distraction irritated her at first, but then she saw it was her mother calling and she quickly answered *"Kaixo ama, zer moduz?"*— She was genuinely glad to hear from her, and she knew her mother would be pleased to be greeted in Basque.

---

[2] Because of the controversy, 'somatic gene editing' (where genes are changed in an existing organism in a way that does not impact its reproductive cells and hence are not 'heritable') and 'germline editing research' (where the genome of reproductive cells—like sperm and eggs—of an organism are edited in the laboratory for experimental purposes, but the organism is not allowed to reproduce) had been the common practice.

"Kaixo Maria. Ondo nago, eskerrik asko." Maria's mother did indeed sound pleased, but knowing Maria's Basque was by now getting rusty, she switched to the Spanish amalgam that they had come to use with each other. "I had a strange feeling last night that I needed to check on you, but I didn't want to wake you up. Is everything okay with you, Maria?"

"Yes, Mama, everything's fine. You haven't been seeing that fortune-teller again have you? I keep telling you it's superstitious nonsense and a waste of your money." Before she had even finished the sentence, Maria already felt a pang of guilt for the condescending tone she had used with her mother.

"Maria, there are things beyond what even your science can understand. Why have you always distanced yourself from the *Calé*[3] blood in my family? Are you so ashamed? You probably couldn't speak a word of *Caló* now if your life depended on it!"

"Probably not… but I didn't mean it that way, Mama. I just worry about you and don't want you to be taken advantage of. As for me, I still have to work and try to succeed in a world that isn't always welcoming to Romanies."

"Well, your father accepted me, and loved me. And we made a happy family together."

"I know, Mama. I'm sorry… please, let's not argue," Maria said, desperately wanting to change the subject before her mother started asking her about when she would get married and start having children.

---

[3] *Calé* (Kale) – based mostly in Spain and Portugal, one of the 5 major groups of Romani people and who speak the Caló dialect.

"By the way, I made some *Bacalao a la Vizcaina* last week using your recipe. It was so good. It reminded me of home."

"That makes me happy *alaba*, I wish I could be there to make sure you eat right all the time. Anyway, I'll send some recipes. Don't forget our food."

"*Eskerrik asko, ama.* I'll call you next week… I have some work now that I have to finish. "Please take care of yourself—and say hello to everyone for me. I love you, *ama*"

"Okay, *agur maitea.* You take care as well."

After hanging up, Maria went to prepare herself a small lunch—all the talk about food and recipes had reminded her that she hadn't eaten yet, and it was already after noon. It had begun raining again, which also reminded her of her last phone call with Dr. Mendez. She wondered when he would call so that they could discuss their story for the Institute's security office, and so sent him a reminder text message before getting back to editing her paper.

Chapter 2: Cachito

Mendez loved the art of Miró. The swirling shapes and colors always somehow reminded him of his childhood visits to his grandfather's farm in Brazil, where he could wander among the exotic-looking plants and various animals, temporarily emancipated from the boredom of schoolwork and his mother's watchful eye back in Argentina. His grandfather—'Senhor Pedro' as the neighbors called him—enjoyed puttering around the farm with his dogs and generally let young Carlos roam freely after he had helped with the morning chores. "A young man needs to go exploring and learn about the real world," was Senhor Pedro's standard response when Carlos' mother would call, worrying about her son as mothers do.

On this Friday, as he often did, Mendez had packed a small lunch and walked the few blocks from the Pasteur Institute Medical Center to the Square de l'Oiseau-Lunaire—a small park named after the Miró sculpture at its center ('the Moon Bird'), which he especially liked because he secretly thought it looked like a balloon animal version of one of those fantastical *alebrijes* of Mexican folk art. Having briefly escaped the demands of his work at the Medical Center, and when the light was just right on Miró's Moon Bird and the children were laughing and playing in the square's playground, he would allow himself to slip into a reverie of carefree memories of his grandfather's farm. As the drizzle of a light rain intruded, the ping of Maria's text message also interrupted.

After the short walk back to his office, Mendez pulled his phone out of his jacket pocket and dialed Maria.

"Hello, Dr. Mendez. Thank you for calling."

"Hello, Maria. I've been thinking about our story for the security office, and it seems to me it would be best to just stick as closely as possible to the story we've been using to explain your visits to my clinic over the last year. Namely, that you've been helping me with analysis and management of my research samples, and in return I let you use some of them for your work and have supported you in an advisory capacity."

"I was thinking along the same lines, but I think there are still a few gaps that we need to fill in. Why would we need to be coming into the clinic in the evenings and on weekends? And how do I explain that there is no record or awareness in my department of me collaborating with you?"

Mendez paused briefly and then replied. "Well, as to your first question, we can simply point out that our collaboration, while professional, was extracurricular to our formal responsibilities at the Institute, so we felt that in good conscience we should do it on our own time. As to your second question, I'm not sure I can be helpful since I don't know how the administration of your department is managed."

"Ok, yes… that makes sense. I'll think of something around the question of my department and send you a note on it by Sunday evening," Maria said, not wanting to drag the call out further.

"That's fine, Maria, although I really don't need to know the specifics. I can just—truthfully—plead ignorance about how the administration works in your department. In any event, let's plan to talk again next Wednesday or Thursday to compare notes, as I'm meeting with the security office on Tuesday."

"Okay, but…"

"Yes?"

"I have to confess that being contacted by the security office has made me start wondering a little about what might happen if the Institute eventually finds out what we've been doing… I'm a little worried, Dr, Mendez."

"That's understandable, Maria, but what we are doing is important, so all the more reason to be extra careful. Speaking of which, I would like you to watch your health and your diet closely until we can resume our little project. No overly heavy exertion or alcohol for now… okay?"

"*Muy bien. Bon week-end, docteur.*"

"*Tú también*, Maria." He chuckled, amused by how she seemed to occasionally like mixing Spanish and French together in peculiar ways.

After Maria ended the call, she poured herself another cup of coffee and decided she needed a break to clear her head. She curled up on her sofa with her headphones, opened the music app on her phone, and hit play on one of her favorite songs—Alejandro Sanz's passionate 'Amiga Mía.' As Alejandro crooned, she took a sip of coffee, wrapped herself with a blanket, and smiled as she thought, "I don't think many women would be able to be just friends with that handsome face and beautiful voice." It's what her college-age self would say to wind up her friends when they were out together and this song played.

≈

By late Sunday morning, Maria had finished editing her symposium paper, doing her laundry, and cleaning-up around her flat, so she decided to walk over to the St-Germain neighborhood for lunch. After browsing through her closet, she put on white cotton trousers, a light French-blue sweater, and matching espadrilles. She then checked herself in the mirror as she accented the ensemble with a scarf in the way that women in Paris seem to pull off so effortlessly, grabbed her shoulder bag and sunglasses, and headed out. Her destination was the storied Café de Flore, one of her favorite places to while away time over a light meal and a cup of tea, and the brief but pleasant walk up to and along the grand Boulevard Saint-Germain put her in an effervescent mood.

After a leisurely lunch, enlivened by the pageant of fashionista passersby out shopping at local boutiques, Maria decided that a change of scenery might help stimulate her thinking. She still needed to work out the story for her meeting the next day with the Institute's security office on why her department was not aware of her collaboration with Mendez. She strolled first further southeast down the Boulevard Saint-Germain, and then turned south on Rue de Seine, which turned into Rue de Tournon, and then finally terminated at the stately Luxembourg Palace and Gardens. It was only a twenty-minute walk, but she felt invigorated by the time she arrived and found a bench to settle into at the park's Medici Fountain, named after Marie de' Medici. Hailing originally from the powerful Italian House of Medici, she had been a significant 17th century patron of the arts, in addition to being the widow of France's King Henry IV and mother of King Louis XIII.

Maria stared blankly for a long while at the fountain's monumental focal sculpture—a rendering from Greek mythology of the jealous cyclops Polyphemus lurking above the lovers Acis and Galatea—and finally an idea for a story came to her. When meeting with Remy Boucher tomorrow she would 'confide' that the departmental manager who controlled funding of projects had made a romantic overture to her, but she had rebuffed him. She would say that subsequently the approvals and funding for her new research idea kept getting delayed, and so when she had told her friend, Dr. Mendez, he had offered to help her to mature her work. And, she would say that she had not told anyone on the team or the departmental manager because she was worried he might get angry and jealous and cause trouble for her and Dr. Mendez. She knew that if she appeared convincingly vulnerable that her little fiction would likely trigger his protective male instinct. Finally, she would ask him to keep their discussion private and to let her continue to try and manage the situation, but she would also ask if she could come see him again if things got difficult for her—she reckoned that would be the perfect final *coup de pinceau*. Feeling satisfied with herself that this was a plausible story that she could sell to Remy Boucher, she tapped out an outline of it in a text to Mendez and headed back to her apartment.

The meeting with Remy Boucher on Monday morning seemed to go as Maria expected it would—she had even rehearsed some of her expressions in the mirror as she was getting ready for work. Remy had introduced himself as a retired policeman who had taken the security job at the Institute as a way to pass time and earn a little extra money, and he seemed genuinely friendly and intrigued by her story, though he kept mostly silent and listened, occasionally arching an eyebrow or nodding his head. After she had finished, he assured her he would handle the matter with discretion, and that he would follow up as necessary once he had also met with Dr. Mendez the next day.

At the end of the day, after an afternoon of routine activities in her lab, Maria sent off the final version of her research paper to the symposium organizers and decided to call Mendez to share her positive impression of the meeting with Remy Boucher. Mendez answered after the first ring.

"*Buenas tardes*, Maria. I hope everything went well?"

"*Buenas tardes*, Dr. Mendez. Yes, I think the stories worked. He didn't really talk much, but I guess that's because he's a former policeman." There was a long pause before Mendez replied.

"I was not aware of that."

"I'm sure it's nothing to worry about—he seemed very nice," she interjected quickly.

"If you say so, Maria… but in my experience policemen are suspicious by nature and rarely accept things at face value."

"Dr. Mendez, I must say I'm surprised that you have so *much* experience dealing with the police—you *must* tell me more," she said teasingly. An uncomfortable silence hung for several seconds before Maria chimed in again "I'm sorry doctor… I hope that didn't sound offensive… I was just trying to lighten the moment."

"*No te preocupes*, Maria," he replied after a moment. "I just don't want some unforeseen misfortune putting at risk the progress we have made in preserving your bloodline."

To Maria, "preserving your bloodline" seemed an odd choice of words, but then again she had heard stranger things emerge when communicating across different languages and cultures. "Thank you for your concern," she said, feeling that it was time to bring the call to an end. "I hope your meeting tomorrow with Remy also goes smoothly. I'll plan to call you again by the end of the week."

"Okay, Maria. *Cuídate.*"

"*Y usted también, doctor.*"

Mendez's meeting the next day with Remy Boucher seemed as innocuous as that of Maria's, and when he spoke with her again later in the week they dissected their respective impressions but could not identify anything of particular concern. In the end, they decided to just carry on with their individual routines and wait to see if Boucher followed up with them. It anyway suited them, as Maria was busy preparing visual materials for her planned symposium presentation, and Mendez had picked up an increased caseload to cover for a colleague in his department who was away conducting field research.

It was a few weeks later, as she was putting the final touches on her symposium slides, that Maria realized that her period was late. It was now the second week of May and although she was normally fairly regular, she did—like most women—occasionally experience irregular cycles and so didn't pay much attention to it, especially as she had not been sexually active for several months. She nevertheless decided to check in with Mendez. She had not spoken to him since their discussions after the meetings with Remy Boucher. She knew he was still very busy with an increased caseload, so she made a formal appointment through his clinical staff to avoid disrupting his schedule.

When the time came for her appointment the following week, Maria walked the short distance over to the Institute's Medical Center and up to Mendez's office area. After checking her in at the reception desk, the clinical assistant on duty ushered Maria into Mendez's office and told her that Mendez would arrive very soon, as he was just returning from lunch. Instead of sitting down, Maria lingered at the side wall of his office, taking in again the old panoramic black & white photographs Mendez had hung there and of which she had grown very fond. There were sweeping and dramatic, almost surreal, Patagonian landscapes and the serene rolling plains of the Argentine Pampas. Other than these yellowing antique photographs however, his office was austere and modern—an ensemble of chrome and glass and leather. The contrast was striking.

"I'm sorry to keep you waiting Maria," Mendez announced as he walked into the office. "It's such a pleasure to see you—and I see you're admiring my photographs again. They're captivating, no?" he said as he walked up beside her, fixing his gaze also on the photographs.

"Yes they are. And I just noticed for the first time that there is some tiny, faded script on the bottom of that one there"—she pointed to a picture of a meadow with a herd of cattle and a small farmhouse in the distance—"but I can't quite make out what it says."

"*Ein neuer Anfang in einem neuen Zuhause*—a new beginning in a new home."

"Oh, I see now. Do you speak German as well, *Herr Doktor*?" she said half-jokingly, "There seems to be no end to your talents."

Mendez laughed. "Only some rudimentary phrases left over from the language classes my parents made me attend in secondary school. I actually found these photographs in an antiques store in Buenos Aires and had to use a magnifying glass and a German dictionary myself to figure out what it said."

It was Maria's turn to laugh. "And here I was thinking there was some mysterious story behind these pictures."

"I'm sorry to disappoint you, Maria." Mendez deadpanned as he went to sit at his desk, motioning to one of the chairs in front of him. "Please have a seat and tell me how you're doing and why you needed an appointment."

"Well, doctor, in general I feel fine, but I wanted to let you know that I'm almost two weeks late for my period, and I'm still not having any PMS symptoms. It's probably nothing, but I thought I should tell you, since I haven't been late like this since we began retrieving my eggs over a year ago."

"And… I guess you haven't… *been* with a man recently?" he asked tentatively.

"No."

"I see. Well, like you said, it's probably nothing to be concerned with, but let me give you a quick examination and take some blood and urine samples, and I'll call you if I see anything unusual, okay?"

"Thank you, Dr. Mendez. I would appreciate that," Maria said, though her gaze had absent-mindedly wandered towards Mendez's locked closet.

Mendez knew what was on her mind. "Don't worry Maria, they are all safe and healthy."

After conducting a routine physical examination and collecting samples from Maria in the adjacent examination room, Mendez went back to his office to wait while she slipped out of the hospital gown she had worn for the examination and dressed again. When she came in, he stood and came to meet her in the middle of the room. "Everything seems fine so far, Maria. As I mentioned, when I get the lab results I'll give you a call."

"Thank you again doctor." And then, in the moment, Maria inexplicably felt an urge to lighten the mood and confide a bit more with Mendez. "I guess I should be happy about not having my period this month. You know, doctor, in the culture from my mother's side of the family, menstruation is considered *mahrime*—ritually unclean—so it seems I will effectively get to experience almost two months feeling *užo*—clean," she said, her tone an amalgam of faux cheer and sincere sarcasm.

"Are those Basque words? I had not heard of those concepts being part of Basque culture," Mendez said, looking clearly perplexed.

"No. They're Romani words… superstitions really. I'm afraid I haven't been completely open about my background. You see, my mother has family ties to a Gitano—Spanish Romani—clan. They call themselves *Calé* actually, but Gitano is the more well-known colloquialism in Spain. Very strictly speaking my mother is a Cascarot, the descendants of marriages between Basques and Romanies, but her upbringing was heavily influenced by Gitano culture. I know it sounds confusing—it still is to me sometimes."

Mendez stepped back, his eyes wide. "But you said you were Basque. Your light skin and your features are characteristically so. Why would you lie?"

Maria was a little startled by his reaction but composed herself. "I didn't lie—I am Basque, and a little more. My father is pure Basque, and it seems I just inherited more of his features than my mother's. Given the prejudices against the Romani people, I suppose I just found it easier once I left for university not to talk about it. People always assumed I was just Basque, or Spanish, or whatever, and it was just easier as time went by to let them go on assuming. But I have come to trust you, Dr. Mendez, and to feel that a man of your depth and worldliness would be above such petty prejudices."

Mendez said nothing, and Maria could feel his gray eyes, now narrowed and intense, examining her. Just as the moment was turning uncomfortable, his clinical assistant walked in and announced his next appointment was waiting in the reception area. Mendez mumbled something to her and turned to walk back to his desk without a word to Maria. Although still confused about what had just happened, Maria realized that she had been effectively dismissed, and so turned and followed the assistant out the door.

The next few weeks became a jumble of routine and distraction for Maria. Her work at the Institute and final preparations for the symposium where she would present her paper kept her busy, but the odd reaction of Mendez in his office and her confusion—including at the fact that he had not yet contacted her about her test results or even responded to her attempts to text and call him—began to morph into anxiety. She was also feeling more fatigued at the end of the day than usual and occasionally having weird dreams. She knew her mother would call the feeling a 'sign' or a premonition, but Maria dismissed the thought as yet more superstition.

And then things began to change. On a Monday morning in the last week of May her phone rang. She recognized from the number that it was an internal call from within the Institute and answered right away, desperately hoping it was Mendez finally calling, but from a different location in the Medical Center. It was not. After she said hello, the gravelly voice of Remy Boucher came on the line.

"*Bonjour,* Dr. Guevara, this is Remy Boucher from the Facilities Security Office. Do you have a moment?"

"Yes, how can I help you, Mssr. Boucher?"

"Please, call me Remy. I have been trying to reach Dr. Mendez for over a week now to follow up regarding some other visitors he has been having. But it turns out he has taken a sudden leave of absence. His office staff said it was something about a family emergency back in South America that required his presence. I wondered if you knew what was going on?"

There was a clear edge to the way he asked the question, and the news that Mendez had suddenly left compounded Maria's unease. "What?" was all she could seem to say at first. Boucher began to repeat what he had said, thinking she had not heard him clearly, but she interrupted. "*Je suis désolé.* I was just surprised to hear Dr. Mendez had left. He is a friend, and I had been expecting a call from him about some laboratory results we had been working on together."

"And do you know anything about recent visitors he has been having, who are not Institute staff like yourself or patients?"

"I'm afraid not. He really didn't talk about his personal life, except for sharing some stories of his childhood."

"I see. Well, if you remember anything that is relevant, please call me," he said, sounding unmistakably more like the veteran policeman he was than the amiable security guard she had experienced in their first meeting. "One more thing, Dr. Guevara. The normal protocol in a situation like this would be for me to inform the senior leader of your department of the situation, given your unorthodox working relationship with Dr. Mendez and your access to restricted pathogens. But given our recent discussion, I will hold off on that for now and ask you to consider a way to bring the matter to the attention of the relevant person in your department—Mssr. DuPont I believe—as soon as possible. Once you have done it, please let me know, okay?"

Maria knew it was not really a question. "Yes, I can do that. Thank you, Remy."

"I will look forward to hearing from you. *Prends soin.*" And then the line clicked off before Maria could respond. She put away her phone, feeling disoriented, and almost unconsciously grabbed her coat. Some fresh air might help… and those new strawberry *galette* pastries at the Carisa Paris bakery looked so delicious.

On Tuesday morning Maria was at her desk thinking about what she would say about Mendez and their relationship to her departmental manager when he unexpectedly appeared in front of her. Olivier DuPont was tall and slender and just beginning to gray at the temples, with wide rimmed glasses and an almost aristocratic air about him that was unusual for a scientist, even a managerial one.

"Good morning, Maria. Could we perhaps have a word in private please?"

Maria's thoughts were racing. Had Boucher had a change of heart and contacted DuPont? What was happening? "Yes, of course, Olivier," she finally managed, and followed him to the same meeting room on their floor where she had met with Mendez after the two of them were first contacted by Remy Boucher.

Once they were seated Olivier began. "Maria, one of the Institute's directors sent me a copy of the paper that you submitted for the ESHG[1] symposium in Vienna. I wish you would have discussed it with me first."

Maria was initially relieved—this was not the topic she was worried he would bring up. "I'm sorry, Olivier. We've all been so busy you know, and I became so immersed in this project that by the time I was finished, I was worried that I wouldn't make the submission deadline on time if I circulated it around for input."

"Normally, it wouldn't be such an issue, but the Institute is getting caught up in the politics of the debate at the EU level about putting further restrictions on certain types of genetics R&D. Unfortunately, what you have submitted—a proposal for exploring a field-based gene drive—has set off alarms. The Institute receives a substantial amount of its funding from the EU and can't afford to put that at risk."

"That's ridiculous. It's just a proposal, and with carefully constructed control and safety parameters. I think you would agree with that," she said, a little too defensively.

"The methodology looks sound, theoretically, yes. Probably even brilliant. But we're talking about public sentiment and politics here, Maria. And the sample lab experiments it appears you have conducted to

---

[1] ESHG – European Society of Human Genetics

generate baseline control data were not part of an Institute-authorized project. I'm not sure I even want to ask where and how that happened."

"Olivier, please. I've been working on this for so long. If this technique can be proven and implemented, it could lead to a breakthrough for reducing the spread of vector-borne diseases like malaria."

"I'm afraid it's out of my hands, Maria. I've been asked to suspend funding for all of your projects until this is sorted out by the Institute's leadership team. You also won't be able to initiate any new lab work or experiments without clearing it with me first."

"Am I being fired, Olivier?"

"No. You are welcome to continue coming into the facility while this is being resolved, and perhaps help out some of the other researchers, if you don't mind. I'm also required to inform you that if you feel you need to raise your case with Human Resources—HR—or the Works Council, that's of course your prerogative."

Maria sat back in her chair, looked out the window, and sighed. "I see. There is one more thing I need to tell you, Olivier." And then she told him, as she had promised Remy Boucher that she would, about how Mendez had been helping her with her research and the proposal that was outlined in the paper and pleaded with him to ensure there would be no repercussions for Mendez. She did not, however, mention their separate 'private' project involving the frozen eggs in Mendez's office closet. Although DuPont looked a little shocked about the involvement of Mendez in her research work, he simply took a few more notes and then excused himself. She sat silently for a long while, looking out the window—and then again felt a sudden specific craving for pastries, although this time she was craving a delicate profiterole instead of the strawberry *galette*. "How odd," she thought.

Although she had felt crushed by being effectively sidelined and spent a few days moping, Maria finally pulled herself together and decided that she had to try and keep busy, even if only as a distraction. After a few awkward discussions with colleagues, she agreed to be an extra pair of hands and eyes to help on some projects that were of interest to her, and by Friday even started to feel that she had established a sort of interim routine. The work was also a welcome distraction from the disappointment of not being able to present her research paper at the symposium in Vienna. Meanwhile, in hopes that Mendez would return soon, and they could resume freezing more eggs, she had continued to avoid alcohol and over-exertion, as he had instructed. Nevertheless, on Saturday morning she awoke unexpectedly and intensely nauseous and barely made it to the toilet to throw up. She assumed it might have been caused by the cheap seafood dinner from the night before, which she reasoned could possibly have been a bit off. But then the mysterious pastry cravings came again. And on Sunday morning the nausea and vomiting were repeated, even though she had not eaten any particularly unusual food the night before. After brushing her teeth, she went to the kitchen to have some ginger ale to settle her stomach, and then sat on the sofa. Getting sick in the morning two days in a row for no apparent reason and having unusual cravings seemed more than coincidence. She shook her head and thought—"it can't be." Slowly she began reconstructing the timeline to her last period and realized the timing fit. She shook her head again—it was impossible.

Finally, Maria decided to go to the local pharmacy to buy a home pregnancy test, as that would quickly confirm that the impossible was indeed impossible and she could then stop thinking about it. She picked up three tests—just to be sure—and then made her way back home, stopping on the way back at a local patisserie for one of their crème-filled chocolate éclairs that suddenly looked so irresistible to her in the window as she was passing by. She laughed at herself but reasoned that she anyway needed something for her empty stomach. As soon as she got home, she used one of the tests and stared at it in disbelief when it showed up positive. She used the second test a few hours later and still the result was positive. Still in denial of what she was seeing, she composed herself and decided to save the last test to use the following morning, grasping at the idea that maybe her hormone concentrations were somehow irregular and fluctuating. But the next morning, the test result was again positive, and again she was nauseous. She stared in the mirror, stupefied, thinking only—"how is this possible?"

After a long, blank moment Maria finally glanced at her watch and realized it was now almost 8:00 a.m. on Monday morning. She gathered herself together, got dressed, and made her way to the Institute. The rest of the morning was a blur to her and, needing some fresh air, she decided to walk over to the nearby park with her lunch, the way she knew Mendez often did. She was secretly hoping she might see him there, but the park was unusually quiet and empty, inhabited only by Miró's Moon Bird sculpture. She sat on a bench, unwrapped a sandwich, and then paused for a long moment, shaking her head. "What is happening, Carlos?" she whispered to herself.

Chapter 3: Take Five

THE ARDITURRI CREEK MEANDERS out of the Aiako Harria Nature Reserve in the foothills of the rugged Pyrenees Mountains and down through the rural hills and valleys that comprise the hamlet of Ergoien in Spain's Basque Country, before it finally feeds into the Oiartzun River and then empties into the Bay of Biscay just east of San Sebastián. Along a secluded area of the creek near the entrance to the nature reserve there sits a cluster of houses and stables hidden behind a grove of trees, and although it is formally part of Ergoien, the people who live in the sequestered little settlement simply refer to it as 'Arditurri.' Arditurri was also the birthplace and family home of Naomie Villar before she met and eventually married Ander Guevara of San Sebastián and moved there to be with him.

Naomie would still come back every summer to Arditurri to spend time with her extended family though, sometimes with Ander and sometimes alone. But after their daughter Maria was born, it increasingly became just Naomie and Maria who would go back while Ander stayed in San Sebastián to tend to the now expanded trucking and freight-forwarding business he had taken over from his father. Arditurri was like another world for young Maria—sometimes delightful and sometimes disorienting—but she always looked forward to the visits. She roamed with the other children along the creek and into the hills, rode horses, and helped her grandparents tend to the goats and sheep. In the evenings when the weather was clear, she would be transfixed by the music and dancing and storytelling around a communal outdoor fire. Although she didn't understand much of the *Caló* they spoke, she still loved listening to them and trying to find opportunities to show off the few words she did know.

That summer in Arditurri had started out feeling like most every other, but Maria was now fourteen and maturing quickly. Indeed, with every summer that had passed she was beginning to feel the widening gap between her life and those of her summer playmates. While they attended a nearby provincial school, Maria was receiving a rigorous education from the Jesuits of St. Ignatius College. While they experienced mostly just the homogeneous rural rhythm of the traditions and rituals of the extended families they lived with, Maria was experiencing the vibrant melting pot of Basque, Spanish, and European influences and friends back in San Sebastián. And while they were immersed in and absorbing the belief systems and worldview of their *vitsa,*[1] Maria's father encouraged her curiosity by bringing home books on classical antiquity and mythology and occasionally taking her with him on business trips around Europe.

It was also that summer when Maria noticed that some of the boys of Arditurri were starting to act differently around her. The good-natured teasing of the past about her struggles to speak *Caló* or properly handle a horse was gradually being replaced by clumsy adolescent innuendo and the occasional wandering hand. She was not completely naïve of

[1] vitsa – clan, or band

course—between her mother's warnings about excitable teenage boys and the stories she had overheard from the older sisters of her friends back in San Sebastián—she knew what was happening. Nevertheless, it was irritating and deepened the sense of the widening gap between her and her 'summer family.'

A few days before Maria and her mother were scheduled to return to San Sebastián, Maria decided to go out riding in the late afternoon. She loved to watch the sunset from the hills above Arditurri and hoped this would be a final pleasant memory of the summer to take back with her. As evening began to fall, she was indeed rewarded by a spectacular burst of oranges and yellows fading into an indigo dusk—even her horse seemed to whinny with approval as she stroked his neck. However, under the fading twilight on the way back she accidentally turned onto the wrong trail and got lost for almost an hour. She was finally able to backtrack her way to Arditurri, but it was already pitch-dark outside by the time she made her way into the dimly-lit stables. By now, feeling hungry for dinner, she quickly dismounted, relieved the horse of his saddle and halter, and guided him into his stall. When she turned towards the door she heard a faint rustling, and then noticed someone was standing in the shadows nearby.

"Who's there?" she said haltingly.

"Alfonso," came the reply, as he stepped forward and stood under a bare, suspended light bulb, grinning mischievously.

"Oh—you startled me. What are you doing here?" Alfonso was undeniably cute but unfortunately he was one of the most belligerent boys in Arditurri, and so Maria usually tried to avoid him.

"Just checking on the horses—and the pretty girl from San Sebastián." He stepped closer, too close. Still grinning, he slipped his arm around her waist.

"Leave me alone Alfonso… I'm not interested, and I'm already late for dinner," she said, nearly spitting at him as she pulled away.

"I don't care. You're not even one of us anyway. You're just a half-breed pretender from the city." *Pretender? Half-breed?* His jeers struck a chord. And then he lunged forward and grabbed at her.

Maria wanted to scream, but Alfonso's unexpected strength and sudden ferocity had shocked her, and she felt herself lose her balance as she struggled with his grip. As she stumbled backwards to the ground he was on top of her in an instant, groping, his breathing feral. Now panicking, her breathing was fast and shallow as Alfonso pulled at her blouse and pressed his arousal against her. With his full weight bearing down on her, all she could muster was a muffled "No… get… off… of me."

Suddenly, Alfonso pulled off of and stepped back from Maria, still breathing heavily, his eyes wide and looking beyond and behind her. Her adrenaline pumping, Maria jumped to her feet, turned, and saw that one of the other older boys was standing there, his hands on his hips, glaring at Alfonso. She had seen the boy around but didn't know his name—only that he came from the Amaya family, who mostly kept to themselves.

"I wasn't really going to do anything to her… I just wanted to have a little fun and scare her," Alfonso said sheepishly.

"Shut up and go home, Alfonso, while you still can," was all the Amaya boy said, and Alfonso immediately turned and ran out of the stable.

"Thank you," Maria finally said as she brushed herself off and straightened her blouse.

"Are you okay?"

"Yes. But please don't tell anyone."

"Alfonso has caused trouble before—maybe this should be brought to the elders. My father would be able to call for the meeting."

"No. I don't want this to cause any trouble, especially for my mother."

"Okay. But don't worry, Alfonso and the other boys won't bother you anymore. I'll see to that. You should go home now too." And with that he turned and walked away.

A few days later, Maria left Arditurri with her mother as planned, wondering if she would ever want to return.

It was now the first weekend of June in Paris and still there was no word from Mendez. Maria had returned to the Café de Flore in hopes that it would lift her spirits, but even its potent charm could not keep her thoughts from spiraling—her carefully constructed and controlled life had unraveled, perhaps irretrievably, over the last month. Her status at the Institute remained in limbo, and a recent trip to the Medical Center there had confirmed that she was approximately one month pregnant, but still with no clue as to the circumstances of conception. At first she was fascinated by the idea that a developing embryo was actually now inside of her. She had immediately looked up what it would look like at this stage—basically a tiny, curved structure about the size of a pumpkin seed. Then there were a few days of frantic searches of various online databases of scientific literature. But there was simply no verified precedent or demonstrated biological mechanism for asexual reproduction[2] in humans. Unsure of what to do next, she decided to make an appointment with an Institute HR representative to see if they had any advice or updates about her case. It was still Sunday though and she could not stop thinking about the results of her pregnancy test, so she decided to open up the calendar app in her phone and scroll back to the window of days around the end of April when she had last ovulated, scrutinizing every calendar entry and searching her memories of those days. Nothing seemed particularly unusual, but her mind was still racing desperately, even irrationally, for a clue. It couldn't be the Immaculate Conception, because she knew she was no Virgin Mary. What about those stories she had heard as a teenager about getting pregnant from sitting on a toilet seat? Had she been raped and had a psychotic break that blocked it out? The only thing even remotely out of the ordinary that had occurred outside of work and away from her normal routine was Gerard Durand's birthday party at Le Bal Blomet, when Brigitte had helped her to get home. Finally, unable to contain her curiosity and even though she knew there was probably nothing new to find out, she picked up the phone and dialed Brigitte's number.

"*Allo?*" came Brigitte's voice, bright and cheerful as usual.

---

[2] Asexual reproduction – or parthenogenesis (from the Greek for 'virgin creation'), where development of an embryo from an unfertilized egg cell occurs. Typically seen only in certain invertebrates as well as a select few vertebrates. While some 'spontaneous parthenogenetic events' do occur in humans, rather than healthy embryos they result in tumors—some even resulting in an anatomically disorganized structure with elements of fat tissue, hair, teeth, and, in rare cases, partially-developed limbs.

"Hello Brigitte. This is Maria. I'm sorry to call you on a Sunday—do you have a few minutes?"

"Yes, of course, Maria. Is everything all right?"

"Generally, yes… but I just wanted to thank you again for making sure I got home after Gerard's party. I hope it wasn't too much trouble. I guess I was just a little curious about exactly what happened, since I can't seem to remember anything after we came back to the table from dancing, and I was not feeling well when I woke up."

"Well, you had the glass of wine that the waiter had brought to you, and then not long after that you started looking sleepy and couldn't seem to speak very clearly. I helped you into the bathroom and splashed some water on your face, but it didn't help. It looked like you might faint, so I found your address on your ID card in your purse—I hope you don't mind—and told the waiter to call a taxi to take you home. But at the last minute I decided to go with you to make sure you got home okay. When we arrived, you could barely stand, so I found your key in your purse and helped you out of the taxi. By that time, I was having a hard time holding you up, but luckily there was a nice gentlemen—he looked like some kind of businessman—passing by the door to your building, and he offered to help me. We got you up to your apartment, and that was about it. Oh yes, I also left that note for you on the counter."

"I see. That was nice of that man to help you. Was there anything out of the ordinary about him?"

"Not really—he seemed very polite. He didn't mention his name and hardly spoke. His French seemed fluent, though I detected some kind of accent. That's not unusual in Paris though. He waited by your door while

I wrote the note for you, and then we walked out of the building together. After that, I got back in the taxi, and he continued on his way."

"Was there anyone else in the hallway or lobby of the building?"

"No."

"Besides being sleepy, did my condition seem unusual… Did I look sick?"

"No, at least it didn't appear that way."

"Okay, thank you again, Brigitte. It was really kind of you to look after me."

"Of course. I'll see you at the Institute tomorrow then? I'm afraid I have to go walk my dog now before he makes a mess in my apartment."

Maria laughed. "No problem. *Au revoir*, Brigitte."

As she hung up the phone, Maria thought about how Gerard's party had not been the sort of social event she would normally go to, but that she had enjoyed what she remembered of it, and that Mendez had anyway probably been right to suggest she attend for the sake of appearances. She had been absent-mindedly doodling and taking notes while talking to Brigitte—an old habit—and finished with the words "good suggestion by Dr. Mendez." She then folded up the paper and shoved it in her purse—another old habit—and headed into the bathroom to take a shower.

On the following Tuesday, Maria was able to meet with Chloé Ducasse, the Institute HR manager who handled her department and as such would also have been notified of the suspension of her project work. When Maria entered her office, Chloé stood to greet her, smiling warmly. "Hello, Dr. Guevara, it's been a while, no? Lovely to see you again. Please have a seat and let me know if you would like some tea or coffee."

"Thank you Chloé, I'm fine. And please, no need for formality… just Maria is fine. It's very nice to see you again as well by the way," Maria said as she took a seat.

"Okay. So tell me, how are things with you, Maria?" Chloé inquired as she settled back into her chair. "I know progress feels slow on your case, but I'm hoping we'll ultimately be able to get things resolved."

"Well, there's been an additional complication… in my personal life. I recently discovered that I'm pregnant."

Chloé could tell from Maria's tone and body language that 'congratulations' might not be the right response. "Oh. I see. How far along are you?"

"Around a month and a half. It's an… unusual situation. I'm trying to figure out how best to manage the decisions ahead of me, given the uncertainty also with my work and position here at the Institute."

"I wish I could be more definitive about when your case will be resolved, Maria, but I'm afraid I can't—it's being handled above my head, to be honest."

Maria sighed and turned to look out the window. "Do you have any advice at all?"

Chloé paused for a moment, sat back, and crossed her hands across her lap. "Well, unofficially…" she started, but then hesitated.

"Please Chloé," Maria implored. "Don't worry, I won't tell anyone what we discuss, and I won't blame you if it doesn't work out."

Chloé looked intently at Maria, weighing up the moment, and then began. "Have you considered taking a sanctioned sabbatical or leave of absence? I'm pretty sure Olivier would not object to it, and between the two of us, we have the authority to sign off on it. You would still officially be affiliated with the Institute, and a few months down the road you can formally notify them of your impending maternity—assuming you intend to keep the baby. Legally then, even in the worst-case outcome of your case, it would basically be impossible for the Institute to take any steps towards letting you go until after the minimum sixteen weeks of maternity leave that you are entitled to—six weeks prior to delivery, and ten weeks after. And, with a little luck, by the time your maternity leave ended, the issue of the EU political sensitivities might even resolve itself in your favor."

Maria sat quietly at first, absorbing and reflecting, and then replied. "I was actually not even aware of that as an option. Let me think about it for a few days. In the meantime, can I call you if any questions come to mind?"

"Yes, of course. Take the time you need, and then let me know what you decide. And please keep this conversation just between us."

Maria stood and nodded. "I will. And thank you again Chloé. You've been very helpful… and kind." She then turned and left to return to the 4th floor of the François Jacob Center building where she was helping a colleague prepare equipment for an experiment.

On the following Thursday evening Maria was still feeling restless and uncertain as she stepped out of the Metro at Sèvres–Babylone Station on her way home from the Institute. She decided on a whim to head around the corner at the station exit and spend some time at Le Bon Marché, the *grande dame* of department stores. Its proximity was another reason she loved her neighborhood—wandering through its cornucopia of shops and boutiques was always a pleasant diversion, and the Ladurée macarons she was craving were a guaranteed antidote to melancholy. Eventually, she somehow ended up on the third floor and wandered into *l'Espace Enfant*—the Children's Zone—an exuberant 17,000 sq. ft. menagerie of toys, books, clothes, and nursery décor. As she walked past the books, she noticed a young boy in bright red suspenders, sitting on a stool and mesmerized as he leafed through 'The Castafiore Emerald,' one of the timeless 'Adventures of Tintin' comic books that many a child in Europe grew up with. Maria paused and smiled—she still had a childhood collection of Tintin comics in a box back at home in San Sebastián—and this particular story was one of her favorites. She remembered it so clearly because she had been moved by its sympathetic treatment of the Romani characters in the story and how it— uncharacteristically for its time—lambasted the prejudices against them. Suddenly, the boy in red suspenders looked up at Maria and smiled widely, holding her gaze for several moments, and then went back to reading his Tintin comic. She did not fully realize it yet, but it was in that moment that she decided what she was going to do.

After her pregnancy had been confirmed at the Medical Center, Maria's initial reaction had been to make an appointment at a women's health clinic to explore her options for terminating the pregnancy. But her meeting with Chloé Ducasse had happened in the intervening time, and she was now having second thoughts. Her feelings had anyway already been in a nonstop swirl of turmoil. Initially, she had felt abortion was the practical choice and would spare her family the embarrassment of her being an unwed mother to a child of an unknown father, and she would also avoid the designation of being 'ritually unclean' for the next nine months, per Romani traditions around pregnancy and childbirth. On the other hand, the cultural stigma around abortion from a once deeply Catholic Spain and her Jesuit schooling still lingered in her consciousness. She couldn't help feeling an undeniable scientific curiosity about—and the flickering of a maternal connection with—the tiny entity now growing in her womb. And now there was the additional factor of what Chloé had shared with her about maternity leave policy. On Thursday night, a few hours after she had returned from Le Bon Marché, she finally decided to call her mother, who picked up after the second ring.

"*Bai?*"

"*Kaixo*, Mama. It's Maria."

"Oh… Maria. It's late. Is everything okay?"

"Well, yes and no. There's a little bit of a complicated situation at work."

"I hope nothing too serious?"

"I may need to take some time off… maybe several months. I'll explain it to you later. But I was thinking I might use the time to come back there to Donostia[3] for a while. I just wanted to check with you first to make sure it would be okay with you and Papa."

"Yes, of course, Maria. You know we love having you here. When would you be coming?"

"Once I make a final decision it will probably take a few weeks to finalize arrangements with my apartment and to tie up loose ends at work. I'll call you back once I have decided one way or the other."

[3] Donostia – Basque term for San Sebastián

"Okay, Maria. I wish you would tell me what's going on, but we'll wait to hear back from you. I love you, *alaba*."

"Thank you, *ama*. I love you, too," Maria finished, feeling a sudden flush of emotion.

After hanging up, she noticed it was almost midnight, so she ate one of the lavender macarons from the box she had brought home, drank half a glass of milk, and went to bed. As she laid down she instinctively spread her hands over her abdomen and murmured, almost subconsciously, "We're going home, *txikito*."

Maria slept more soundly than she had for a long time and knew as soon as she woke up that Friday morning what she was going to do. After a quick breakfast of scrambled eggs with chorizo sausage and coffee, she sent a text message to Chloé asking her to put in motion the option they had discussed. She then additionally called the women's health clinic to cancel her appointment. Maria had decided she was going to take a leave of absence, go back to San Sebastián for the remainder of her pregnancy, and try to put her life back in order. She even began to wonder one evening, while she was looking at her naked form in the mirror, whether she should begin documenting her pregnancy in more detail—in the event it would actually result in the first known case of true human parthenogenesis. She then shook her head and laughed out loud at herself as the thought of writing a research paper on her own pregnancy briefly crossed her mind.

The next few weeks were a blur of preparation and packing, punctuated by a few sentimental lunches with colleagues and weekend strolls through St. Germain, as well as a consultation with an obstetrician at the Medical Center. Finally, in the middle of the last week of June,

Maria was on the platform at the Gare Montparnasse train station, boarding the high-speed TGV. In about five and a half hours, she would arrive in Hendaye, a French city at the border with Spain, and then switch to the Euskotren for the final forty-minute ride to San Sebastián. As the platform attendant blew the final boarding whistle and the carriage doors closed, she finished hoisting her carry-on bag onto the overhead rack and settled into her seat by the window.

A little more than an hour after leaving Paris, as the train was crossing the Loire River near Tours, Maria had drifted into a light nap, coaxed by the gentle swaying of the train and the hearty vegetable soup and toasted baguette she had enjoyed at a bistro near the train station in Montparnasse before departing. But just as the train had crossed to the southern bank of the Loire, a high-pitched ping woke her. She pulled her phone out of her jacket pocket, her head still resting against the window and her eyes half closed, but then sat up straight when she saw the name on the message notification that had generated the ping—Dr. Mendez.

DM
Have you heard anything more from Boucher or the Institute's Security Office?

MG
No. I heard you were back in South America—when will you return? Why haven't you replied to my earlier texts and emails?

DM
An urgent personal matter needed my attention.

MG

I was waiting to hear back from you on my test results, but I don't need them now—I went back to the Medical Center, and they confirmed I am pregnant. How is that even possible?

DM

You should terminate the pregnancy. I will contact you again when I return to Europe.

MG

I have taken a leave of absence due to an issue that has been raised by the Institute about my research. I'm on my way back to San Sebastián now and plan to carry on with the pregnancy.

DM

Why would you want to keep the baby if you don't even know who the father is? Be sensible.

MG

I'm perfectly capable of handling things myself. It's my body and my decision to make.

DM

…

MG

Hello?

Maria waited for a while and then realized there was not going to be a reply from Mendez.

Several hours later, Ander and Naomie Guevara were sitting patiently on a bench at San Sebastián's Amara Station, waiting for the Euskotren to arrive from Hendaye. The other *donostiarres* milling about the station could not know that this quiet, older couple was feeling at once happy and anxious; happy that their daughter would be arriving soon, but anxious about what may have happened to cause the unexpected return. Ander silently took Naomie's hand and gripped it tightly as they spotted the train in the distance making its final approach to the station.

The Guevara family home sat on the eastern slope of San Sebastián's iconic Monte Igueldo, with a sweeping view overlooking the crescent-shaped La Concha Bay and its beautiful beach. Ander's father had built a house there once he had established the family business many years ago, and when the cost to do so was still modest. In more recent years, given the coveted views and the location being adjacent to the popular Antiguo neighborhood—the oldest in San Sebastián—Ander would get regular calls from property agents asking if he was interested in selling. He was not, nor was Naomie. "This is our family home, and it will stay in the family," was his standard response to every property agent, after which he would thank them for calling and hang up, smiling. Naomie knew he secretly enjoyed turning them down, especially when it was an *atzerritar*—a foreigner.

Only a few days after she had arrived, Maria had settled in and was now enjoying a mid-morning cup of coffee on the small upper balcony of the house, where she never tired of the view or the sweet, creamy fragrance of the flowering gardenias on the hillside below that would drift up and mix with the ocean breeze. It felt good to be home and to be able to take in again the familiar and comforting surroundings of her childhood. Her father had left early, as usual, to his office in town and her mother had gone down to the market to pick up fresh fish, bread, vegetables, fruit, and some of the delicious *txistorra*—Basque sausage— that she had asked for. Their conversation the day before about her job had been brief, with Maria only vaguely alluding to 'funding cuts at the Institute which had affected her area of research.' She knew that they, and especially her mother, suspected she was not telling them everything, but she had deftly changed the subject, coaxing them to fill her in on the latest local news and gossip.

Maria also knew it would not be long before she would have to tell her parents she was pregnant, but she couldn't understand it herself yet, let alone explain it to them. She told herself that she just needed a little more time to figure out what had happened. She stood up then and went over to the balcony railing, closing her eyes as she tilted her head up to enjoy the warmth of the morning sun. Interrupted by the sound of footsteps from the road below, she then leaned over the balcony expecting to see her mother coming back from the market. But instead, it was a just a tall man walking by, wearing a guayabera shirt, sunglasses, and a fedora-style Panama hat. "Another lost tourist," she thought, and then turned and went back into the house.

Chapter 4: Summertime

THE SUMMERS ARE GENERALLY mild and pleasant in the south of Poland, but there was nothing pleasant about this place in 1943. The new medical officer had arrived at the beginning of the summer, eager to advance the work and theories of his mentor, Dr. Otmar von Verschuer, Director of the Kaiser Wilhelm Institute for Anthropology, Human Heredity, and Eugenics in Berlin. Verschuer was already famous for his pioneering use of a twins methodology for human genetics research, but he was still very pleased that his protégé was now in a position to easily acquire the kind of 'twin materials' that the current conditions in Europe had made so difficult to procure. He was elated when he began to receive specimens even sooner than expected, as it turned out this new medical officer had already received authorization for conducting 'anthropological investigations' as part of his new assignment.

Doctor von Verschuer's promising and ambitious protégé was Doctor (and recently-promoted SS Captain) Josef Mengele, who was now the medical officer responsible for the *Zigeunerlager* ('Gypsy camp') located in the Birkenau subdivision of the enormous Auschwitz concentration camp complex. Soon after his arrival he had set about gathering up twins, most of them children, from among the existing camp population and from the regular train arrivals. Besides sharing data and specimens with von Verschuer, Mengele also eventually hoped to use his 'research' at Auschwitz to produce his *Habilitation*—the second, post-doctoral, dissertation required to become a professor in Germany. As such, now that he had several experimental studies up and running he felt he needed to eventually widen the genetic 'sample populations' he was working with. Birkenau's *Zigeunerlager* was at this point mostly populated by the *Sinti* group[1] of Romanies predominant in Germany and Austria, as well as the *Roma* group of central and eastern European origin. He was therefore especially pleased when a train arrived in early September that unexpectedly included some *Calé* from northern Spain along with the expected *Manouche* from France.

After the Spanish Civil War of the late 1930s, Spain's *caudillo* General Francisco Franco and his Nationalists had begun rounding up suspected supporters of the Republicans, and the Romanies among them—already discriminated against in Spanish society—were treated especially harshly. As a result, some fled to France where, in a stroke of tragic irony, many were eventually rounded up by the occupying German forces and the collaborators of Vichy France. Some even more tragically ended up on trains headed east to the industrial-scale concentration camps like Auschwitz. And so it was that by September of 1943 Mengele's Romani 'sample population' came to include some *Calé* from Spain.

It was September 13th, to be precise, when the two young boys were brought shaking with terror into Mengele's office, having been separated

---

[1] Romani groups – there are 5 major Romani groups in Europe, each with differing dialects and traditions, and each in turn inclusive of a number of sub-groups. The 5 major groups, and their predominant location in Europe, are: the *Roma* of Central/Eastern Europe & the Balkans; the *Sinti* of Germany, Austria and Northern Italy; the *Calé/Kale* of Spain & Portugal; the *Manouches* of France & Italy; and the *Romanichals* of the UK.

from their parents the day before. "Well, well… what do we have here?" Mengele said, smiling.

The nurse who had shepherded the boys into Mengele's office responded, "*Zigeuner* twins from Spain, age 7, sir."

"Excellent. They look healthy, but let's do a full examination to be sure. I want to see which would be the best candidate to be the control subject, and which should be used for the experiments. What are their names?"

"The family name is Amaya. This one here is Silvanus, and the other is Danior."

"How do you know which one is which?"

"I marked them on arrival when we were recording the family information provided by the parents. See? An 'S' on this one's shoulder, and a 'D' on the other's," she said as she turned them to stand sideways to Mengele and pointed at their shoulders. The marks were still raw but had started to heal into scars.

"Very well. We'll finish the examinations today and then begin with the procedures tomorrow morning. I'll meet you in the examination room. Please take the subjects with you. I need a few minutes to gather up my instruments."

"Yes, *Herr Doktor.*"

The next day marked the beginning of a descent into an unimaginable abyss of physical and psychic trauma for the Amaya twins. Danior had been chosen as the control subject, and so it was Silvanus who bore the brunt of the physical suffering resulting from Mengele's bizarre 'experiments.' There were surgeries (including amputation and organ removal) without anesthesia, injection of chemicals into the eyes in attempts to fabricate blue eye color, and, for some subjects, deliberate exposure to deadly diseases like typhus and tuberculosis. Danior had to helplessly endure his brother's screams and pleading from the adjacent room during the day, and, if Silvanus was still conscious, his sobbing next to him at night. When Silvanus finally succumbed, Danior was relieved that his brother's suffering had come to an end and sometimes wished he could have joined him, as the screams and sobbing then became part of his regular nightmares.

Miraculously, Danior later emerged as one the tiny handful of Romanies that somehow escaped the final wholesale extermination of the over 4,000 remaining Romanies at Birkenau on the single fateful evening of August 2nd, 1944, though the details of that night were something he refused to discuss for the remainder of his life, even with his closest family members. Overall, only about 2,000 of the estimated 23,000 Romanies that had been sent to Auschwitz during the war survived. And, of the roughly 3,000 Jewish, Romani, and other twins in total that were subjected to medical experiments there, only about 200 survived. The survivors tried as best they could to keep their story alive and to bear witness to the reality that across Europe over 500,000 Romanies were killed as a result of the *Samudaripen* ('mass killing,' or genocide) perpetrated against the Romani people by the Nazis and their collaborators. Many Romanies remember it as *O Baro Porrajmos*—The Great Devouring—and the shadow of its impact still echoes across the generations.

≈

After helping her mother put away the groceries from the market, Maria had decided to start researching some of the universities and organizations in the United States that were on the leading edge of genetic engineering research. In the event her position at the Pasteur Institute became untenable, she wanted to have some alternative options to pursue, and the Americans seemed to be less restrictive in their approach to regulating this important frontier of research, focusing mostly on restrictions around heritable genome editing of *human* embryos. Although she felt that restrictions on scientific inquiry in general were usually rooted in vague religious or philosophical 'superstitions' and slowed progress, she understood the hold that these beliefs had on people. Not coincidentally, she then turned and looked down the hall at her mother, who was busy tidying up the living room. "Are we having a visitor, Mama?"

"Yes, it's Vadoma. She'll be here any minute," Naomie said cheerfully.

"The fortune-teller? You know how I feel about that. Please don't give her any money."

"Maria, please be respectful. You talk about her as if she's a carnival act. The real *castañera*[2] like her practice an ancient tradition, and only charge the *payos*,[3] not us," Naomie said. "I only occasionally give her a small gift out of appreciation."

Maria couldn't help rolling her eyes, but she had turned her head so her mother wouldn't see. It was just then that she heard three sharp knocks on the front door. "She still has that knobbled old walking stick," Maria thought, shaking her head.

---

[2] castañera – the Caló term for a fortune-teller

[3] payos – the Caló term for a non-Romani person. The more widely-known Romani term is 'gadže.'

"Come, let me take a look at you," Vadoma said after she had entered and spotted Maria. "Your mother told me you had come back for a visit, and I've been looking forward to seeing you."

"*Bienvenido*, Señora Vadoma. I hope you are well?" Maria said, trying to be polite.

"*Si, gracias*… although I'm a little slower running after my chickens than I used to be." She laughed. "Come closer, let me give you a hug."

Maria smiled and embraced Vadoma. "Please, have a seat. Can I get you some tea?"

"Yes, thank you."

"Don't worry—I'll get it," Naomie chimed in, heading for the kitchen.

Vadoma then silently surveyed Maria from head to toe, a quizzical expression eventually forming among the deep features of her face. "Have you told your mother yet?" she said.

"What do you mean?" Maria said, looking confused.

"You know what I mean," Vadoma said as she dropped her gaze to Maria's stomach.

Maria thought she was maintaining her composure, but, almost imperceptibly, her eyes had widened, and her posture shifted. "What?"

Vadoma laughed. "It's not only the eyes that can see, girl, and not only the ears that can hear. But don't worry, your secret's safe with me. You don't have long before she'll be able to tell though."

Just then, Naomie came walking back with a tea service and some polvorón cookies for the three of them. "So, who's ready for some of my fresh polvorón?" she said, smiling broadly as she set the tray down on the table in front of them.

≈

The offices of Guevara Freight were located adjacent to the railyard and commercial harbor in Pasai Antxo, a small suburb a few miles east of San Sebastián. Maria had not been there in years and, after the previous day's encounter with Vadoma, was looking forward to getting out of the house.

"Thank you for taking me with you today, *aita*. I've been looking forward to spending some time with you," Maria said as they pulled into the parking lot.

"And me as well, *alaba*," Ander said cheerfully as he put the car in park, unbuckled his seat belt and opened the car door. But just then, Maria reached over and put her hand on his arm.

"*Aita*—there's some things I think I may need to talk with you about later… maybe tonight. Okay?"

"Yes, of course, Maria."

Maria loved the warm smile he always gave her. She knew its source was the unconditional love of a father for his daughter, and always felt it in his presence. She leaned over and kissed him tenderly on the cheek. "*Eskerrik asko, aita*. Okay, I guess we should go in now."

"*Bai*. And keep working on your *Euskara* my dear—it sounds like you're a little out of practice," he said teasingly as he got out of the car. Maria grinned at him and laughed, taking his arm as they walked into the front office of Guevara Freight.

Elixane, the matronly office manager, almost jumped out of her seat and came around the counter to embrace Maria. "Little Maria… you're all grown up into a woman now!" She was beaming. Elixane was the queen bee of the office, complete with a floral print dress, Oxford pumps, reading glasses on a neck chain, and her hair pulled up and fastened firmly into a bun on the crown of her head—all clean, tidy, and eminently sensible. Originally from the adjacent suburb of Errenteria, she had started out many years ago as a part-time receptionist while raising her children, and had gradually become a right hand to Ander, learning the details of the business and helping him as he expanded the business. Now that her children were grown and her husband retired and underfoot at home, she clearly preferred spending her days at Guevara Freight. "I'm so glad you came to visit. Your father talks about you all the time; he is so proud you know," she said, smiling widely and throwing a knowing sideways glance to Ander.

Maria blushed briefly, not knowing exactly how to respond "Thank you, Elixane. It's good to be back. I hope all is well with your family?"

"Yes, of course. They have me making sure of that!" she replied, her chin up and her hands planted firmly on her hips. "Now, let me show you around. There have been quite a few changes, but one thing that hasn't changed is that your father needs to get his coffee and look over the morning schedules and manifests."

Ander laughed and waved to Maria as he turned towards his private office. "Don't worry, Maria, you're in good hands. I'll catch up with you shortly."

"Let me show you what we've done with the logistics control room—I think you'll be very impressed," Elixane remarked as she opened the door at the back of the front office and motioned for Maria to follow. The room was a hive of activity, but what caused Maria to stop and stare—even as she was still smiling in bemusement at Elixane's enthusiasm about a logistics control room—was the bank of huge computer display screens almost covering two walls of the room. The cork bulletin boards that she remembered, with papers pinned all over them, were gone. There were screens with maps dotted with blinking icons showing truck, ship, and train locations, as well as screens that looked like the displays in airports, but showing freight shipment names and departure and arrival times.

"This is amazing. When was this all installed?" Maria asked, still surveying the room.

"Well, it all began not long after that awful COVID pandemic. Your father initially just wanted to have some updates done on our existing computer systems, and so he gave a temporary contract to a bright local boy—Xavier—who had just graduated with a computer science degree from that tech university in Barcelona. But then Xavier told him about how some of his friends worked for a company that had received EU COVID relief funds for small businesses, and so he and your father worked together on an application and got a pretty good amount for us. It turned out that there was a lot of support available for businesses making investments in new technology. So Xavier designed this whole set-up, and it's made a huge difference for us. It took almost two years for the full transition—he said it was partly because there's something called 'Artificial Intelligence' running the system that had to be 'trained', but I have no idea how it works. After the new system was up and running and your father saw what it could do, he hired Xavier full time."

"Wow. Very impressive."

"There's more. Follow me!" Elixane gestured towards the door to the warehouse loading dock, and they walked out to where a row of trucks was parked. "See?"

"See what?" Maria said, looking left and right, thinking she had missed something and suppressing a giggle at how Elixane was giving a tour of a freight company as if it were the Moncloa Palace.

"The trucks, they all run on the *hidrógeno*—I think 'fuel' something?"

"Fuel cells. It's wonderful… but it must have been expensive to make the changes?"

"Yes, but there was also some EU money available for making these 'green investments'—that's what your father called them. So the cost to us was not too bad. And the fuel and maintenance costs are so much cheaper than for those dirty old diesel trucks, so it was worth it."

"I'm really happy to see the business is doing well, Elixane. And I can tell you've been a big help to my father."

"It's been my pleasure. He is such a kind man, and this place has become like a second family to me." Elixane's tone then turned quieter and more serious. "But you know Maria, your *aita* is not getting any younger. I know he eventually wants to retire, but he worries about what will become of the business. As do I."

Before Maria could reply she heard footsteps and saw her father approaching.

"So, what do you think?" Ander said. "Guevara Freight has caught up with the twenty-first century, no?"

"It's amazing, *aita*. You have done so much."

"I've had a lot of help as well," he said, looking over and smiling warmly at Elixane. "Right, come with me now and let's go for a drive and then get some lunch. Elixane has things under control, and I know you don't want to hang around here all day."

After they made their way to the car and were pulling out of the company parking lot, Maria noticed a man sitting at the bus station on their block. He had one of those expensive cameras hanging from a strap around his neck, but what really caught her eye was what he was wearing—the same guayabera shirt, sunglasses, and Panama hat she had seen on the man walking by her house the other day, and which now seemed even more out of place to Maria in this industrial neighborhood. As they drove right by him, she looked closer and noticed his hair was blonde, and then in the rearview mirror she saw he had lifted his camera and was pointing it in their direction. "A strange place for a tourist to be taking pictures," she thought to herself. And she couldn't shake the feeling that he had been looking right at her through his sunglasses as they drove by.

'Break bread and then break the news.' Maria remembered watching a distinguished retired ambassador being interviewed on French television, talking about how he would handle difficult and delicate conversations. 'Preferably after the main course and a few glasses of wine, but before the stimulus of a sweet dessert' he had explained, exuding the relaxed and confident savoir-faire that was a result of a lifetime of diplomacy, an elite education, and an elite family name. Maria blinked and the moment came back into focus—it was dinner time now at the Guevara home and Maria and her parents had just finished a main course of hearty lamb stew.

"Now how about some dessert… I have some fresh pantxineta in the refrigerator," Naomie said, beginning to push her chair back.

"Wait, *ama*, there's something I'd like to talk with you and *aita* about first."

Naomie pulled back up and rested her forearms on the table, clasping her hands together. She glanced at Ander and then turned her gaze to Maria. "Of course, Maria. Dessert can wait."

Maria took a deep breath and began. "Paris and my work has been wonderful, but things have gotten… complicated. Some of it is my fault, but some of it I don't fully understand yet. I was doing some research work that I think could eventually make a big difference to the lives of a lot of people, but it was without the full knowledge of the Institute. Unfortunately, my research got caught up in the EU politics around genetic engineering that the Institute is having to navigate, so my work and funding got suspended while they review my case. I was well-intentioned, but I should have known better than to get so far ahead in my work without the right approvals. That's the part that is my fault."

Ander set down his wine glass. "We did have a feeling that something might be wrong, but it doesn't sound like you were fired, so why did you decide to leave Paris?"

"Since all I could do while waiting for a resolution of my case was act as a glorified assistant to other researchers, I decided to take a leave of absence. It was embarrassing."

Naomie had already sensed there was more. "But packing up and coming back to Donostia seems a little extreme. You said there was something else, something that you said you didn't understand yet?"

"I'm not quite sure where to begin. I don't want you to be disappointed or worried," Maria said, looking at her father.

Ander looked at Naomie and then back to Maria. "Go ahead, Maria. You are our *alaba,* and we love you. Nothing will change that."

"Well, I met this medical doctor at the Institute," Maria began, and then noticed her mother's expression had brightened. "It's not like that, *ama.* He's an older colleague and a friend, originally from South America. Dr. Mendez—Carlos Mendez—is his name. I've been so busy with my work for the last few years that I started thinking about freezing some of my eggs—as a kind of back-up plan." Ander had arched an eyebrow but kept silent. "Anyway, once I got to know Dr. Mendez better I confided in him what I was planning to do, and he offered to help me, which I accepted."

After a few moments of silence, Naomie interjected, "I suppose I can understand how your scientific mind led you to that decision, as unusual as it may sound to us. But it sounds like you knew what you were doing, and, with your education, you would have known what was involved. So, what is it really that has happened that you don't understand, Maria?"

"I'm pregnant, and I have no idea how it happened." Maria could feel tears welling up in her eyes and tried to hold back. But the weight of the last few months was too much. "I feel like my life has been falling apart, and I don't know what to do."

There was a stunned silence, and then Naomie finally spoke. "Maria, what do you mean you don't know how it happened? Were you seeing anyone? Could there have been some kind of mistake when you were doing this… what do you call it… egg freezing?"

"No, *ama.* No boyfriends, no casual encounters. And with the egg freezing, they take them *out.* There's no chance one got accidentally dropped into my uterus along the way."

"Maria, please," Ander winced quietly. He could see his wife trembling with emotion and knew he needed to inject calm into the discussion. "But then how could it be possible?"

Maria dropped her head and closed her eyes. "I'm sorry. It all just suddenly feels so overwhelming. I looked up all the available research and all I could find is some vague theoretical speculation on biological mechanisms that *might* exist to trigger asexual reproduction… but there's no known cases or experiments that have been done. I honestly have no idea what has happened… and I'm a little afraid, *aita*." And then the tears came again, and Ander, pulling Naomie along with him, stood and came over so that they could embrace and comfort their daughter.

"We'll figure this out together, Maria. Don't worry." Ander said.

"Thank you, *aita*. You know, lately I've had this strange feeling that I'm being watched—it's probably just my hormones and emotions getting the best of me. But I feel safe now here with the both of you."

Naomie made a mental note to consult Vadoma and then remembered the dessert. "Now, let's have some of that pantxineta," she said, trying her best to sound cheerful. She then headed for the refrigerator while Ander cleared the table and set out fresh plates.

Mendez was tired and irritated. The flight from Buenos Aires to Madrid was over twelve hours long, and the train ride from Madrid to San Sebastián had taken another five hours. He had just checked in to the Hotel María Cristina, the stately *Belle Époque* icon sitting astride the Urumea River where it finally empties into the Bay of Biscay, but his mind was elsewhere. It was now the beginning of the second week of July and things had most definitely not been going as he had planned.

"There's nothing I can do tonight though," he thought to himself, and finished the glass of Rioja that he hoped would help him fall asleep.

Not long after he had showered and dressed the next morning, the text message Mendez had been expecting arrived. It included an address, the picture of a house, and a brief message—'she's at home… I'll pick you up in front of the hotel in twenty minutes.' He set his phone down, took a sip of coffee, and continued with the remainder of the room service breakfast that had been delivered several minutes before. "No need to go out on an empty stomach," he thought as he then slipped on his jacket and headed for the door.

Waiting in front of the hotel was a sleek new AC raVE, all in black, including the opaque window tint. AC—Automòbil Catalunya—was a recent Spanish start-up company based just outside Barcelona that had introduced a breakthrough in high density solid-state battery technology and taken the European market by storm. The raVE ('VE'—*vehículo eléctrico*) was their latest offering and its range on a full charge was 1200 kilometers (~750 miles), well beyond the previous generation of electric vehicles. Mendez slid into the back seat and nodded at the reflection of the driver in the rearview mirror. "Hello, Ulrik. A nice car you've chosen, though not very inconspicuous," he said as he buckled his seat belt.

"Yes, but it is very fast doctor," Ulrik said through a thin smile as he hit the accelerator pedal, and the car launched forward like a silent rocket.

Mendez was briefly taken by surprise as the sudden and extreme acceleration pressed him back into his seat. "Slow down, Ulrik. I just had breakfast, and the last thing we need is attention from the local police." Ten minutes later, Ulrik eased the car to a stop on the side of the street in front of the home of the Guevara family and pushed the gear selector up to 'park.'

Ulrik looked up at the rearview mirror, catching Mendez's eye. "You must convince her to terminate the pregnancy, doctor. Otherwise, I may be forced to take more drastic measures. The DNA in that… abomination… inside her could eventually be traced back to me, and then ultimately linked to you."

"Yes, I know, Ulrik—that is a future *possibility*. But DNA from a crime scene would become a definite *reality* that is immediately available to investigators. This is a complicated situation, and I need you to keep calm and not make it more complicated."

Ulrik's blue eyes narrowed. "I don't need lectures about keeping calm, doctor. May I remind you that it was *your* sentimental beliefs about the Basque race that got us into this predicament."

"And that is why I flew halfway around the world to make this intervention. I realize that I should have done a more thorough check of the origins of her DNA, but the window of opportunity was narrow, and I took the gamble." Mendez had dropped into a lower, more placating tone, wary of triggering Ulrik's short temper. "Now, let me get on with this," he said as he reached to open the door.

Maria was enjoying the view again from the upper balcony when she noticed the black sedan pull up and park across the street. She couldn't see through the tinted windows, but after a few minutes she saw a strangely familiar figure step out from the back seat. It's impossible, she thought to herself. What would he be doing here? She stood up and leaned as far over the balcony railing as she dared, squinting to try and focus on the figure walking across the street now towards the front door of the house. "My God, it's him," she said under her breath, as she wheeled around and headed for the stairs.

Mendez was just about to knock when Maria opened the door and stepped out onto the porch, closing the door behind her. "What are you doing here, Dr. Mendez?" she said, feeling an odd mix of relief at seeing him and anger at his behavior since their last meeting in his office.

"I was on my way back to Paris and thought I would take a detour here to check on you. Should we perhaps go inside to talk?"

"If my mother sees you it won't be until after she's fed you lunch that you'll be able to leave. And she is a very curious woman."

"I see. Well, how are you doing, Maria?"

"I suppose I'm fine, all things considered. I'm trying to figure out how to get my life back together. And of course there's this," she said as she placed a hand on her stomach. "Do you have any idea how this could have happened?"

Mendez was noticeably stiff, and his tone clipped. "No. Did you consider my recommendation to terminate?"

Her face flushed red with anger. "Quite the bedside manner you've got there doctor. No. This pregnancy will buy time to get things resolved with the Institute, and in any event I'm not getting any younger, so it's probably anyway time to get started with becoming a mother."

"Maria, after the samples I took from you showed that you were pregnant, I ran a maternal serum screening on your blood. That fetus is at high risk for congenital defects—that's what I came here to tell you. You really should terminate."

"I saw an obstetrician at the Institute's Medical Center before I left. He didn't mention anything like that."

"It's possible he didn't run that particular test if you didn't ask for it or indicate to him any family risk factors."

"Well, with all due respect, I think I'll get a second opinion. I have an appointment with a local obstetrician next week and will ask them to run the test to be sure," Maria answered stubbornly.

Mendez's gray eyes flashed angrily, and he stepped in close to her, speaking in a hushed but vaguely menacing tone. "Don't be stupid, Maria. There could be serious complications… you may be in real danger. Terminate this pregnancy. Now." For emphasis he poked her stomach with his index finger.

Maria was stunned and speechless for a moment but then stepped back. "I think you should leave." And then over Mendez's shoulder she saw the *castañera* Vadoma coming up the walk to the house. "I have company arriving," she finished somewhat curtly, relieved to have an excuse to end their conversation, but still feeling confused and conflicted.

Mendez turned and walked away, passing Vadoma without saying a word. Vadoma stopped in her tracks when she saw him and stared directly at his face as he walked by. When she reached Maria she was wearing a dark expression. "Who was that, Maria? There is something about him that does not feel right. You must be careful in your condition."

"Just a lost stranger. But you're right, something about him did not feel right," Maria responded as she opened the door for Vadoma. "Please come in, Señora Vadoma—I'll tell my mother you're here."

"Thank you… but it was you that your mother asked me to do a reading for," Vadoma said as she walked into the house while Maria held the door for her.

"What… Why?" Maria said as she closed the door.

Vadoma tapped her walking stick on the floor and motioned for Maria to follow her. "Come girl. I know you are not interested in things beyond the reach of your senses or reasoning power, but I can assure you that they are interested in you. I'm sure you can spare a little time to indulge the wishes of your dear mother and this tired old woman in front of you. Oh, and would you be so kind as to close the curtains and put a few candles on that table in the sitting room please?" Maria let out a resigned sigh and turned to prepare the room, with Vadoma smiling softly as she watched.

Maria and Vadoma then sat at the table, across from each other, illuminated only by the candlelight and the slivers of daylight that were able to leak through the drawn curtains. "I have to admit I've never had this done before… what should I do now?" Maria asked almost at a whisper, feeling at once skeptical and curious.

"Nothing dear," Vadoma replied, her tone gentle and calming. "Clear your mind and steady your breathing—you may find that focusing on the flame of the candle can help to still your mind," she continued as she waved a small bundle of smoldering dry sage leaves in the air between them, and then recited something unintelligible.

"What is that for?" Maria asked, her senses now stimulated by the novelty of the experience.

"Don't worry. It's just a little precaution… to cleanse the space around us of negative energy," Vadoma replied. "Now please, Maria, try to clear your mind," Vadoma added as she set the sage in a small ceramic bowl and reached into the pocket of her dress to pull out what looked like a deck of cards and put them on the table. Maria saw that they were Tarot cards, and Vadoma asked her to then shuffle the cards and set ten of them on the table. There was a long silence as they both stared at the cards.

"Do you think there is a message there for me?" Maria finally whispered, unable to contain her curiosity.

"Hush, girl. It cannot be rushed or forced. It must allow itself to be revealed to me." Vadoma then closed her eyes, took a deep breath, and recited a few more unintelligible words. A few moments later her eyes opened, and she smiled. "We can begin now... do you know about these?" she said as she pointed to the cards.

"Not really, Señora Vadoma. I only know they are Tarot cards."

"Well, listen closely then, and pay attention." Vadoma turned over the first and second cards—the Tower and the Ten of Swords—and her expression tightened. "It appears you may have been betrayed by someone close to you... and could be in danger."

Maria's eyes widened. "In what way... what does that mean?" she said, still somewhat skeptical but also beginning to feel that she didn't know what to believe since finding out she was pregnant.

"That I cannot see, but the betrayal is linked to the danger you are in." Vadoma then turned over the third card and fourth cards—the Page of Pentacles and the Hermit. "Your ambition and desire to control events may have put you in danger—but will also help you in your search for the truth, if you can listen to your heart as well as your head." Maria nodded her head, but to her scientist's mind this just sounded like vague generalities. Vadoma turned over the next four cards and then shook her head. "Not much is coming through from these, except that it seems some greater conflict is around you." She then turned over the final two cards—The Chariot and the Empress. "You must find someone you can trust and be willing to give up some control. If you can do that, there will be a good final outcome that is also nurturing." Vadoma paused again and then leaned forward. "Now, give me your hands and close your eyes," she said gently. Maria closed her eyes and rested her arms, palms up, on the table and Vadoma grasped her hands and chanted more of the unrecognizable words, several times over. Suddenly Maria began feeling strange, as though Vadoma's voice had expanded and filled the room and was somehow entering her consciousness not through her ears, but upwards from her chest. Vadoma smiled knowingly. "Very good. Empty your mind and open your heart. That is the wider realm around us that you feel touching you now… it is the gift of your mother's blood that flows within you. Can you remember all of that?"

"Yes, I think so," Maria replied, feeling slightly dizzy.

"Good. And remember also that more may now reveal itself to you in your dreams."

"I will," Maria said as she stood up and steadied herself, struggling to reconcile her usual intellectual skepticism with the electric current of intuition that she had just experienced, and which now lingered as a palpable presence. "Thank you for the reading, Señora Vadoma. I hope you'll excuse me—I think I need to go out and get some fresh air. I'll ask my mother to come down and look after you." As she walked out the door, the puzzling behavior of Mendez kept surfacing among the whirl of her thoughts.

≈

The following weekend was *Karmengo Jaiak*[4] in San Sebastián and a welcome diversion for Maria. She had always enjoyed going to see it as a young girl, and she was sure it would cheer her up now. The center of the festivities was in *la Parte Vieja*—Old Town—adjacent to the wharf there. Small bands would march through the streets playing traditional Basque music, accompanied by colleagues wearing carton-pierre[5] *gigantes* and *cabezudos* ('giants' and 'big heads'). The crowd-pleasing highlight of the Saturday afternoon though was a competition among young locals to try and wriggle to the end of a greased mast that was held horizontally over the water and grab the Basque flag that was there before falling into the water. Later, in the plaza near the wharf, there would be traditional Basque dancing where spectators were encouraged to participate, though some preferred to simply watch from nearby tables while enjoying freshly grilled anchovies and some local Txakoli white wine.

Maria strolled breezily through the familiar streets of her childhood in a billowy white linen dress, a wide-brimmed floppy straw hat, and sandals. After stopping for an ice cream cone at Pastelería Oiartzun, she walked the few additional blocks up to the section of *Portu Kalea*—Port Street—that passed by Constitution Plaza, where she knew there would be an excellent view of the parade making its way down to the wharf. As she waited and finished off her ice cream, her thoughts drifted back to the unsettling warnings of Vadoma and the equally unsettling behavior

---

[4] Karmengo Jaiak – The Festival of Carmen, patron saint of sailors and fishermen

[5] carton-pierre – a heavy, molded type of papier-mâché resembling plaster and used to make decorative ornaments in imitation of wood, stone or metal

of Mendez. "This is all just too strange to be real," she thought, but then the approaching music and clamor of the parade brought her back into the moment. She took a deep breath and then slowly exhaled, letting her senses absorb the atmosphere of celebration.

Ulrik was tense and uncomfortable. He had followed Maria from the Guevara home to *la Parte Vieja* and, once he saw where she had positioned herself, had used a restaurant bathroom to change into a traditional local costume he had rolled up in his backpack. He felt ridiculous, partly because he was not able to find something that fit his tall frame and so the sleeves of the white shirt and the hems of the white trousers both ended a few inches above where they should have. Thankfully, the shopkeeper had at least showed him how to properly tie the red sash around his waist and the red scarf around his neck, but the traditional red beret looked like a mushroom cap on his head as he had tried to tuck his hair up into it and then pull the back and sides down, hoping to cover his blonde hair. "What a mess Mendez has made of this situation," he thought, as he positioned himself around a corner a block away from Maria. Mendez had already left for Paris and had told him to go back to Sweden and await further instructions. But Ulrik's irritation had now metastasized into a malevolent fixation, and he had decided to take matters into his own hands. "God damn that doctor and his delusions," he grunted under his breath as he reached inside his shirt to grip the hilt of the hunting knife hidden there. The leading edge of the parade was approaching.

Maria smiled with delight when the fanciful *gigantes* leading the procession came into view just up the block from her. The music echoed up and down the street and, true to tradition, the mischievous *cabezudos* were chasing people about and swinging at them with a dried hog's bladder fashioned into a balloon at the end of a cord. As the music and the din of the crowd echoed past Constitution Plaza, Ulrik flexed his jaw and began to make his move. At first he was walking and then broke into a slow jog as he got closer to Maria, zig-zagging around people in the crowd with one hand still tucked inside his shirt gripping the knife. It was then that Maria noticed him, laughing at first at how odd he looked, but then noticing the blonde hair and strange expression on his face, looking straight at her with unmistakably blue eyes. Startled, she stepped back but was met by the wall of the building behind her and a throng of people on either side. Then she saw Ulrik pull the knife out and palm it. Her eyes went wide, and her mouth opened, but she couldn't seem to get a sound out as he closed in. When Ulrik saw that she had seen him and looked terrified, his tight lips spread into a smirk, his pulse racing with anticipation and adrenaline.

Edrigo had always been something of a troublemaker and so he loved being a *cabezudo* for the festivals. Normally the *cabezudo* is supposed to chase children and young girls and try to scare them and sometimes smack them with the hog's bladder, but when he saw the tall strange-looking foreigner jogging through the crowd he couldn't help himself. He launched the bladder. It hit the stranger at the ankles, causing him to stumble just as he was approaching a curb. The stranger's left foot then caught the curb, sending him tumbling onto the sidewalk. At first Edrigo started to laugh but then he heard an old man yell and point to a large hunting knife that had clattered out in front of the foreigner.

Maria was frozen for a moment and time seemed to stand still. She now realized this stranger was after *her*. When Ulrik then shook his head and started to push himself up, she finally pivoted to the side and pushed her way through a group of people, working her way down the block and darting into a small restaurant that she knew had a back exit. In the meantime, several local men had begun to surround Ulrik, but he had been able to reach his knife and wave them back. When he heard police whistles in the distance he sprinted off, cursing and knocking over several people and *gigantes* in his path.

Stopping a few times to catch her breath and reorient herself, Maria had made her way through side streets and alleys to Kafe Botanika, which sat on the west side of the Urumea River overlooking the elegant María Cristina Bridge and its four sculpture-crowned sixty-foot obelisks. She had hunkered down at a small table hidden behind a huge leafy plant in the back of the cafe and was sipping a cup of tea now that her hands had stopped trembling, and her heart had slowed to a more normal pace. She wondered whether the stranger who had looked like he was going to attack her might have been some kind of foreigner on drugs who had come for the festival and gotten out of hand. But she also couldn't shake the feeling that he had been specifically coming after her. But why? When he had fallen to the ground she had noticed two peculiar tattoos on his forearm—one was a simple 'C18' and the other was a vertical arrow inside of a diamond-shaped outline. She sketched them out quickly on a napkin to be able to jog her memory later. As she took another sip of tea, it dawned on her that he had looked familiar, and her mind kept drifting back to the man she had seen twice around town wearing the guayabera shirt and Panama hat, the unexpected visit from Mendez, and the words of warning from Vadoma. "What if it's not all a coincidence… what could this all be about?" she said to herself softly, almost absent-mindedly, while peering through the big leaves in front of her and towards the front of the café. Just as she was wondering whether she should file a report with the police her phone pinged. She had received a message.

Dr. Guevara, this is Remy Boucher from the Institute. I'm sorry to disturb you on a weekend, but I wanted to ask you to please call me this week when you have a chance. I have done some more checking on Dr. Mendez's visitors and have some cause for concern. In the meantime, please be careful.

Maria at first considered calling right away, but realizing she was flustered and that it was Boucher's day off, she instead sent a text confirmation that she would call soon. Almost as an afterthought, she took a picture of the writing and the rough sketch she had done on the napkin and sent it as well, asking him if the images on the napkin had any meaning to him. She then signaled the waitress for the bill and decided to call a taxi instead of walking back home along the beach the way she normally enjoyed. About halfway through the short ride back she looked down and noticed her hands were trembling and so clasped them across her lap, whispering in the direction of her midsection, "We're going to have to be more careful *txikito*. I don't know what it is, but something strange is going on, and it doesn't feel right."

Chapter 5: Night and Day

NEARLY THREE MONTHS BEFORE the incident at the parade in San Sebastián, Mendez was feeling invigorated by a frisson of anticipation as he rode through the streets of Paris in a taxi in the dark, chill hours of that April pre-dawn morning. His thoughts drifted again, as they had so often recently, to vivid memories of his grandfather talking about human genetics and the promise of eugenics. He had been particularly fascinated with theories about the Basque race and how their genetic and linguistic uniqueness, distinct among other Europeans, seemed to validate his theories of racial purity. With great enthusiasm, his grandfather had showed him two 8mm movies from 1944 by Herbert Brieger, a German director who shared a belief in these theories—'Im Lande der Basken' ('In the Land of the Basques') and 'Biscaya südwärts' ('The South of Biscay'). Both movies romanticized the Basque people and their heritage, and a voice-over in the latter went on to pose the central question that had come to preoccupy Mendez like it had his grandfather: "Where did these people come from? Nobody knows. Maybe from those who built the Tower of Babel, from the Phoenicians, from Atlanteans, the Finns, or the Mongols. In any event, the most popular theory says they came from the Iberians."

Mendez pulled out his wallet to pay the driver as the taxi glided to a stop on the Rue de la Chaise in front of Maria's apartment building. Relieved that he could see Ulrik was already there waiting for him, he grabbed the handles of the black leather Gladstone bag on the seat next to him and stepped out, motioning towards the building entrance. "Is everything in order?"

"Yes, doctor. Whatever it was you gave me to put in her drink at that jazz club worked perfectly. Stefan was here as planned when the girl arrived and was able to confirm that she was unconscious by the time he had helped her colleague—I think her name was Brigitte—get her upstairs. He also assured me that there were no hallway cameras and that he had prepared the door so that we would be able to enter her apartment."

"Good. Do you think this colleague of hers would be able to identify Stefan?"

"It seems unlikely, but as a precaution he has taken an early flight out of the country."

"All right then, let's get on with it… I want to be out of here before dawn," Mendez remarked impatiently as he stepped into the building. They had both already put on latex gloves.

Once they entered Maria's apartment, closed the curtains, and found her still unconscious on her bed, they began to prepare for the procedure. They had meticulously rehearsed and so were able to work quickly and without speaking. Mendez gently opened a metal container in his bag that held two of Maria's eggs that had been thawed, fertilized, and genetically enhanced—they were now fully-fledged embryos. As Ulrik undressed Maria and then spread and elevated her legs with pillows and sofa cushions, Mendez set up the small portable ultrasound device and wand that he had brought to help guide the placement of the embryos into Maria's uterus. He then carefully transferred the embryos from their container into an embryo transfer catheter, lubricated it, and nodded to Ulrik, signaling that he was ready to begin the procedure and that Ulrik should hold Maria steady.

As Ulrik knelt behind Maria's head and pressed down on her shoulders Mendez placed the ultrasound wand with his left hand on Maria's lower abdomen and quickly adjusted the controls on the main console until the image on the display came into focus. He made a final slight adjustment of the wand to center the image over the cervix and uterus and then, holding the wand in place, he picked up the embryo transfer catheter with his right hand and began to slowly guide it into Maria. As the ultrasound image showed the catheter began to emerge from the cervix and into the uterus, Mendez slowed even further. Once he was satisfied he had reached an optimal location, he deposited the embryos, waited for a moment to observe, and then slowly pulled the catheter out. After wiping the residual lubricant from Maria and the catheter with a paper towel, he nodded to Ulrik, this time signaling the procedure was complete. While Mendez packed up his equipment, Ulrik re-dressed Maria and arranged the pillows, cushions, and duvet as close as he could remember to how they had been when they arrived.

After they had made their way back down to the ground floor and stepped out onto the sidewalk, Ulrik could no longer contain his curiosity. "Was everything as planned? Do you think it will work?"

Mendez stopped and allowed himself a satisfied smile. "Yes, Ulrik. The seeds of our plan have been planted." He then turned and walked away into the dark and silent streets.

No one was home when Maria arrived back at the Guevara household after the short taxi ride from Kafe Botanika. She had hurried inside, looking up and down the street to see if anyone was watching, and then locked the door and closed the curtains. She thought about calling the police to report the incident at the parade and the foreigner with a knife, but then remembered that she had heard police whistles approaching the scene as she had fled and there had been plenty of bystanders. She came to the conclusion that the police must already have the man in custody and that it would be unlikely she could add anything beyond what others had reported. She decided to wait a few days, find out what Remy Boucher wanted to talk about, and then check in with the police to see if they still needed a statement from her. It was anyway late on the Saturday of a festival weekend, and she reckoned the police on duty would not appreciate having to fill out even more paperwork right at this moment. Suddenly feeling hungry, she made her way to the refrigerator and found some leftover Porrusalda vegetable soup. She knew it must have been made by her father as it was one of his specialties and it had salt cod in it, which he always used to brighten its flavor. As she let it heat up on the stove, she poured herself a tall glass of fresh apple juice and made a fresh salad from the produce her mother had brought home the previous day. The meal was delicious and familiar—just what she needed. After washing up, she went up to her room to try to clear her head and think about what she should do next, but it was not long before she dozed off under the comforting influence of the Porrusalda.

On Sunday morning, Maria woke early. She could tell her parents were already awake because the television was on. She padded down the stairs, still in her pajamas, rubbing the sleep out of her eyes. "*Egun on ama, aita.* Is there any coffee ready?"

"*Bai laztana.* In the kitchen. There's also some eggs and sausage you can heat up if you're hungry," Naomie replied. "You must have had a big day—you were already asleep when we came home. Did you see this news of what happened at the festival in Old Town yesterday? It seems we can't even have a simple parade these days without someone ruining it."

Maria was already in the kitchen pouring her coffee, but stopped and took her half-filled cup into the living room so she could see the television. "I did hear there was some commotion," she said coyly as she took a sip of coffee, not wanting to alarm her parents.

"Apparently some maniac foreigner with a knife was running amok in the middle of the parade. Some people are saying that they think he was on drugs, but others said it looked like he was actually after someone in particular and then ran away when the police came. Unfortunately, they didn't catch him, so they're asking people to be on the lookout for suspicious characters."

Maria was staring at the television screen and almost dropped her coffee cup. "*Mierde,*" she mouthed silently.

Ander had looked up when Maria came into the room and saw the sudden change in her expression. "What's wrong Maria—you look like you've seen a ghost."

"I think I have, *aita*. I was there, and that foreigner almost attacked me. I didn't say anything because I assumed the police had caught him, and I didn't want to worry you."

Ander and Naomie stood up, their eyes wide. "Why would he want to attack you, Maria," Ander said, as he guided her to sit down on the sofa.

"I don't know, but it feels like strange things have been increasingly happening to me. First this pregnancy, then the unexplainable behavior of Dr. Mendez and his visit here, the premonitions from Madame Vadoma, the feeling that a stranger is following me, and finally this attack."

Naomie glanced at Ander and then back to Maria, unable to hide her alarm. "Maria, what are you talking about? Why haven't you told us about this? I remember you mentioned Dr. Mendez as a colleague in Paris, but you never told us he had come here. And what is this about a stranger following you, and Vadoma's premonitions?"

Maria then told them everything. When she finished, Ander took her hand. Speaking gently but firmly, he said, "Maria, I'm going to take the day off from work tomorrow and go with you to the police station so you can give them a statement and as much information as you can remember about the foreigner. Until then, stay home here with us please and don't go out, okay?"

"Okay," Maria nodded, unable to think of an alternative. "But I have an appointment on Tuesday with an obstetrician, and I think I should still go."

"That's fine. I'll tell Elixane that I'll also be gone part of Tuesday, so that I can take you."

"Thank you, *aita*. I'm so sorry that I have upset things around here."

"It's not your fault, Maria," Naomie said, sitting down next to her. "I think I'll also go with you to the doctor, if you don't mind."

"Of course, *ama*." Maria squeezed her mother's hand, suddenly feeling emotional.

Naomie then looked across Maria to Ander and said in a soft but serious tone, "I think I'm going to check in with Vano, just in case." Ander nodded his head—he knew it was not a question.

Maria turned, curiosity furrowing her brows. "Who is Vano, and what are you going to call him about?"

"Don't worry about it now, *alaba*, I'll tell you later. Now, let me warm you up some breakfast. Remember, you're eating for two now!" She put on a wide smile, patted Maria on the stomach, and then stood up and went into the kitchen.

The ride to the police station on Monday morning was uncharacteristically quiet. Traffic was light as many people had taken the day off to rest after the festival weekend, and inside the car Maria and her father, usually chatty with one another, were still feeling a little overwhelmed by recent events. After a long silence, Ander finally interjected, "Maria, I'm a little worried about whether it's safe for you here in Donostia. If that stranger that tried to attack you was actually the same person you said you saw by our office and walking by the house shortly after you returned here, then he knows where you... we, live. I'm not really worried about myself," he added with a little forced bravado, "but the safety of you and your mother is another matter." Maria knew he was being instinctively protective and was probably right. She nodded silently.

At the police station, Maria gave a statement with as much detail about the incident at the parade as she could remember, including a copy of the sketch she had made of the curious tattoos visible on the stranger's forearm. She then also told them about seeing a potentially similar looking stranger near their home and near her father's business, additionally describing the distinctive Panama hat and guayabera shirt he was wearing. Maria left out the visit from Mendez as the two matters seemed unrelated and she didn't want to complicate the statement unnecessarily. Once the session was finished, the policeman gave Maria his telephone number, asked her to call if she remembered anything further or if there were any more suspicious incidents, and thanked her for coming in. As Maria stood up, she paused for a moment. "Can I ask what happens next please?"

"Of course. We'll give all this information to the detective that was assigned to the case yesterday. She will follow up on it along with the other information we received from bystanders who saw what happened. We'll also be checking with Interpol to check if any notices have been issued on persons of interest that may fit the description of the suspect. If there are any relevant developments, we will contact you. In the meantime, I urge you both to be cautious of your surroundings. If you don't already have one, consider installing a basic security system at your house and"—he looked at Ander—"at your business. In addition to the peace of mind, on the off chance that the suspect returns we might get lucky and have a security camera capture his image. The latest systems are inexpensive and easy to install. I'll give you a list of the ones we recommend." He then handed Ander a slip of paper with the information on it and walked them to the door, thanking them again for coming in. After leaving the police station, Ander took Maria and drove straight to a local hardware store to purchase one of the home security system kits on the policeman's list.

When they arrived home, Maria remembered that she needed to respond to Remy Boucher's text message, so she decided to call him while her father unboxed the new security system kit and read the instructions. She stopped in the kitchen to make a cup of the local sloeberry-infused black tea she had been delighted to find in the pantry a few days ago. Then she went upstairs and dialed Boucher's number.

"Oui, Allo?" came the rough-hewn voice that Maria now found somehow familiar and reassuring.

"Hello Remy, this is Maria Guevara. I received your message on Saturday… is this a good time to talk?"

"Ah, Dr. Guevara… Maria. Yes, I'm glad you called. Is everything okay with you?"

"Well, yes and no, Remy. It's been lovely to spend time with my parents again, but something frightening happened this weekend," Maria said, trying not to sound emotional. She then went on to describe what had happened in much the same way she had described it to the police that morning. However, this time she included her recollection of the unsettling visit of Mendez to San Sebastián and his unexpected behavior in Paris before she had left—though she still did not reveal that they had been freezing her eggs. "So, you can imagine after all that I am very curious to hear what you have discovered."

There was silence on the line for a few moments and then Maria heard Remy exhale heavily "*Zut.*" After another moment he began. "Before I go on, can I ask you where you saw those markings that you sent me after you responded to my text?"

"They were tattooed on the forearm of that stranger that I think was trying to attack me at the parade on Saturday. I saw them pretty clearly when he fell down."

"*Merde.*" Remy paused and then carried on. "After Dr. Mendez's sudden absence, my old policeman's nose started twitching, so I checked into his visitor logs. At first nothing looked unusual, but then I found a few after-hours visits where the companies logged with the visitor names turned out not to exist. With a little backchannel help from an old protégé who now works for DGSI,[1] we determined that the names were also probably fake, as one of them was a known alias for a senior figure in a violent transnational organization that's on the DGSI watchlist. It's called Combat 18, sometimes abbreviated to C18, and they are basically neo-Nazis. Given the other tattoo image, there is no doubt in my mind that the man who tried to attack you is part of that organization and may have been the same one visiting Dr. Mendez in Paris."

"What about the other tattoo?"

"That other image—the arrow inside a diamond outline—is the symbol of the Nordic Resistance Movement. They have tried to masquerade as a political party in Scandinavia, but they are essentially another far-right neo-Nazi group. Like C18 they embrace violence, but

[1] DGSI – France's General Directorate for Internal Security, responsible for counter-espionage, counter-terrorism, countering cybercrime and surveillance of potentially threatening groups & organizations.

C18 is more of a paramilitary and even terroristic organization. C18 started in England and has since spread within northern Europe. The Nordic Resistance organization has so far remained active mostly only in Scandinavian countries. From what I am hearing though, European state security organizations have been increasingly worried about these groups starting to align and spread their tentacles. I don't know why your attacker had tattoos from both groups, but it can't be a good sign, and it almost certainly means he is quite dangerous and violent, Maria."

"Yes, I noticed. And I guess that would explain the blonde hair and blue eyes. But I'm struggling to understand what any of this would have to do with me?"

"I don't know yet. But it seems we have to at least consider the possibility that it may have something to do with Dr. Mendez. He is potentially the common connection in all of this. And you mentioned that his behavior towards you had become unusual?"

"Yes, but he was always so kind and helpful with me… until…" Maria said, her voice trailing off.

"Until what?"

"Until that day I went to see him in his office after I had found out I might be pregnant. I ended up telling him about the Romani blood on my mother's side, which seemed to surprise him."

"You are aware that the Nazis hated the Romanies almost as much as they hated the Jews, right?"

"Vaguely, I guess. I don't know the whole history. Are you saying he may be a Nazi?" The potential horror, the complexity, of the situation was starting to become clearer to Maria.

"I don't know what he is, but it's almost certainly more than what's on the surface. I think you may need to consider going somewhere else for a while… I'm not sure it's completely safe there if dangerous people know where you are living."

Maria chuckled ironically. "My father said the same thing. He's installing a new home security system as we speak."

"I don't want to frighten you, but these are not the kind of people that would be deterred by a few cameras and an alarm system. Maria, I'm afraid I have to go now… but let's stay in touch. I'll let you know if I find out anything more, and please do likewise."

"Thank you, Remy. I'm sorry if all of this has caused extra work for you."

"Not to worry… what else do I have to fill the hours here anyway besides watching the security monitors and doing the rounds to make sure the doors are locked? *Au revoir*, Maria."

Maria and her parents arrived on Tuesday morning at the office of Dr. Danel Otxoa just as it was opening. She had booked the first available appointment of the day. After she had signed in and filled out a screening form, a nurse took her to an examination room, checked her vital signs, and gave her a cotton hospital gown to change into and a cup to provide a urine sample later. Dr. Otxoa came in shortly after and performed a standard examination and an ultrasound, drew some blood, and asked her some more detailed questions about her medical history and the timeline since her last period. He was a soft-spoken older man with a gentle and calming manner—which is probably why Naomie had said he was the most popular obstetrician in town. As he was finishing up he pulled off his gloves, looked over his shoulder as he was washing his hands, and said reassuringly, "Everything seems normal so far Señorita Guevara—I'll let you know if we see anything notable from the tests that will be run on your samples. Do you have any questions or concerns?"

"Well, I wanted to make sure the tests you run will include a maternal serum screening. A doctor I saw in Paris said he did one in May and saw some risk factors for congenital abnormalities."

Otxoa turned now squarely towards Maria with a curious look on his face. "Doing a serum screening that early would be highly unusual and almost certainly inconclusive. We usually only do it after 10 weeks. Given you are coming to the end of your first trimester it will anyway definitely be on the panel of tests we will run for you now. In any event, if it's possible, please see if you can have copies of your medical records in Paris forwarded to me."

"And the ultrasound… anything unusual?"

"Everything looks normal so far for this stage, although it's still early. If you want to know the gender of the baby we won't be able to determine that conclusively for another six or seven weeks. I can tell you that you don't have multiples… I mean twins. Anything else?"

Maria thought for a few moments and then asked, "I'd like a detailed DNA test on the baby please… is that something you can help with? I don't mind paying extra." She also wanted to ask him if he had ever heard of any cases of human asexual reproduction but decided that it might sound a little delusional—which wasn't something she wanted him to make notes about in her file.

"There is something new we've been doing trials on in partnership with a lab in Madrid. I would need to take a sample from your placenta in addition to your blood, and then send it off to Madrid. Getting the results will take a little longer than the other tests."

"I know. Genetics is one of my research areas," Maria said matter-of-factly.

Otxoa's eyebrows arched slightly. "Oh, I see. Then it's *Dr.* Guevara, I presume?"

"Yes, but not a medical doctor. Anyway, let's go ahead with the DNA test, please. Would it be possible to take the placenta sample now?"

"Yes, I suppose so. Is there anything in particular you're looking for?

"Everything, doctor. I want to find out as much as I can about this baby."

≈

Naomie was in the passenger seat tying her scarf, and Maria was sitting in the back, lost in thought as they drove away from Dr. Otxoa's office. Had Dr. Mendez lied about the maternal serum screening test? And if so, then what was the real reason he was so insistent that I terminate my pregnancy? And how did he know where to find me in San Sebastián? Suddenly she realized her father was talking to her, while looking at her in the rearview mirror, like he used to do when he would drive her to school as a child.

"Maria… Maria. Are you listening to me?"

"I'm sorry, *aita*, I was thinking about something. What were you saying?"

"I thought it would be good for you—for all of us—to get out of the house for the day, so we've packed a lunch and are driving up to Pagoeta Natural Park. It's a quiet day. Everybody else is at work."

Maria was delighted. Pagoeta Natural Park—only a thirty-minute drive southwest of San Sebastián—had beautiful walking trails and scenery, including a botanical garden, prehistoric cave sites, and of course the eponymous Mount Pagoeta. "What a wonderful idea! Thank you, *aita*. I hope it won't be a problem for you to be away from work again today?"

Ander laughed. "Maria, you've met Elixane. She's got things running so smoothly there that I think I'd have to be gone a week or more before they noticed!" They all laughed, relieved to finally have a moment that felt light and carefree, and Ander then turned on some music while they enjoyed the rest of the leisurely drive through the familiar Basque countryside and villages.

Almost exactly thirty minutes later, Ander pulled into the parking lot of the park's visitor center and announced, "Here we are!"

"Yes, we can see, Ander." Naomie teased, turning with a conspiratorial grin towards Maria, who was trying not to laugh.

"Very funny ladies I see that I've got with me today," Ander deadpanned as he stepped out of the car, looking at his watch. "Why don't we check in at the visitor center, have a walk through the botanical garden, and then have lunch at the picnic tables over there," he said, pointing toward the far side of the building. "After that, we can go for a nice afternoon hike, okay?" They both nodded and then headed for the visitor center restrooms.

Later that afternoon, after they had worked their way up a trail through the trees and into a lush hilltop meadow with a sweeping view of the mountains in the distance, Ander signaled that they should stop for a moment and rest. He put his hands on his hips, stared into the distance wistfully, and said in a hushed voice, "I love this land of ours." Naomie put her arm around Maria's shoulders and gave her an affectionate squeeze.

"Ander, now that we're here and all together, maybe it's time now that we have a talk," Naomie said, and Maria then realized that they had brought her up here to talk about something. Probably something serious. They were sweet, she thought, but predictable in the way that people get as they grow older.

"Maria, we have an idea of where it might be safe for you, at least until the police can find out what's happening," Ander began.

Naomie jumped in, impatient to get to the point. "The Amaya family in Arditurri… do you remember them? They mostly kept to themselves, but they are distant relations of mine, and their son—Vano—has connections that not even others in Arditurri know about. I spoke to them yesterday while you were at the police station with your father. They offered to provide you sanctuary, at least for a while. It is a tradition of ours. Vano is coming to Donostia tomorrow to meet you so we can all discuss it together. I know this is a bit sudden, but with everything that has happened, we felt we needed to find a place to keep you safe, at least for now."

Maria crossed her arms, feeling at once hesitant and vulnerable. She preferred being in control of her own circumstances. "That's very kind of them, but I only have a vague recollection of them, and I'm not sure I want to go to Arditurri. It feels so… remote."

Ander interjected, "That's part of the point, Maria. At least keep an open mind until you speak with Vano. Please?"

Maria paced for a moment and then turned to Naomie. "*Ama*, you mentioned this Vano person has connections… what did you mean by that? What kind of person is he?"

"Vano is not that much older than you… maybe five- or six-years difference. You probably saw him around Arditurri as a child but just don't remember the name. No one in Arditurri outside his immediate family really knows him well, as he travels a lot for his job and doesn't socialize much." Naomie's voice trailed off a little nervously and she glanced over at Ander. He nodded, a prompt for her to carry on. "What I'm about to tell you must remain only among us. Do you understand?

"Yes."

"I'm serious, Maria, it's very important."

"Yes, *ama*. I promise not to talk about it with anyone," Maria said, trying her best not to sound petulant.

"Vano works for the CNI."

Maria's arms unfolded and dropped to her sides. "What! The spy agency?"

"Oh, they do domestic intelligence as well," Ander half joked.

Naomie held her daughter's gaze and nodded silently.

When Maria stepped out of the shower the next morning, she stared at her reflection in the mirror for a long while after she had toweled off. She knew she was no beauty queen, but she had also never really been particularly unhappy with her looks. She kept herself fit, had a nice figure, a pleasant face and healthy hair, and—when the mood struck her—she knew she could attract men as effectively as most women. Her attention at this moment, as it turned out, was on her lower abdomen. She could not see any noticeable changes in her body yet, but she knew there was a living, growing child in there, and was still trying to process the complex thoughts and emotions that had begun to accompany that realization. Just then a light knock came on the bathroom door, interrupting her musings. "Yes?"

"It's me Maria," her mother chirped. "Can you come down and help tidy the house after you are dressed please? Vano will be here soon, and I want to finish preparing lunch."

"Yes, *ama*. I'll be down in about ten minutes, okay?"

"Thank you, dear."

About thirty minutes later, and once Maria had finished putting the rooms on the ground floor in order, she joined her mother who was in front of the stove in the kitchen. "That smells like pil-pil, *ama*," she said, slipping her arm around Naomie's waist and giving her a gentle squeeze. "You must be in a good mood," she added teasingly. It was *Bacalao al pil-pil*, a dish that looks simple but takes some work to prepare correctly. It consists of salt cod, first cooked in olive oil with garlic and chili peppers, and which releases a gelatin that is then used to emulsify a creamy sauce that is prepared separately. The sauce is then finally spooned over the cod before serving. It paired perfectly with the remaining unopened bottle of white Txakoli wine that was in the refrigerator.

"Well, Vano has made a special trip here to see us, so the least we can do is provide him a nice meal. And it's been quite a while since I've seen him or his family. Can you please set the table, Maria?"

"Yes, of course."

It was not long after they had finished preparations that the expected knock came on the front door. Naomie wiped off her hands with her apron and hurried to the door, beaming. "That's him, Maria," she said, and then opened the door.

Vano Amaya was waiting on the porch with a small overnight bag he had set down beside him. He was of average build and a bit more than average height, and was wearing perfectly-fitting jeans, a crisp white cotton shirt, a linen Navy blazer, a closely-trimmed beard, and a wide smile. After receiving an affectionate hug from Naomie and exchanging greetings, he stepped into the house and spotted Maria. "Ah, this must be Maria. It's been a long time, no?"

Maria's first reaction was that this man's hair was a little too long, his outfit too stylish, and his manner too charming for him to be a government employee. But she held her tongue and offered her hand politely, "Yes, and you must be Vano. It's a pleasure to meet you. Thank you for coming… we have some lunch prepared. Can I get you some wine?"

Vano shook her hand, looking mildly amused. "Yes, thank you," he said, as he set his overnight bag by the sofa. "Let me just wash up, and I'll join you at the table."

Once lunch and an acceptable interval of small talk about the weather, their families, and recent travels had passed, Naomie started gathering the dishes to take back to the kitchen. Maria began to stand and help, but Naomie put her hand on Maria's shoulder. "I think you two should talk now. I'll take care of things in the kitchen."

"Are you sure, *ama*?"

"Yes. And speak openly with Vano—he and his family have our trust."

Maria and Vano pulled away from the table, moved into the living room, and sat across from one another—Maria on the sofa and Vano on an armchair. After a brief awkward silence, Maria began. "I'm sorry, but I can't seem to remember having met you. When did we meet?"

Vano paused for a moment, and his gregarious manner seemed to recede a bit. He looked down, and then back up, directly at Maria. "In truth it was only once, but I remember it clearly."

"And?" Maria said, a little impatiently.

"You must have been only about fourteen. It was that night in Arditurri, in the stables, when I found you trying to fight off that jackass Alfonso."

Maria was flabbergasted—this was the last thing she had expected. "That was you? I knew then that you were from the Amaya family, but I didn't know your name. And you look so different now."

"We both grew up. And I have this now," he said as he stroked his beard.

"I meant to find you later and thank you, but…"

"But you never returned to Arditurri."

"I'm sorry, Vano. And thank you again. Did you ever tell anyone about what happened?"

"No. You asked me not to."

"Not even my mother?"

"You asked me not to tell anyone."

It was in that moment that Maria realized that she could trust this man, and her demeanor softened. "Out of curiosity, whatever happened to Alfonso?"

"He's still a jackass, as is the rest of his family."

Maria almost snorted with laughter. "Is he still in Arditurri?"

"No… I think he moved down south in Andalusia somewhere."

Their discussion carried on and Maria recounted what had happened to her since April in Paris. Vano listened intently, only occasionally asking a question for clarification. He had heard much of the story via Naomie on the phone but wanted to hear it directly from Maria. When she came to the end of the story she took a sip of the tea she had brought with her and then set it down slowly and deliberately. "Are you sure your family would not mind me staying with them for a while?"

"Well, it's just me and my parents. They are getting old now, and I am away a lot due to my work, so they are very much looking forward to seeing you again and having someone around the house. They don't get out much, and we Amayas have always been a little at the periphery of the community there in Arditurri."

"Why is that?"

"It's a long story… why don't we save that for the drive to Arditurri."

"When should we leave?"

"Tomorrow morning. It'll be safer for your parents if you're away until we can figure out what is going on and who is involved. Also, I need to be in Madrid in a few days and then Lyon after that."

"Oh. Can you tell me more about your work, Vano? Is it interesting?"

Vano laughed and stood up. "In due course Maria, in due course. Let's take things one step at a time, okay? Right now, this situation is about you."

Maria gave a resigned sigh. "Okay. Let's go for a walk then… I'd like to get out of the house for a while. I just need to go freshen up and get ready."

A few minutes later Naomie joined Maria upstairs while she was changing and sidled up next to her, looking at her in the mirror. "How did it go? He's handsome, and charming as well… don't you think?" she asked mischievously.

Maria exhaled and turned to face her mother. "*Ama*, my goodness! You said we're related to the Amayas. But yes, objectively, I guess he is handsome. And nice."

Naomie could see that Maria had blushed slightly but pretended not to notice. "It's a very *distant* relation Maria," she said with a knowing smile as she reached into her pocket. "By the way, Sra. Vadoma prepared this for you… for protection." It was a small black pouch called a *putsi*, hanging from a leather cord. She opened it to show Maria the contents— a stone with a hole in it, a seashell, and a fine piece of paper with a spiral drawn on it—and then closed it tightly and began to fasten it around Maria's neck. "Wear it next to your skin and keep it with you always."

Maria sighed, "*Ama*, you know I don't believe in this stuff. Talismans… amulets… relics of old superstitions that provide only false hope."

"Don't worry, Maria. What is real and what we believe are sometimes very different things. Humor your mother and just wear it… even if only for my sake."

PART II:

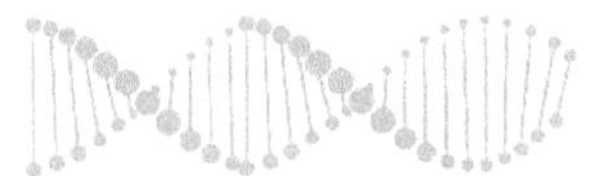

QUICKENING

From the cadenced roar of the waves

and the wail of the wind,

from the shimmering light

flecked over woodland and cloud,

from the cries of passing birds

and the wild unknown perfumes

stolen by zephyrs

from mountaintops and valleys,

there are realms where souls

crushed by the weight of the world

find refuge.

—From the Cadenced Roar of the Waves (Rosalía de Castro)

Chapter 6: Au Privave

THE DRIVE TO ARDITURRI never took longer than forty-five minutes unless there was road construction or a traffic accident, but to Maria it always felt longer. It was as if she was leaving one world and entering another. The night before, Ander had brought home one of his signature dishes from his *Txoko,*[1] and the four of them ate and drank and talked late into the evening, ending on a wistful, melancholic note. In the morning, there had been tearful farewells and promises and the usual proverbs of parental advice, and then Vano had finally urged that they should get going to avoid traffic. But before leaving, he asked Maria for her phone as she was getting in the car and took it back inside the Guevara home. When he came back, he pulled another phone out of the glovebox and handed it to her.

"What's this... and where is my phone, Vano?" Maria asked, clearly irritated.

"We can't take a chance that your phone might be being tracked. That's a burner phone I've prepared for you. It's got an encrypted VPN

---

[1] Txoko – a traditionally Basque male members-only gastronomical society where men come to cook, eat, and socialize.

for when you need to access the internet, and the phone number is not registered."

"What if someone like my parents or Remy Boucher is trying to reach me? They don't have the number for this phone."

"Don't worry, any calls or text messages to your original phone will get routed to this phone via a phone number anonymizer link that I already set up for you. And when you make outgoing calls from this phone it will look like it's coming from your original phone *and* appear to be linked to its location."

Maria put her sunglasses on, clicked her seatbelt into place, and turned to Vano with a slightly sheepish expression. "Well, thank you… I guess. I hope it works." Vano nodded and put the car in gear, pulling away while Maria's waving parents receded in the rear-view mirror.

Just as they were leaving the city limits of San Sebastián, Maria reached forward, turned the volume down on the radio, and said in a teasingly mock-serious tone, "So, Sr. Vano Amaya. You have me at a disadvantage. It was clear from the conversation last night that my mother has pretty much given you the details of my entire life story, but I know next to nothing about you and your family. Since it seems we are going to be spending more time together, maybe now is a good time for you to fill me in?"

Vano laughed deeply, holding up one hand, palm out. "Okay, Okay, Maria. I see now what your mother meant about you having an inquisitive mind… let me think for a minute about where to begin."

"Well, if it's easier, maybe start by telling me about your family. You mentioned yesterday that they had been on the periphery of the Arditurri community?"

"Yes, I suppose that's a good place to start, but we'll have to go back in time a few generations. And this is just between us… okay?"

"Yes, of course. I really am interested to know more," Maria answered, inwardly pleased that her coaxing had paid off.

"During the Civil War,[2] the Amayas were supportive of the Republican government and—"

"When you said you had to go back in time, you meant it," Maria remarked, sounding surprised.

Vano looked slightly irritated. "Do you want to hear the story or no?"

"Sorry," Maria responded contritely. "Yes. Please go on."

"The Amaya family suffered, Maria. Some even got caught at the bombing of Guernica in 1937 when Franco and his Nationalists invited their friend Hitler to test his *Luftwaffe's* new aerial bombing techniques. When the Nationalists finally won in 1939, they started hunting down Republican partisans and sympathizers. After going into hiding for a while, my great-grandfather took his family—his wife and twin sons Silvanus and Danior—across the border into France, thinking they'd be safe. But it wasn't long after France fell that the Nazis and their French collaborators started hunting Jews and Roma, rounding them up, and sending them to concentration camps. The family was eventually sent to the 'Gypsy Camp' at Auschwitz because the doctor there—Mengele—was doing so-called 'genetic experiments' with twins. The only one that survived was little Danior—my grandfather." Vano paused for a moment, but kept his gaze straight ahead, his knuckles tight on the steering wheel. The silence was thick with unspoken implication.

---

[2] Spanish Civil War (1936–1939)

Maria struggled for words. "I… I had no idea Vano. I don't know what to say."

"No need for words, Maria. It happened. Now you know. There's more, if you're still interested."

"Yes."

"When my grandfather—Danior—grew up, he wanted revenge, or at least some kind of justice. So he became a sort of freelance Nazi hunter. He was so good at it even the Mossad[3] contracted with him to help on some of their hunts and gave him asylum in Israel when they learned of his full story. He had refused to return to live in Spain while Franco and his Nationalists were still in power, so my father was actually born in Tel Aviv. The family finally moved back to Spain in the mid-1980s. By then my father, having grown up with people—literally around the house—from Mossad and other friendly intelligence agencies that were part of my grandfather's social circle, kind of naturally drifted into this 'family business' in the shadows that I now also find myself in. Mengele had been my grandfather's greatest obsession though, his 'white whale' like Ahab's in Moby Dick, but he never caught him. It haunted him."

"So what happened to Mengele," Maria asked, by now completely captivated by the story.

"He had gone into hiding in South America, first in Argentina and then eventually in Brazil, where he died. He had taken another wife and then a mistress there, and some say he even fathered more children— nobody knows for sure. When a break in the case finally came in the 1980s through family connections in Germany, they were able to track

---

[3] Mossad – the national intelligence agency of Israel, responsible for intelligence collection, covert operations, and counter-terrorism.

him down, but he was already dead and buried. By the early 1990s, DNA testing had developed to the point that they could confirm it was Mengele. His skeleton is actually stored at the São Paulo Institute for Forensic Medicine."

"That's… an astonishing story Vano. And not at all what I was expecting. But what about the relations of the Amayas in Arditurri with the rest of the community? Why the distance?"

"Some of those families had been, believe it or not, supporters of Franco and the Nationalist regime. Including the family of that little bully Alfonso that attacked you in the stables. Even though my father finally returned to live in our ancestral home in Arditurri when he came back to Spain, he never really trusted some of the neighbors, and they never knew quite what to make of us. Old suspicions and distrust don't die easily in our culture—you know that."

"My mother never told me any of that."

"A lot of people would rather just forget all those bad times and not let their children get pulled into old rivalries and feuds. It's understandable. With my family, though, there is no hiding from it."

"*Caray.* This is a lot to take in, Vano. One more question?"

"Sure, go ahead."

"How did a *Calé* boy from Arditurri end up working for CNI?"

Vano allowed himself a pensive smile, though his eyes remained fixed on the road ahead. "Well, like I said, there were already a lot of connections in that world through my grandfather and then my father. I idolized them and wanted to follow in their footsteps. My father insisted I get a good education first, so I studied history, languages, philosophy, and psychology at university. Then he made a few introductions that helped me get an interview. And the timing was good because CNI was setting up an undercover unit to monitor potentially dangerous old Francoist fascists. The idea was to infiltrate their modern-day offspring movements, and so it helped to have people that could easily blend into different environments and cultures. We had the additional benefit of being able to access my grandfather's old network, which included people in Romani communities throughout Europe. My father had maintained those relationships, and it became my turn, in a sense. We were a goldmine for CNI once they figured out the extent of our network and depth of our hatred for anything that smelled of fascism or Nazis. My grandfather used to say that we Amayas can never let the memory of his brother Silvanus be forgotten."

"And why do you trust me enough to tell me all this?"

"I thought your last question was the last question." Vano laughed. "Maria, your mother must have told you there is some connection between our families. The Villars were the only other family in Arditurri that my father really trusted. You are potentially in danger now, so it is our tradition, our responsibility, to help you—that is our culture. And if it does turn out to be some kind of modern-day Nazis or similar group that is involved, then eliminating that threat will be especially satisfying to us. Now, let's try and enjoy the rest of the drive—what's left of it." He then reached forward, turned the radio volume back up, and began singing along with the music, to Maria's dismay.

≈

Mendez was furious. Back in his apartment in Paris now, he had just got off the phone with Ulrik Eklund and learned of the botched attack in San Sebastián. He paced around his living room for a few minutes, pausing occasionally to peer through the curtains, and then pulled his phone back out of his jacket pocket. He scrolled through his contact list and pressed 'call' on the name of Stefan Lang.

"Hello?" came a soft-spoken response after a few rings.

"Hello Stefan. Where are you now? Are you free to talk?"

"Ah, *Herr Doktor*. Yes. I am in Zürich."

"And is your phone encrypted?"

"Yes, of course."

"Good. It seems we are in need of your services again. Ulrik generated some unexpected and unwelcome noise in Spain. We need someone to go there and, with a little more finesse and subtlety this time, try to find out what the police know, and to also see if the girl is still there. If not, we need to know where she has gone. Is that agreeable to you in line with our usual arrangements?"

"Yes. That shouldn't be too difficult. We have people in Spain."

"*Exzellent*. Keep me updated please. I will text you the information you will need."

"*Danke. Wir sprechen uns später.*" And with that the call was over.

Mendez had already decided what he needed to do next. It was late on a Sunday morning at the peak of summer holiday season in France, so there would be no one around his office at the Institute's Medical Center, and only a minimum required staffing in the adjoining clinical areas for emergencies. "Perfect timing," he thought to himself, as he needed to take away and dispose of the cryogenic chamber in his office closet—including the remaining frozen eggs it held—without curious staff seeing him. Luckily, he had left the two-wheeled hand cart he used to bring the chamber to the closet in there with it.

Mendez had rented a van and, after the brief drive from his apartment, parked it in the visitor parking area closest to the entrance of the Medical Center. After swiping his badge, entering the building, and making his way to the wing where his office was located, he was relieved to see that indeed no one seemed to be around. Everything appeared to be as he had left it. He unlocked the closet and there, too, the chamber and the hand cart remained exactly as he had left them. After peeking his head out into the hallway one more time to make sure no one was around, he unplugged the chamber, shoved the blade of the handcart beneath it, and wheeled it out. As he drove away from the Medical Center, he breathed an audible sigh of relief—it was only a short drive to the Hospital Paris Saint-Joseph, just across the cluster of train tracks leading into the Gare Montparnasse station. Once there, for appearances sake, he did some damage to the chamber with a hammer that he had brought along and then manhandled the it into one of the hospital's big industrial waste containers by its rear loading dock. He knew it wouldn't look out of place when the garbage workers came to take the hospital's waste containers away. They would just assume it was some damaged equipment from the hospital.

Mendez then drove back towards the hospital, but this time passed by it and parked on the Rue Borromée just around the corner from his favorite park. He grabbed the wrapped sandwich and bottled water on the seat next to him, walked into the park, and found his favorite bench for looking at the 'Moon Bird' sculpture. By the time he had unwrapped his sandwich he already felt more relaxed. Back at the Institute, Remy Boucher was also just about to eat his lunch when his phone pinged with a message. The tiny motion-activated camera that he had hidden in

Mendez's office after the unsettling call with Maria had sent an alert that there was new footage to view.

≈

Two days after arriving in Arditurri, Maria was still asleep when a soft knock came on her door early in the morning. "Yes?" she finally replied.

"It's Vano. I've made some coffee. I have to leave later for several days and wanted to talk about a few things, if you don't mind."

"Sure. Give me a ten minutes to freshen up. Do you always wake up so early?"

"Yes. You'll get used to it," he replied.

"Probably not."

When she joined him at the kitchen table, he poured her a cup of coffee as she sat down. She noticed he had his laptop open with a small microphone plugged into it. "What's that for?" she said, pointing to the microphone.

"I'd like to go over everything that happened to you around the time that you think you became pregnant, just to make sure I haven't missed any details and have it saved for future reference. I've got some software that will automatically transcribe what's said into a written transcript. I won't share it with anyone—it will only be for us to use to compare notes. Okay?"

"I guess," Maria replied and then took a sip of coffee. "But before we begin, where are you going?"

"I have some briefings on another case I have to attend at CNI headquarters in Madrid. It'll be a good opportunity to do some research on the compartmentalized system files there that we keep firewalled from remote access. After that, I'm going to Interpol headquarters in Lyon to speak with a liaison."

"Research about what? Me?"

"No. I've already done a pretty thorough background check on you. You're clean."

Maria could tell he was not joking. "I see. So what will you be checking on then?"

"Carlos Mendez, C18, that other tattoo, and whatever might jump out from our conversation that sounds like it needs more follow up. Can we start now please?"

"Yes." Maria sighed and then began going over the details of what had happened since April, including some background on how she had been freezing her eggs with Mendez's help. Vano mostly listened, but occasionally interjected with a question.

After Maria had finished, Vano leaned back in his chair, laced his fingers behind his head, and looked up at the ceiling for several seconds, as if searching for something. He then dropped his gaze back to her. "Wait. You mentioned Mendez seemed fascinated—in a positive way— by your Basque heritage. Did he ever explain why?"

"Not really. Except one time he mentioned something about having read how the origins of Basque DNA were unique and… 'pure' was the word I think he used. I remember thinking that was an odd way to describe it. But then again, he sometimes had an odd way of expressing himself, so I didn't think too much of it." While Maria spoke, she could see Vano was scribbling some notes in addition to the recording.

Vano stopped scribbling and looked up again.

"Doesn't it also seem unusual then, perhaps even relevant, that it was only after you told him about your Romani blood that he started acting strangely?"

"That's what Remy Boucher said when I spoke to him. He even mentioned something about how Nazis hated Romanies after I told him about the C18 and other tattoo, and I guess the story of your grandfather corroborates that. But if Dr. Mendez is somehow involved with some modern-day neo-Nazis, and Nazis were fascinated with Basques, then why would they have bombed Guernica? That is the heart of the Basque Country. None of it makes sense to me." Vano jotted down some more notes, including a reminder to himself to look into the history of the Basque Country during World War II and to try to develop a deeper profile of Mendez.

"What can you remember about what he told you of his past? Before coming to work at the Pasteur Institute."

"Nothing that seemed unusual. Mostly anecdotes about his childhood split between growing up in Argentina and visiting his grandfather's farm in Brazil. He got his MD at the University of Buenos Aires and then later a PhD in Biochemistry. He then went to work at HUG-CELL—the Human Genome and Stem Cell Research Center—at the University of São Paulo in Brazil. I think they call it 'Genoma' now. He became quite well known for his work in human genetics in general, and infectious and tropical diseases in particular. That's how he came to the attention of the Pasteur Institute. They eventually offered him the equivalent of a tenured residency, which is how he ended up in Paris."

Vano poured them both a fresh cup of coffee. "This grandfather in Brazil. What did he tell you about him?"

"The grandfather on a farm? How would that be relevant?"

"It's probably not. But sometimes hints are hidden behind little details."

"He said the neighbors called him Senhor Pedro and that he encouraged Mendez's interest in biology and later genetics, even teaching him some of the basics."

"Fascinating. Senhor Pedro. Peter. Did he mention a last name?"

"No. I assumed it was Mendez, the same as his. But then again…" Maria's voice trailed off. "I vaguely remember now that he mentioned that it was his mother's father, so I guess the family name would have been different. Anyway, is there a reason we're going down this rabbit hole?"

"Like I said… hints and details. One more question about Mendez—how old would you say he is?"

"Early sixties, I would guess."

"That would fit," Vano murmured, seemingly to himself.

Maria was becoming exasperated. "Fit what, Vano?!"

"It's probably just a very bizarre coincidence, but Josef Mengele—*the* Josef Mengele—lived in hiding in Brazil in the 1960s and 1970s and one of the false identities he used was posing as a Swiss national by the name of Peter Hochbichlet. He lived in several different locations—including farms—over that period, all in the São Paulo region."

The room went quiet for a moment and Maria stared at Vano in disbelief. "Vano, are you saying Dr. Mendez is the grandson of… Josef Mengele?" She intended to sound skeptical, but her voice wavered, ever so slightly.

"That's not what I'm saying," Vano retorted. "What I'm saying is that at this point we can't rule it out, Maria." He scribbled a few more notes, pushed his chair back, and then stood up and paced around the kitchen a few times.

"Anything else? I'm getting hungry."

"Just one more thing—"

"You must have excelled in interrogation training at CNI," Maria interrupted, breaking the mood with a laugh.

"I did," Vano replied, smiling back at her. "You said you made a sketch of those tattoos. Can you show it to me?"

Maria went into the bedroom and brought back her purse and reached inside. But when she pulled out the sketch, another slip of paper fell out with it. It was the doodling she had done while talking to Brigitte, and which included the words '… good suggestion by Dr. Mendez.' Maria let out a percussive "Hm," and then said, "I forgot about this."

"What is it?"

"I doodled this absent-mindedly when I was talking to my friend Brigitte about that night I passed out after going to that jazz club. I remember thinking that it had been a fun night, all things considered, and a good suggestion by Dr. Mendez that I attend. But now that I think of it, how would he have known about it? We're in completely different departments. And that night was the only unusual thing I can remember happening to me in the window of days it would have been possible for me to get pregnant."

Vano crossed his arms and began, "Like I said, Maria—"

Maria interrupted again "I know, Vano. Hints and details."

≈

Mendez tapped his fingers rhythmically on his knee as the shiny black electric Mercedes he was riding in glided to a halt. He was a confident and sometimes arrogant man, but today he was tense, and not at all looking forward to this meeting. As he stepped out of the car the imposing, almost menacing, spires of The Dolder Grand hotel towered above him. Perched on a hillside above Zürich, this historic location had been the meeting place for the Council for more than eighty years, except during the hotel's renovation from 2004 to 2008. A favorite of royalty, celebrities, and statesmen from around the world for decades, The Dolder Grand was not just a bastion of European refinement and Swiss efficiency, it also provided the exacting kind of security and discretion that the Council required when they met. Mendez made his way into the lobby, settled into one of the white leather sofas near the front windows, and ordered a double espresso from the lobby attendant. As the attendant went away to fulfill his order, Mendez reflected on the pleasure of being in a place so well-run that even the lobby attendants somehow knew the perfect moment to approach a patron and had the perfect blend of reserve and graciousness in their demeanor.

The Council of the Nine Realms ('the Council') had been inaugurated in 1950, rising from the ashes of defeat in World War II and the turbulence of five momentous post-war years. A new State of Israel had been proclaimed and admitted to the recently-created United Nations; the Berlin Airlift, the creation of NATO, and the first atomic bomb test by the Soviet Union had signaled the beginning of the Cold War in earnest; the World Bank had been established, with the US Dollar replacing the Pound as the world's reserve currency; Mao's communists had won the Chinese Civil War; and the Marshall Plan, the Council of

Europe, and the Organization of American States had been launched. The tectonic plates of geopolitics had been broadly reorganized, and so the Council's founding members felt their multi-generational work of creating and installing a 'purified' ruling class that would eventually enforce a 'proper hierarchy' across the major realms of humanity it governed could begin (again).

The members of the Council oversaw operations in nine global regions—Europe, North America, Orthodox Eurasia, South America, Oceania, East/Southeast Asia, South/Central Asia, North Africa and the Middle East, and Sub-Saharan Africa. The Council acted mostly informally, but the member for Europe was the permanent Chairman and would vote when a tie-breaking vote was needed on major decisions. In terms of operations and liaisons, the means justified the ends, so even the 'abominations' of Jewish and communist states would be used as leverage to manipulate events towards their end goal. But they had become impatient with slow progress and seized on the promise of advances in genetic engineering as a way to accelerate the creation of a new kind of 'master race.' That is where Mendez had come to the Council's attention. His family connections through his grandfather had gotten him the kind of audience with, and warm reception from, the Council that was rarely given, and where he had laid out his plans. But today, he knew they would not be happy to hear about what had happened with Maria Guevara. He knew he would be, as his mother used to say when she was angry at him, on thin ice on a hot day.

Mendez's phone vibrated once—the signal for him to come to the meeting room. Typical of the bland, anodyne meeting rooms set up for business clientele, there were water, coffee, and tea pitchers in a serving nook to the side, and extra pens and pads of hotel stationery spread around a large boardroom table encircled by leather office chairs. The nine men seated around the table wore suits and hair styles in varying shades of grey, and held stony expressions on their faces. Mendez sat down, suppressing a sardonic smile as he thought about the irony of this scene vs. philosopher and Holocaust survivor Hannah Arendt's famous quote about 'the banality of evil.' He clasped his hands in front of him and was about to begin to speak when the Chairman put his palm up, signaling that Mendez should remain silent.

"We are aware of the current state of affairs, so there is no need to recount that here," the Chairman intoned. "How long until your alternative plan can be operational?"

"You mean engineered cloning?" Mendez said, trying to hide his surprise.

"Yes."

"I can't do it where I am working now. I would need to have another dedicated lab set up. Once that is done, at least three months, maybe six, to get the replication process tested and systematized. After that, production could begin. And I would need some support staff."

"I see." The Chairman looked around the room and asked, "does the Council concur?" All nodded. He then went on, looking directly at Mendez, "You are to proceed expeditiously, but carefully. But first, the loose ends of the current affair need to be… *cauterized*. All of them. The girl, the Norseman… anything or anyone that could lead back to you and therefore us. Do you understand?"

"Yes. Where will we be able to locate the new project though? I have a few ideas but haven't worked out any details."

"Budapest. Our little project to distance Hungary from the EU and NATO and into a non-aligned posture has been successful and allowed us to move people, money, and equipment across their borders with almost no scrutiny. We have secured a lease option on a suitable building on the outskirts of Budapest through one of our anonymous holding companies. You'll be given the information of a local contact to whom you can provide a list of what you will need to set up the lab. One more thing—we have recruited a brilliant young Czech researcher. He will work side by side with you, so that you can share your knowledge with him. We need to prepare for the next generation of our work."

"But—"

"Thank you for your time Dr. Mendez," the Chairman interrupted, and then pulled an envelope out of his pocket and set it on the table." Here is some additional information you will need and updated bank account details. Please keep us apprised of progress—I'm sure you will honor the legacy of your grandfather."

Mendez realized the meeting was over and that he was being politely dismissed. He stood up, straightened his jacket, and walked over to pick up the envelope in front of the chairman. He then turned to the rest of the table to nod and say, "Thank you gentlemen," as he opened the door to leave. As he walked back to the hotel lobby he couldn't help but think that he was potentially a 'loose end' in the eyes of the Council as well, but that they still needed him—at least for now.

≈

While Vano was away in Madrid and Lyon, Maria passed time by immersing herself in reading. There were academic papers on genetics and synthetic biology that had been published online in the last few months that she wanted to catch up on, her continuing review of various research institutions that could be an alternative to employment at the Pasteur Institute, an occasional scan of news sites to keep up with current events, and an increasing list of reference sites she had begun to bookmark on pregnancy and early childhood development. When she needed a break from reading she would help Naiara and Guaril—Vano's parents—around the house or take a walk in the woods behind their house. Vano had advised her to try to avoid making her presence known to the rest of the Arditurri community for now, which suited her as well—the privacy and stillness of her surroundings and the quiet time spent reading or chatting with Vano's parents all felt like a welcome antidote to the turbulence of the last few months. Her earlier worries about feeling uncomfortable being back in Arditurri had turned out to be unfounded.

Naiara and Guaril Amaya were a kind and hospitable couple, but more introverted than Maria's parents. They were careful not to talk much about the neighbors, politics, or Guaril's work before retirement, deftly changing the subject or suddenly remembering some random chore that needed to be completed when those topics came up. And although they were obviously proud of Vano, they would mostly only talk about his childhood exploits, letting on nothing about his adult life. Maria finally came to understand that these were people who had spent a lifetime being careful about sharing information, and that a few days of prying was not going to open them up, so she stopped probing so directly. She desperately wanted to know more about the connection between their families but didn't want her hosts to feel she was being intrusive.

And then one pleasant summer afternoon when Guaril had gone out to tend to their vegetable garden, Naiara invited Maria to join her for tea and motioned for her to sit down at the kitchen table. Maria somehow sensed the moment might be ripe and obliquely asked about their family history. She was pleasantly surprised when Naiara, after a long pause, then smiled gently over her teacup and replied softly, "It's a little complicated Maria, but I'll try to untangle it for you."

"Thank you, Sra. Amaya," Maria replied as she leaned forward attentively and squeezed some lemon into her tea.

"You see, your mother's grandfather Eduardo Villar and Guaril's maternal grandfather Antonio Navarro were close friends who went off together to fight with the Republicans during the Spanish Civil War while they were still only in their late teens. After the war, Antonio got married and had a daughter—Flora. But then the White Terror[4] came and Antonio was rounded up by Franco's BPS.[5] He died in prison, probably tortured to death… but he never betrayed Eduardo. Antonio's wife was grief-stricken and ended up committing suicide, making Flora an orphan. When Eduardo heard about what had happened, he and his wife took Flora in and raised her as one of their own."

"So that's the Aunt Flora my mother used to talk about?" Maria almost blurted out.

"Yes. Although she was not your mother's aunt by blood, the Villar's always cared for her like one of their own. She was actually Guaril's

---

[4] The White Terror – the violent political repression, including executions, which was carried out by Franco's Nationalist faction during the Spanish Civil War and by his ruling regime in the decade after the war.

[5] BPS – Franco's 'Political-Social Brigade,' which acted as a de facto secret police in charge of persecuting and repressing opposition movements.

mother—Vano's grandmother. You see, through his network, Guaril's father Danior eventually learned of Flora's tragic story while he was still living in Tel Aviv. Moved by the echoes in the story of what had happened to him and his family, he invited the Villar family to bring her and come visit him. Danior and Flora—perhaps because they had both lost their parents to tragedy—were immediately drawn to one another and ended up falling in love and getting married. And so, Flora became the connection between the Villar and the Amaya families. A connection not of blood relation, but of honor."

"I think I understand now what my mother was hinting about when she spoke of our family relations. Vano and I are not really related… we just share some interwoven family history."

"Yes, Maria, but the shared history is quite a strong bond. Now let me prepare us a little *merienda*—you must be hungry by now," she said, glancing at Maria's midsection. "Can you be a dear and ask Guaril to wash up and come join us?"

"Of course. And thank you again for sharing that family history with me. I don't know why my mother never told me."

"Naomie was funny that way. It was like she wanted to protect you from the ghosts of the past. But I think she finally realized that sometimes those old spirits can become our guardian angels, no?" she said with a soft twinkle in her eye, and then turned toward the sink and put on her apron.

≈

Maria was sitting on the porch of the Amaya home the next day, enjoying the early afternoon breeze and still ruminating on the family history Vano's mother had revealed to her, when her phone rang. She didn't recognize the number and so answered with a clipped, "Yes?"

"Hello. This is Dr. Otxoa from San Sebastián. Is this Srta. Guevara?"

"Oh… yes. Hello Dr. Otxoa."

"I'm calling to give you feedback on your recent test results. Is this a good time to speak?"

"Yes, thank you. Please go ahead."

"Everything came back well within normal ranges, including the Maternal Serum Screening test. Whatever test they did for you back in Paris must have generated a false positive, which is not surprising actually. It would have been premature timing for that test."

"That's very good news. Thank you, Dr. Otxoa. And do you know when the DNA test results will be ready?"

"It turns out they finished the analysis faster than I expected. But given the complexity, the lab in Madrid asked if you could call them so they can first take you through the results over the phone and then send you the detailed files afterwards. I'll text you their telephone number and the Test Identification Number to refer to. I hope you're feeling well. In any event you may want to book a follow-up appointment and another ultrasound for next month. My assistant can help you with that if you call the front desk."

"I'm fine, thank you for asking. I've been able to get some much-needed rest. And thanks for the reminder. I will give your assistant a call."

"Excellent. Goodbye Srta. Guevara."

Maria stood up, walked to the porch railing, and crossed her arms. "So, Dr. Mendez had lied about the serum screening test and the risk of congenital defects in the baby," she thought to herself. "But why? That would mean he had another reason for wanting me to terminate the pregnancy. Why would he care one way or another, especially to the extent of making a special trip to San Sebastián to insist on it?" Maria shook her head, still unable to make sense of his behavior.

Maria decided to go for a walk down the path that meandered through the woods behind the house and had just returned when her phone pinged with the message from Dr. Otxoa with the contact information for the DNA lab—'Mapa de Vida' in Madrid. She went into the house to grab a bottle of water, a notepad, and a pen and then came back out and settled back into the chair on the porch. After taking a drink of water, she dialed the number Dr. Otxoa had sent her.

"Mapa de Vida, this is Elena speaking," came a woman's voice on the other end.

"Hello. My name is Maria Guevara. I am a patient of Dr. Otxoa in San Sebastián, and he gave me this number to call regarding the results of my DNA test."

"What is your Test Identification Number please?"

"Just a moment," Maria said as she re-opened Dr. Otxoa's text message, and then read out the number.

"Thank you. Please hold while I transfer you to the analyst who handled your test."

"Okay," Maria murmured and then took another drink of water.

After about thirty seconds a male voice came on the line, "Hello Srta. Guevara, I am Jorge Gomez, your case analyst… I'm just pulling up your test results now."

"Hello Jorge. I was surprised when Dr. Otxoa told me the results were ready—I thought it usually took longer?"

"It did until recently. But we now have an agreement with BSC for access to their quantum supercomputer. That, combined with our proprietary AI-enabled gene mapping software, has really accelerated our turnaround time."

"BSC?"

"The Barcelona Supercomputing Centre."

"Oh, I didn't even know about it. Anyway, I'm curious to hear about the results of the analysis—specifically about the father of child and of course the child itself."

"Well, let me start off by saying this is probably one of the most interesting cases I've ever analyzed. First off, the father's DNA is of more-or-less pure Scandinavian origin. If you drew a circle around southern Sweden and Norway, and then Denmark also, that would basically center the ethno-geographic locus. The report we send you will of course provide a lot more detail. But the Scandinavian DNA is not really the particularly interesting element."

"What is it then? What about the child... are there any red flags?"

"Quite the opposite. The child appears to be... remarkable. I've never seen a profile like this before."

"What do you mean?"

"There are multiple instances of certain key top-percentile characteristics, most notable being the expected muscle density, intelligence level, immune system strength, and cardiovascular efficiency."

"How is that possible?"

"In my experience, it's essentially an impossible outcome in the universe of natural random hereditary mutations to have this many simultaneous optimizations. If I had to guess, the genes of this child have been engineered. There is also some indications that there may have been some more subtle epigenetic programming. We only saw hints of it because we've been developing computer simulations on epigenetics and the AI program registered some hits. We would have to do some more runs with BSC to be sure."

The line went quiet for a moment and then Maria almost gasped, "What?!"

"I'm sorry... I realize I got a little carried away with the technical detail. I can explain what I meant by epigenetics if it helps."

"I know what it is but thank you anyway. This is all just a bit much to take in."

Jorge cleared his throat nervously. "I'm sorry Srta. Guevara, I didn't mean to sound insensitive. If you don't know how the potential... intervention... happened, then this may be a matter for you to take to the authorities. Due to EU privacy restrictions, we are not allowed to share your information with anyone except you."

"Please just send all of the files, including the raw data, to me at the email address in my file. I want to take some time to review it in more detail."

"Yes, of course. Is there anything else I can do to help or any other questions I can answer?"

"Will it cost me anything to have you do that additional epigenetics analysis you mentioned with the BSC computer?"

"I think we can cover the cost. The data may actually help refine our simulations. Are you okay for us to use the data in that way as long as we anonymize it?"

"Yes. Go ahead. And please send me the results when you're done. Thank you, Jorge, you've been very helpful."

Maria sat silently for a long while after the call was over, her thoughts spinning. There was only one person who could have done this, she thought as she stood up. "Mendez. *Hijo de puta*," she muttered as she turned to go back into the house. "I guess that probably rules out the possibility that I'm the first woman since the Virgin Mary to experience an immaculate conception." But her anger receded, and a cloudy uneasiness began to settle in as the door closed behind her—"what exactly is incubating inside me, and what might it cause? I have to figure out what is happening."

Chapter 7: Impressions

REMY BOUCHER FELT MORE frustrated each time he replayed the video footage from Mendez's office. He couldn't make out what the cylindrical metal canister was that Mendez had wheeled out of his office. By himself. On a Sunday. *"Fils de pute,"* he muttered, shaking his head. "What are you up to now?" After pacing around his small office and finishing his coffee, he suddenly stopped, snapped his fingers, and exclaimed "Félix!" He then marched down to the Facilities & Supply Department in the basement of the Medical Center and nearly barged through the door.

"Remy! You startled me. What are you doing here?" Félix was the manager of the Facilities & Supply Department and not accustomed to surprise visitors in his basement habitat—especially a surprise visit from the head of security.

Remy laughed and grasped Félix by the shoulders, "Don't worry, *mon ami*, you're not in trouble. I just need your help with something."

"Of course. What is it?"

Remy took out his phone, navigated to the video from Mendez's office, and gave the phone to Félix. "What's that thing he's taking out of his office? It looks like it could be some kind of lab equipment."

Félix brought the phone close to his face and squinted as he watched the video loop a few times. "It looks like a cryo chamber."

"What's a cryo chamber?"

"A cryogenic chamber. It's mostly used to freeze biological specimens and products for storage, using liquid nitrogen. Stem cells, semen, eggs… that kind of stuff. Researchers here work with this type of equipment all the time in their labs. But why would he have it in his office closet?"

"That's what I was wondering. And why did he then take it? That's potential property theft, or at least improper use of Medical Center equipment. You must have some kind of physical asset registry for the Medical Center, no? Lists of things like computers and lab equipment with serial numbers that show which people or departments they're assigned to. Can we take a look at that?"

"I don't need to," Félix said, reaching for a catalog on a shelf above his desk.

"What? Why?"

"That's not one of our cryo chambers," Félix responded flatly as he set the catalog down on his desk, leafed through it for a few seconds, and then pointed to a picture. "This is the only kind we buy. You can tell by the differences in the height and the latch cover assembly. It appears you have a mystery on your hands Mssr. Boucher."

"*Merde*," Remy grunted. He turned and began walking for the door and then stopped suddenly and tapped on his phone.

"Something else?" Félix asked tentatively.

"Just an old *flic's* hunch," Remy mumbled as he attached the video clip to a text message to Maria captioned 'any idea what Mendez was doing with this?' He hit 'send,' then turned and walked out the door, leaving Félix with a puzzled expression and a cup of coffee that had gone cold.

≈

Stefan Lang—Mendez's fixer who was now in San Sebastián to assess the situation—was pleased with the contents of the package brought to his hotel room personally by the AN liaison. AN (*Allianza Nacional*, or National Alliance, a Spanish neo-Nazi organization) were eager to make a good impression on someone they knew had connections with The Council and had delivered as promised. One of their 'members' worked for the Spanish National Police at their headquarters in Madrid and so had access to their country-wide incident reporting and tracking system. Accessing reports of the incident involving Ulrik at the festival parade in San Sebastián and then printing them out had taken only a matter of minutes. Two days later, Stefan was now sitting in his hotel room reading through the pages and taking pictures of them. When finished, he called Mendez.

"Yes?" came the reply after one ring.

"The police here still list Ulrik as an unidentified suspect. Nobody was actually injured, so it has not been assigned a high investigative priority."

"Good."

"However, the girl filed a report and provided a description of Ulrik, which included those tattoos he has on his arm."

"*Verdammt!* I kept telling him to have those removed or to at least keep them covered. That idiot might as well have given them an engraved invitation to come looking for us! He may be a perfect physical specimen, but I should have given him an IQ test before I decided to use his DNA. What about the girl?"

"I'll be doing some surveillance starting tomorrow."

"Good. Keep me updated."

"Of course." Stefan hung up the phone, burned the printouts of the police reports one by one, and then flushed the ashes down the toilet. What he could not know was that, while in Madrid, Vano had requested an encrypted flag be attached to the incident report file, and once it had been accessed and printed out, an alert had been sent to Vano.

Maria had fallen deeply asleep on the sofa while reading, coaxed by a floral afternoon breeze drifting softly through the screened windows and the beef stew and *mollete* bread rolls Naiara had prepared for lunch earlier. So when Vano entered the house and the spring-hinged screen door smacked to a close loudly behind him, she woke with a start and then stood to look towards the door. She was about to ask him how his trip had gone when she caught him pass a glancing gaze down her body and then back up to meet her eyes. It was only then that she remembered that she had fallen asleep in shorts and a T-shirt, but with no bra because the ones she had brought with her were now beginning to feel uncomfortable as her breasts had continued to swell and become tender. "You're back!" she said, blushing faintly. "Give me a minute to put something on and you can tell me all about your trip. There's some leftover stew on the stove if you're hungry."

"I was… just wondering why you had a *putsi* hanging from your neck," Vano called after her as he walked toward the kitchen, not sounding at all convincing. "I had the impression you didn't believe in that sort of thing."

"He's a quick thinker—I'll give him that," Maria thought to herself, smiling as she wrapped herself in a thick robe. "I'm not sure I do, but it's harmless, and anyway my mother gave it to me and asked me to wear it. She said Sra. Vadoma had prepared it especially for me."

Once Maria had joined him at the kitchen table, and he had finished his bowl of stew, Vano began to share what he had learned during his trip. "The background on the stranger's tattoos that your friend at the Institute…"

"His name's Remy Boucher, but I'm not sure I would call him my friend. He's in charge of security there."

"Well, it sounds like he is concerned for you, which is a good sign. Anyway, the background he gave you on the meaning of the tattoos checks out. And Interpol found an archived record from Sweden that mentioned those same tattoos. For some reason there were no photos in the file though, which may mean the person who was mentioned in the file was brought in for questioning but was not arrested. Some guy named Karl Larsson. I think we should check the name with Sr. Boucher and see if it matches a name on Mendez's visitor logs at his office, okay?"

"I agree. But he's going to wonder where I got the name."

"Let's figure that out later. Now, another thing I found out is that the story of Mendez's university education and research work in Sao Paulo checks out, but there seem to be no records available from before that and no records at all regarding his parents, let alone grandparents. Zero. No trace. Which in this day and age is unheard of unless they have been deliberately expunged. Are you sure he never mentioned the names of his parents?"

"No. I mean, yes… I'm sure. He only ever vaguely referred to his mother in Buenos Aires and that his parents made him attend language classes."

"Did he say which language?"

"German, I think. It came up when I was looking at the landscape photos from South America in his office—one of them turned out to have some German writing in the margin."

They looked at each other silently and intensely for a moment and then Vano went on, "There's one more thing. I went to the *Biblioteca Nacional* in Madrid while I was there to dig around in their archives about Nazi activities in the Basque Country after the Civil War. It turns out there was a small but influential group of 'race theorists' that had become fascinated with the idea that the Basque genes had some kind of ancient, mythical origins, maybe similar in their thinking to that of their so-called master 'Aryan' race. That influential group included Josef Mengele."

"But what about the bombing of Guernica?"

"I don't think the two things are mutually exclusive. Their theories about the Basque race appear to have matured later, and Guernica was anyway an early political and military expedient for Hitler. It was an opportunity to keep a kindred fascist in power—and to test the aerial bombing techniques the Nazis had been developing—ahead of the wider conflict they were already planning."

"I probably should have paid more attention to my history classes." Maria stood up and then filled the tea kettle with water. "I'm going to make some tea—do you want some?"

"Sure. Thank you. By the way, have you found out anything new while I was gone?"

"As a matter of fact, I have," Maria said. She set the kettle on the stove and turned up the heat. She then went on to tell Vano the details of her conversations with Dr. Otxoa and Jorge Gomez about her various test results. She finished just as the tea kettle began to whistle.

They were both silent as she poured the hot water into their cups and they dropped their tea bags into them. Finally, Vano looked up and asked quietly, "Maria, you have a scientific mind. Given all we've discovered, do you have a theory of what is going on?"

"I think so. And with your CNI training you must also have a theory too?"

"Yes… but you go first," Vano said as he lifted his cup.

"Okay. Let's say Mendez is in fact Mengele's grandson. Mengele infects him with his sick theories about race but also with this weird idea of historical echoes between the Aryan and Basque races. Mendez meets a Basque girl—me—and can't help wondering what the result would be of combining the genes of the two races. Conveniently, he also gains access to the girl's eggs because he is helping her to freeze them. The temptation is irresistible. So he then finds some healthy Scandinavian sperm donor, does a little extra genetic optimization, and… voilà!" Maria dramatically gestured towards her stomach. "But then when I tell him that I also have Romani blood, he's not so happy anymore and wants me to get rid of the baby. I just don't understand why he was so careless as to have not run a full analysis on the origins of my DNA."

"Confirmation bias. When people—even very smart people—are obsessed, they tend to see what they want to see. You didn't 'look' Romani to him, and I suspect he just could not imagine the idea of a Romani scientist. But tell me, how could he have impregnated you without you knowing it?"

"It had to be that night that I almost passed out at the club and was knocked out by the time I was put to bed in my apartment. It must have been planned somehow, and he must have found a way to get into my apartment while I was unconscious."

"Is that possible?"

"The procedure itself is pretty simple. I'm just wondering how he was able to arrange for me to get drugged—which is what must have happened—and how he got into my apartment."

"You told me previously that some stranger helped your friend Brigitte get you upstairs. Maybe that wasn't just some random stranger. Maybe Mendez had help."

Maria paused for a few moments, looking up at the slowly-rotating ceiling fan. "Perhaps. But it still doesn't explain how I got drugged."

"What do you think Mendez's motives were?" Vano interjected.

"Weren't you listening? He wanted to conduct an actual experiment on an idea that had fascinated him since childhood, and I was the guinea pig."

"So, all that trouble just to create one hybrid, genetically-optimized child as an experiment?"

Maria stared at Vano blankly and then shook her head. "I don't know. You're the expert when it comes to criminal motives and the thinking of these neo-Nazis, or whatever they are. What is your theory then?"

"Mostly the same as yours. Except I think Mendez had bigger plans. He didn't want to stop with the creation of just one child. He wanted to begin the creation of a new master race—that's the way these people would think—starting from some sort of 'genetic alloy' fashioned from the Aryan and Basque races that he had clearly inherited an obsession with. Psychologically, I would say he was trying to fulfill the perceived wishes of his grandfather. And now he is furious that the culmination of his work has been sullied by Romani blood and so has decided it must be disposed of. But he realizes that the child you are carrying is also evidence, so he hopes that it can be destroyed in a way that can't lead back to him—hence him wanting you to get an abortion. You then tell him you are not going to get an abortion, which clearly provoked him. Soon after, a stranger with neo-Nazi tattoos and blonde hair—and who may have been following you earlier—tries to attack you with a knife. That seems like more than a coincidence, Maria."

"*Mierde*. It feels surreal Vano, but unfortunately it's also beginning to make sense"—Maria exhaled—"But why did he choose me to be the host? He could have just as well used another woman as a surrogate after fertilizing one of my eggs and optimizing the embryo."

"Control. He knew he could keep a close eye on you. He doesn't seem like the type who would want to go through whatever official process there is for matching with a surrogate… too many questions. And would he risk his little genetic marvel being carried by the type of woman who would do it unofficially? No doubt he wanted to minimize the number of people involved, which was probably why he also ended up using that blonde psychopath as a sperm donor. In the end, I think he also maybe had some fascination with your being Basque and being the birth mother—and gambled that since you eventually wanted to be a mother anyway that you would come to embrace the pregnancy. Whatever the scenario, no matter how strongly this points to Mendez, there are details that don't add up."

"You're probably right."

"But even if what we suspect is true, Maria, we still have some tricky unanswered questions. Who was the person who tried to attack you, and does he in fact have a direct connection to Mendez? And where is he now? Also, if you did get drugged that night, who was involved? And who was that stranger who helped Brigitte carry you up to your apartment? Are there more people working with Mendez that we don't know about yet?"

Maria looked up at the fan again and then back at Vano. "All this time… I was just a science experiment to him. A lab rat that provided an egg and a womb…" she said, her voice trailing off. She absent-mindedly clutched the *putsi* hanging from her neck. "What should we do next?"

"I'm not sure yet, but I think we need to try and figure out what they might try to do next. While you, and especially that baby, are still alive they will be feeling exposed."

Maria felt an unexpected rush of conflicting emotions—there was first an instinctive surge of maternal protectiveness, and she clasped her hands over her stomach. "I won't let them hurt my child." And then came a cold shudder of fear. "My God, Vano…my child! What if he's…? Could he be…? Am I…? Maria held her breath as the implications began to consume her. But then a hard, rational resolve rose in her as she finally exhaled. "Whatever terrible thing they were hoping to make this child into, I won't let it happen."

≈

Stefan Lang drove slowly by the home of Ander and Naomie Guevara, and then by the offices of Guevara Freight, noting that external security cameras had been installed at both locations. Preferring to avoid having his image captured, he decided to drive back to his hotel to think about how best to determine the location of the girl without exposing his presence unnecessarily.

Just as he was passing through the neighborhood of Intxaurrondo on the GI-20 West highway, traffic ground to a halt—the contents of a large flatbed truck involved in an accident had scattered across the roadway about fifty meters ahead and there was nowhere to exit. He would have to sit it out until the mess was cleared. He rolled down the windows, turned off the car's main battery to conserve power, activated the auxiliary so he could monitor the local news on the radio, and tilted his seat back to a comfortable recline.

"I wonder if the Council really understands what people in the field like me have to deal with… doing their dirty work so they can keep their hands clean," he muttered to himself. He let his eyelids close to catch a light nap.

The Council had long used men like Stefan Lang to execute activities that would further prepare and advance their agenda. And what an agenda it was. Early on they had recognized that however 'magnificent' the aims of the Third Reich had been, they were limited by the people and human capabilities they had at their disposal at that particular time. The Council also took their lessons from history. Leaders with superior abilities like Darius (I), Alexander, Qin Shi Huang, Augustus Caesar, and Genghis Khan, along with their exceptional military leaders, could take their empires to a zenith, but their achievements would inevitably begin to dissipate in the hands of less capable successors. The eugenicists of the Third Reich had of course also recognized this problem and initiated the *Lebensborn* Program[1]—but without the availability of genetic engineering technology, they simply ran out of time. Normal human generational cycles of 12 or more years before being able to achieve reproduction were just too long. So the Council had to bide its time and wait for the technology of genetic engineering to catch up with their aspirations to engineer and accelerate the creation of a ruling class, a true master race, with nothing left to the chance and vagaries of normal human heredity and natural selection. This new 'Homo Optimus' would be the apex of humanity, and its rightful leaders for millennia to come. In the meantime, the Council would have to patiently lay the groundwork of finance, global networks, and political conditions that would support the emergence of their *Neue Ordnung*—'New Order' when the time came. And they needed loyal men like Stefan to execute that groundwork.

Stefan woke with a start when the car behind him honked. The cars ahead of him had started to move again. He readjusted his seat, turned the power back on, and eased the car forward into the flow of traffic. By the time he reached his hotel room he had already decided what he was going to do. After a little online searching he found the home telephone number of the Guevara family. Using his anonymized virtual phone number, he called and Naomie answered.

"Bai?"

---

[1] *Lebensborn* Program – A program initiated in 1935 by Heinrich Himmler and the SS where post-pubescent German and Nordic girls deemed 'racially pure' were put in group homes, essentially birthing centers, and encouraged to give birth to as many children as possible, and where the fathers—also having been assessed as 'racially pure—were usually SS officers.

In the best French accent he could muster, Stefan replied, "Hello. My name is Jean-Louis Pillet with the Pasteur Institute in Paris. I was trying to reach Dr. Maria Guevara—is she there by chance?"

"No. But you can give me your number, and I'll ask her to call you back when I see her next."

"It's very important that I speak with her. Is she still in San Sebastián? If not, do you know where I can reach her?"

Naomie went silent for a moment and then replied hesitantly, "What did you say you do with the Institute, Mssr. Pillet?"

"I'm afraid I have another call coming in. Thank you for your time Sra. Guevara," he said, and then quickly rattled off his anonymized phone number to Naomie and hung up, swearing under his breath.

≈

Over another breakfast earlier than she was used to, Maria found herself enjoying the sight of Vano from across the table while he stared seriously at the screen of his laptop computer. He was undeniably attractive and fit, but she had met a lot of men like that. There was something different about this man—and she suddenly realized it had started to pull at her. A relaxed confidence, a mind that was sharp and yet unlike hers, a quick smile, and a sense of purpose and loyalty that felt as solid and deeply-rooted as an old oak tree. She shook her head, as if trying to wake up, took a sip of coffee, and thought to herself—almost mouthing the words—"I better keep myself from getting too close to *this* slippery slope." Just then, Vano said, "What is this?" and sat back, his brow furrowed with a curiosity.

"What?" Maria replied, startled.

"I was going through all the emails from the last several days while I was traveling and realized there was one here I missed reading. As a precaution, I had the police report of the incident at the parade in San Sebastián flagged in the system. It appears someone accessed the file."

"That doesn't sound so unusual. Maybe they're doing some follow up investigation?"

"It was accessed by a terminal at the National Police headquarters in Madrid and printed out. Since no one was hurt in the incident, something like this would be considered a low-priority matter and left to the local authorities in San Sebastián to handle."

"Oh. Maybe someone in Madrid had heard about it and was curious?"

"Maria, those guys have way too many major cases already and not enough people. They are not sitting around in their leisure time browsing low-priority reports from local municipalities. And they're definitely not printing them out for bedtime reading."

"Okay, then why did you put a flag on the file? What do you think happened?"

"When I was on my way to Madrid, I listened to the recording I made of that conversation you and I had about Mendez and neo-Nazis and everything that had happened in general since April, including the incident at the parade. I decided that if there was indeed someone involved behind the scenes, they would want to know exactly how much the police have found out, so that they can manage their risks. That's how they would be thinking. And the only way they could find out would be to get a full copy of that report—so I put a flag on it, just in case. I think we now need to factor into our thinking the possibility that there is someone on the inside who got them a copy of the report."

"On the inside? Of the National Police headquarters in Madrid?"

"Don't sound so surprised, Maria. Sometimes people get compromised or just go rogue. It happens. Statistically it's inevitable in a large organization. That's why the police have internal affairs units. I'll call someone I trust and ask them to look into it discreetly."

Maria sat back, took another sip of coffee, and then suddenly leaned forward. "What if this person in Madrid contacts my parents, sounding official, referring to the report, and asking about me? They might even try to trick my parents into telling them where I am."

Vano arched his eyebrows and nodded. "You're probably right, actually. How did a scientist end up with detective instincts?"

"It was just a logical inference," Maria shrugged nonchalantly, not wanting to let on that she was pleased that he was impressed.

"Maybe you should call your mother and tell her that if the police contact her she should be polite but say that you've gone on a trip, and she doesn't know where you are. She should alert your father as well."

Maria nodded and stood up, taking her dishes to the sink. "Okay, but I'm going to take a shower and get cleaned up. Maybe you should too," she said teasingly as she looked him up and down and walked away barely containing a laugh at the surprised look on his face.

Later that morning, they reconvened at the kitchen table and Maria called Naomie. "*Egun on ama.* I'm here with Vano, and I've got you on speakerphone, okay?"

"Oh. Yes… that's fine. Good morning, Vano," Naomie said warmly.

"Good morning Sra. Guevara," Vano replied with equal warmth.

"I'm glad you called. I wanted to let you know that someone phoned from the Pasteur Institute in Paris looking for you, Maria. He said it was important. He said his name was Jean-Louis Pillet, and he gave me a phone number to pass along."

"I don't recognize that name. Did he say what he does for the Institute?"

"No. I asked him, but right then he said he had another call coming and had to go. After everything that's happened, it felt a little odd, Maria. Anyway, here's the number," Naomie said, and read out the number Stefan Lang had provided.

"Thank you. We'll check this out. In the meantime, we wanted to tell you to make sure not to tell anyone where I am. Even if the police contact you or *aita*, just tell them I went on a trip, and you don't know where I am. That's what Vano suggested. Okay?"

Naomie paused for a few seconds and then replied. "Yes, I guess so. If that's Vano's recommendation, then that's what we'll do. What is going on?"

Vano jumped in, "Thank you, Sra. Guevara. Don't worry—it's just a precaution. I promise I'll explain later."

"Okay, well you two take care. I need to go pick up a few things at the market. Tell your parents I said 'hello,' Vano."

"I will. Goodbye Sra. Guevara," Vano replied, closing the call.

Maria went immediately and got her laptop—now protected by an encrypted VPN program Vano had installed—and brought it back to the table. She logged into the Pasteur Institute employee portal. "If there is anyone named Jean-Louis Pillet at the Institute he'll be in the employee directory."

Vano nodded and opened up his laptop as well. "While you're doing that, let me check that phone number your mother passed on."

After some searching, Maria looked over her screen at Vano, shaking her head. "There is no one with that name at the Institute."

Vano finished with his own search and then peered back. "And that phone number is fake as well. It's an anonymized virtual number… a common tool among criminals."

"What do you think is going on, Vano?"

"If they have the police report, then they will have the statement you made, and will know you can ID the guy who tried to attack you. I think they're looking for you… and the baby. I'm worried that the next time they contact your parents, it might be in person, and they might not be so polite with their questions."

Maria recoiled. "We can't let this thing put my parents in danger, Vano. Or yours, for that matter."

"Yes. So I think you need to resurface in Paris and make your presence known to Mendez. To draw these people away from Spain and the Basque Country."

"Are you proposing to use me as bait?" Maria said, looking a little aghast.

Vano couldn't help but smile. "Just a tiny bit, Maria. Don't worry, I'll be with you, and I have some friends in Paris that we can trust. Okay?"

Maria crossed her arms and then finally, hesitatingly, replied, "Maybe… but you're going to have to tell me exactly what you're planning, and I am going to have a say in what happens as well."

"Of course."

"Oh, and speaking of Paris, I just remembered that I need to reply to Remy Boucher. He sent me a text with some kind of surveillance video of Mendez taking the cryo chamber—the one with my eggs in it—out of his office. He's asking if I know anything about it. We can also give him that Larsson name you got from the Swedish police files to see if it matches any names on Mendez's visitor logs."

"What are you going to tell him? I mean about the cryo chamber and where you got the Swedish name?"

"I don't know yet. But I'm tired of these *bastardos* making me feel scared and out of control of my life. And now they are potentially threatening my family. I'm tired of being on the back foot and in the dark—maybe it's time we try to take some action and turn the tables." Maria put her hands on her stomach. "With every day of this pregnancy that passes, I'm going to become more physically vulnerable, and it's going to be harder for me to help you. But if we work together, I'm sure we can figure a way through this. Your mother told me the story of the connection between our families—they wouldn't want us to be forever running in fear from these people."

Vano stared at Maria for a long time, sizing up her conviction, and finally just nodded his head. "If you're up to this, so am I, Maria."

Maria tilted her head and met his eyes. "What were you thinking just now? Were you so surprised at what I said?"

"A little bit. Given your Villar heritage, I was just a little surprised it took you this long to get your blood up." Vano replied with a faintly mischievous smile.

Maria matched his smile for a moment and then countered dryly, "There's one more thing you need to keep in mind—we have to be very careful with Mendez. With his knowledge and the kinds of things he has had access to in his field of work, there are a hundred ways for him to kill."

Chapter 8: Body and Soul

Maria and Vano had packed their suitcases and placed them by the front door and were back now at the kitchen table enjoying a mid-morning cup of coffee, though the previous day's conversation was still lingering between the lines of their small talk. The train departing San Sebastián for their journey to Paris would be leaving in the afternoon, so they would have to leave Arditurri soon and were trying to absorb the last few hours of being in the quiet and secluded Amaya household. Maria eventually set her cup down and interjected, "I should probably reply to Remy Boucher before we leave."

Vano nodded. "Good idea. And I think you should tell him everything."

"Everything? Are you sure we can trust him completely? If I tell him about what I was doing with Mendez… about freezing my eggs… that's probably breaking some kind of Institute rules that he might feel compelled to report, no?"

"I think we can trust him. If he was crooked, he would have cashed in while he was still a cop and wouldn't be working a security guard job in retirement at a place like the Institute, where there is no extra angle for pocketing money. Besides, I ran his name; he comes up squeaky clean. Of course there's still a risk, but I think given our situation it's a risk worth taking. I'd like to think that once he hears the full story he might be inclined to forgive your little deception. If you don't mind, I'd like to join you on the call... to introduce myself and help explain the situation."

Maria picked up her coffee cup, took a long sip, and then set it down and finally exhaled, "Okay, Vano. But I hope you know what you're doing here—my status with the Institute is already on shaky ground."

"Everything is on shaky ground right now, Maria. We need to turn the tables, remember? We could use an ally inside the Institute."

"All right... let's get it over with." Maria sighed as she hit the 'call' button on Boucher's listing in her phone contact list.

"*Oui? C'est Boucher,*" came the now familiar and rough-hewn voice of Remy Boucher.

"Hello, Remy, it's Maria. I'm on speakerphone. I'm responding to the message you sent. Are you free to talk now?"

"Ah, Maria. *Oui.* Now is good."

"Before I start, I want to introduce you to someone in my extended family who has been helping me look into what has been happening. We left my house in San Sebastián and came to his family's house to the south near the mountains. His name is Vano Amaya."

"I see. I assume he's there with you now?"

"Yes, Remy. Now about that video clip you sent..." Maria began.

"Hello, Mssr. Boucher. This is Vano Amaya. It's a pleasure to make your acquaintance. And allow me to thank you for how helpful you've been to Maria. I want to be completely open with you from the beginning—I do indeed share a family connection with Maria, but I also work for Spain's CNI... I assume you know what that is?"

There was a long pause before Remy finally replied, "Yes."

"Let me give you my ID number in case you would like to check my bona fides. Maria says you have a friend in DGSI—he can verify the number and name through Interpol as I also liaise with them in an official capacity." Vano then slowly read off a string of numbers. "Did you get that?"

"Yes."

Maria was about to begin speaking, but Vano continued. "I also want to give you a name—Karl Larsson. I understand Maria told you about the tattoos she saw on the man that tried to attack her. I was able to find an archived Swedish police report—associated with the name Karl Larsson—that described those same tattoos. There were no pictures though, so I assume he was just brought in for questioning and not arrested. The case appeared to be related to a broader investigation of organized trafficking of unregistered firearms, so maybe they were trying to cultivate him as an informant."

"What am I supposed to do with this name? I'm retired from law enforcement and just look after security here."

"Maria mentioned that there had been some potentially suspicious entries in Mendez's visitor logs. We were hoping you could check to see if this name matches one of the entries, and if so we can then look for known aliases associated with the name."

"I guess I can do that. I'll have to find the copy I made of the logs and get back to you, though."

"Thank you. I wanted to also share with you our thinking about Mendez's background and recent behavior. You see…"

Remy interrupted pointedly, "Maybe it's time you let Maria talk… I'd like to hear from her."

"Yes, of course, Remy," Maria jumped in. She then described in detail their suspicions about Mendez and what he was trying to do, including how it related to his recent behavior with her.

Remy was again silent for a long while and then exhaled. "So, I guess that explains the cryo chamber in Mendez's closet—it had your eggs in it?"

"Yes."

"So, you lied to me about having a problem with your boss and hid the fact that you were freezing eggs with Mendez, even after we talked about him being potentially dangerous. Why should I trust you now?"

"I'm sorry, Remy. I was scared, and my job was—is—already at risk. I was worried you might feel compelled to report me and that if you didn't, your job would also be at risk. I couldn't see a good way through either scenario, and so I… But none of that really matters anymore. Someone pretending to be with the Institute contacted my parents looking for me, so Vano and I have decided to come to Paris in order to draw attention away from San Sebastián. If Mendez comes back to Paris, it's possible he may visit his office at the Institute, so we felt you needed to know. I was hoping we could follow up with you again when we return to Paris."

"When are you arriving?"

"Tonight."

"Let me think about it. You can call me again tomorrow."

"And the name on the visitor logs?" Vano chimed in.

"Yes, yes. I'll check the name you gave me against Mendez's visitor logs. *Au revoir* for now." Boucher made clear the call was over.

≈

Shortly after the Euskotren had left San Sebastián's Amara station, Maria took a drink from the water bottle she had pulled out of her backpack and gave Vano a gentle nudge. "Hey. Don't go to sleep yet. I want to talk about what we're going to do when we get to Paris."

Vano sat up with a start and looked around their section to check if there were other passengers sitting nearby. "Now?"

"Yes. First, I want to know where we'll be staying."

"Drancy."

Maria's eyes widened. "In the 93?[1] Isn't that dangerous?"

Vano laughed, "Only for the *payos*, not us. I have a friend there—Kashi—who leads an influential *Romungro*[2] community in Drancy that has established itself alongside the broader *Manouche* population of Paris, and who has agreed to let us stay with him and his family. No one will think to look for us there. Not Mendez, not the police… no one. And if someone does come, Kashi's people will see them coming long before they get near us. It's a little over six miles from the center of Paris… close, but not too close."

"And his family won't mind?"

---

[1] The 93 – a colloquial reference to the Seine-Saint-Denis department (the 93rd) of the Greater Paris *métropole*; it is considered one of the more notorious of the *banlieues*—working-class areas/suburbs around the periphery of large French cities.

[2] Romungro – a sub-group of the broader Roma group of Romanies originating in central/eastern Europe, the Romungro are also the largest Romani sub-group in Hungary.

"No. He owes me a favor anyway. And there's something in Drancy I want to show you that you might find interesting."

"In Drancy? It's kind of a ghetto isn't it?" Maria replied, incredulous.

Vano's jaw clenched almost imperceptibly, but his tone bit unmistakably. "Maybe, but there is some history there beyond what most people see. It's also where the Nazis set up a transit camp during the war. Jews and Romanies that had been rounded up were interned there before being shipped off to concentration camps. Along with a memorial[3] center, one of the buildings of the old Cité de la Muette housing complex they used—and where my grandfather and great-grandparents were held before they were sent to Auschwitz—is still there."

Maria flushed with embarrassment and looked down at the floor. "I'm so sorry, Vano. I had no idea. I didn't mean to sound like such a snob."

"Never mind. Anything else?"

"Well, I was wondering what exactly we should do initially… I mean regarding Mendez."

"Like we discussed, we need to first make our presence in Paris known to him—but carefully. And we need to see if he is even actually in Paris. I was thinking you could send him a text message saying that you want to meet. We can then stake out the location and see who he brings with him—I want to get a better idea of what and who exactly we're up against before we plan too far ahead. Once we hear back from Remy about the name we gave him we can also see if there is any

---

[3] The Drancy Shoah Memorial – inaugurated in 2012, retraces the history and function of the transit detention camp set up by the Nazis in Drancy, as well as the daily lives of those interned there.

connection to known aliases and their associated locations. In fact, it might be a good idea to meet with Remy and compare notes face to face. Maybe he would even be willing to get Mendez's home address in Paris for us out of the Institute's files."

"What would you do with his address?"

"I'm not sure yet, but it would be good to have the option to at least monitor it, or even take more aggressive steps if needed."

"You mean like breaking into his apartment?"

"Maybe. If that becomes necessary."

"I get the feeling that would not exactly be official CNI business."

"Officially, I'm just here following up on some leads related to an extremist group that may have infiltrated the Spanish National Police. This Mendez thing is off the record for now."

"I guess that all sounds fine, but I think we also need to see if we can get into Mendez's computer files."

"I'm not a hacker Maria, and we don't have enough on Mendez yet to be able to get authorization for that kind of technical support from CNI, let alone permission from the French authorities to deploy it in Paris. It's a longshot, but I guess we could see if Remy could help in getting access to Mendez's work files. It would be asking a lot of him though, and Mendez was probably anyway careful about what he kept on his work computer."

Maria looked out the window at the passing countryside for a few moments and then turned back to Vano. "I may have an idea but let me think about it some more."

"Fine. Can I take a nap now?"

"Sure, but we'll be arriving in Hendaye in about twenty minutes."

"Great," Vano responded dryly as he crossed his arms and closed his eyes.

Aside from jogging through some light rain and picking up sandwiches and coffee at a station kiosk, Maria and Vano's transfer at the station in Hendaye from the Euskotren to the TGV was rushed but uneventful. By the time the TGV had reached its cruising speed of over 300 km/h, Vano was well into his coffee and wide awake, staring out at the passing French countryside. "It's ironic, isn't it, Maria?" He finally said, turning to her.

"What's ironic?"

"That the very products of human creativity and intellect, like science and technology and commerce, can erode our humanity if left unchecked or put in the wrong hands."

Maria's eyebrows raised. "Hmm… I see the train ride has put you into a philosophical mood. Well, don't forget that the lives of humans would also be a lot shorter and more brutish without things like modern medicine. Would you want to live in a world without a polio vaccine or anesthetics?"

"Absolutely not, but that's not really what I mean. What I mean is that there has to be some kind of moral element to what we create. I don't mean moral in the religious sense—I just mean a recognition of the uniqueness… the dignity… of humanity, and the need to protect that. A recognition that just because you *can* make something, or do something, doesn't always mean you should. And that moral imperative gets more important as our technological capabilities become more far-reaching—we have to be careful with fire, but we have to be *really* careful with hydrogen bombs, no?"

"I suppose. But we also need scientific inquiry. We don't want to go back to a world like the one where Galileo was put on trial by the Catholic church for suggesting that the Earth revolved around the sun do we?"

"No. But without guardrails, our humanity risks being flattened by technology and markets. Unless we're all *first* recognized as human, each richly contoured by a unique combination of emotions, imagination, empathy, intuition, and values, we run the risk of being packaged, categorized, labelled, and ultimately used as consumers, markets, users, audiences, workers, test subjects, patients… lab specimens. Do you see what I'm getting at?"

"The irony of my situation and how Mendez planned to use me—and my little *txikito*—is not lost on me, Vano," Maria replied coolly.

"Good," Vano said, almost as if it were a benediction, and the remainder of the journey passed mostly in silence.

Ander Guevara had received Maria's text message from the train while he was still at work in his office at Guevara Freight, and he had summoned Xavier straight away. "Have a seat Xavier," he said, motioning to one of the chairs in front of his desk as Xavier entered the room.

"Good morning, Sr. Guevara," replied Xavier, nodding politely as he sat down. He was a wiry and tousle-haired young man in jeans and a faded T-shirt with the logo of a local band—*Metalezko Mutilak* ('Metal Boys')—emblazoned across the front. Given these distractions from convention, people often missed the intensity of his eyes and the deep intelligence behind them. Ander had not.

"How is everything with the IT systems today?"

"All good. I've been running some diagnostics since we added the additional security you requested, and everything checks out so far."

"Very good. Xavier, the reason I asked you to come to my office is that I need to ask you a favor. A personal favor. But it has to be something that stays just between us."

"Of course, Sr. Guevara. You've done so much for me; how could I refuse?"

"This is quite an… unconventional… favor Xavier, so you may want to hear me out before you commit." Ander leaned forward, resting his forearms on his desk with his hands clasped.

Xavier paused and then cautiously replied, "Okay. I guess I'm very curious now."

"I've told you about my daughter Maria, no?"

"Yes, the scientist… in Paris, right?"

"Yes. Well, I don't know how to put this, but some bad people there have been bothering her. Maybe it's better if I don't give you too many details. Anyway, it's not something that she can just solve by going to the police. One of the people in particular—let's call him Mr. X—may have connections with some extremely dangerous people."

Xavier's eyes had widened. "But how could I help?"

"Maria thinks she can find out more about these people and what they may be planning by getting into Mr. X's computer. Maria is not easily dazzled when it comes to technical matters Xavier, but after Elixane showed her how you had transformed the systems here at Guevara Freight, she was very much impressed. She seems to think you might know a way—or might know someone who knows a way—to remotely access the information in Mr. X's computer, ideally without being detected."

Xavier replied, his voice lowered, "Sr. Guevara, if I understand you correctly, that's hacking and could be illegal."

"I know, Xavier. I wouldn't be asking if Maria—and maybe me and Sra. Guevara—weren't potentially in danger. This Mr. X came to our house here in Donostia not long ago looking for Maria and we think someone may have followed her here, too."

"And the police can't help?"

"At this stage no—I wish I could explain more. On this you can trust me—I wouldn't ask you if there was any other way. And you have my word that I would never tell anyone you helped me with this."

Xavier was silent for a while, fixated by Ander's pleading gaze. Finally, he looked down and replied, "I have a friend—"

"It's probably better I don't know his name," Ander interrupted.

"Okay, but *she*—not he—is a genius in applied cryptography. I met her when we were both at university and she does freelance work now for big companies that are dealing with ransomware attacks or industrial espionage."

"Do you think she would be willing to help… to travel to Paris?"

"She won't need to. And I won't need to tell her much."

"What do you mean?"

"She invented something she calls an ESK—an electromagnetic skeleton key. All I have to do is see if she will let me borrow it."

"How does it work?"

"Well, with respect Sr. Guevara, it's pretty complicated, and I'm not sure even I understand every part of it. But essentially, all you have to do is get this little box she built—about the size of a pack of cigarettes—near the computer you want to get into. It uses electromagnetic induction to create a connection to the hard drive and then transmits a signal to someone nearby—within, say, Wi-Fi range. That person's phone or laptop then acts as a relay to send the signal to a computer—a really big computer—in her basement, that she built and programmed herself. The program uses a combination of quantum cryptography and artificial intelligence, which for people who do computer security, is pretty scary technology. There's probably almost no computer hard drive in the world that would take longer than a few minutes to get hacked and copied by this program once the signal is connected."

"That sounds fascinating, Xavier, although you were right—I didn't understand most of it. Clearly, Maria's instincts about you were right. Do you think your friend will let you borrow this… ESK thing? We will need to send it to Maria in Paris and tell her how to use it."

"I think so, Sr. Guevara. Give me a few days—I'll need to go to Barcelona."

As was their custom, Kashi and Esma Kolompár had welcomed Maria and Vano to their modest, but tidy and cozy, apartment in Drancy with a fulsome meal and warm hospitality. After lingering at the dinner table following the main course, they finally moved to the living room to enjoy some tea and continue talking. Esma had disappeared for a moment, but then reappeared with four servings of a traditional flan dessert, to the delight of all. As Maria eagerly finished her first bite she turned to Esma. "It's so delicious Esma… and flan is my favorite dessert. How did you know?"

Esma smiled coyly and replied with a whisper, "Didn't you know that all of us *gitans* are fortune-tellers and psychics?" When she saw Maria's confused look she glanced over at Kashi and then Vano, and then the three of them yelped with laughter. "I was just joking Maria. I'm so sorry… I thought you understood," she finally said soothingly, after seeing that Maria had flushed with embarrassment.

Maria smiled generously and waved her palm to dismiss the tension. "Don't worry about it Esma… It's my fault. It's been good for me actually to reconnect with this part of my heritage—including the humor. Vano is definitely keeping me on my toes with that," she finished, throwing Vano a mischievous side-eye.

"Funny *and* handsome—a devastating combination. Be careful, Maria." Esma grinned. Kashi gave an exaggerated faux scowl, and then they laughed again, all together this time.

Maria took a sip of tea and, eager to change the subject, looked over at Kashi and asked, "You mentioned earlier that your family name is Kolompár. It doesn't sound French or Spanish, and it's not a name I've heard before… Where does it come from, if I may ask?"

"Hungary. It's actually a fairly common name among the Romanies there."

"Oh, were you born there?"

"No, I was born in Paris. My great-grandfather fled Budapest with his wife and their son—my grandfather—after Hungary joined with the Nazis and the rumors of round-ups of Jews and Romanies began to circulate. They were given shelter for several years by a Romani clan in Istanbul and then decided to move to Paris after the war, when it became clear that the Soviets were going to take control of Hungary. With the fall of the Soviet Union and after Hungary joined the EU in 2004, some of the extended family returned to Budapest, but my parents preferred it here and stayed, along with me."

"That's quite a story. I guess I can see why you two get along," Maria said, her expression pensive as she alternated her gaze between Kashi and Vano, wondering what other secrets these two men shared.

Just then Esma yawned. When Vano noticed he stood up, looking at his watch. "I'm sorry, Esma, we've kept you up late. We should let you and Kashi get to sleep."

Esma waved her hand. "Don't worry, Vano. We've enjoyed catching up with you and meeting Maria. I'm just sorry we have only one guest bedroom to offer, so you'll have to share the room I'm afraid."

Vano glanced awkwardly at Maria and then turned back to Esma. "I don't mind sleeping on the sofa. Do you have an extra blanket and pillow?"

"Of course," Esma replied, and then turned to Maria with another conspiratorial grin. "Funny, handsome, *and* chivalrous? My, my, my… you better keep an eye on this one." After she had left the room Kashi rolled his eyes, shrugged his shoulders, and silently mouthed 'sorry' to Maria.

Maria stood up and replied laughingly as she headed for the bedroom, "Good night everyone, it's been a lovely evening."

After washing up and changing into a light cotton nightgown, she switched off the light and settled down to sleep. Her thoughts jumped aimlessly for what seemed a long while around the events of the last months, but then she finally drifted off to sleep, unconsciously clutching the *putsi* that still hung around her neck.

Vano was up early the next morning, as usual, and knocked softly on the door to the guest bedroom. "Yes?" Maria replied sleepily.

"I've made a pot of coffee. I think we need to talk about how we're going to make your presence in Paris known to Mendez, and we also need to get in touch with Remy Boucher."

"Okay, okay. Do you ever just sleep in, Vano?"

"Not usually."

About twenty minutes later, Maria emerged into the kitchen and patted Vano on the back. "Good morning, *madrugador*. Where's Kashi and Esma?"

"Kashi went to work and Esma had to go run a few errands. She'll probably be back around noon. Here's your coffee," he said as he finished pouring her a cup and set it in front of her.

Maria sipped her coffee and then set it down. "They are really nice people, Vano. I enjoyed the evening with them." She paused and then continued, "Can I confess something to you?"

Vano looked up, his expression bemused. "Well, I'm not a priest or a policeman, but I suppose so."

"Very funny, *señor agente secreto*. What I wanted to confess is that I've been feeling a little guilty."

"About what?"

"It's just that... you and your family, and now Kashi and Esma... you've all been so kind to me. I spent so many years being silent about or turning away from the heritage of my mother's family and these connections, and now when I'm in trouble, you've all been there for me. I wish I had known earlier about all of this... all of *our*... history."

Vano sat back and looked at Maria for a while, feeling moved by her words, but still reflexively gauging her body language and sincerity. Finally, he replied. "I'm not sure it's the absolution you're looking for, but it's good to have you back among us, Maria. As my father used to say—we need to know where we came from and what we are made of, if we are to meet life's difficulties with confidence. Don't let what happened with Alfonso in Arditurri so many years ago ruin your memories and your connection with our people. You can always find your way back home, like my grandfather Danior did."

Maria was taken aback for a moment. Vano's insinuation at first felt slightly intrusive, but admittedly triggered a resonant chord." I suppose what happened with Alfonso did contribute to why I never went back to Arditurri. I guess I just didn't want to be the cause of any family conflicts there… and I definitely wanted to avoid ever seeing him again. Maybe over time, in trying to forget about what happened, I let go some of the good along with the bad," she added as her voice trailed off, unsure what to make of the feelings that this surprisingly perceptive man had surfaced.

"I understand," Vano replied. He sensed Maria's unease and so decided to change the subject. "Let's get to work now. What are you going to tell Mendez about being back in Paris?"

"I was thinking that I would send him a text and just tell him what he wants to hear—that I've reconsidered our conversation about my pregnancy after having thought more about it and the implications for my career, and that I'm back in Paris looking for a doctor to do the abortion. It will be a lie of course, but it should buy us some time and draw attention away from San Sebastián for now."

Vano nodded approvingly. "Psychologically that's probably a good first move. But given the fact that he went to the trouble of following you to San Sebastián—and likely had you followed while you were there—I would expect he'll be looking to find a way to confirm you've actually terminated the pregnancy."

"I could tell him that once I have confirmed an appointment for the termination that I'll contact him again so that we can plan to talk or meet again after it's done. I could frame it such that I would be looking for his advice on how to get my life back on track after getting all the pregnancy business behind me, including starting to freeze my eggs again, which he knows would imply that he would have the opportunity to give me a physical exam."

"But he got rid of the cryo chamber, didn't he?"

"He doesn't know that we know that, and he will no doubt play along at least until he can examine me to make sure I've terminated the pregnancy."

"Okay, that may work actually. Any thoughts on what we should do in the meantime to find out more about what he's been up to? Also, we're going to need to think through if, when, and how we might actually approach him in person."

"I think that's your department, Vano," Maria said as she pulled out her phone and began tapping out the text message to Mendez.

Mendez had just finished submitting his application for a residence permit at the Hungarian embassy in Paris when he felt his phone buzz, signaling that he had received a message. He thanked the clerk and walked out of the building, down the steps, and the short distance back to the grand Avenue Foch. He decided to enjoy the walk up towards the Arc de Triomphe, where he could more easily catch a taxi and also take in the stately old palaces and chestnut trees that lined the avenue. He smirked as he pulled his phone from his jacket pocket. He was wondering how many tourists that wandered down this avenue appreciated the irony that the Jewish Rothschild family and banking dynasty had once had a mansion at one end, and the Nazi Gestapo had later set up their headquarters in occupied Paris at the other end. Almost next door to the current location of the Hungarian embassy. When he saw the message was from Maria he stopped walking and read it several times over. He then went to his contact list, scrolled to Stefan Lang's name, and pressed 'call.'

"*Hallo, Doktor,*" came Stefan's thin but deliberate voice.

"Are you still in San Sebastián, Stefan?" Mendez asked, too impatient to waste time with polite greetings.

"Yes. I've been watching the Guevara home and business, trying to work out the best way to determine the girl's location. It may be necessary to get a little more… persuasive… with her parents."

"Forget about that—you need to come to Paris right away. She's returned here and sent me a message just now. We need to clean up loose ends here so I can get on with setting up the new operation in Budapest—the Council is getting impatient. I've already submitted my resignation with the Institute and started making inquiries with moving companies."

"What about Ulrik?"

"I'm going to call him to come to Paris as well."

Stefan paused for a moment. "He's a little unpredictable, *Herr Doktor.*"

"Yes, the Council also thinks so. That's why I'm asking him to come to Paris… so we can try to kill two birds with one stone, if you see what I mean."

"I do."

"Good. Call me when you arrive."

≈

Remy Boucher had just returned to his desk when his phone rang. He saw it was Maria calling and answered on the second ring. "*Bonjour*, Maria. *Ça va?*"

"*Ça va bien, merci.* Is this a good time to talk, Remy?"

"*Oui.*"

"We're back in Paris now and wanted to get in touch with you. We're thinking about what our next move with Mendez should be."

"I'm not sure how much I can help with that, but I did check that name you gave me—Karl Larsson—against Dr. Mendez's visitor logs and it matched. I cross-checked again with my contact at DGSI, and that name was indeed the one I mentioned that had turned out to be a known alias for a member of C18 that's on DGSI's watchlist. I think you've found your man."

"What's his real name?"

"Ulrik Eklund."

"Do you have a picture of him?"

"I just sent it to you."

Maria looked at the picture from Remy and caught her breath. "*Hijo de puta.* That's him. The one that came at me at the parade."

"Are you sure?" Vano interjected.

"Yes," Maria replied.

Vano continued. "Well, that's progress. We have a name and a picture. Thank you, Mssr. Boucher."

"There's more," Boucher replied. "I checked with HR to ask if there were any changes to Mendez's status at the Institute. They said he just recently submitted his resignation and didn't leave a forwarding address or give any information about where he was going."

"We need to find out where he's headed. I think there's something happening that's bigger than just Mendez. Can we come see you in the next few days?"

Remy paused and then replied, "If that's what Maria wants to do."

"Thank you so much, Remy," Maria joined in, her tone underscoring her gratitude that Remy had decided to look past her earlier little white lies. "By the way, I've sent a text message to Mendez letting him know I'm in Paris, in order to draw his attention away from San Sebastián. So he may show his face at the Institute trying to check up on me."

"Please be careful if you see him. He likely wants to cover his tracks and not leave any loose ends," Vano added.

"Yes, Yes. Of course," Remy replied impatiently. "Call me when you decide when you want to come by and meet. I have to get back to work now. *À tout.*"

Chapter 9: The Sidewinder

REMY BOUCHER WAS FEELING uneasy as he waited for Maria and Vano to arrive at the Institute. He had agreed to meet with them but was still uncertain how involved he should get with the two Spaniards. As a former policeman, he knew there was no real hard evidence on Mendez that he could use to get the authorities involved. There was some suspicious behavior and suspicious visitors yes, but no evidence of a crime. He was worried that he had already crossed the line a bit by putting the hidden camera in Mendez's office, and now that Mendez was leaving the Institute there would be even less justification for him to be involved going forward. He definitely did not want to be seen as an accomplice to a Spanish intelligence agent operating—probably unofficially—on French soil. But he had also learned long ago to pay attention to his instincts, and they were telling him that something much bigger than Institute protocols and investigative procedures was at stake here.

When Maria and Vano arrived, Remy met them at the reception desk, signed them in, and took them back to his small office. There were two wooden chairs in front of his desk, and he motioned for them to have a seat. "Welcome to *chez* Boucher," he quipped sardonically as he settled into his chair.

"Thank you for seeing us, Remy," Maria replied.

"I'm pleased to finally meet you, Mssr. Boucher," Vano added.

"Likewise," Remy replied out of politeness, though not with any noticeable warmth. "As I mentioned on the phone, Mendez is leaving the Institute, so I'm not sure it's going to be appropriate for me to have much involvement going forward… unless of course something happens here at the Institute." He had already calculated that he wasn't going to close and lock the door completely, knowing that the information he was gathering about these two unusual Spaniards could prove to be useful if things got out of hand.

Maria and Vano looked at one another for a moment and then Maria turned to Remy. "That's understandable, Remy. You've already been more helpful than I deserved. We were just wondering about one more thing, though."

"What is that?" Remy asked cautiously.

"Well, is there any way to check into whatever files he left on the Institute's server? There may be some clues there about what he's been up to."

"Sharing that with you two would be a pretty major breach of Institute policy, but it's a moot point anyway."

"Why?" Vano interjected.

"Because I've already asked the IT department manager to see what's remaining on the server and to archive it, and he came back and said Mendez seems to have found a way to delete his files from the server. Every single one of them."

"*Mierde*," Vano scowled.

Remy laughed. "Indeed. But you're in France now *mon ami*—it's '*merde*.'"

Vano smiled and nodded his head in acknowledgement, realizing from Remy's body language that the meeting was effectively over. "Can we keep in touch?" he said as he stood up, tapping Maria on the shoulder to follow.

"Sure, feel free. What do you plan to do now?" Remy asked, looking at Maria.

"I'm not sure yet. I guess we'll try to find out where Mendez is and what he's up to," Maria replied.

Remy reached forward to shake Maria's hand. "Good luck, my dear, and please be careful." He then shook Vano's hand and walked them both to the exit, opening the door for them and giving them a small wave as they left.

"Well, that was a waste of time," Vano said under his breath as they walked away from the Institute and towards the metro station.

"Maybe not," Maria replied. She opened her hand and unfolded a small slip of paper that Remy had surreptitiously placed in her palm when they shook hands.

Vano stopped and cocked an eyebrow. "What is that?"

"It looks like an address."

"Where?"

"In the Passy neighborhood… It's in the 16th arrondissement. A very *chic* and very expensive neighborhood."

"Mendez's apartment?"

Maria smiled. "Probably," and then whispered softly, "Thank you, Remy."

At that exact moment Stefan Lang was calling Mendez from a bench on the sidewalk across the street from the Pasteur Institute. He had been watching the entrance and seen them go in, and then saw them exit, escorted by Remy Boucher. And he had taken pictures of all of them to send to Mendez. "Should I follow them?" he said when Mendez answered.

"Not this time. We need to find out first who that is with her. I do, however, recognize the person that walked them to the exit—it's the Institute's head of security. I think we need to ask him a few questions."

"What do you suggest?"

"Come to my apartment and let's discuss how we can, shall we say, *encourage* him to tell us what he knows about those two."

It had taken some persistent tailing, but Stefan Lang had finally found an opportune time and place to plunge the small syringe provided by Mendez into the side of Remy Boucher's neck. After a brief struggle, Remy had collapsed to the sidewalk and was loaded into an unmarked panel van that had rolled up next to them. When he began to slowly regain consciousness later, he realized he was completely naked and bound to a cold metal chair. Looking around for some kind of visual clue as to where he was and what was happening, he could find none and released a primal howl of rage, shaking his body violently and pulling at the cords that bound him.

"Ah… I see you have finished your nap Mssr. Boucher," came a voice from behind.

Remy knew immediately who it was and grunted, "Mendez. *Bâtard!*"

Mendez laughed, "Actually, technically speaking, you are correct Remy. Do you mind if I call you Remy?"

"*Vas te faire foutre.*"

"Well, now that we have the greetings out of the way, I suppose we should get to work, no? I am going to ask you some questions, and you—one way or another—are going to answer. I could of course make this easier on you by giving you some barbiturates to make you more conversational, but what would be the fun in that?" Mendez rolled a small metal trolley table in front of Boucher, on top of which were spread an array of surgical instruments.

At that moment Remy knew he was going to die—there was no way Mendez could do this and let him live. He bowed his head for a moment, whispering a farewell and wishes of happiness to his granddaughter Amélie, and then looked back at Mendez with cold contempt. "Let's get it over with then."

Mendez smiled thinly, picked up a scalpel, and approached Remy slowly as Stefan Lang suddenly appeared from behind to assist. "Now, let's find some nerve endings, shall we?"

Remy's screams remained trapped with him in the subterranean room they all occupied now, as Mendez's knowledge of anatomy allowed him to elicit an escalation of agony that no person could long endure. It was when Mendez drove a slender, nail-like stainless steel spike into the nerve at the root of one of his teeth that Remy coughed out the passcode to his phone along with some blood. But it was only after a blunt force castration and then strips of skin being peeled from his face that he finally revealed what he knew about Maria and Vano. Eventually he descended into incoherence, and ultimately—mercifully—unconsciousness. Without hesitation, Mendez then finished his grim work with a deliberately brutal and messy *coup de grâce*—leaving an unmistakable message. Stefan then dutifully began cleaning up the scene and loading

Boucher's body into a makeshift plastic body bag while Mendez picked up Boucher's phone and tapped out a message to Maria.

"Did you find something else, *Herr Doktor*?" Stefan asked. He was now wrestling the plastic body bag and its gruesome contents into a larger canvas duffle bag.

"No. We just need to set out the bait now for our friend Ulrik so that we can finish this business, and I can leave," Mendez replied as he hit 'send' on the message to Maria and then pulled out his own phone to call Ulrik.

"Very well," Stefan intoned as he attached the duffle bag to a hand cart with bungee cords and wheeled it out of the room, heading for the van.

It had turned out to be a very busy day for Maria. First, there had been a quick registration with a local obstetrician near Drancy that she had found, in case any complications arose while she was in town. Next, she and Vano had gone to a DPD France[1] location in the suburb of Gennevilliers to pick up a package her father had sent to her. And now she was back at the apartment of Kashi and Esma Kolompár, scanning through the DNA analysis files Mapa de Vida had finally emailed to her, while Vano sat across from her reading the instructions Xavier had written up to accompany the ESK box that had come in the package from her father. Needing a break, she sat back, looked at Vano, and finally asked, "So, have you figured out how we can use that thing?"

---

[1] DPD France – a subsidiary of the European parcel delivery network DPDgroup

"We'll have to get it into Mendez's apartment and near his computer. And then one of us will have to stay near the building with our phone or laptop to act as a relay for the signal. We'll also need to coordinate the timing of that in advance with Xavier so he can make sure his friend's system in Barcelona is ready to receive and process the signal. Complicated, but doable. I may need to enlist Kashi's help. What did you find out?"

"Mendez, or whomever he was working with, really went all out on the genetic engineering on this baby. The EPOR gene was modified for increased endurance. The MSTN gene was modified for strength and muscularity. The LRP5 gene was modified for bone strength. The DEC2 gene was modified to require less sleep. The—"

Vano interrupted. "I get it. He made a turbocharged version of a human being."

Maria gave a little eyeroll. "That's a colorful metaphor for it I guess, but there's more. The individual gene modifications add up to a modification of the child's genotype. But the analysis Mapa de Vida did points to something more subtle that was done as well… some combination of epigenetic programming."

"What is that?"

"It's a little bit complicated. The physical manifestation of our inventory of genes—our genotype—is influenced by the surrounding environment and results in a phenotype, which is our observable characteristics and behaviors. This occurs through what's called gene expression—where the information stored in our DNA is converted into instructions for making proteins or other molecules. Gene expression acts as both an on/off switch and a volume control for a particular gene.

So epigenetics is the study of how environment and behavior can cause changes in overall gene expression and how this ultimately manifests as unique phenotypes."

"It's a little confusing, but I think I follow the broad idea. But what then is the epigenetic programming you mentioned?"

"The ultimate fine-tuning tool of genetic engineering. Real frontier stuff. Up until now, we could mostly just manipulate the *composition* of the genome—the genotype. This next level of engineering would be manipulating the *output* of the genome. Imagine if you could reverse engineer and trigger the patterns of gene expressions that would result in an even more precise set of desired characteristics and behaviors, which previously had only arisen as a result of interaction with the environment over time. Things like height, hair and eye color, immune system response, and even certain personality traits."

"So, a kind of hot-wired feedback loop?"

"Very roughly speaking, yes. But I've only ever seen theoretical analysis and computer simulations about it in technical journals. I've never heard of someone actually figuring out how to do it with a complex organism like a human."

"What kind of personality traits are we talking about?"

"Well, the AI analysis from Mapa de Vida put in the framework of something called the Big Five. I'm not really familiar with it."

"Ah yes, the Big Five personality traits. I remember that one from my psychology classes. Extraversion, Openness, Conscientiousness, Agreeableness, and… um… Neuroticism, yes, each on a sliding scale of low to high."

"I see. So anyway, the Mapa de Vida analysis suggests a personality with contours that would tend towards being stable, organized, extroverted, and secure—likely a strong or even charismatic leader type. And all of this additionally packed into someone tall with blonde hair and blue eyes. Mind you these are just theoretical models they are working with."

"How predictable. Sounds like they definitely went for the 'master race' stereotype… or I guess phenotype?"

"Very funny… I see you're a fast learner. Well done," Maria replied laughing, unable to contain her amusement at the self-satisfied look on Vano's face. Though still feeling conflicted about her situation, she managed a smile and murmured with a downward glance, "You really are something special, aren't you, *txikito*?" Just then her phone pinged with a message. When she looked at it, her eyebrows furrowed.

"What's up?" Vano asked.

"It's Remy. He wants to meet tomorrow in the Bois de Boulogne,[2] by the LV museum.[3] It's his day off, and he's taking his granddaughter first to the children's amusement park that's nearby—the Jardin d'Acclimatation—and then he'll meet me near the museum after her mother picks her up. And he wants me to come alone. He says he has some new information to share with me."

"Interesting," Vano muttered cryptically.

"What do you mean?" Maria probed.

[2] Bois de Boulogne – At over 2000 acres, almost 2.5 times the size of New York's Central Park, Bois de Boulogne is the largest park in Paris. It was originally a royal hunting grounds and part of the greater Forest of Rouvray.

[3] The Louis Vuitton Foundation art (mostly modern and contemporary) museum and cultural center.

"Nothing really. He's probably just still a little suspicious of me. You should go and see what he has to say. I'll come along and wait for you nearby, but out of sight."

≈

The Louis Vuitton Foundation museum is a masterpiece of contemporary architecture in a long line of masterpieces by Frank Gehry. It's ship-like exterior includes 12 glass 'sails,' which cover the concrete clad gallery spaces, and it was the fulfillment of Gehry's wish to "design, in Paris, a magnificent vessel symbolizing the cultural calling of France." Maria loved it because it also reminded her of Bilbao, a city near the ocean in Spain's Basque Country and the location of another one of Gehry's masterpieces—the Guggenheim Museum Bilbao. She lingered for a moment near the entrance pavilion, enjoying the dazzling dance of light on the glass sails from the late afternoon sun, and then finally turned to cross the Ave. du Mahatma Gandhi. Once she had crossed she carried on directly into the wooded area of the Bois de Boulogne via the Rte. Sablonneuse path and after about twenty meters turned left on the All. des Maronniers path. After walking about another three hundred meters, she finally came to the location where the text from Remy Boucher's number had told her to wait for him—a small clearing at a kind of triple intersection where the All. des Maronniers path crossed a small stream and also met with another path. She looked around and then took a seat on the bench on the side of the clearing, checked her watch, and pulled out her phone to check her messages. There was only one that had come in recently—from Remy Boucher, mentioning he would arrive shortly.

Maria tilted her head up to the warmth of the sun and closed her eyes briefly, letting her thoughts wander. She wondered what Remy's granddaughter was like and what it was like for him to take her to an amusement park, and she wondered what her own child would be like. She put her hand on her abdomen and rubbed the barely-detectable bulge that she had only recently noticed. Not long after, she spotted a figure approaching in the distance from the opposite direction on the path and stood up, expecting it would be Remy. As the figure got closer, she could make out that it was a man, but he seemed too tall to be Remy Boucher. Probably just someone out for a walk, she thought and turned aside, not wanting to appear to be staring. A moment later, she heard the footsteps of the stranger begin to quicken into a run and she looked back, startled. In an instant, Maria recognized the blonde hair and scowling visage—the same one that had come at her in San Sebastián—and started to run, yelling "*Au secours!*" hoping someone would hear her, even though there didn't appear to be anyone around. Just when it sounded like the footsteps were right behind her, she heard a muffled 'thwup' sound and a grunting groan. Almost simultaneously, Vano leapt onto the path from the tree line where he had been watching and pulled her to him, protectively wrapping his body around hers.

"You're safe now Maria… take a deep breath," Vano said, still holding her tight.

"What in the hell just happened, Vano?" Maria replied, shaking from the surge of adrenaline that had hit her system.

"What happened is that I just took that bastard down," came another familiar voice from the tree line. And then out walked Kashi, grinning and holding up something he was carrying and looking back towards Ulrik Eklund, who was writhing and moaning on the ground with what looked like a short arrow in his abdomen.

"Kashi? What are you doing here?" Maria asked, taken aback.

Vano jumped in, "That message supposedly from Remy didn't feel right to me. He had made it clear to us that he didn't want to be involved anymore and asking you to meet him outside the Institute just didn't fit my read of him. So I asked Kashi to tag along and to be prepared for a worst-case scenario." Vano then looked over at Kashi and motioned towards Ulrik, "Finish him, before he starts screaming too."

Kashi nodded and pulled another one of the short arrows out of his backpack, loaded it into his weapon, and launched the arrow through Ulrik's throat. "That should keep him quiet," he said grimly as Ulrik's body twitched a few times and then was still.

Still disoriented by what had happened, Maria stared at Ulrik's body for several seconds and then turned to Kashi, "What is that thing?"

"A compound crossbow. Very powerful. Designed for deer hunting, but works equally well on Nazis," Kashi replied, grinning as he folded up and shoved the crossbow into his backpack. "Nice and quiet too."

"Clean shots. Well done, Kashi," Vano said as he pulled a pair of latex gloves out of his pocket and began putting them on as he walked towards Ulrik's body. "We should take these arrows back with us though—no need to leave evidence lying around." He then pulled the arrows the rest of the way out through Ulrik's chest and throat and wiped as much blood as he could off of them using Ulrik's shirt tail. "We need to get out of here now… before someone sees us."

"Wait," Maria interjected tersely.

"What? We need to leave Maria… right now."

Maria ignored Vano and turned to Kashi, reaching her hand towards him. "Give me one of those arrows—a clean one, and don't touch the tip. And do either of you have a clean plastic bag or another one of those gloves… unused?"

Kashi looked at her quizzically for a moment and then pulled an arrow from the quiver in his backpack as Vano dug out a fresh latex glove. "What are you going to do?"

"Get a little evidence of my own," she said as she walked over to Ulrik's body. She leaned over Ulrik and first took a picture of the tattoos on his arm, and then used the blade on the arrowhead to scrape some flakes of his skin and drops of his blood into the opening of the glove. She then carefully tied up the opening and put it in Kashi's backpack. "This is all I need to get a DNA analysis. We can go now."

Kashi hesitated for a moment and turned to Vano. "Shouldn't we take his phone? There might be useful information on it."

Vano shook his head. "No. I don't want to take a chance that we get followed, in case his phone's being tracked by Mendez or whoever else he was working with."

Once they were well into the tree line and working their way back towards the LV museum, where Esma was waiting with a car, Maria stopped unexpectedly and planted her hands on her hips.

Vano turned, an urgent look on his face. "What's wrong, Maria? We need to keep going."

"Why didn't you tell me you were suspicious about that message from Remy? You really did use me as bait didn't you?"

"No. Well, maybe just a tiny bit… but you were never in any real danger. Your body language had to look genuine—like you didn't suspect anything—because they were probably watching you from a distance at first."

"They?"

"I think we need to assume there may have been someone else with Ulrik… watching to see what happened. He didn't seem the type to be able to pull this off all by himself."

"Mendez?"

"Maybe… I don't know. Come on now, we have to go, Maria."

"Don't ever do that to me again, Vano. I mean it," Maria replied angrily as she turned and continued on towards the museum. At that moment, Stefan Lang was also making his way through the trees, moving away from the vantage point where he had watched the events unfold at the clearing, but east towards the bus stop near the entrance of the Jardin d'Acclimatation.

≈

William Tell, who famously used a crossbow to shoot an arrow through an apple sitting on his son's head, hailed from Bürglen, a picturesque little village that sits among the foothills of the Swiss Alps. Hans Rudolf Giger, a more recent and more anonymous resident of Bürglen, now maintained an elegant chalet there, which he had used over the years as a private retreat from the hustle and bustle of Zürich. The chalet was perched on a hill just above the village and set back among the trees and when Giger was away in Zürich a local caretaker would occasionally check on the chalet. But when he came to Bürglen, his personal assistant, Lina Bormann, would join him to attend to his needs and keep the chalet in order—Lina referred to Giger as 'Chairman' though, because he was the Chairman of the Council of the Nine Realms.

Early in the evening following the dramatic events in Paris' Bois de Boulogne, a gentle knock came on the glass door of the wood-lined sauna in the back of Chairman Giger's chalet, where he was relaxing after a long day. He looked up, knowing already that it was Lina. *"Hallo?"*

"Herr Vorsitzender, Stefan Lang is on the line."

"Give me a moment," Giger replied as he stood up, toweled the sweat off his naked body, and stepped out through the door that Lina had now opened for him.

"Here you are, sir," Lina said in her usual measured and courteous tone as she handed the phone to Giger, unfazed by his unclothed form.

Giger spoke into the phone, *"Ja?"*

Stefan knew Chairman Giger liked to get straight to whatever business was at hand. "The Norseman is dead. It happened in Paris, in a park. I took his phone before I left. There's nothing that could lead the authorities back to the Council."

"Good. And the girl?"

"She was there, but she had help. Someone apparently connected to CNI in Spain, and we think with potentially some kind of family connection to the girl. Him we were expecting, but there was a third, unidentified and armed, person with them. That's the one who killed the Norseman before he got to the girl."

"She got away?"

"I'm afraid so, yes."

"How much do you think they know?"

"Nothing about the Council, but still too much. They know the connection between Mendez and the Norseman now and seem to be piecing together more about Mendez and her pregnancy."

"How did you find that out?"

"We interrogated the security man where she and Mendez work after we discovered she was talking to him. That was another loose end that has now been put to rest."

"This is getting messy, Stefan. The girl connects to Mendez, and he can connect to the Council. And now someone from CNI is involved? We cannot be exposed—our time is near."

"I understand, *Herr Vorsitzender*," Stefan replied, his tone deferential.

"Work with Mendez to finish this business so we can get the Budapest project off the ground. Let him continue to think that you are working only for him and keep a close eye on him. These scientist types are sometimes a little too independent and unpredictable."

"*Jawohl.*" Stefan sensed the call was coming to an end and didn't want to draw it out further with any unnecessary commentary.

"Keep me updated… and deal with whoever is helping the girl if it's necessary but avoid triggering the attention of CNI or any other authorities." Giger finished curtly, and then hung up.

A few moments later, Lina appeared in a form-fitting jumpsuit. "Are you ready for your massage sir?" she said as she dimmed the lights and pulled a bottle of oil out of a warming device.

"Yes," Giger said as he walked, still unclothed, over to the massage table at the other side of the room and lay down. "And remind me afterwards to call the Austrian."

≈

Maria woke early and abruptly. She didn't usually dream—or at least didn't usually remember her dreams—but this one she remembered vividly. She had been in what appeared to be some kind of restaurant, with music playing, and was holding a baby. A waiter holding a baby bottle filled with milk had approached her, taken the baby from her, and started feeding it, murmuring, "This will put you to sleep." Maria had felt apprehension in the dream though, as the waiter was not smiling and had pulled the baby with a jerk from her arms. And he was blonde. The meaning hit her as she woke up like an electric shock—Ulrik Eklund had been that waiter in the jazz club that had served her wine, drugging her, and he was the father of the child she was carrying. A few seconds later the words that the *castañera* Vadoma had ended Maria's tarot card reading with echoed in her head, "*And remember also that more may now reveal itself to you in your dreams.*"

Maria put on her robe, briefly freshened up in the bathroom, and went out into the living room of the Kolompár's apartment to wake Vano, who was still asleep on the sofa. When she placed her hand on his shoulder, he sat up suddenly, rubbing his eyes and looking at his watch. "What's wrong?" he mumbled, looking around warily.

Maria sat down in the armchair next to the sofa, crossing one leg over the other and pulling her robe tight against the morning chill, and replied, "Nothing, Vano, I just wanted to tell you about my dream. Why would you think something was wrong?"

"Because *I'm* always the one that has to wake *you* up, Dr. Guevara" Vano teased, poking her shoulder with an outstretched finger. "Now, tell me, what was this dream?"

After Maria finished recounting the dream and her feeling of what it meant, as well as the memory of Vadoma's reminder that had come to her, she watched for Vano's reaction. "Well? What do you think? Am I just imagining things?"

Vano stared at her curiously for a few moments and then tilted his head to the side. "What do I think? I think that six months ago you would have dismissed the dream as just a dream. I think that whether you realize it or not, what has happened to you in the last few months has reawakened your *Calé* blood… and it is speaking to you. Can I ask you a personal question, though?"

"I'm not sure there's anything personal left that you don't already know but go ahead."

"Knowing what you now know about the baby—how it was conceived without your consent and the intentions behind that—why have you decided to keep it?"

"What do you mean by that?" Maria shot back, her tone at once sharp and defensive.

"I'm not judging you, Maria. I just think that it's important for you, and the child for that matter, that you're honest with yourself about why you're still going ahead with this. You're choosing the more dangerous path in the short term, and eventually the child is going to have questions about where he came from and who his father is."

Maria met his eyes, and the room remained silent while Vano's words hung in the air for a long while. Finally, she replied, "This is *my* child now, Vano. As each day passes I feel his presence in me and my connection to him growing. Mendez may have thought he was manipulating what was happening, but I am taking back control of my life and my body and this child. Maybe spending time with you and Vadoma has opened me up somehow… I didn't believe in fate before, but I'm starting to be open to the idea, and if there is such a thing then this situation and this child is it. If there really is a bigger purpose behind what has happened, I want to know what it is. And if there is something truly special about this child, beyond even his genetic enhancements, I want to find out… and help him with it. Anyway, I had always planned to be a mother, and I'm not getting any younger." As she finished and her own words trailed off, she suddenly realized she was also trying to reassure herself. Could it also be that there is something malevolent or even evil growing inside me? After all, it was designed with that purpose. But she refolded her resolve—'science and technology is amoral… what matters is what we do with it,' she almost forced her inner voice to repeat. The unease seemed to dissipate… though not completely.

Vano paused and then finally nodded his head in reply. "Fair enough. If it's clear to you, then that's all that matters. Is there anything you need to do today?"

She then pulled out her phone. "I have an idea."

"What?"

"I'm going to send the picture that Remy sent to me of Karl, or Ulrik, or whatever his name is, to Brigitte, and see if she thinks he looks like the waiter that served me in the club that night."

"Even if it was, it doesn't really matter Maria—he's dead now."

"I know. I just want to see if it was actually him that night. And if it was, then we'll know that there isn't some other mysterious person out there who drugged me."

"With these people, there's always more of them out there." Vano grunted as he stood up. He walked behind her and unexpectedly gave her a friendly peck on the top of the head and then headed into the kitchen. "I need some coffee, Maria. Do you want some eggs and sausage for breakfast?"

"Yes, please," she chirped, suddenly realizing that the pitch of her voice had gone up, and she was smiling widely just because of the little peck he had planted on the top of her head. "Must be the hormones," she muttered to herself and shook her head.

"Did you say something?" Vano called out from the kitchen.

"No," she replied as she hit the 'send' button on the message to Brigitte.

Several minutes later a reply came back.

Hi Maria, It's good to hear from you! I hope everything is ok with you?
Yes, the man in the picture looks like the waiter we had at the end of the evening, but I can't be 100% certain. What's going on—where did you get that picture?

By the way, your friend Dr. Mendez came by the lab looking for you the other day.

B.

Thank you, Brigitte—The story behind the picture is a little too complicated to go into here, I'm afraid. Regarding Dr. Mendez, if he comes around again, please let me know, but please don't tell him you've been in contact with me. It's complicated—I promise I'll explain later. I hope everything is going well with you and the others at the lab.

I miss all of you.

Take care,
Maria

Maria then went into the kitchen to join Vano and showed him the text exchange. "Look at this."

"He's persistent; I'll give him that," Vano scowled. "Now, let me finish making us breakfast. I'm hungry."

"We are too," Maria smiled and patted her stomach. She went back into the living room briefly to turn on the television and then came back just as Vano was pouring two fresh cups of coffee while the sausage sizzled on the stove. And then the morning news report coming from the television caught their attention.

"Police are reporting the discovery of two bodies in Paris last night, both of which appear to be murders. One was an unidentified male found in the northern part of Bois de Boulogne with deep puncture wounds in his abdomen and throat," came the animated voice of the news anchor. "The other was found on the sidewalk in front of La Gitane bar in Paris' Belleville neighborhood. The gruesome discovery was made by a resident of the neighborhood who said it looked like the victim was a middle-aged man that had been mutilated or tortured. The police have not released the name of the victim at the request of the family for privacy, but we can now confirm, based on information from anonymous sources in the police department, that he was a retired policeman. In addition to the investigations, police have stepped up patrols and are asking the public to be vigilant of their surroundings. There is no confirmation yet as to whether or not the two murders are connected."

Maria and Vano sat in stunned silence for nearly a minute. Finally, Maria spoke up, her voice unsteady, "Do you think it was… Remy?"

Vano reached to turn off the stove and then turned back to Maria. "Of course it was Remy. Those filthy animals butchered him and then left him to be found in front of a bar called La Gitane—The Gypsy. That was no coincidence Maria—it was a message to you… to us. And they no doubt tortured him to get everything he knew about us out of him, and to be able to get into his phone so they could send you that message asking to meet in the Bois de Boulogne. We have to assume now that they know about me, and that we both know too much."

Maria lowered her head and closed her eyes as she felt tears welling up. "This is my fault, Vano. I'm the reason they came after Remy. My God… his poor family."

Vano reached across the table and gently rested his hand on Maria's hand. "It's not your fault, Maria. Remy was being Remy up until the end… he made his own choices and acted on his own accord. You couldn't have forced him even if you wanted to."

Maria looked up, tears on her cheeks. "Perhaps. But in the end he died a terrible death because someone was trying to get to *me*." They sat in silence for a long while then. Maria's gaze was downcast and distant. Vano continued to hold her hand.

Finally, Maria looked up. Vano gave her a searching look, trying to gauge her state. "I think our coffee has gone cold. I'll make a fresh pot and scramble some eggs to go along with the sausage I almost burned," he said as if thinking out loud, giving her hand a little pat as he stood up. He wanted to get her talking about something besides Remy, so, as he huddled over the stove, he asked, "What do you think we should do next, Maria?"

Maria willed herself back into the moment. "I think we need to use that device Xavier sent to us and get into Mendez's computer before he tries to leave Paris. We know he's already resigned from the Institute. After what happened last night, he's probably afraid we might go to the police and name him as a potential suspect or accomplice. After Remy was killed, Mendez thought he'd be able to have me killed me in the park. But now he'll be feeling exposed. If we can get into his computer, we might find out where he's going and what else he's up to."

Vano turned away from the stove for a moment and nodded. "Let me speak to Kashi and Esma, but I think we can pull something together in the next few days. We'll need to do a quick reconnaissance of Mendez's apartment building first. Something tells me we haven't seen the last of him though," Vano said as his gaze dropped down to Maria's abdomen. "He seems determined to get rid of the remaining evidence of what he's done—to you and the baby—and I don't think he's going to give up after just one try. You know too much now. But you're probably right that he'll be looking to get out of town for a while, at least until he can determine whether you've talked to the police. However, he had this Ulrik fellow working for him, so it's possible that he may have other people in Paris working with him and still trying to find us. We need to be careful and—"

Maria had been nodding in agreement while Vano was speaking but then interrupted, almost absent-mindedly. "By the way, Remy mentioned he had gotten some of his information on that Ulrik character from an old friend that now works for DGSI. Do you think we should try to find out who that was and make contact?"

Vano arched an eyebrow as he finished preparing two plates of the now-cooked eggs and sausage, set them on the table, and sat across from Maria again. "Maybe. Let me work on that. Let's eat now… we have a lot to do."

Chapter 10: September Song

Kashi and Esma were getting ready to leave for the day when Maria emerged from the bathroom, wrapped in a robe, after a long, hot shower. The initial shock of the news about Remy Boucher's murder had subsided, but the atmosphere in the apartment remained subdued. Kashi turned and waved as he opened the door and stepped out. "You two should stay in today. Let me see if my network can pick up anything from the street on what's happening. I've put eyes outside Mendez's apartment building, the Pasteur Institute, and the police station handling the murder investigations."

"And there's plenty of food in the refrigerator—help yourself," Esma chimed in as she closed the door behind her.

Maria walked over and stood near Vano, her hair still damp and her skin still flushed from the hot water. She paused for a moment, watching him as he finished folding up the blanket that he used while sleeping on the sofa, and then asked, "So, what shall we do today?"

Vano turned, reached out, and gently grasped Maria's shoulders. "We're going to have to do some planning if we want to get into Mendez's apartment and computer, but I don't want you to feel like you have to rush past what just happened, Maria. How are you feeling?"

Maria was surprised by her reaction to Vano's touch. She felt as if she was somehow starting to fall into his warm gaze and that time was slowing. She shook her head, as if to wake herself up, and finally replied, "Angry… and a little vulnerable, to be honest. But I think I'll be okay."

"Good." Vano said, smiling gently. He then pulled Maria to him, gave her a comforting hug and a peck of a kiss on the damp tousle of hair at the top of her head.

Vano was almost a foot taller than her, so Maria had turned her head and rested her cheek against his firm chest. Her breathing deepened and then suddenly she felt an unexpected wave of desire washing over her. She pulled at him and whispered under her breath, "Oh, Vano… what would I have done without you?"

Vano had sensed the change in Maria's body and her breathing but was not sure what he should do. He dropped his head down beside hers, kissed her gently on the cheek, and then said, "I'm not sure if this is right, Maria. I don't want to take advantage of you."

Maria looked up, deep into his eyes, and replied softly, "Please kiss me, Vano. After all that's happened, I need to feel something good… some joy, some passion… some hope."

Vano clutched her tightly and kissed her. Softly at first, and then more intensely as her lips and her body responded to his. As his breathing quickened in sync with hers she could also feel his arousal growing against her and she reached to caress it, the stimulation of the sensation causing him to inhale sharply. He kissed her even harder and then pulled back slightly and whispered, "Are you sure?"

Maria locked eyes with him and then untied her robe and let it fall to the floor. "Yes." She stroked his thick, taut forearms and then took his wrists and pulled his hands to her full breasts. "I'm sure."

In one effortless motion, Vano swept Maria up into his arms, carried her to the bedroom, and laid her gently on the bed. He kissed her breasts gingerly for a moment and then stood to undress. "You know… It's been a while for me, Maria."

"Me too. I haven't been with a man for a very long time… not even when I got pregnant," she chuckled.

Vano smiled back at her. "It's good that you're able to laugh about it." He was fully undressed now.

Maria looked over Vano's lean, lithe form and his intensely erect manhood and then pulled him to her. "Come here, *guapo*."

Vano positioned himself over her and began kissing her, first on the mouth and then on her breasts, and then working his way down her torso. He then murmured into her abdomen, "Don't worry, I'll be gentle."

Maria stroked his hair, and her hips arched upwards as his kisses reached her inner thighs and then touched on the aroused and glistening flesh of her tender folds. She moaned and then replied, "You don't have to be *too* gentle."

Their first round of making love was intense, though didn't last overly long, as they both climaxed quickly. After a brief rest they made love again, this time more leisurely, and more intimately as they explored one another. After they were spent, Vano turned to her, stroking her hair, and said, "That was very good."

"Yes, it was." Maria smiled. "I guess it's true what they say about pregnancy making you *cachondo*."

Vano put on a mock hurt expression. "So, I didn't have anything to do with it?"

"Oh, you most certainly did, Sr. Amaya." Maria laughed. "By the way, how is it that you're still single? You seem like something a girl could get used to."

"All the traveling and need for secrecy… it's not a good recipe for long-term relationships, Maria." Vano stood up and put on a robe.

"No lingering regrets about one of the short-term relationships, then?"

Vano turned and bent over Maria, kissed her forehead, and stroked the back of her head. "How about I don't ask you about your past relationships and you don't ask me about mine? *And* I'll go make us some coffee. Deal?"

"Make some sandwiches too, and you've got a deal." Maria laughed.

Vano gave her a faux scowl and turned to leave the bedroom towards the kitchen. "Okay, *fine*."

Esma and Maria had been happy to come to Passy and act as 'lookouts' for Vano and Kashi two nights later, now that the reconnaissance and planning for their little operation had been completed. Mendez's apartment in that posh Parisian neighborhood was located on the Rue Benjamin Franklin[1] and near the Trocadéro Square,

---

[1] Rue Benjamin Franklin – named in recognition of Franklin having lived in Passy for the nine years he was in Paris on a diplomatic mission seeking French support during the American Revolution.

with its magnificent views of the Eiffel Tower. As Esma drove past the address Maria had received from Remy Boucher, Maria craned her head out the window to take in the building and then pulled back in, letting out a low whistle. "He must have inherited some of that looted Nazi gold, because there's no way you could afford to live here on an Institute salary."

"Let's stay focused please," came Vano's voice through her wireless earphone. All of them were wearing one and were connected to one another via an encrypted four-way conference call that they had dialed into earlier. Their reconnaissance had established that for the last two nights Mendez had left his apartment at exactly 8:00 p.m. to walk to a nearby restaurant and returned about ninety minutes later. Assuming Mendez's arrogant and controlling nature also made him a creature of habit, Vano had planned around it. Vano's voice came across the line again, "It's 7:30… let's all get into place."

Esma parked on the side of the street, put a 'city government official' parking pass on the dashboard, and gave Maria a mischievous grin as she pulled the handle to open her door and step out. "I don't know where Kashi finds things like this… I guess it's probably better I don't know. I'll see you back here when we're done." She shut the car door and then walked away towards the restaurant where Mendez would be having dinner—and where she had also booked a dinner reservation in order to keep an eye on him.

Maria turned in the opposite direction, crossed the street, and took a seat on a park bench that was at the southwest corner of the Trocadéro Gardens, where the Rue de le Tasse intersected the Rue Benjamin Franklin. From there she had an unobstructed view diagonally back across the street to the entrance to Mendez's apartment building, which would allow her to alert the team when he was leaving the building and when he was coming back into it. Directly in front of her and abutting Mendez's apartment building was the Rue Franklin Apartments—an eight-story art deco icon with a rooftop terrace and garden. Vano and Kashi had earlier made their way into the building, wearing white hard hats and dark blue coveralls that proclaimed '*Service de l'Urbanisme— Sécurité et Conformité des Bâtiments*' in large white letters on the back. Once on the roof they had been able to hide themselves until sunset in a closet-sized garden tool shed that was tucked behind one of the taller shrubs. It would then be relatively straightforward to climb over to the adjacent rooftop of Mendez's building and lower themselves down on to the balcony of Mendez's apartment, which sat on the top floor. Kashi would wait on the balcony and use his second phone to link the signal from the ESK device to the system in Barcelona that Xavier and his friend had configured for the operation and would be monitoring. In order to avoid interrupting the relay signal or getting accidentally cut off from the local four-way conference call, Kashi had brought a third burner phone so he could communicate directly with Xavier. Vano had insisted on being the one to enter Mendez's apartment—that was the role with the most risk, and he felt he had already asked too much of Kashi.

At 8:01 p.m., Maria's voice came on to the conference call, "He's leaving the building." Esma had just been seated at her table and was going over the wine menu, and Vano and Kashi emerged slowly from their garden tool shed, scanning the terrace to make sure no one else was there. After another ten minutes of stealthy movement, they were finally crouched on Mendez's balcony, checking the window frame for alarm sensors and peering inside the darkened apartment.

"Well?" Kashi asked, sounding a little impatient.

"No visible alarm sensors."

"Really?" came Maria's voice.

"I'm not surprised actually. It's the hubris of the arrogant and over-educated. They don't realize where their blind spots and vulnerabilities are until it's too late," Vano replied matter-of-factly. It hit a little close to home for Maria, but she held her tongue.

"Can you see inside?"

Vano pressed close to the glass, peering in again, and then pulled back. "Enough to see that he's got most of his things packed up in boxes and waiting for the movers. Looks like we got here just in time. I'm going in." He then pulled a small pry bar from an inside pocket of his coveralls and popped the balcony door open, waiting a few seconds to see if there was any sign of an alarm being triggered. There was none. Before going in he turned and nodded to Kashi who nodded back and hit 'call' on Xavier's number that he had saved on his burner phone.

Xavier picked up after the first ring. "*Hola*, this is Xavier."

"No names," Kashi whispered. "We're in… stay on the line please."

Vano was working his way through the apartment with a pen light and in the bedroom finally came across a desk with a pile of papers on it and a closed laptop computer. "I found it," he said. "Do I need to open it up or press the power button?"

Kashi relayed the question to Xavier and then relayed the answer back to Vano, "No, just press the power button on the ESK device until the blue light comes on and then set it right next to the computer."

A few seconds later, Vano's voice came back, "Okay, done. What now?"

"Wait," Kashi replied, checking that the Wi-Fi Direct indicator on his relay phone was on and ready to receive. A second later a text box popped up 'Allow ESK device to connect?' and Kashi hit 'Allow.' Per the instructions Xavier had provided earlier, he then opened a custom app on the phone called 'Data Transmission Tool,' and a dialog box opened, asking for a phone number. He tapped in the number he had saved that linked to the system in Barcelona, double-checked it, hit 'send,' and then set the relay phone down on the small wrought iron bistro table that was beside him on the balcony. Kashi spoke into the burner phone to Xavier. "Everything looks set… tell me when you start receiving the signal."

"It looks like it's coming in now," Xavier replied. "Give us a minute to initiate the program on the main computer so we can feed in the signal."

"Sure, do what you need to do. But let's try not to cut it too close." Kashi looked at his watch—it was almost 8:30 now—and then added, "To give ourselves some margin we should try to be getting out of here in forty-five minutes or less."

"Okay," Xavier replied just as Vano rejoined Kashi on the balcony, gently closing the door behind him.

"Any luck?" Vano asked.

"The signal's gone through, and they've linked it to their computer. I guess we have to just wait now and see if it works. It's times like this I wish I hadn't given up smoking—I could use one."

Vano smiled and rested his hand on Kashi's shoulder. "I know what you mean, my friend. I am in your debt for all this, Kashi. You have my marker."

"Good. I'm pretty sure I'm going to need it someday."

About ten minutes later, Kashi heard Xavier's voice, though barely. "*Hola*. Hello. Are you there?"

Kashi had forgotten he had put the burner phone back in his pocket and quickly pulled it out. "Sorry, yes. I'm here. Any progress?"

"Yes, we've finally gotten into the hard drive and are downloading a mirror image of its contents, which may take a little time. It's encrypted, but we can always crack through that later."

"Okay, thanks. Keep us updated, Kashi replied and then repeated the details of his conversation with Xavier into the local four-way call.

Twenty minutes later, Esma came into the call. "It looks like our friend may be finishing a little early tonight. Are you almost done up there?"

Vano and Kashi looked at one another, and then Vano replied to Esma, "Hopefully yes. Let us know when he's on the move."

Kashi pulled up the burner phone again. "Are we almost done from your end? It looks like we might have less time than we planned for."

There was a pause, and then Xavier replied, "We're at least seventy-five percent through the download, and I think it's speeding up a bit now. Another ten or fifteen minutes should do it."

Kashi looked at Vano. "Another ten or fifteen minutes. It might get tight, my friend."

Vano wanted to keep the team calm. "Don't worry. We'll make it. We've been in tighter spots."

"If you say so, my friend," Kashi replied, not sounding entirely reassured.

Five minutes later, Esma came on the line. "He's asked for the bill and is getting ready to leave. You've got maybe ten or twelve minutes left, gentlemen."

After another five minutes had elapsed, Kashi was growing impatient and spoke into the burner phone. "We're almost out of time here… have you got it all yet?"

"Maybe five more minutes," Xavier replied.

"*Merde,*… it's going to be close," Kashi whispered, to no one in particular.

Several minutes later, Maria's voice came on the line. "Hello? Can you hear me? I see him coming up the street now. He'll be at the entrance to his building any minute now."

Just then Xavier's voice came through again on the burner phone. "We're pretty much done on this end. The end-of-transmission lock down sequence has begun. You can shut off the device in exactly sixty seconds from… *now.*"

Vano looked at his watch and then made his way back into the apartment.

Maria's voice came back onto the line thirty seconds later. "He's at the building entrance and getting his key out. You better get out of there now."

Exactly thirty seconds later Vano emerged back onto the balcony with the ESK device in his hand, closing the door behind him. He shoved it into Kashi's backpack and boosted Kashi up to the ledge above them. As Mendez was coming up the elevator Kashi reached down and grasped

Vano's arm, pulling him up. They then disappeared into the darkness back to the Rue Franklin Apartments roof garden and down to the street, where Esma and Maria were waiting in the car in front of the building.

Mendez was enjoying his morning coffee on the balcony of his apartment when his phone rang. He had just left a message with the building maintenance supervisor about the door to the balcony, the latch of which for some reason was not inserting properly into the door frame and thought it would be the supervisor returning his call. When he looked at his phone though, he saw it was Stefan Lang calling. "Yes?" he answered, after pressing the green 'Accept' button and turning on the speakerphone so that he could continue with his coffee.

"*Guten Morgen, Herr Doktor*," Stefan replied. "It's been a few days now, and I was wondering what your plans were, and if I can be of assistance."

"*Hallo*, Stefan. Right at this moment, my plans are to finish my coffee. After that, I have a few more things to pack before the movers come," Mendez replied, a bit facetiously.

"I meant regarding the girl, *Herr Doktor*."

"Yes, I know Stefan. I haven't forgotten," Mendez retorted, an edge of irritation in his voice. The humorless Lang was beginning to bore him, and he was tiring of the messy drama involving Maria. He was anxious now to put it and Paris behind him as his mind increasingly wandered forward, eager to delve back into his research and the project he would be running in Budapest. But the Council's wishes were clear—the girl was a loose end they couldn't abide.

"If you would indulge me, I have a few ideas."

Mendez took a sip of his coffee and a deep breath of the crisp September air, and then replied, "Go on."

"Well, we don't know where the girl is, so we need to flush her out. I could phone in an anonymous tip to the police about the security man having two unusual visitors at the Institute, not long before he was found dead. They may have been careless enough to sign their names in the visitors' log, and then the police could use that to name them 'persons of interest.' If not, we could probably manufacture some other plausible way to make the police aware of their names."

"So?"

"So then it's not just us looking for them—it's the police. And if they come to the police station, either voluntarily or otherwise, we will be alerted."

"That sounds fine but could take a while. What are your other ideas?"

"I'd like to ask our associates in Spain to try and discreetly find out more about the CNI agent that appears to be helping her. I'd like to assess what the exposure—and potential leverage—is around the involvement of this person."

"I suspect this is probably a personal or family thing with him. But fine… let's see what your friends can find out. Anything else?"

"I think you should contact the girl. Try to leverage communication into proximity."

"What? I'm the last person she would want to talk to right now."

"I'm sure that a subtle reminder that you know the whereabouts of her parents would change that. Once you have her on the phone, make it clear that the situation must be resolved one way or the other and that you can finish things painlessly for her and the child or cruelly, with her parents involved as well." Mendez's eyebrows briefly flicked upwards, and he responded with a single, silent nod, acknowledging Lang's cold calculus.

It had taken almost 30 hours, but the AI-driven quantum cryptography program running on the computer in the basement of Xavier's friend in Barcelona had finally worked its magic. The encryption on the mirror version of Mendez's hard drive had been cracked and the files were now all accessible. Xavier had loaded them all onto a separate, secure server and then sent Maria a password-protected link so that she could remotely access the server.

"Well? Anything interesting?" Vano asked Maria as he walked into the kitchen of the Kolompár apartment, where she had been sitting for hours poring over the files from Mendez's computer.

"A lot. Have a seat."

"That much, huh?" Vano sat down across from Maria. "Okay… I'm listening, *cariño.*"

Maria looked up, slightly surprised, though with a tiny smile. "Really? Already with the romantic nicknames?" she teased.

"You don't like it?"

"I didn't say that. But let's just be discreet around Kashi and Esma. We've already overdrawn from their hospitality—no need to make them feel we've turned their guest bedroom into a rendezvous spot as well."

Vano chuckled. "Okay, Okay… but I think they, or at least Esma, would be fine with it. And probably even pleased… or at least amused."

Maria rolled her eyes and then looked back down at her computer. "Can I continue?"

"*Por favor.*"

"I found a folder called 'Eugenesis,' which caught my eye. It's a very specific, and somewhat archaic, term. It's the quality of having strong reproductive powers, particularly as it relates to the fertility of hybrids that have been created between different species or races."

"I've never heard of that. Are you sure he didn't just misspell 'eugenics?'"

"Based on what's in the folder, I'm quite sure. But I'm also pretty sure that his clever, twisted little mind intended the proximity of meaning."

"Tell me more."

"The overall plan was to use genetic engineering and—more generally—synthetic biology and ultimately cloning, to fast-track the creation of a new, hybrid 'master race.' So, you were right about that—it wasn't just about using me to create some kind of experimental Basque-Aryan hybrid."

"What is it with these Nazis and their goddamned master race delusions?" Vano asked rhetorically. "And what is synthetic biology?"

"I guess a simple way to describe it would be a multidisciplinary scientific approach to redesigning organisms for various purposes by engineering them to have new abilities."

Vano shook his head slowly from side to side and muttered, "When the Promethean fire in the hands of man does alight, the inferno of God's anger will ignite."

"What was that?"

"Just a line of an old poem I was reminded of."

"Sounds pretty dire."

"I know," Vano replied matter-of-factly.

"You know, Vano," Maria continued, "the whole 'master race' impulse is in some sense not really surprising. In an evolutionary sense."

"What do you mean?"

"We're primates. Primates are social animals but are also generally tribal by nature and tend to create dominance hierarchies. We humans have evolved, but not as much as we'd like to think."

"If you say so. Was there something in the files that explained how you fit into the 'master plan?'"

Maria smiled and shook her head at the pun. "In the 'Eugenesis' folder there was a file called 'Inception.' That was about me, or should I say the plan about how to use me. The child inside me was to be the seed from which this new master race would be propagated. There would be variations then engineered from the base seed and optimized towards fulfilling specific functions, which would be key to maintaining overall control of a new global order. Leaders, soldiers, scientists, engineers, managers, and even some that would be designed as breeders and caretaker companions." She sat back and blinked a few times, as if a realization had just hit her. "Sort of like a controlled gene drive into the human population," she finally added, speaking more out loud to herself than Vano, as she reflected back to the research paper she had eagerly submitted, and which proposed a controlled gene drive experiment within a mosquito population—the same proposal that Mendez had helped her to mature.

"And I guess we antique humans would end up as the ones doing the menial work and physical labor... like slaves?"

"That's how it appears. And speaking of dominance hierarchies, the plan was that this seed child would become the first 'alpha'—the first overall leader of the new hybrid race," Maria said, resting her palms over her stomach. "I guess that's why it… he… was optimized in so many ways—in order to function as the 'alpha male.' No need now for an ultrasound to find out the gender."

"My god, Maria… is there something in the files about the father?"

"He doesn't use names. There's a reference to 'the Swede,' and in another section 'the Norseman.' From what I can gather he was chosen based on his so-called 'racial purity' and physical characteristics. I'm pretty sure it will turn out to be my now deceased stalker. Anyway, we'll know for sure when I can get his DNA analyzed. Maybe Vadoma was right when she said things would be revealed in my dreams," she added, her tone at once incredulous and curious.

"How was he planning to organize all this? He couldn't do it all himself… there must be other people involved, people with access to money and power. And where would all this manufacturing of a master race occur? He couldn't do anything of this scale inside the walls of the Pasteur Institute."

"As far as I've been able to determine from the files, they're setting up some kind of operation in Budapest. That's probably where he's headed next. Without the seed child, he'll have to go straight into engineered cloning. And there are clearly others he's involved with, but he's very careful in all the references. He uses metaphors or some kind of codewords."

"For example?"

"He refers a few times to 'the Rat.'"

Vano's eyes went wide for a moment, and he stood up abruptly. "Show me," he said as he came around and stood behind Maria, peering at the computer screen.

"Here"—Maria said pointing at a document on the screen—"and here. I don't really understand the context. For example, this one says, 'confirm Rat funding.' Was he planning to do some kind of experiments with rodents?"

"No." Vano replied in a low tone.

"That sounded very certain."

"'Rat' means 'Council' in German. He's talking about the Council."

"What's that?"

"Something I've only heard rumors of, almost like some kind of urban myth. Something sinister, like those New World Order conspiracy theories you find on the internet. But this New World Order would be dominated by a master race and overseen by a ruling Council."

"That sounds kind pretty crazy."

"That's what I thought too."

The afternoon had started to turn cold, and Vano buttoned up his jacket as he sat sipping a double espresso at Carisa Paris bakery, waiting for Maria to rejoin him. She had come to drop off the skin flakes and blood residue she had collected from Ulrik with Brigitte, who had agreed—somewhat reluctantly—to run a DNA analysis on them. The Pasteur Institute was just around the corner and down the block, so it was not long before Maria had returned. As she approached, he noticed that her expression and body language appeared agitated. "How did it go? Everything okay?" he asked gingerly as she arrived and took a seat on the stool next to him.

Maria looked around and then replied in a hushed tone. "Not really. Brigitte said that between the time I contacted her yesterday and coming here today, the police had visited the Institute and were asking about me. She heard about it from our department manager, Olivier DuPont. He told her that the police had indicated that I am a 'person of interest' in their investigation of Remy's death and that they want to speak to me. She was very nervous and nearly refused to go through with running the DNA analysis for me. In the end she agreed, but I doubt she'll be willing to do anything more for us after that."

"That's understandable from her perspective. I think we should avoid talking to the police for now though—they're no doubt under intense pressure to produce some suspects for the two murder cases, and we would be convenient targets," Vano said. He finished his espresso and stood up. "Let's go for a walk and think this through… I'm getting cold just sitting here, and we could use the exercise."

They turned to the right on Blvd. Pasteur as they exited the bakery and after a few blocks angled north onto the broad and park-like Avenue de Breteuil, which terminated at the grand 'Les Invalides'—a large military museum complex and the opulent final resting place of Napoleon Bonaparte. They walked slowly, enjoying the view, and Vano eventually slipped his hand into hers, giving an affectionate squeeze and adding, "I think I feel warmer now." A bit surprised by how delighted she felt in that moment, Maria smiled and looped her arm through his, pulling him close to her.

Just as they had passed the Louis Pasteur monument at the center of the Esplanade Jacques Chaban-Delmas roundabout, the mood was interrupted by Maria's phone pinging to signal an incoming text message. She pulled her phone out of her coat pocket and then stopped abruptly when she saw who it was from—Mendez. The message was brief, but she let out an audible gasp before she had even finished reading it.

"What is it?" Vano asked, alarmed by her reaction.

"It's Mendez. He wants to talk. And he reminded me that he knows where my parents live. Do you think that's a threat?"

"Yes."

"What should I do?" Maria asked, trying not to sound as frantic as she felt.

"I have a friend in Bilbao that I can ask to go to San Sebastián to provide a little added security for your parents. In the meantime, we need to slow Mendez down and buy a little time to work out a longer-term solution."

"How?"

"Give me a minute to think," Vano replied and then took her hand and started walking again, his pace brisk. Just as they were approaching the intersection with Avenue Duquesne he stopped. "I think I have an idea. It's pretty heavy-handed, actually, but it's pretty simple."

"Yes?"

"Mendez doesn't know we've gotten into his computer. We can put him on the back foot by threatening to go public, or to the authorities, with what we have, including his connection to Ulrik and our suspicion he killed Remy Boucher. Tell him we have people watching your parents' house and if anyone suspicious comes near them or finds you, the files will be released. And mention the Council—I want to see how he reacts to that."

"Should I call him now?"

"Yes, before he has a chance to make any further moves."

Maria took a deep breath and called Mendez's number. After a few rings he picked up. "Hello, Maria. I see that I have gotten your attention."

"What do you want Carlos?" Maria replied angrily.

"Ah, finally you call me Carlos. How ironic, no? Listen, why prolong the inevitable and additionally put your family in danger, Maria? Let me finish things for you and the child. I will ensure that it's quick and painless. After that, you have my word that we will leave your parents alone."

"You sick bastard."

"Being emotional won't help, Maria. You're running out of time and need to make a choice before it's too late."

"Actually, it's you that needs to make a choice, Carlos. I know what you've done and what you are planning."

"Is that so?" Mendez replied mockingly.

"Yes. I know that you impregnated me, and that Ulrik—the now deceased Ulrik—was the father. You did it on the night of that birthday party... where Ulrik drugged me at the club. And he was the one that tried to attack me in San Sebastián and tried again in the Bois de Boulogne, no doubt on your orders. Am I getting warmer?"

"Impressive detective work, but it doesn't change the situation or the choice you're faced with, Maria."

"I am also pretty sure you killed Remy Boucher in order to try and get to me. Perhaps I will report that to the police?"

Mendez laughed. "Go ahead… there is no evidence one way or the other, and I'm sure they would love to speak to you, being a 'person of interest' as you are."

"That was you that triggered that, wasn't it?" Maria replied, trying to control her anger.

"Maria, it's irrelevant at this stage. Stop grasping at straws. You need to make your choice now."

"I have your computer files, Carlos. All of them. Proof of what you did to me and your link to Ulrik—the other murder that I'm sure you're aware the police are very interested in. I know about the modifications you made to the child and why. And I know about your link to the Council… or should I say the 'Rat.'"

The line was silent for several seconds before Mendez finally replied, venom in his voice. "You're more resourceful—and troublesome—than I expected, but I suppose that other Gypsy scum from Spain has helped, no? Trust me, we will find out more about him, and he will face consequences as well."

The anger in his voice told Maria she had struck a nerve, so she dug in. "A copy of the files, including an outline of what we know, are in the hands of a third party, and we have someone in San Sebastián watching my parents. If anything happens to me, or anyone comes near them, the files will be released to multiple authorities. So it is you that has to make a choice now, Carlos."

"What exactly are you proposing?" Mendez hissed.

"Some kind of truce, I guess. You disappear and leave me and my family in peace. And I'll keep the files hidden and my mouth shut."

There was another long pause, and then Mendez said, "That's quite a gamble you're making, Maria… with your parents' lives," he replied threateningly.

"And yet, you haven't said 'no,'" Maria responded, sensing her leverage.

"I'll get back to you," Mendez said angrily.

"Why? Do you need to check with the Council? Who are they anyway, Carlos?"

Mendez inhaled sharply. "*Schlampe,*" he said and hung up.

Maria looked up. Vano was smiling. "I'm impressed… you're a natural."

"Most every woman is a natural in dealing with angry men, Vano."

"So, what about the Council?"

"Oh, judging from his reaction it's real all right. I think the fact that we stumbled on to it was the thing that shook him most. That's when he hung up, when I started picking at that. What now?"

"We head back to Kashi's place and plan our next moves. This is getting bigger than both of us. I need to call my friend in Bilbao and also widen the circle on this with a few trusted colleagues at CNI headquarters—the murder investigations will potentially be bringing some unwelcome heat around my name. And I think it's time we tried to check in with Remy's friend in DGSI and see if he can help at all. I'm a little out on a limb here in France. And you need to write a summary of what we know and send it to Xavier so he can add it to the files and set up the 'dead man trigger' that you bluffed Mendez with on the files. I'll give you some secure email addresses for target recipients that you can pass on to Xavier."

≈

Mendez had not been looking forward to the call with Hans Rudolf Giger, but he knew he needed to inform Giger about his conversation with Maria, including the fact that she had hinted at awareness of the Council.

"How much does she know?" Giger asked sharply.

"I think nothing more than the word," Mendez replied.

"Make your way to Budapest immediately. We need you to initiate the project there and start instructing your new Czech colleague."

Mendez's jaw tightened but he swallowed his pride for the moment. "What about the girl? What should I tell her?"

"Tell her you accept her terms. Over time she will become complacent, and we will be watching for the opportune moment to find where she's hidden the files and then deal with her. Someone will be in contact with you soon. Tell them everything you know about her and the situation," Giger replied curtly, and then hung up. He then looked over at Lina Bormann, who was across the room. "When will the Austrian arrive?"

Bormann turned and came closer, a clipboard cradled in one arm. "Tomorrow, sir."

"Very good."

Chapter 11: Autumn Leaves

FRANZ EDER STILL LIVED in the secluded family compound in the forested highlands west of Vienna where he had spent his childhood. After the war, his remaining immediate family had taken the maiden name of his great-grandmother Lisl and sequestered themselves away to rural anonymity. Lisl's husband—Franz's great-grandfather—had been the notorious Ernst Kaltenbrunner,[1] a name that still haunted post-war Austria, and which Franz's grandparents knew would stigmatize the family for generations and attract endless unwanted attention. With the help of some sympathetic local officials, the birth certificates of Lisl's children conveniently 'disappeared,' and new ones were created to show that they were born out of wedlock to an unknown father. As the decades passed, only a handful of people outside the family knew the truth— Hans Rudolf Giger was one of those people, but he simply referred to Franz as 'the Austrian.'

---

[1] Ernst Kaltenbrunner – A high-ranking Austrian SS official in the Nazi regime and considered a major perpetrator of the Holocaust. Kaltenbrunner became the third and final head of the Reich Security Main Office (RSHA), which oversaw the main security and intelligence agencies of the SS (the *Geheime Staatspolizei*—or 'Gestapo', the *Kriminalpolizei*—or 'Kripo,' and the *Sicherheitsdienst*—or 'SD'). Shortly after Germany's surrender, Kaltenbrunner was apprehended in a mountain cabin in Austria and found guilty of war crimes and crimes against humanity at the Nuremberg trials, where he was subsequently sentenced to death and hanged.

The Council had quietly monitored the families of former high-ranking Nazi officials for years, partly as a security measure and partly as a way of identifying and grooming new talent for future recruitment. Franz Eder's preternatural intelligence and athletic ability had brought him to Giger's attention early on, and expert instructors had been dispatched to the Eder family compound in the Vienna Woods to supplement Franz's development with additional tutoring in martial and military arts, economics and finance, espionage tradecraft, psychological and propaganda operations, and language training. His formidable skills had then been further forged through a crucible of increasingly complex and dangerous field and political operations on behalf of the Council over the years. Eventually he had become a trusted protégé to Giger and had ultimately been put in charge of the Council's overall security and intelligence operations, echoing the role in the Third Reich of Franz's great-grandfather Ernst Kaltenbrunner. This was no accident of course—Giger believed that there was a sort of symmetry in history's episodes and that he was, in his own way, grafting branches from one episode into another even greater one. He even believed that Franz might one day be his successor, although he had not shared this thought with anyone.

After the flight from Vienna to Zürich, a private car shuttled Franz Eder directly to Giger's chalet in Bürglen. Lina Bormann was waiting at the door and motioned towards the dining room as he entered. "Welcome Herr Eder. The Chairman is waiting for you to join him for dinner. You can leave your bag here—I will take it to the guest quarters."

Eder nodded slightly and set his bag down. "*Danke schön*, Lina."

"*Bitte schön*. It's always a pleasure to have you visit," Lina replied sincerely. She knew Giger and his idiosyncrasies well and had observed that he was invariably in a better mood when Eder was around.

Eder passed through the foyer of the chalet and turned into the dining room where Giger was waiting. A large fire was roaring in the fireplace against the October chill, and Giger was just finishing pouring two glasses of wine. He picked one up and handed it to Eder, smiling almost imperceptibly, "Ah, you've arrived, Franz… it's good to see you. Come warm up and have a drink—it's a lovely Margaux. We have a lot to discuss."

Several days had passed since Maria's phone conversation with Mendez on the Avenue de Breteuil, and both she and Vano were now feeling restless. Mendez had sent Maria a perfunctory text message indicating agreement to her proposed 'truce,' and Brigitte had emailed to her the DNA analysis of the sample from Ulrik, which—once Maria compared it to the Mapa de Vida profile of her child—confirmed he was the biological father. At this stage, it had become simply a matter of verifying the conclusion to which the circumstances and her intuition had already led her. The hospitality and support of Kashi and Esma Kolompár had continued without reservation or qualification, but Vano and Maria knew that the time was coming to move on—before their presence became a burden or a danger to their hosts. Maria also knew that their growing intimacy would be hard to hide, especially from Esma.

Maria and Vano had gone out for a walk, partly to stretch their legs and also so they could speak privately. Although Kashi had insisted that one of his local contacts accompany them in order to keep an eye out for suspicious characters, the 'chaperone' dropped back to an inconspicuous distance and just out of immediate earshot when Vano shot him a glance and a quick nod. They made their way finally to the Drancy Markets, a sort of farmers market housed in a warehouse-like building near the center of Drancy. After they had bought a coffee from a kiosk and wandered among the fresh produce and meat and flowers for several minutes, Maria finally stopped and turned to Vano. "It feels like it's probably time for us to move on and let Kashi and Esma have their apartment to themselves again. I'm just not sure what I… we… should do next."

Although Maria had not phrased it as a question, Vano knew it essentially was. And he had enough experience with women to know that the future of their relationship was on her mind as well. "I've reached out via Interpol channels to Remy's friend in DGSI. Ideally, I'd like to meet with him before we finalize any plans, especially if we decide to leave Paris. Whatever happens though, I want to make sure you're safe, Maria," he said, reaching up to rest his palm tenderly on her cheek.

"Thank you, Vano," Maria replied, looking up at him, smiling warmly, and running her own palm over her midsection. "I've been thinking about maybe returning to San Sebastián for a while to check in on my parents, and also given my condition. It doesn't seem like there is much else I can do until the baby is born, and I hear back from the Institute about my job. And maybe it's a good chance for you to spend some time back in Arditurri as well… it's only a short drive to San Sebastián you know," she added, wondering if he would notice the subtly flirtatious tone she had thrown in at the end.

Vano gripped Maria's shoulders and held her gaze, almost pleadingly—he knew she wasn't going to want to hear what he was about to say. "Maria, I don't think we can trust that these people will give up so easily. They'll back off for a while but eventually they'll look for a way to find those files we copied—and us. We know too much now. But you'll be safe with your parents for a while, especially with my friend from Bilbao watching over you."

Maria stepped back, her tone now disappointed and bordering on consternation. "It sounds like you're already planning something. I thought we agreed that we would make decisions together. I know I look strong and like I have everything under control, but I'm also a little frightened, Vano. I feel safer with you around."

Vano looked down. There was a long pause before he replied. "I wouldn't be suggesting it if I didn't think it was safe. I wouldn't let anything happen to you, Maria, and I trust my friend—who's also an experienced agent—completely. Of course, you would have to agree before we do anything though… I'm not trying to force you. And in any event, like I said, I want to talk to this DGSI fellow before I make a move."

"What kind of move? I can tell you're thinking of something."

"I want to go to Budapest… to find out more about the reality of the Council, and to stop Mendez and their plans. I feel like every day that slips by, their tentacles spread further."

Just then, the minder that Kashi had assigned to them approached, his expression urgent. "We need to go back to Kashi's place now. We've received word through our network that there have been some people poking around in a few of our communities in Paris and asking about you two."

"The police?" Kashi asked.

"Possibly, but not uniformed. And they didn't identify themselves."

≈

The DGSI headquarters building is located in the Levallois-Perret neighborhood of Paris, just a mile northeast of the spot in the Bois de Boulogne where Ulrik Eklund had died. On the third floor of the building, Agent Jean-Luc Sarfati was at his desk reviewing the dossier on the Remy Boucher murder that he had finally received from the Paris squad of the National Police's Criminal Brigade—the investigating authority—when his phone rang. He picked up the phone and declared brusquely, "*C'est* Sarfati."

"This is Cécile at the reception desk, Mssr. Sarfati. Your guests have arrived."

Sarfati's tone softened. "*Merci beaucoup,* Cécile. Could you please escort them to the ground floor meeting room for external visitors and I'll be down in a moment. Would it be possible to also check if there is fresh coffee and tea in the meeting room?"

"*Bien sûr, monsieur.*"

Maria and Vano had already helped themselves to a cup of coffee by the time Jean-Luc Sarfati arrived to join them in the meeting room. They stood to introduce themselves and shake hands. Sarfati motioned towards the chairs. "*Bienvenue à la* DGSI. *Asseyez-vous s'il vous plait.*"

"Thank you for agreeing to see us, Agent Sarfati," Vano began.

"Please, call me Jean-Luc—we are after all in a similar business, no? Your bona fides that Interpol provided were impressive, and your family story precedes you… especially that of your grandfather. It seems we both have families that were affected by that dark chapter of history."

Vano, looking puzzled, glanced at Maria and then turned back at Sarfati. "I'm not sure I follow you, Jean-Luc."

"Sarfati is a name common among Jews of French origin, and many ended up in the camps."

"I see," Vano nodded, the connection now clear.

Sarfati turned to Maria. "I understand that you came to know Remy, and that you have an idea who might have killed him?"

"Yes. Remy was a good man… he tried to help me. It all still feels a little unreal."

"He was indeed a good man, and an exceptional mentor to me when I began my career. Have you spoken to the police investigating the case?"

"Not yet."

"And I guess it's also safe to assume that you two may have some knowledge of the other murder that occurred… the one in the Bois de Boulogne?"

Before Maria could say anything, Vano rested his hand on her arm and replied, "Possibly."

Sarfati sat back in his chair and paused for several seconds, surveying them both carefully, and then replied, this time his tone more serious, "As a courtesy to Mssr. Amaya here I am generally conducting this as an off-the-record meeting, but I am still bound by the law when it comes to dealing with evidence of a serious crime. Before we go any further, I need to ask you why you haven't gone to the police, and I also need to advise you that you should consider getting an attorney."

Maria pulled her arm away from Vano's hand and sat forward, her eyes fixed on Sarfati's. "Mssr. Sarfati, these people have impregnated me without my knowledge, tried to kill me twice, threatened my family, and it seems are still looking for me, so—with all due respect—I'm not interested in attorneys or talking about the finer points of law. We need to stop them, and we were hoping that you, as someone Remy obviously trusted, might be able to help us."

Sarfati was taken aback at first by Maria's response—as a seasoned DGSI agent he was used to a certain level of deference from civilians caught up in criminal investigation—but his curiosity had been piqued. He bit back his irritation, arched an eyebrow, and replied, "You have my undivided attention, madam. I would be sincerely interested to hear more about these circumstances and how you believe they intersect with the case of Remy Boucher. And what exactly do you mean by 'these people?'"

"Have you heard of something called 'The Council?'" Maria asked.

Sarfati's face tightened. He turned his gaze to Vano, who gave him a knowing nod. "Where have you heard about this, and what do you know about it?" Sarfati shot back.

Maria again held his gaze. "It seems from your reaction that you have heard of it. That criminal that you confirmed to Remy was on the DGSI watchlist as a member of C18—Ulrik Eklund—was also working with the person who we believe impregnated me, probably with Eklund's help, including as a sperm donor. We believe they also later killed Remy because he had helped us and knew too much. This person I'm talking about is additionally connected to the Council and is on his way to Budapest as we speak. By now you probably also know that Eklund was the person found dead in the Bois de Boulogne. He was the one who twice tried to attack me. There's more context behind all of this, but those are the key circumstances."

Vano leaned in. "Just to be clear on why we didn't immediately go to the police, Jean-Luc—I found out that these people appear to have a mole at the Spanish National Police headquarters in Madrid. I'm not suggesting that the French police have been infiltrated, but we just wanted to talk to someone first that we were sure we could trust. The Council—or whoever these people are—appear to have a formidable network and resources."

Sarfati was silent for a long while, sizing his two visitors up anew, and then finally stood up, took his overcoat from a rack behind the office door, and turned back to them. "Perhaps we should go for a walk and get some fresh air. There's a nice café that's not far." His tone was still brisk but had eased. "If you two are about to make things considerably more complicated for me, we might as well do it over a decent cup of espresso."

After a short walk to the café and then a long discussion, a tacit rapprochement and then a plan began to come together over a second round of espressos and croquants, a delicious French cousin of the classic Italian biscotti. Maria and Vano had told Sarfati the whole story of Mendez and how he likely killed Remy Boucher, but they carefully sidestepped explaining exactly what they knew about Ulrik's death, as they had been relieved to sense an unspoken 'don't ask/don't tell' posture from Sarfati on the matter. As a first step in the plan, Sarfati felt there might be more information to be found within Mendez's files. "Maria, if you can have your friend transfer a copy to me, I can have our forensic cyber analysts look for things like metadata, hidden sub-files and coded messages. Our specialists are magicians when it comes to finding those kinds of things."

Maria nodded. "That shouldn't be a problem. Is there anything else I should do while I'm back in San Sebastián?"

"First, neither of you should let on that you were aware someone was looking for you among the Romani community here. And when you get back to Spain, make a point of going about a regular routine every day in a way that doesn't appear like you think you're being watched or followed. We want to buy some time and let them think things have settled down."

Vano jumped in. "Don't worry, my friend from Bilbao will still be around and keeping an eye on you and your parents. If you see something suspicious, just tell him. Anyway, we know it's the files they're most worried about right now. And I have an idea how we can divert their attention towards that and maybe at the same time expose some of their operation in Madrid."

"How would you do that?" Maria asked, and then took a bite of her croquant.

"I can have someone file an addendum to the incident report involving Ulrik—the one that was accessed by someone at the National Police headquarters in Madrid. In the addendum, it would mention digital evidence and files potentially related to the case that have been secured from a confidential source in Paris and that are now stored on a portable hard drive. We can have your friend in Barcelona put a copy of Mendez's files on the portable hard drive to make it seem authentic, and have the drive placed in a storage room in the police headquarters there in Madrid, accompanied by a tracking device. It will be irresistible bait for our little mole and his associates in Madrid once he comes across the addendum in the incident files. We can then see where their dirty little tracks lead back to. In the meantime, I will be in Budapest with eyes on Mendez and to size up what is happening there. And if I'm lucky we may get some more leads into his contacts with the Council and their operations."

Sarfati nodded in agreement, but then added, "You must be very careful my friend. Hungary has increasingly become the wild west, or the wild east I should say, of Europe over the last few years. The far-right political movement has almost completely consumed their government and the local Interpol and intelligence networks there are no longer considered reliable partners. This is quite sensitive, but you should also know that an agent with our sister agency for external operations—DGSE—is now missing and presumed dead while he was on an operation that started in Switzerland but where his last known location was in Budapest."

There was a long pause, and then Maria finally interjected, "Mssr. Sarfati, if you don't mind me asking, you haven't mentioned yet how and what you know of the Council."

Sarfati looked around the café, checked his watch, and then replied, "I'm afraid this is not the place to go into those details, and I'm already running late for a meeting I'm supposed to be attending. Perhaps we can all have dinner together before you both leave Paris, and talk more about it then… *d'accord?*"

"*C'est bon.*"

≈

Manicured into the northeastern shoreline of Lake Zürich is the elegant Chinese Garden of Zürich, a gift from the city of Kunming to its sister city. As instructed, Stefan Lang was waiting in the garden's central pavilion, the collar of his black leather coat pulled up against the chill wind coming off the lake and his gloved hands stuffed deep into the coat pockets. He had been passing time trying to spot the goldfish in the garden's pond, but so far they seemed to be hidden away. "Probably trying to find someplace warm," he muttered to himself.

A moment later Franz Eder approached and stepped into the pavilion beside Lang. "You're on time as usual, Stefan. Thank you."

"I wouldn't dare keep you waiting, Franz," Lang replied, only half joking.

Eder nodded and then continued. "Look, it's cold, so I'll get right to it. This business with the Spaniards has become a distraction to the Chairman. The larger affairs of the Council need his full attention, and he wants Mendez completely focused on his laboratory work in Budapest. He was giving Mendez some wider than normal accommodation due to his family history—which is why you were assigned to Mendez and given a direct line to the Chairman. But going forward, you'll resume reporting directly to me. We've been given the task of cleaning up the remaining loose ends of Mendez's little Basque folly."

"That's a relief, actually. So, what's next?"

"I need you to go back to Spain and work with your contacts there to try and get more information on this CNI agent who's been helping the girl, while also keeping an eye on her movements. Our overall first priority though is to find out where they're holding the files that they copied from Mendez's computer, which I believe are most likely somewhere secreted among their circle of family or friends. You need to ensure your presence is not exposed—we need to find the location of the files first and then decide a plan of action. If the files are sent to the authorities, we can probably use our networks to manage things, but if they are leaked to one of the press outlets that we don't have eyes in, then we have a bigger problem to manage."

"Understood. And where will you be?"

"In Budapest. I need to make sure Mendez is able to get his project up and running as quickly as possible and without distraction. My instinct tells me that now that the CNI operative knows something of what's planned in Budapest, he'll find it hard to resist making a move... and so I'll ensure a little reception is waiting." Eder was gazing over the pond now, a thin smile creasing the lower half of his face.

"*Sehr gut,*" Lang intoned.

"Oh, look," Eder then remarked suddenly, pointing towards water, "there's one of the goldfish."

Lang shook his head and patted Eder's shoulder. "You always were the lucky one, Franz. Let's go get something warm to drink now."

Chez Janou is a cozy and welcoming restaurant serving delicious, fresh, and unpretentious Provençal cuisine. Sarfati was waiting outside for Maria and Vano when they arrived in a taxi and stepped quickly over to open Maria's door. He extended a hand to help her as she pulled herself from the back seat. She was nearly six months pregnant now and increasingly feeling the changes in her body. She took Sarfati's hand to steady herself as she stepped out and then smiled self-consciously but warmly as she said, "*Merci*, Mssr. Sarfati."

"*De rien*. And please, call me Jean-Luc, at least over dinner. I think you will enjoy the food here—it's just a pity you won't be able to enjoy the wine with us as well—they usually have a nice selection." Sarfati then reached over to shake Vano's extended hand as he was coming around the back of the taxi from the other side. "*Rebonjour, camarade*."

Moments after they had entered the restaurant, the hostess hurried over to Sarfati, having clearly recognized him. "Welcome back, Mssr. Sarfati… it's such a pleasure to see you again after all this time. The table you asked for is ready, and Mssr. Cadieux is very much looking forward to seeing you." She helped them hang their coats on a coatrack near the door and then motioned towards a table in a secluded corner of the restaurant. "*Après vouz, s'il vous plait*."

After they had been seated the hostess returned to her station by the front door and their waiter appeared with a basket of fresh, warm bread and mineral water. "If you would be so inclined, Mssr. Cadieux has recommended a special dish for your main course tonight that is not on our normal house menu—Provence-style duck breast with figs. It's additionally seasoned with a bit of balsamic vinegar, honey, rosemary, and a little cinnamon. Before that, I would suggest starting with our fresh baby spinach and goat cheese salad. Would that be acceptable?"

Vano and Sarfati nodded and then looked over to Maria, who enthusiastically agreed. "That sounds wonderful actually—thank you. And since I won't be having any wine could I please have some cranberry juice?"

"*Bien sûr*, madame."

Sarfati then motioned at the waiter. "Could we see the wine list please?"

The waiter made a show of looking around and then smiling conspiratorially. "If you don't mind, Mssr. Cadieux has also selected a bottle for you from his private cellar, compliments of the house."

Sarfati paused for a moment and then finally nodded. "I suppose just this once, since I am with guests. *Merci*." The waiter then nodded in response, turned, and returned to the kitchen.

Maria and Vano exchanged amused glances, and then Maria, unable to contain her curiosity, nudged Sarfati mischievously. "It seems you're something of a celebrity here, Jean-Luc. Is there more that we should know? Will there be paparazzi waiting outside when we leave?"

Sarfati turned slightly red, but before he could respond, Hugo Cadieux came barreling out of the kitchen, a huge grin spread across his face, with a decanter full of wine in one hand and an empty wine bottle in the other. He was a short, stocky, balding man with an impressive waxed and curled moustache. He wore an immaculate white chef's smock, with the name 'Hugo' impeccably embroidered above the breast pocket in an elaborate script. "If Hercule Poirot had become a chef instead of a detective, he would look exactly like this," Maria thought to herself.

"*Bienvenue* Jean-Luc!" Cadieux exclaimed. "I see you have brought friends with you," he added, smiling at Maria and Vano. "Good. I will be preparing something special for you all. And to start things off, I have a very special bottle of wine for you to enjoy—a fully matured Grand Cru Musigny Burgundy from Domaine Georges Roumier." He set the decanter on the table and presented the bottle for them to view.

"*Merci beaucoup,* Hugo… it's very nice to see you again. As always, I am humbled by your hospitality. I'm afraid I have to admit though that I'm not familiar with that wine, but I trust your judgement of course."

"In this case, your ignorance is understandable Jean-Luc. Only about three hundred bottles a year of this elusive little beauty are produced, from a tiny 1000 square meter slice of the greater Georges Roumier Domaine, and it needs a few decades in the cellar to fully mature. As such, it is *very* hard to acquire one of these bottles, and the curse is that once you've tasted it, you'll find it hard to be satisfied with any other Burgundy. As you can see, I've taken the liberty of already decanting it for you, so that you wouldn't have to wait." Cadieux poured a small amount into Sarfati's glass so that he could taste the wine.

Sarfati held the base of the wine glass against the table, gently swirling the glass to open up the bouquet of the wine, and then held the glass up to his nose to take it in. Next he took a drink, set the glass down, and waited a moment to savor the complexity of the wine's finish. Finally, he sat back in his chair and looked up at Cadieux. "*C'est un énorme vin, mon ami.*"

"*Oui. Je sais,*" Cadieux replied confidently, but also pleased at Sarfati's reaction. He then poured a half glass each for Sarfati and Vano, and finally turned to Maria with a sympathetic expression. "I'm so sorry you won't be having any, madame."

"Well. I may take just a very tiny sip from one of the gentlemen's glasses, if they'll allow it," Maria replied.

"How could they not?" Cadieux beamed. "Now, if you'll excuse me, I need to go finish preparing your duck. The waiter will be out with your salads shortly. And I have a final surprise for dessert, if you're up to it." He said with a wink and headed back to the kitchen.

Maria then turned back to Sarfati again. "So? What is the story with the VIP treatment here, Jean-Luc?"

Sarfati hesitated for a moment, looking a little embarrassed, and then finally replied, "Hugo is the owner here. A few years back he was getting extorted every month by one of the local organized crime gangs for 'protection' money. I was on the squad that sent that particular gang to jail, and so he feels grateful for that. I was just doing my job though—Hugo deserves a lot of credit for having the courage to come forward and being willing to testify against them. We kind of became friends along the way, and the information he occasionally picks up from the streets is helpful. And I love his food to be honest. On his part, I think he sleeps a little better knowing that I pop in once in a while to check on him and that I'm only a phone call away. Developing these kinds of relationships is something I learned from Remy Boucher, back before I joined DGSI—when I was a junior police officer working with him… may he rest in peace."

"I see. This all makes sense then." Maria nodded knowingly, just as the waiter was setting down their salads and condiments.

"Bon appétit… can I bring you anything else for now?"

"Maybe some more bread, please," Vano replied, noting that Maria had eaten three pieces already.

"I'm eating for two, and he seems especially hungry tonight," Maria added a little sheepishly.

Vano then turned to Sarfati. "Is organized crime still a big problem here, Jean-Luc?"

"*Le Milieu*[2] has been around for a very long time, in one form or another. Gangs come and go, and we've disrupted a lot of their ability to operate in a centralized way, but it's impossible to wipe them out completely."

"Why is that?" Maria asked.

"Because we are constrained by the boundaries of laws and procedure and morality, and they are not," Sarfati replied. "And their incentive structures—both positive and negative—supercharge their motivation and behaviors relative to ours. Technically speaking, they have an advantage in both the scope of their operational dynamic range and in the intensity of their performance motivation. In the early days, the Zemmour family was the dominant gang in Paris. And then when they started dying out, the Hornec family gang ascended. Lately, the Corsican mafia has been sporadically trying to make moves into Paris, but their real stronghold remains in the south of the country." Sarfati stopped to take a few bites of salad, a sip of wine, and then looked up with a bemused expression. "In that sense, our impromptu alliance here is a little ironic, no?"

"I don't follow you," Vano replied.

"Well, here we are in Paris, like the Zemmours and the Hornecs, but representing different dimensions of our cultures. The Zemmours were Jewish—like me, and the Hornecs are Romani—like you… though we all get painted with the same brush, unfortunately, since most people don't even understand the difference between an Ashkenazi Jew like me and Sephardic Jews like the Zemmours. Just like they don't understand the difference between *Calé* like you and *Manouches* like the Hornecs. But

---

[2] *Le Milieu* – a general term for organized crime in France.

in the end, every culture and every group has its positive and negative aspects—like the concept of yin and yang, photographic negatives of one another. We have ended up on one side, for whatever reason, and they on another… but remain strangely bound to one another's orbit." Sarfati took another drink of wine and laughed. "Forgive me, it appears this extraordinary wine is bringing out the philosopher in me."

Maria thought for a moment about asking Vano if Kashi Kolompár had connections to the Hornec gang, but decided it was probably better for now not to reveal his name or their connection to him to Sarfati. Instead, she decided she would finally try a small sip of wine from Vano's glass. As if on cue, the waiter suddenly appeared with their *plat principal* of duck breast, and they proceeded to focus on absorbing its subtle deliciousness, switching temporarily to some small talk about the weather and local politics.

When they were nearly finished, Hugo reappeared, still bursting with energy. "So? How did you like it?"

"*C'était magnifique*, Hugo," Sarfati replied ebulliently. "And the wine paired perfectly with the duck. You are truly talented."

Cadieux was beaming. "*Merci*, Jean-Luc. And now I can reveal that your surprise for dessert will be my special *crème brûlée à la pistache*. Your waiter will be out with it in a moment—I just need to go and put the torch to it."

"You are spoiling us, *monsieur*… I love anything with pistachio," Maria interjected with sincere delight. Cadieux bowed graciously and headed back to the kitchen.

Once the waiter had returned with their dessert and then went to prepare some espresso, the conversation turned serious again. After a first creamy spoonful of the *crème brûlée*, Sarfati turned to Vano. "So, Vano… do you mind if I ask you—unofficially—if CNI has sanctioned your activities here, and on what basis?"

"Initially it was more of a personal… family matter," Vano replied, glancing over at Maria and then back at Sarfati. "But once I reported back on the bigger scope of what we were discovering, CNI asked me to stay on the case. Their first interest of course is Spanish national security—it is thought that the Council probably played an indirect role in the armed ETA[3] Basque separatist movement of several decades ago and the more recent Catalonian independence movement. Spain would be strategic geographically for them as a smuggling corridor into Europe from Africa and a naval gateway to the Mediterranean, especially since we finally got control of Gibraltar back from the British last year."

"But I thought ETA was a far-left movement?" Maria interjected.

"Which made it easier for the Council to cover their tracks. They weren't interested in ETA *per se*… it's about trying to destabilize the political environment to the point where they are able to install people in the central government friendly to their agenda and who promise to 'restore law and order.' Like we believe happened in Hungary."

"So, an understandable concern for CNI, I suppose," Sarfati added matter-of-factly as he took another spoonful of his *crème brûlée*.

After the waiter brought their espressos, Vano took a sip and then sat back in his chair. "So, Jean-Luc… when we last met, you mentioned you would be able to talk more about the Council over dinner. Dinner is almost over, but I don't think we're in any hurry—what can you tell us?"

---

[3] ETA – *Euskadi Ta Askatasuna* ('Basque Homeland and Liberty')

"It seems you two already know quite a bit… probably more than us when it comes to their activities in human genetics. We've been focused on trying to understand how they operate. You're right about efforts at political destabilization—it seems to be a major focus for them. We've found—I can't tell you how, and I'm trusting in your discretion with this information—a web of dark money, communications, and logistics conduits that feed into just about all of the surging far-right or populist movements across the globe. It's staggering really—the National Rally party here in France, AfD in Germany, UKIP in Britain, the America First party in the U.S.… The list gets longer every year. And there appear to be regional nodes… we think between 8 and 10 of them. Everyone thought it was the Russians, but that was a diversion, a decoy. Our latest theory points to a nexus leading back to somewhere in Switzerland, but we're not sure. That was why DGSE deployed an agent to Switzerland—the one who later disappeared in Hungary. In the end, we want to be able to strike a blow to their networks, likely at the nodes, to disrupt their operational capabilities. But our map is still incomplete. We're also concerned about who in our own government—and other governments—may be compromised. We have found a few, but we're sure there are many more. Some died mysteriously when we started getting too close, so we think they probably have developed some kind of intelligence and direct-action capability."

"Also operating from Switzerland?" Vano asked.

"We're not sure. Our AI models that have analyzed and correlated many terabytes worth of travel and location data centered around these mysterious incidents point to Central Europe. That's ten to twelve countries though. However, the probabilistic models seem to converge around an east-west axis that runs across Hungary, Austria, and Switzerland—still a huge area. It's partly why I'm very interested to see what we can find in this Mendez fellow's computer files that could help us narrow our focus."

Maria leaned in, still a little perplexed. "Jean-Luc, I thought DGSI only focused on France's internal security?"

"I'm part of a combined DGSI-DGSE task force. I indeed am primarily working on the domestic dimensions, but I am included in the general briefing sessions."

"Why are you willing to share all of this with us? It seems pretty sensitive."

"Because I have a good instinct about people. Because I had you both checked out pretty thoroughly. And because frankly our progress has been too slow, and we always seem to be several steps behind. But, as chance may have it, you two may have given us a brief opening to get closer to some of the real players in this sprawling hydra. Good intelligence work, like good police work, recognizes the value of improvisation when opportunity arises."

Vano looked at Maria and smiled wryly. "In the parlance of the intelligence world, Agent Sarfati is developing us as 'assets.' The question is, how can he help us?"

Sarfati scowled briefly, then eased his expression. "Fair enough. After all you've been through, you have reason to be careful. First, I have just now shared a lot of sensitive information with you. Second, once we analyze Mendez's computer, I will make sure to share with you whatever new information we find. And third, I'm going to give you a few names that you will find helpful. One of them is a high-ranking Spanish official—who also has connections to NATO—that we are certain has been compromised by the Council… I am sure CNI would be interested in that. The other name is a DGSE asset in Budapest that is very resourceful and who you can contact for help if the need arises. Okay?"

"No names for me?" Maria chimed in.

Sarfati looked at Vano and then back at Maria as he pulled a card out of his jacket pocket. "Madame, I can assure you that you will be in very capable hands with this gentleman, especially once you are back in Spain. However, here is my private number—if you call, I will answer. And while you're in France we'll be keeping an eye on you and monitoring the location information on your phones. Don't be alarmed—it's just in case something else unexpected arises and you need our help. Now, let me take care of the bill and bid Hugo *adieu*."

A little nonplussed, Maria took the card and nodded. "*Merci* Jean-Luc, also for the lovely dinner."

It had been an enjoyable evening, but when they all finally made their way to the door and the spell cast by their charming host and his food began to recede, their farewells were muted. The sprawling scale of the menace they faced had begun to sink in.

Maria had done some stretching exercises to relax her back muscles and applied some cocoa butter to her abdomen and breasts—now a nightly routine as her pregnancy had matured—and was in bed watching a variety show on TF1 while Vano was showering. They had booked a room in an unassuming hotel near Gare Montparnasse, as Maria's train bound for Spain would be departing early in the morning. Given Sarfati's revelation that he would be 'keeping an eye' on them while they were in

France, they also didn't want to give away Kashi Kolompár's location by staying with him. Vano had been able to get a message to Kashi to explain and Esma, wearing a comically large blonde wig and sunglasses as a disguise, had brought their bags and dropped them off with the hotel concierge.

Vano finally emerged from the shower and slid into the bed next to Maria, kissing her lightly on the cheek and resting his hand on hers. "I have to admit I'm going to miss you, Maria."

"Hmmm… you smell good Vano—I think I'll probably miss you too," Maria teased, giving him a gentle nudge.

"So, what's on your mind besides that ridiculous song and dance routine on the television?"

"They're pretty good actually… perhaps you're just a little jealous of that man's tight and sparkly outfit?"

"Not likely."

"Well, what was on my mind was the realization that I had been missing out on a lot of joy and appreciation by not embracing all of my heritage and not being more aware of the histories they represent. I wanted to thank you for opening me up to all of that."

"I'm glad I could be of service," Vano replied, kissing Maria again—this time on the neck.

Maria turned to her side and snuggled backwards into Vano's embrace. "And what do you think, Vano? Are we… is this, becoming serious?"

"I think it may already be," Vano replied, reaching around to gently caress her breasts.

Maria felt his manhood then suddenly grow firm against her buttocks and she arched her hips backwards into it. "I think you're right," she smiled.

"Are you sure it's okay?" Vano whispered, his breathing now heavier.

"Very," Maria replied as she guided his warm fulness into her.

Chapter 12: When October Goes

It was a crisp autumn day in Madrid, cool but sunny, and Stefan Lang had indulged himself by spending some time in the Prado Museum—the Louvre of Spain—before settling in to wait for his contact. As a 'fixer' for the Council, Lang knew that he needed to close out this messy business in Spain, and the loose ends it had created—like the potential exposure of Mendez's computer files—soon. He had found the perfect bench to enjoy the afternoon sun in the Royal Botanical Garden that is adjacent to the museum and was halfway through his coffee when Inspector Luis Delgado of the Spanish National Police finally arrived and sat nonchalantly beside him.

"I see you've been enjoying some of the treasures of Spanish culture," Delgado said quietly, having spotted the museum brochure sticking out of the breast pocket of Lang's coat. Delgado was off duty and in plainclothes, but his sensible shoes, ill-fitting suit, and rigid bearing were a giveaway to a practiced eye.

Lang sighed, rolled his eyes—conveniently shielded by dark sunglasses—and intoned the agreed countersign, "Velázquez's 'Las Meninas' is a masterpiece."

Delgado's posture relaxed slightly as he replied with the final agreed countersign, "Your eyes do not deceive you." He then pulled a large manila envelope from within the folds of his coat and gently placed it on the bench next to Lang, all the while looking straight ahead. "Welcome to Madrid, Sr. Lang."

Lang stiffened with irritation. "No names."

"As you wish."

"So, what have you been able to find?" Lang asked, barely disguising his impatience.

"This CNI agent you're looking for is a ghost. We fed the name you gave us into the system, and it drew a complete blank at first. Which means he's probably been scrubbed and is doing primarily undercover work. The good news is that we know CNI only runs a small number of agents in that way because it takes so much effort within the bureaucracy to maintain their cover and the confidentiality of their activities. Given what appears to be some kind of connection to the girl though, we've narrowed it down. It wasn't easy, but we think we've found traces of local financial transaction records that lead back to CNI front companies and point to what looks like three of these 'ghost' operatives deployed in the Basque Country. It should be just a matter of time now. I've put three of our best National Alliance people on the ground, one chasing each of the leads."

"Good. But make it six… they should operate in pairs. In case something happens to one, the other will still retain whatever is the latest information they have discovered, and you avoid a setback in progress."

"We'll need more funds to afford that."

"I know," Lang replied flatly. "Just do it please. And what about the other matter?"

"That was a little easier. There are *very* few people in Spain outside of academia, government, and business with the skills and equipment to remotely hack into your associate's computer and break the encryption on his files. We have some people that operate on the periphery of that world, so putting together a short list of names was not difficult. Once those names and their locations were triangulated against travel and call records between Paris and Spain during the time window in question, we were able to zero in on one particular well-known freelancer."

"Do you have the details of his location?"

"*Her* location is in Barcelona. We've got someone on the way there to do some reconnaissance. The details are all in the envelope."

Lang picked up the envelope and slid it into his inner coat pocket and then stood up, "Very good, Inspector. Contact me when you have more information to share—I'm staying at the Santo Mauro."

Delgado stood up and turned to Lang, "I think you will enjoy your stay in Madrid. Almagro is a very nice neighborhood, and that is a very nice hotel. You are a stone's throw from some excellent restaurants in Salamanca."

"Oh, and one more thing," Lang began.

Delgado interrupted politely, holding his hand up. "Yes, I know—add a second person to the reconnaissance in Barcelona." Lang nodded in reply, and they then turned in opposite directions and walked away.

Having returned again to the relative calm of San Sebastián and the home of her parents—and prompted by the increasing physical manifestations of her pregnancy—Maria had booked an appointment with Dr. Otxoa, the local obstetrician she had seen previously, for another full check-up. She knew that the next three months would take a toll on her body and also realized that the almost constant stress of the last six months had probably already taken an extra toll. As she was finishing up dressing after the examination and waiting for the doctor's final feedback, she couldn't help herself from worrying about what he might tell her. Finally, she heard a light knock on the door and responded, "Come in."

"I'm glad you came back to see me, Sra. Guevara. Everything looks very good with the baby—he looks quite strong and healthy, actually."

"Thank you, doctor… that's such a relief."

"However, I have a little concern about you. It's nothing too serious, but I've given you a list of mineral and vitamin supplements you should pick up from the pharmacy and start taking every day. Your lab work showed some deficiencies, especially with respect to iron, calcium, and B vitamins. I suspect your diet over the last months has not been as balanced as it should have been, no?"

"Guilty," Maria replied. It was a response to his question, but also how she felt. Had she been so wrapped up in the intrigue with Mendez and her adventures in Paris that she hadn't been taking good enough care of herself and, by implication, the baby? The question wormed in her conscience.

Dr. Otxoa sensed her anxiety and gave her a cheerful pat on the back. "Don't worry—it's nothing terribly serious. It's quite common with first-time mothers, in fact. Just please make sure to take those supplements and eat healthy. The next three months will place increasing demands on your body. Call me if you have any questions or anything unusual comes up. In the meantime, you can make an appointment with the receptionist for your next check-up." He was smiling reassuringly and held the door open as she made her way out of the examination room.

Xavier was waiting in the reception area and stood when she came out of the doctor's office. "Everything okay?" he asked.

"Yes, thank you, Xavier. Also for bringing me here and waiting for me. Let me make a next appointment and then we can go. I need to stop at a pharmacy on the way back to pick up a few things, please."

"Sure, no problem. Sr. Guevara… I mean your father… anyway gave me the rest of the day off in return for taking you to your appointment and then back home."

Once they were in Xavier's car, Maria turned to look in the backseat and saw a backpack. "Is it in there?" she asked.

"Yes. I had my friend in Barcelona put a copy of all the files on a portable hard drive, just like you asked when you called from Paris. What are we going to do with it?"

"I am going to give it to someone who knows what to do with it. It's probably safer for you not to know any more than that."

Xavier nodded, though looked mildly disappointed. "Okay… I suppose that makes sense."

Almost immediately after Xavier dropped Maria off with the backpack in front of her parents' house and drove away, an electric sedan pulled up silently to the sidewalk beside her, and the driver's window descended. She turned and looked into the darkness of the car. "You must be Vano's colleague from Bilbao. I didn't even notice you following us."

"I wouldn't be very good at my job if you had," came the driver's voice in reply.

Maria handed the backpack to him, feeling relieved to be rid of it. "Is there anything else you need from me?"

"No. I'll take it from here. We can bait the trap now with this little device. I'll be monitoring things overall, but you should still keep an eye out for anything that looks or sounds unusual. And keep your doors and windows locked and the alarm turned on, please."

"I most definitely will. Good night."

And so it was that three days later Inspector (and National Alliance mole) Luis Delgado received an automated email alert signaling an update to the case file he was monitoring—the one regarding the reported attack during the parade in San Sebastián a few months ago. When he logged into the system and reviewed the case file, he saw that an addendum had just been posted about new evidence that had been secured from a confidential source. The addendum indicated that the new evidence appeared to be some kind of encrypted digital files on a portable hard drive and was now in a locked evidence storage room in Madrid police headquarters—just three floors below him. Before going down to look at it though, he pulled out his phone and sent a quick voice message to Stefan Lang. "It seems we may have a new development. I'll call you after I have looked into it." He then opened his desk drawer, grabbed the card key that gave access to secure areas of the building— like the evidence room—and headed for the elevator.

László Kolompár was a second cousin to Kashi Kolompár and had ended up back in his family's home city of Budapest after their extended sojourns in Istanbul and Paris. He lived in Újlipótváros, a residential neighborhood on the east (Pest) bank of the Danube River and just across from Margaret Island, a green urban oasis of parkland and recreation facilities that sits in the middle of the river. He particularly liked that the neighborhood was off the tourist radar screen but still close to the city center and Nyugati Station, one of Budapest's three main railway terminals.

It was a Sunday and the morning just after his arrival, but Vano was already glad he had taken Kashi up on the offer to connect him to his family while he was in Budapest. "Your hospitality is much appreciated, László. What is this dish by the way? It's delicious."

László had an easy, infectious smile and leaned back, spreading his arms wide. "That my friend is *búbos rántotta*—stacked Hungarian-style scrambled eggs made with sour cream, milk, a bit of lard, some rye bread, bacon, chives, and salt. And you are most welcome to stay as long as you like. Kashi has vouched for you, and that's good enough for me. How is your Romani[1] *by* the way?"

"A little rusty, I'm afraid."

"Mine too. We Romungro mostly speak Hungarian."

"Well, at least we have that in common. How did you learn to cook like this, László?"

"I spent a few years working as a sous-chef in one of the nicer hotels in Budapest while I was working my way through university. It kept me fed and put some money in my pocket. And it turned out there was no shortage of girls who wanted to date a guy that knew how to cook well. Maybe that's why I never got married—I can feed myself and choose when I do or don't want to have a woman around."

---

[1] Romani – the common language/lexicon of the Romani people, with roots in Sanskritic languages (e.g., Urdu and Panjabi), and which has multiple dialects.

"Don't you want children?"

"Oh, I have some of those, but they're with their mothers. It's better that way."

Vano laughed and took a deep drink of his coffee. "Are you busy today, László?"

"Free as a bird my friend. What's on your mind?"

Vano pulled out two slips of paper and set them in front of László. "I was wondering if you could drive me to this address so I could take a look around and maybe take a few pictures?"

László looked at the address and then quickly replied, "Sure. That's in Csepel—the twenty-first district—in the south-central part of the city. It was a pretty run-down heavy industrial area for years after the end of the Soviet Union, but the city and the central government have been investing in trying to turn it into a tech manufacturing and innovation zone… things like robotics, biotech… that sort of stuff. They've also turned some of the old warehouses into spaces for local artists and reclaimed some of the riverfront area and turned it into parks, which is pretty cool." László finished his last bite of *búbos rántotta* and then picked up the second slip of paper. "And what's this? It looks like a name."

"Yes. Someone in Paris gave that name to me and said I could contact her if I needed help here in Budapest. I have no reason to question the motives of the man who gave me the name, but I would like to see if I can find out more about her before I make contact. Do you have any… *friends*… in town that could check her out… discreetly?"

László smiled his big, easy smile and stuffed both slips of paper in his shirt pocket. "Leave it with me. There's just one favor I want in return."

"What's that?" Vano asked tentatively.

"If she's attractive, I get the first shot at asking her out."

Vano shook his head and chuckled. "No problem. That's the last thing on my mind."

Looking a little surprised, László leaned forward and searched Vano's expression. He then sat back and cocked an eyebrow. "Hmmm… now that was a little too easy. It seems someone else has already captured your heart, no? It's written all over your face."

Vano felt a faint flush for the first time in many years and was surprised by it, but decided not to respond, even though he knew that in itself was a giveaway to what he was now realizing was a surprisingly perceptive László Kolompár. "I really appreciate your help, László. I'll clean up the dishes and then we can go—okay?"

At that same moment, in a nondescript windowless building in Csepel, hidden behind a nine-foot security wall around its perimeter, Franz Eder was finishing his own cup of coffee and monitoring the feeds from the property's security cameras. Some were visible and some were hidden, and they provided views of every part of the exterior of the building as well as the exterior of the security wall. There were also motion sensors that triggered the system to separately save images triggered by the sensor for later viewing, otherwise the system would erase the camera data every three days to make room for the next three days of recordings. Eder had just finished testing the remote link of the system to his phone and was satisfied everything was in order. He could hear Mendez rattling around in the next room, barking instructions to his new Czech understudy, as they unboxed and begin assembling a final truckload of equipment that had arrived.

"*Ist alles in Ordnung, Doktor?*" Eder turned and called out.

"*Ja. Fast fertig,*" Mendez replied. "And what about your little project? Do you really think it's a good idea to just wait and hope one of them comes here?" Mendez had walked into the room with Eder and was wiping his hands with a small cloth towel.

Eder set his coffee cup down and swiveled in his chair to face Mendez. "My good doctor, this is what I do. A good hunter knows how to track his prey. But a master hunter *understands* his prey and waits at the place where he knows from experience they will come. In the African savannah if you wait by the watering hole, the gazelle will eventually come to you. After what he has seen in your computer files, our little Spanish gazelle will be drawn here like a moth to a flame, visions of heroic deeds in his head, and we will be waiting."

Llúcia Savall had just unlocked the door to her townhouse in the bohemian Gràcia neighborhood of Barcelona when she was forcefully grabbed from behind, a large black garbage bag was pulled over her head, and she was shoved into the foyer of her home. In a low voice, someone a few feet in front of her warned her not to scream as the person that had grabbed her now zip-tied her hands behind her and locked the door. She knew immediately it was not some kind of local gang—the person talking to her was not speaking any Catalan and even his Spanish was clumsy, with a heavy accent that sounded vaguely German. "What do you want?" she finally blurted out.

"Sra. Savall, listen to me carefully. Where are the files that were stolen from the computer of Dr. Carlos Mendez in Paris?" came the voice again. It was Stefan Lang, and he was impatient to finish cleaning up the messy distraction Mendez had triggered.

"I don't know what you're talking about. How do you know my name?" Llúcia shouted in the direction from which the voice seemed to be coming. A second later she was struck with a blow to the side of her head which nearly knocked her over and made her ears ring.

"Please do not waste my time or this will become more unpleasant than you can possibly imagine. Tell me where the computer equipment is that you used to decrypt and store the files. and give me the protocols for accessing it all. As a precaution, we have someone watching your family in Sabadell." Lang paused and smiled when he saw Llúcia stiffen at the mention of the small city about twelve miles north of Barcelona where her parents and younger brother lived. "Good. I knew that would get your attention. Now, shall we get this over with?"

"Yes."

"Are the servers that store your security camera feeds in the same room?" Lang asked.

"Yes… the hard drives that hold the camera data can be easily disconnected and pulled out," Llúcia replied, anticipating what Lang planned to do.

As the technician that had accompanied Lang was finishing up about thirty minutes later, Lang pulled out his phone and called Franz Eder to provide an update. "We're almost finished here with retrieving the files," Lang said when he heard Eder answer.

"Good. Any complications?" Eder asked.

"None so far. We've recovered the source for the files that were sent to the police in Madrid via our contact there, but we can't be certain that

she hasn't made more copies. Shall I probe further with some…
enhanced interrogation?"

"No. At least not yet. This woman clearly has some unique skills that
could be useful to us, especially since we can use her family as leverage.
She may be recruitable—that's something we need to explore first before
getting heavy-handed. Once you are back in Switzerland and your
technician has had a chance to go through and review both sets of files,
call me if you find anything unusual."

"Understood."

"Oh, and Stefan," Eder added.

"Yes?"

"Given the caliber of her skills, we've been assuming she was
contracted for this little project by the CNI agent, but perhaps your
contacts there in Spain can look into whether there are other connections
that we might be missing. And be ready to come to Budapest if I need
you."

"Of course."

"*Sehr gut.* I'll be in touch," Eder finished and then hung up.

Alain Corbin almost burst into the office of Jean-Luc Sarfati after he
knocked on the door and Sarfati called out "Enter."

"I've found something," he said excitedly as he opened his laptop and
put it in front of Sarfati.

Sarfati didn't know what to make of what was on the screen and
looked up at Corbin. "You're going to have to explain it to me Alain."
Corbin was the forensic cyber specialist that Sarfati had tasked with

analyzing the copy of Mendez's files that Maria had arranged through Xavier to have transferred to DGSI.

"He was using a technique called 'Matryoshka folders' to hide some additional files."

"I have no idea what that means."

"Like the nesting Russian dolls… the Matryoshka dolls. Hidden files within hidden files within hidden files. I think I've found them all—there were not that many and whoever did it made the mistake of using a similar placement and burrowing pattern. Probably so it would be faster for them to find and dig them out later. Some of it is technical and scientific stuff, but there are two files that looked very different from the others."

"How so?" Sarfati asked as he leaned forward, trying to make sense of what he was looking at."

"Here is the first one," Corbin said as he punched a key on the keyboard, and a file opened with a long list of names, aliases, telephone numbers, and what looked like codewords and bank account information.

"*Merde.*" Sarfati exhaled as he began to recognize some of the names and realize the implications of the list. Government and military officials, politicians, corporate executives—the scope was staggering and global.

"That was my first reaction, too."

"Alain, has anyone else seen this?"

"No, and I have taken it off the main server and put it only on my laptop."

"I have to think about how to handle this. For now, you show no one, and tell no one, and keep this thing with you at all times. Do you understand?"

"Yes."

"Now, what about the other file?"

Corbin opened the second file with another keystroke and pointed to it while he spoke. "I don't understand a lot of this, but it was hidden in a subfolder called 'Inception' that had to do with some kind of genetic modification of a baby, so it seemed a little out of place from the other things I found that looked more research-oriented. Anyway, it mentions how something called an 'HBB gene' has been modified with something called a 'clock gene' to cause it to mutate and stop working properly after about three hundred days. The word 'fail-safe' is used in the description, but it took me a little while to figure it out because the German equivalent for the word was used in the file."

"And what would all that mean?"

"Well, I'm not a biologist so I can't be certain, but I did do some online research. The HBB gene provides instructions for making a protein that is a key component of the hemoglobin in red blood cells, which transport oxygen throughout the body. Mutations in the HBB gene can affect its ability to bind with and transport oxygen. It seems the purpose of all this was so that if the mutation is not fixed before the three hundred days from conception run out, the baby would basically end up asphyxiating and no one would know why."

"So, basically within a month or less after it's born?"

"It would appear so. Thus reducing the likelihood of ever creating a linkage back to the perpetrator of the mutation. The question is why.

Why go to all the trouble of creating a genetically-engineered child and then risk it all with this? Were they that worried about being found out, or was there another reason?"

"I don't know. But couldn't someone just use the information in the file to create the fix to the mutation?"

"Again, I'm no biologist, but I think the actual technical details to be able to do that were put in another file, which I so far have not been able to find. There is only a reference to a shipping list and a box number—eighteen."

"Anything else?"

"That's the highlights."

Sarfati opened his desk drawer, pulled out a thumb drive, and handed it to Corbin. "Okay, good work, Alain. Keep digging for that other file please—in the meantime, put a copy of those two files on this thumb drive for me before you leave."

After Corbin had left, Sarfati sent the file about the HBB gene modification to Maria to review, along with a cover note to explain what his analyst had thought it might mean and asking her what the technical information for fixing the mutated gene would look like so that they could search for it with more precision. He also mentioned the reference to the shipping list and box number that Corbin had found. He then grabbed his hat and coat so he could go out for a walk and think about if and how he should warn both Maria and Vano that the list of names that Corbin had found was going to make things more complicated—and dangerous—for all of them.

≈

László Kolompár had parked two blocks away from the walled and windowless compound in Csepel that Vano was interested in seeing. Vano had then moved to the back seat to unpack from a duffle bag and assemble what looked to László like a complicated piece of equipment. He took a long drag of his cigarette and then turned to Vano. "What is that thing? I thought you just wanted to go by the building and take some pictures."

"It's a remote-controlled drone with a camera attached, which can take video or stills. That way, I can have a look from above and see behind that wall," Vano replied and then coughed as the smoke from László's cigarette drifted into the back seat. "What are you smoking László? It smells like a dirty sock."

László laughed. "It kind of tastes like one too, but you get used to it. It's an old local brand—'Symphonia.' A favorite of performative masochists."

"To each his own, but could you roll down the window please?"

"Sure," László replied and lowered the rear windows, letting the chill, damp outdoor air of late October gradually dilute the warm smoky interior of the car.

After another ten minutes of assembly and set-up, Vano finally grabbed the drone and controller, stepped out of the car, and turned back to László. "I'm going to go launch from that partially-enclosed bus stop across the street from the target building. It's Sunday, so I assume most everything around here is closed but keep an eye out anyway."

≈

Behind the nine-foot walls and inside the windowless building, Franz Eder had just finished a sandwich and his third cup of coffee for the day and was absent-mindedly scrolling through news feeds on his phone when he spotted movement on one of the external cameras. He put his phone down, sat forward, and zoomed in with the camera controller. The movement was around the bus stop across the street, and he watched as a dark-haired figure set something on the ground on the sidewalk outside the bus stop and then sat down on the bench inside. Suddenly the thing on the ground slowly lifted up, first vertically, and then slowly maneuvering towards the wall. Eder smiled when he realized it was a drone because he knew that whoever was in that bus stop would be completely focused on operating the remote-control module. "I see my little gazelle has arrived," he said quietly to himself and then without hesitation stood up and grabbed the Steyr SSG 69[2] rifle that was hanging on the wall, cycled the bolt to chamber a round, and headed for the storage area door on the back side of the building. Although the SSG 69 had been replaced by the SSG 08 model after 2015, he still preferred the SSG 69. It was the rifle he had learned to shoot with when he was young and was most comfortable with. It also had the extra benefit of looking more like a basic hunting rifle to the untrained eye, whereas the newer model looked very much like a tactical, militarized weapon.

László had just finished relieving himself behind a tree near where he had parked and was walking back towards his car with his head down as he lit another cigarette. When he reached the car door, he stopped for a moment to take a drag from the cigarette and look around. Something moving in the distance caught his peripheral vision. He quickly pulled

---

[2] Steyr SSG 69 – Austrian-made bolt action 7.62x51 mm sniper rifle that resembles a hunting rifle. Introduced in 1969, it was continuously manufactured until 2015 due to its reputation for accuracy and reliability.

out his phone, opened the camera function, and zoomed in. The cigarette almost fell from his mouth when he saw a figure crouched at the corner of a wall, aiming a rifle at Vano. He threw his phone back in the car, reached in to honk the horn twice, and was pulling his pistol from his jacket pocket when he heard the rifle shot echo around the adjacent buildings. "*Fattyú!*" he yelled as he fired three shots at the crouched figure, jumped in the car, and sped over to the bus stop, unlatching the passenger door on the way.

Luckily, Vano had taken the round in the shoulder. If he had not turned to look towards László when he heard the horn, the round would have hit its intended target—his heart. But he was still seriously injured and struggled to pull himself into the car. Another shot rang out and shattered the rear passenger window, so László stomped on the gas before Vano even had a chance to close the door behind him. As he drove off, he heard a final round hit the back of the car. Vano was using his right hand to put as much pressure as he could on the wound in his left shoulder to slow the bleeding and turned to László. "Will the hospital report this to the police if I come in with a gunshot wound?"

"Yes."

"Do you know someone else who can fix me up?"

"Yes," László replied and smiled his big, easy smile. "And if you're nice, she'll read your fortune afterwards."

"Thank you, László… I owe you one. By the way, was that you that I heard firing a pistol?"

"Yeah. I've got an old FÉG 9mm I carry sometimes, lucky for you."

"Lucky for me…" Vano mumbled and then began to feel dizzy.

At that moment, Franz Eder was back inside the windowless building and was speaking into his phone, leaving a voicemail for Stefan Lang. "Come to Budapest as soon as possible. The Spaniard is here, and it appears he has some local help."

László and a woman Vano did not recognize were standing over him in László's apartment when he finally woke up. His arm was throbbing, but he could see that it had been expertly bandaged and so began to try and sit up. The woman gently placed her hand on his chest and shook her head. "You must rest."

"Vano, this is Zsófia. You probably owe your life—or at least your arm—to her," László remarked, relieved to see Vano's condition looked to be improving.

"Thank you, Zsófia. Is there any way I can repay you for your help?" Vano asked, surprised at the effort it took to speak.

Zsófia was closing up her bag and first looked over at László and then back to Vano. "You can get him to send more money to help with our daughter, and to come spend more time with her."

László put on a wounded expression. "I just think your parents don't like me because I'm not Vlax[3] like you."

"They don't like you because you're not being a very good father László," Zsófia retorted. "And my situation is a little embarrassing for

---

[3] Vlax – the 2nd largest sub-group in Hungary (after the Romungro) of the Roma group, and, in general, a sub-group who speak the Vlax dialects of the Romani language. The most common Vlax dialects in Hungary are Cerhari and Hungarian Lovari.

my uncle, who now is a respected elder and often presides in *kris*[4] proceedings.

"I'll give him a good long lecture, madam… I promise," Vano chimed in, and then immediately had to bite back a smile when László, having moved safely behind Zsófia's back, exaggeratedly rolled his eyes and shrugged his shoulders like a naughty schoolboy being scolded. "Is there anything I should be aware of in terms of taking care of my shoulder?" he then finally asked.

"I've left some extra dressings, antiseptic, antibiotics, and something for the pain, as well as a list of instructions. There's also a list of things you can have László pick up for you at a pharmacy. If there are any sudden changes he can call me. Otherwise, I'll be back in a few days to check on you," Zsófia replied and then added, throwing a sharp glance at László, "and we'll see if your lectures have had any effect by then."

As Zsófia was about to leave, László reached out to put his hand on her shoulder, and in a gentle voice said, "I promise to do better, Zsófia. Thank you for this. You know, I mentioned to him your other gift. Did you sense anything in his future?"

Zsófia looked a little irritated and replied, "You know I don't do that for strangers."

"He's not a stranger… at least not anymore. And he's one of *us*, Zsófia."

Zsófia paused and looked for a few moments at Vano and then down at her watch. "I have to get to work, but I guess I have a few minutes."

---

[4] kris – a traditional 'council of elders,' or court, among Vlax communities, convened to resolve disputes on the basis of 'Romanipen,' the traditional values and code that Romanies are expected to abide by.

She then walked over and sat next to Vano, put her left palm over his heart, and closed her eyes.

Vano was too weak to protest and anyway didn't want to appear ungrateful to this woman who had tended to his wound without questioning what had happened, and so he took a deep breath and closed his eyes. A few moments later, Zsófia stiffened and stood up, her countenance noticeably darkened. She took his hand and then spoke gently, almost tenderly. "The one you love also loves you. But you must tell her soon… time is running out. Protect her, and that which she carries." She then grabbed her bag, turned briskly, and headed for the door, stopping for a moment to whisper something to László before she left.

"What was that all about?" Vano asked, looking a little bewildered.

László looked a bit like he had seen a ghost, but composed himself and replied simply, "Let me get you some tea, my friend. Maybe she's a little out of practice."

It was not long after he had finished his second cup of tea when Vano's phone rang, and he saw it was Maria calling. He answered it immediately. "Hello… is everything okay there?"

"I'm afraid not. I got a message from Xavier—his friend in Barcelona called him to say that she had taken her family and gone into hiding for now, because someone managed to track them all down. They grabbed her at her home, took the computer equipment with the files, and threatened to kill her and her family if any other copies of Mendez's files were released in any way."

Vano uttered a *Caló* swear word under his breath and then replied, "What about the portable hard drive—was that planted as planned?"

"That seems to have been accomplished, but your friend from Bilbao came by this morning and asked me to pass on a message to you since you weren't answering your phone. He said the tracker that was put inside the hard drive doesn't seem to be working. At least for now."

"Has Sarfati found anything in the files? Maybe there's something in there that can help."

The line was silent for a few moments and then Maria replied, "More bad news. He found something all right." She then went on to tell him about the time-delayed mutation mechanism in the baby's HBB gene that Mendez had engineered.

"But you can just modify it after the baby is born right? I mean, that's your area of expertise, isn't it?"

"Yes and no. To fix it I would need to know the specific transcription factors he used in designing the combined HBB and clock genes so that I can tailor the repair—there won't be enough time to reverse engineer it by trial and error. But the breakdown of the transcription factors was not in the files from his computer. There was only some clues that suggest they ended up in some hardcopy files that were part of the items shipped to his lab in Budapest. Why would he have done this?"

"He's a psychopath, Maria. It's about control. Here's what I think—he saw you and the baby as one of his experiments, but from the beginning he also knew human behavior and events can be unpredictable, so he built in a mechanism that he could use to manipulate the one behavior which is completely predictable—the primal instinct of a mother to keep her baby alive. What I don't fully understand though is why he wanted you to abort the child once he found out about your mixed heritage. Why not just let the baby be born and allow his little genetic modification to end the child's life?"

"The modification he made is pretty exotic, and I'm not sure anything exactly like it has even been tried in a lab, so he could not be a hundred-percent certain it would work. Like you said, I guess the threat that it represented was the back-up leverage he expected to use to control me in order to get cooperation, or access to the child, or whatever, once it was born. But once he didn't want the child anymore, he wanted to be completely certain that it—and the evidence its DNA carried—was destroyed so it couldn't be traced back to him and the Council's activities. But the reality we have to deal with is that it may work. Vano, I don't know what your plans are, but you have to keep Mendez alive—at least until we get the information on the transcription factors that we need. You have to find a way to get into that lab and find those hardcopy files. Sarfati thinks it's in a box that was labelled number eighteen on the shipping manifest."

Vano took a deep breath and replied, "I'm afraid it's me that has some bad news now, Maria." He then described what had happened and his injury.

"My god, Vano, are you doing okay?"

"I think so, but I don't know how long it will be before I'm mobile again and both arms are useful. I need to think of a plan B."

The line was silent for a long time, and then Maria finally replied, "I'm coming to Budapest."

"Maria… don't be crazy. What can you do in your condition?"

"What can you do in yours? Should we just give up?"

"I said I was going to try and come up with a plan B."

"Fine. If I'm there, I can help you with that. Anyway, since they think they have all of Mendez's files back, there's nothing to keep them now from coming to try and kill me, so if I hang around here I'm kind of a sitting duck and endangering my parents. Even your friend from Bilbao will not be able to stop them if they send enough people—like what happened to Xavier's friend. I'm coming to Budapest, Vano—I have to at least try to save this baby."

Vano knew from her tone that there was no use arguing with her, and that she was anyway right in her assessment. He sighed and then replied, "Do me one favor before you leave then."

"What's that?"

"Go see my father in Arditurri. Face to face—away from my mother. Tell him everything. He may have some advice, and if something… happens, I want him to know the truth. Promise me."

"I promise."

"Thank you. And there's something else I need to tell you, Maria, but not over the phone. So take care of yourself, and I'll see you soon."

"Goodbye, Vano. I'll see you soon." Just as Maria was hanging up she felt her baby kick. She smiled and rested her hand on her stomach, thinking about how strong he seemed, and then she looked out the window of her bedroom in San Sebastián at the rainy sky of the last day of October and allowed herself to cry.

PART III

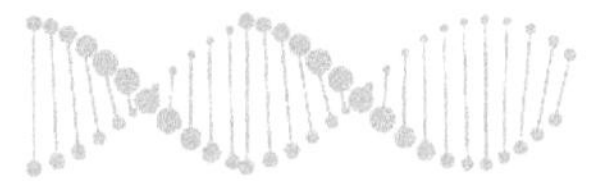

CULMINATING

The soul of man,

It is like water:

It comes from heaven,

It mounts to heaven,

And earthward again

Descends

Eternally changing.

If the pure jet

Streams from the high

Vertical rockface,

A powdering spray,

A wave of cloud

Splashes the smooth rock

And gathered lightly

Like a veil it rolls

Murmuring onward

To depths yonder.

If cliffs loom up

To stem its fall,

It foams petulant

Step by step

To the abyss.

Along a level bed

Through the glen it slips,

In the lake unruffled

All the clustering stars

Turn their gaze.

Wind woos

The wave like a lover,

Wind churns from the ground

up

Foaming billows.

Soul of man,

How like water you are!

Fate of man,

How like the wind.

—Song of the Spirits over the Waters (Johann Wolfgang von Goethe)

Chapter 13: Kind of Blue

HANS RUDOLF GIGER HAD left the bucolic comfort of his chalet in Bürglen to preside over an important meeting of the Council in Zürich, accompanied, as always, by the watchful presence of his personal assistant Lina Bormann. The Council member responsible for North America—John Rudel—was due to provide an update on progress in the region and Giger was particularly keen to hear the assessment. The Council's plans were generally progressing well in Europe and several other of the Nine Realms, but Giger knew that ultimately they had to achieve a tipping point within the vast infrastructure of financial, military, and technological power of North America in order to trigger an irreversible global momentum towards their objective of global hegemony.

John Rudel was tall, stocky, and bearded. His wide, flat accent coupled with his stereotypically extroverted American mannerisms blended with his physical features to create a kind of perfect camouflage for the environment within which he operated. But Giger understood the formidable and cunning man behind the camouflage and had been instrumental in his appointment to the Council. John Rudel had proven to be daring and ruthlessly effective in his own right. After a crisp twenty-minute overview of key financial and operational details, Rudel finished up his summary with a flourish, noticing that Giger was nodding approvingly. "We have finally consolidated our strategic land acquisitions and political influence in the Northern Rockies region of the U.S. under the cover of the American Redoubt[1] program. We're working through a coalition of the Seven Mountains[2] Christian nationalist movement, survivalist networks, and White nationalist militias. Operations to further extend the network of de facto control from this base are underway. The next milestone will be consolidating a north-south corridor running from central Canada down to the southern U.S. border and the Gulf coast. The push would also begin moving eastwards, with the ultimate goal of increasing our ability to isolate the Pacific and Atlantic coasts of the continent at a time of our choosing."

"What main challenges do you foresee?" Giger asked.

"In the north-south axis of expansion of influence, the challenges will be mainly in the U.S. states of Colorado and New Mexico, as well as a few cities in Texas. In our push to the eastern milestone of the Mississippi River, it will probably be just the state of Minnesota," Rudel replied and then added, "and of course in both directions there will be the additional challenge of determining the best approach to use around Native American tribal lands, which are substantial, and with their community leaders."

---

[1] American Redoubt – a political migration movement that originated in 2011, designating the U.S. states of Montana, Wyoming, Idaho, and the eastern portions of Washington and Oregon as a 'safe haven' for conservative Christians.

[2] Seven Mountains – a Christian dominionism movement that came to prominence in 2013, whose followers believe they have a mandate to seize control of the 'seven spheres' of society: family, religion, education, media, entertainment, business, and government.

Giger followed up: "And what do you need in order to address these challenges John?"

"Mostly money. We're buying land and political influence, which is not cheap. And where there is stronger resistance we need sophisticated multichannel influencing programs and expanded militia capabilities and activities. Perhaps some additional tactical and training support for our militias from Franz Eder's team and a broader cyber capability."

Giger looked up pensively for a moment and then replied, "Please put the details into a brief proposal outline and share it with Lina. She can then syndicate it with the rest of the Council to make sure everyone is on board with the details and budgets remain equitably balanced."

"Thank you, and should—" Rudel began, but was interrupted by Giger.

"And please also attach a summary of how this all will specifically enable tangible access to the broader levers of power in the continent and the relevant timelines. You have outlined operations that, while substantial, are still somewhat regional in nature. I think we can all see indications of the linkages, but it will be helpful to be more explicit, especially after what happened with that January fiasco in Washington, D.C. ten years ago. We all know the COVID pandemic disrupted planning and logistics, but did we learn from that? Can we be more explicit about contingencies this time? The resulting investigations and political backlash set us back several years. Now, may I suggest we all take a thirty-minute break? I have a few phone calls I need to attend to." And with that Giger stood up and walked to a small anteroom adjoining the main meeting room, his phone already pressed to his ear.

Franz Eder was on the other end of the line. "We've had an incident here. The CNI agent arrived as expected but appears to be getting some local help. I believe he's injured, but I don't know how seriously. I have mobilized Stefan Lang to come to Budapest."

"Any impact on the work of Mendez?" Giger sounded irritated.

"Not so far."

"Do what you can to motivate Mendez to speed up progress and also find a way to check and ensure that he is fully instructing his apprentice on every step. I will reach out to our friends in government there to get you some help in hunting the CNI agent. *Und pass auf deinen Arsch auf.* Any progress on the recovery operation in Spain?"

"Yes, it looks like Stefan and the local assets he was working with have recovered the computer equipment holding the files. It's been taken back to Switzerland for further examination. The local assets in Spain have also narrowed down their search for the identity of the CNI agent. We're hoping for a breakthrough soon."

"Good. In general I think we need to ramp up efforts to consolidate our influence in the Iberian peninsula, but let's hold that discussion for later. And what about the girl?"

"Now that we have the files, it's likely she can be considered… expendable. But to minimize our risk of exposure I would just like to see what our technicians in Switzerland find on the computer equipment before we make a move. She has turned out to be more resourceful than we expected."

"Fine. Keep me updated. And by the way, John Rudel will be looking for some more support for his operations in North America."

"That shouldn't be a problem—I have a few sleeper cells that have yet to be activated."

"Good—we'll speak later then," Giger replied and then hung up.

Vano was already seated when Sára Weisz arrived at the stylish Sarki Fűszeres café and deli near Szent István park at two o'clock, as they had agreed. She recognized him immediately from the picture he had texted to her and sat across from him after he had stood to shake her hand. "An excellent choice—I'm impressed," she said. "Most foreigners aren't aware of this little gem." She raised her hand to signal the waiter.

"Thank you, but I have to confess it was a local friend that recommended it to me."

"Hmm… honesty *and* modesty out of the starting gate. That is a good sign," Weisz replied half-teasingly. Her raven-black hair was pulled back tight against her head and away from her pale complexion, intensifying the effect of her already penetrating green eyes. As if on cue, the waiter appeared to take their order for coffee and pastries.

"Sára, Jean-Luc Sarfati gave me your information and said I could reach out to you if I got into difficulty here," Vano began.

"Yes, he alerted me that you might be in touch," Weisz replied, looking at his arm held in place with a makeshift sling. "And it seems you have indeed already run into some difficulty."

"The thing is, Sarfati didn't really tell me anything about you, but he said I could trust you."

"You can, and I'm sure the people you had asking around town about me didn't turn up any red flags or you wouldn't be sitting with me here now, right?" Weisz asked, smiling when she saw his reaction. "It's okay,

I would have done the same thing… but I wouldn't rely too heavily on those people if I were you—they're streetwise, but amateurs when it comes to the business we're in."

"You have my undivided attention," Vano replied somewhat warily, and then sat back as the waiter set down their coffee and pastries.

"I used to be a field agent for the Hungarian National Security Office—the NBH. I know you know who they are, because I know who you work for. I met Sarfati years ago when we were collaborating through Interpol on a cross-border case involving arms trafficking by neo-Nazi groups. But when the government here took that hard right turn a few years ago, I started to get sidelined. It turns out that an accomplished female agent of Jewish heritage who was pursuing right-wing extremist groups no longer fit the *zeitgeist* of the current government. My security clearance got revoked and I ended up in a basement office doing clerk work for the facilities maintenance department. You know, ordering toilet paper and cleaning supplies, that sort of thing."

"I see. Why didn't you just quit and leave?"

"Because I knew that's what they wanted, and because the job means I still have access to the building—more than they know. I still think there's hope for this country, but only if people like me don't give up. And of course, I still have rent to pay every month."

"And so, you ended up with a relationship with the French intelligence services? I guess that makes sense… I think."

"That's not something we're going to talk about, Mr. Amaya. Suffice to say that when there are aligned interests and common adversaries, working with allies is a practical choice. Now, Jean-Luc gave me the highlights of the situation you and the Basque scientist are facing—how can I help?"

Vano paused for a moment to reflect and then replied, "Two things for now. I need to get a copy of the building plans, permits, schematics—whatever is available—for a building in Csepel. I'll text you the address."

"That shouldn't be a problem. What's the other thing?"

"Maria Guevara—the Basque scientist—is on her way here. I know this is a lot to ask, but can she stay with you? I think together we are too much of a target, and I don't want to impose on my friend here anymore than I already have. Also, she's entered the last trimester of her pregnancy, and in my current condition I'm worried that I can't fully look after her."

"Yes, I can do that."

"Thank you, Sára. And I mean that sincerely—Maria and I have an indirect family connection."

"No problem. But you know what this means in our business, right?"

"Yes. I owe you a favor."

"No. You and Sarfati *both* owe me a favor. Tell him that when you next talk to him," Weisz replied and then finished her coffee as she stood up to leave.

"I'll be in touch. Be careful, please."

Weisz looked bemused. "Don't worry about me, this is my city. And like my more famous ancestral relative, I have a knack for getting out of tight spots."

Who's that?"

"Erich Weisz," Weisz replied, still bemused, knowing he would not recognize the name.

"I'm drawing a blank."

Weisz's green eyes twinkled mischievously as she looked back at Vano over her shoulder while walking away, "You would know him by the American stage name he adopted—Harry Houdini. And now my friend it's time for me to make my escape—I'll be in touch soon."

Vano finished his coffee, paid the bill, and made his way to a quiet bench at the nearby Szent István park, where he then sat down and called Sarfati.

"How did your meeting go?" Sarfati asked when he answered.

"She was helpful, thank you. She says we both owe her a favor, though."

Sarfati laughed dryly. "As usual."

Vano then summarized what had happened over the last few days and ended up by asking, "How are things on your end—do you think you can arrange for some more help? Getting into that building and getting to Mendez is going to be a challenge—especially in my current condition."

"Things have gotten more complicated than I expected. The list of names our technicians found in Mendez's files and the implications of those connections are wider than I previously imagined. There are trip wires everywhere, Vano. The ace we have up our sleeve is that we have a copy of the files, and it appears they don't know it yet. The problem is that now we don't know who we can trust to tell about it—at least not yet. Until I can thread that needle, Sára's assistance is all I can offer for now. Is there something CNI can do to help?"

"That was going to be my next call, but honestly Eastern Europe is not an area where they maintain much of an operational presence outside the usual embassy and consular cover roles for information gathering. I'm almost certain that pulling together a tactical team from that lot is a non-starter."

"I see. Well, let's stay in touch. Fate is fickle and has a way of changing unexpectedly."

"Tell me about it," Vano sighed as he hung up.

Mattin Ezpeleta was just entering the outskirts of Bilbao when he spotted the tail. Since Maria had departed for Budapest, and he wasn't having to keep an eye on her, he had agreed with Vano that he would head back to Bilbao to take a few days off and to check in with the CNI branch office there. He had a few years less experience than Vano, but still cursed himself for not noticing the tail earlier. All he could make out initially was that there were two men in the car following him. What he could not know was that this was one of the teams of National Alliance operatives that had been dispatched by Inspector Luis Delgado to track down and uncover the identities of the three CNI agents they believed were operating under deep cover in the Basque Country, one of which they hoped would be Vano, or at least would lead them to Vano. But what Delgado did not realize was that as a result of accessing the electronic police report a few months ago regarding Ulrik Eklund's attempted attack on Maria in San Sebastián, he had triggered the system flag Vano had arranged to attach to it and was now being monitored by the Internal Affairs ('IA') department of the National Police. That meant that they had been monitoring calls to and from his phone and therefore had the phone number of the passenger in the car that was tailing Mattin Ezpeleta. That also meant they could monitor its location via GPS.

Vano was back at László Kolompár's apartment resting, having just cleaned and put fresh bandages on his shoulder wound, when the call came in from the IA agent supervising the investigation of Delgado. "This is Vano," he grunted, still grinding his teeth at the pain that had shot through his shoulder when he leaned forward from the sofa to pick up the phone.

"Agent Amaya, do you have any idea why someone that Inspector Delgado is communicating with might have just driven from San Sebastián to Bilbao?"

"I think I might. How long would it take to get a GEO[3] team up north?"

"Once authorized, a five-man GEO Operative Action team can be ready to go on the tarmac at Torrejón Air Base outside Madrid in a few hours. From there, roughly an hour flight, depending on the location of an available airstrip. The GEO superintendent will need to authorize it though, and the team lead will require a mission brief before loading up so they can properly equip."

"Okay, after we get off the phone, call the GEO superintendent and ask him to start getting a team together to deploy to Santiago de Compostela for a potentially hostile capture operation. Text me his number and tell him that I'll call him personally in thirty minutes with details."

"Santiago de Compostela? He's going to have a lot of questions."

---

[3] GEO – *Grupo Especial de Operaciones*, the specialized tactical unit of Spain's National Police Corps, responsible for counter-terrorism operations and support to selected Spanish police security and interdiction operations.

"I know. Just do it please. I'll let you know the details as soon as I can, but I have to make another call right now," Vano replied as he was hanging up. He then immediately dialed the phone of Mattin Ezpeleta. "Hello, Mattin. Where are you now?" he jumped in as soon as he heard the line open.

"I'm on the AP-8, just outside Bilbao," Ezpeleta replied as he toggled to speakerphone mode. He knew it must be urgent since Vano had not used their usual call sign and countersign protocol before starting.

"Are you being followed?"

"Jesus Christ, how could you know that already? I just noticed it myself."

"I'll explain in a minute, Mattin. How many of them are there?"

"Two, in a black sedan, plated 8632 XRW."

"I need you to take them on a pilgrimage."

"Santiago de Compostela? That's nearly a six-hour drive."

"Take it slow, and make it seven hours—we need to buy some time. A GEO 'reception committee' is going to be waiting to pick up your new friends, but it needs to be pulled off with some finesse so that they don't tip off their handler in Madrid. Do you know where the cargo terminal is at the airport there? There's an old makeshift safe house hidden in the substructure."

"I can find it."

"Good. Start heading in that direction, and I'll call you back with more specifics. And keep your sidearm chambered and on you Mattin. After what happened in Barcelona I have a feeling that these guys are not run-of-the-mill thugs." After Vano hung up he saw that the IA agent he had spoken to earlier had, as requested, texted him the GEO superintendent's number. He was about to dial it when another call came in from the IA agent. "Yes? Was there a problem with the superintendent?"

"No, he's alerted a team and is waiting for your call. The reason I called you back is that it appears the tracking device we put inside the hard drive that we planted for Delgado to find has suddenly started working and is transmitting a signal."

"Where is it?" Vano asked.

"Zürich."

Alain Corbin had just left Sarfati's office when the call from Vano came in—Sarfati had sent a message asking Vano to call him when he was able to speak freely. "Thank you for calling back so quickly," he said as he put the phone to his ear.

"No problem. Has there been a development?"

"Yes. Our forensic analyst appears to have found some additional evidence in Mendez's files. Evidence that Mendez, or someone working for him, was conducting surveillance on Remy Boucher in a timeframe proximal to his murder, which would seem to support Dr. Guevara's belief that Mendez was involved in the murder. It's not ironclad but could be the beginning of a basis for an extradition request."

"I suppose that's encouraging but doesn't change the timeline or the situation on the ground here that I'm dealing with. Is there anything else?"

"It appears Mendez made pretty regular trips to Switzerland while he was living in Paris. Also, I was curious if your plan to plant the hard drive in Madrid and then track it had turned up anything yet?" Sarfati asked tentatively.

"You're timing is uncanny Jean-Luc. Let me guess—Mendez's Switzerland trips were to Zürich, right?"

"Yes, how did you know?"

"The tracker was not functioning but just started working again and has turned up in Zürich."

"And the DGSE agent that went missing was in Switzerland before he went to Budapest," Sarfati thought out loud, feeling as if an important piece of a very complicated puzzle was coming into focus. "Can you arrange to get us patched into the tracker location so we can follow it as well?"

"Yes, but you're going to have to find a way to get me some kind of help here Jean-Luc. Time is running out for Maria and her baby, and I'm in no condition now to try and break into what has turned out to be a high-security facility that Mendez is holed up in here. Sára thinks she can get me the building plans, and she is going to let Maria stay with her, but I can't ask her to risk getting more involved just because I was careless enough to get injured."

"I see. So you're asking for a trade?"

"If you choose to see it that way, fine. But after what happened to Remy I think you want Mendez as bad as we do, and it looks like he might even be a link to finding out more about what's going on in Switzerland and what happened to your DGSE agent. Hell, maybe your agent might even still be alive, and you could position this as a recovery or rescue operation. You must have someone in your private address book you can trust to work outside the system."

"You are canny my Spanish friend; I'll give you that. I can't make promises, but there's a contractor that DGSE has used for non-attributable activities. A veteran of the Foreign Legion and later an operative for GIGN,[4] he was recruited by a small private 'security' company that does sensitive support work for DGSE. I will have a quiet chat with my counterpart on the task force and see if something can be arranged—off the books. But you must also understand that means no cavalry is coming if things go sideways."

"Sounds like we have a deal. And as a gesture of good faith I will arrange that you receive a link to the tracking device in the next few hours."

"Thank you. So are your contacts in Madrid going to move on the mole in the National Police now that you have the tracker working?"

"Soon. We've got a little bit of a fox hunt to finish first, including with that name you gave me and"—Vano stopped midsentence for a few seconds and then came back on the line—"I'm afraid I have to go now Jean-Luc… a call from Maria is coming in—she must have arrived. Call me when there is an update on when my newest French friend will be coming."

"*À bientôt mon ami.*"

≈

There had been a lot of time to think. First, Maria had made the trip to Arditurri and stayed overnight to speak to Vano's father as he had requested. Then there was the six-hour train ride from San Sebastián to

---

⁴ GIGN – *Groupe d'Intervention de la Gendarmerie Nationale,* France's elite paramilitary unit responsible for counter-terrorism, high-profile security/protection & surveillance, and hostage rescue operations.

Madrid, and then finally the three-hour flight from Madrid to Budapest. Perhaps triggered by the brief trip back to Arditurri, her thoughts kept circling around a familiar theme—her identity. But this time, rather than the psychological brambles she would usually encounter in ruminating over the topic, she began to feel a mélange of pride and nostalgic childhood memories emerge. And when her thoughts turned to Vano, those feelings were heightened by the memories of his voice and his touch. Across the empty hours of travel the realization hit her about how the connectedness that family and cultural ties provide is so meaningful—especially during difficult times—and how she had either taken it for granted or just ignored it. It was only now, as she longed to see Vano again and reflected on the vulnerability of not just herself at this late stage of pregnancy but the child inside her, that she fully understood—and felt—this need for a sense of belonging. And as she thought again of the tapestry of her childhood experiences around both her mother's and father's families, she began to see more clearly how those roots and the various facets of the cultures that she had been immersed in provided the formative foundation of social connection and validation that all humans need. She was so moved by the thought that she took out a small notepad and a pen from her backpack and wrote "hypothesis: family and culture, along with their attendant customs and rituals, combine to provide the meaning and purpose that we humans crave as an antidote to the prospect of mere bleak and brute existence." As if to accentuate this final reflection, Franz Liszt's rhapsodic *Liebesträume* ('Dreams of Love') *No. 3* began playing over the plane's intercom as the purser announced their imminent arrival at the airport named after the celebrated 19th century Hungarian classical composer.

Sára Weisz had a picture of Maria that Vano had provided to her and was waiting outside the baggage claim area when she spotted Maria exiting. She walked up and extended her hand, smiling, "You must be Maria."

Maria was startled at first and then remembered Vano's message saying that a dark-haired woman named Sára would be picking her up. "You must be Sára," she replied, returning the offered handshake.

"I hope you had a good flight. Do you need help with your suitcase?" Weisz added as she glanced over Maria's unmistakably pregnant figure.

"I'm fine, thanks. I could use the exercise."

"Okay, let's go then. Your friend Vano is waiting at my apartment."

Maria felt a slight twinge at the thought of Vano being in this very attractive woman's apartment, but then brushed it aside, also remembering his injury. "I want to thank you for letting me stay with you—I hope it's not an imposition," she added politely.

"No problem at all—I could use the company. By the way, my apartment is in the Felhévíz neighborhood, on the Buda side of the river, right across from the area in Pest where Vano is staying. They're connected by the Margaret Bridge."

After the thirty-minute drive from the airport and helping Maria access the entrance to her building and the elevator, she turned and waved. "It's number 34C—on the third floor, just to the left when you get off the elevator. I need to go meet someone to pick up the building plans I promised to Vano. Please make yourself at home—I'll be back in about an hour."

Vano had heard the elevator and was waiting in the hallway when Maria reached the third floor. He was smiling widely, though his arm was still in a sling, and Maria's heart quickened when she saw him. She left her suitcase standing by the elevator and rushed to embrace him, but then pulled away when he winced in pain. "Oh, I'm so sorry, Vano. I was just, you know… very happy to see you. How is it doing?"

"It's getting better," Vano replied and then added, "I missed you too, Maria. Let's get your things inside now. Have you eaten?"

"Yes, they fed us on the plane, but I could go for a cup of coffee. Just show me where everything is, and I'll make it."

Vano pointed across the room. "Just around that corner, past the entrance to the bedroom."

"Should I be worried that you know where the bedroom is in the apartment of this mysterious woman? She's quite beautiful, don't you think?" Maria asked as she headed towards the kitchen, trying unconvincingly to sound as if she was teasing.

"Objectively, yes… but from what I have observed so far, I think she would be more interested in you than me, actually," Vano replied.

"Oh… I see. Well then, my wounded knight, I've been very curious since we last spoke. What was it you needed to tell me in person?"

Vano had come quietly into the kitchen, approaching Maria from behind, and she almost jumped when he reached to take her hand using his good arm. "Maria, a lot has happened between us. And I'm not sure what's going to happen next. But I'm going to do everything I can to help you *and* your baby. But if something does happen to me, I want you to…" Vano hesitated and looked down.

Vano's serious demeanor had caught Maria off guard. "You want me to what, Vano? Is it something to do with your parents?"

Vano looked up again and held her eyes for several seconds and then finally said, "I want you to know that I love you, Maria."

It took a moment for Vano's words to sink in. Maria looked confused at first, and then a smile spread across her face. She carefully embraced him, reaching up with gentle, murmuring kiss. *"Te amo, mi querido."* As they held one another in the quiet of Sára's apartment, Maria felt safe and happy and was beginning to see a future for herself again. She was tempted to ask Vano how he felt about becoming a father, or at least a father figure, but didn't want to interrupt the moment. She knew he would be wonderful though.

Inside the windowless building in Csepel, Mendez's new Czech protégé Petr Novák was watching quietly and taking notes as Mendez alternately scribbled text and figures on a large whiteboard and then spoke with barely disguised impatience as he pointed to his scribbles and figures for emphasis. "So you see Petr, the main problems to be solved do not have to do with the actual process of cloning. That is straightforward and, as you are aware, the techniques for successfully cloning a human through somatic cell nuclear transfer were worked out a few decades ago. The first key problem a project of this scale has to address is what are the different *types* of humans you want to clone and therefore which *characteristics* do you want to specifically engineer their genotypes and phenotypes to express. Given the almost infinite potential permutations, the choices have to be narrowed down to a manageable number of archetypes. The other main problem is basically designing the overall logistics."

Novák stopped writing and looked up. "Logistics?"

"Yes, logistics. And I don't mean the sourcing of a starting selection of oocytes and sperm to prime the process. That's already in progress, as I explained earlier," Mendez said, waving toward the whiteboard.

"Using the DNA database we've compiled," Novák echoed.

"Correct. Using front companies that appear on the surface to be research entities partnered with obscure universities, we have gained access to a network of women's health clinics and sperm banks across Eastern Europe—and the DNA data they routinely collect. From there it's just a matter of letting the computer do the work to narrow down and select the best candidate oocyte and sperm combinations that can then be used for further optimization in the laboratory."

"So the logistics problem is at the back end of the process?"

"Precisely. We're not quite yet able to grow embryos in large numbers into a fully-developed fetus in the lab, so we need real wombs attached to real women—a lot of them… fifty to start off our pilot location with. And they need to be healthy, compliant and kept in a supervised and secure environment."

"Surely not here?" Novák asked incredulously.

"Of course not," Mendez retorted. "Under the guise of a private religious foundation for poor unwed mothers we have secured a suitable facility, and some additional modifications are in progress to bring it in line with our needs. You'll need to travel there soon actually on my behalf—to have a look and let me know how the final works are progressing. It's a nice little lake retreat about a three-hour train ride southwest from here. The property we acquired is in the hills above the city of Keszthely, on the far western shore of Lake Balaton."

"Any particular rationale behind that location?"

"The location in the hills is secluded enough to not attract attention, and anyway the locals down in Keszthely are used to seeing strangers around town—a lot of tourists come to visit the lake so they don't pay much attention to them. Among other things, Keszthely has a local hospital, a train station in the center of town, and there's an airport only about six miles outside the city. Also, it's not too far from either Budapest to the northeast or Graz in Austria to the northwest—something Franz was pushing for. And it's big enough to accommodate a future wing for the artificial womb technology that will be operational at the scale we need in a few years, after which we won't need human wombs."

Where did the artificial womb technology come from? I wasn't aware it was already so mature."

"Sporadic research has been going on for quite a while in different locations, but after that EctoLife[5] concept video went viral at the end of 2022, we quietly leveraged the interest that had been generated and worked behind the scenes to put together a major research consortium that would actually develop the technology. It turned out there was no shortage of interest—or money—from countries facing population decline. Japan, South Korea, the Baltics, several eastern European countries, Italy… they're all struggling with the problem and very worried about what it may mean for their future economic and political stability. And of course, there were some organizations in Europe and North America—organizations more closely aligned to us—willing to

---

[5] EctoLife – a concept video describing a large-scale, AI-assisted artificial womb + genetic engineering facility. The video was released in December 2022 by Berlin-based science communicator, director, and producer Hashem Al-Ghaili.

invest anonymously in a technology with the promise of generating a lot of White babies."

"It sounds well thought out. But where will you get those initial fifty 'compliant' women for the pilot?"

"I will fill you in on that later. But suffice to say the problems we had with the woman in Paris won't be repeated."

Just then Franz Eder was walking past them and chimed in sardonically, "Let's hope not, but nevertheless it would appear that some of those problems have followed you here, *Herr Doktor*."

Mendez turned to Eder; his jaw clenched. "Well, then thank God a 'specialist' like you is here then—let's just hope you hit your mark next time." Eder simply laughed at the remark as he continued on into the next room and closed the door. "Now, where was I?" Mendez then asked somewhat rhetorically as he turned back towards Novák.

"Actually, I was going to ask you about the archetypes you mentioned earlier. How are those determined?"

"Oh yes… that was a crucial step. Through a shell foundation we commissioned some studies by historical anthropologists to construct a profile of the archetypes that had proven necessary to efficiently control large societies." Mendez then turned and began writing them down on the whiteboard, reading them out as he wrote them. "First, you need leaders of course, both civilian and military. Second is the diplomats and spies archetype—they have more in common than first meets the eye. Third comes scientists, engineers, architects, and designers—the common thread being a combination of high-level technical and creative capacity. Fourth are skilled technicians, in the broadest sense of the word—doctors, nurses, computer programmers, machinists, etc. Fifth are the managers, administrators, and planners that are necessary to run organizations and bureaucracies. Sixth are the soldiers and police, and finally the seventh archetype is the caretakers, companions, and breeders."

"That's only seven archetypes—why do you need to start with fifty women?"

"We create three groups of redundant archetype specimens as a contingency, but that also have different source material in order to create some degrees of genetic separation. And one male and one female is created for each archetype."

"That still only adds up to forty-two."

"Yes, I am aware of the math, Petr. There will be an additional special group of eight—four females and four males—that have certain variations on the archetypes and that would be kept 'in house' for comparison, advisory, and experimental control purposes once the others are deployed."

"Very clever. And efficient. But who will be doing all the menial work?"

"The *untermenschen* of course—there will still be plenty of those around for a while, though we'll have to watch out for the troublemakers."

Novák nodded and allowed himself a thin smile, "Until we find a final solution, I suppose?"

"Yes. I am in fact already working on the *ultimate* solution—some very specific heritable genome editing that we'll then be able to propagate through undesirable populations using a targeted gene drive. Within a few generations we could effectively drive those populations into extinction. I'll share the details with you later—now let's get back to work."

≈

The flight from Marseille to Budapest had been uneventful, and Achille de Saint Marc was settling into his hotel room when he received the location confirmation on where the weapons cache had been placed for him by a local DGSE asset with assistance from Sára Weisz. Sarfati had flown to Marseille to brief him personally on the assignment before he left, so he knew it was either very important or too sensitive to discuss over the phone, or perhaps both. But he still would have to wait to retrieve the cache until after nightfall, so decided to have a glass of wine and try to get a few hours of sleep. As he often did in quiet moments like this, he reflected on how he had ended up as a quasi-mercenary for western intelligence agencies. The obvious part of the answer was the formidable skillset he had acquired in his service with the Foreign Legion and then GIGN. The less comfortable part of the answer was the realization about himself—he liked to work alone simply because he found it hard to trust anyone and chafed at taking orders. Being treated with a kind of constant watchful suspicion throughout most of his 'official' career simply because of his name had not helped either. But it was a name from which there was no escape. His father's great-uncle had been Hélie Denoix de Saint Marc, the commander of the 1st Parachute Regiment of the Foreign Legion in Algeria in 1961 when they joined with a group of generals that had decided to rebel against the French government's decision to allow Algeria to begin moving towards independence. The local mutiny was eventually put down, de Saint Marc was arrested, and the 1st Parachute Regiment was permanently disbanded. Although sentenced to ten years in prison, he served only five and was eventually 'rehabilitated' by the system, partly in honor of his military service in Indochina and before that as a member of the French Resistance in World War II, where he had been captured by the Nazis and nearly died in Buchenwald concentration camp. Young Achille de Saint Marc was mesmerized by the legend of his forebear and from the time he was a boy was determined to become a Legionnaire and earn the white kepi. But the name his father had given him had turned out to be ironically prophetic. He was indeed a fierce warrior like the Achilles of Greek legend but, like Achilles, he also had a vulnerability—the shadow that followed his family name.

While Achille de Saint Marc was napping at the modest Hotel Metro, across the river in Sára Weisz's apartment, Vano was making notes on the margins of the schematics that Weisz had secured of the windowless building in Csepel. Huddled around the table with him were Maria and Sára, pointing out particular features of the building layout and helping to hash out ideas. Vano would be meeting with de Saint Marc the next day and wanted to contribute by being prepared to come to the meeting with some ideas on accessing the building since he knew he would not be able to participate due to his injury.

In another part of Budapest, Franz Eder and Stefan Lang were meeting with a local official who, after a call from Giger to the Interior Minister, had been dispatched to help them look for Vano. And back in Arditurri, Guaril Amaya had just finished a call with an old friend who was now retired from Mossad. After what Maria had told him when she came to visit, he knew his son might need help and so had decided to call in the marker earned by the Nazi-hunting exploits of his own father—Danior Amaya. It had been a quick call because the Israelis were true to their word and, unsurprisingly, still relished the prospect of going after Nazis and their modern-day ilk. The currents of history, like the course of the River Danube, were now bending inexorably towards Budapest.

Chapter 14: Gone Till November

Maria laughed with delight as she watched the little boy in red suspenders playing in the park by the river. The moment felt so light and happy, and she was captivated by the boy's carefree joy as he ran and tumbled in the grass under a cloudless sky and a warm sun. And then suddenly the boy stopped and collapsed to the ground, gasping. She ran to him, thinking he was choking, but he was not. Still gasping, the boy's skin began to turn a sickly shade of bluish-grey, and Maria screamed for help as she knelt beside him. As if from nowhere she heard a voice tell her, "The boy needs your help, Maria. You can help him breathe."

"But I don't know how to give CPR to a child… what do I do?" Maria called out in desperation, although there didn't seem to be anyone near her.

"Eighteen breaths is all it will take," came the voice again.

Maria immediately blew eighteen breaths into the boy's mouth and then looked around, asking, "What now?" But the voice was gone, and the boy sat up, his skin returning to its normal shade. The boy stared at her and smiled, though it seemed he had an odd, almost triumphant expression that unsettled her. "I can keep him from that path," she thought for no apparent reason. But then she heard a loud crack, like a gunshot, and threw her arms around the boy to protect him. She somehow realized the boy was no longer in danger though and looked up to see a stricken dove, snowy-white against the azure sky, plummet into the nearby river. A sudden wave of grief engulfed her as she watched the dove being carried away from her by the river's current—and then she woke up. After taking a moment to sit up and pull her hair back, she reached for her phone and called Vano.

"You're up early," came the reassuring sound of his voice.

"What was the number of that box that Sarfati mentioned from Mendez's shipping list?"

"Eighteen… why?"

"We have to get to it, Vano."

"Yes, I know. We will—that's why we're here, Maria."

Maria went quiet for a moment and then asked, "What do white doves mean?"

"White doves? Love, peace, that sort of thing. Why? Are you sure you're completely awake, Maria? Maybe you should have some coffee and call me back."

"Yes, you're right. Let me get some coffee, and I'll call you back," Maria replied, absent-mindedly grasping the *putsi* around her neck and then realizing that tears were streaming down her cheeks, though she didn't exactly know why.

Although he was exhausted by the time he left the safe house that was hidden in the cargo terminal of Santiago de Compostela's airport, Mattin Ezpeleta immediately began making calls—the interrogation of the two AN operatives that the GEO team had successfully captured had been an intense and layered psychological exercise, but ultimately fruitful. The first call was to his counterpart agent based in Vitoria-Gasteiz, the charming and nearly 900-year-old capital city of the Basque Country, located in its south-central region. For secure calls they used a proprietary application that operated through a dedicated second SIM card on their CNI-issued phones, as well as individual call signs. Ezpeleta was *Ikuste Hiru* ('Watcher Three') and the agent he was calling in Vitoria-Gasteiz was *Ikuste Bi* ('Watcher Two'). *Ikuste Bat* ('Watcher One') of course was Vano Amaya. After the second ring a voice came over the line, "*Ikuste Bi—libre.*"

Ezpeleta then knew they could speak freely and responded similarly, "*Ikuste Hiru—libre.*" If the opening greeting had been *lanpetuta* ('busy') instead of *libre*, that would be a signal that the speaker had people around him and coded language or a postponed call would be necessary.

"Any news? I'm dying of boredom here."

"It looks like some AN operatives, with help from a mole in National Police headquarters, have zeroed in on us. GEO rounded up a pair that were following me and, based on the information I got out of them, I think they put people on your tail as well. The GEO team is on their way to Vitoria-Gasteiz to coordinate with you to set up a similar capture operation."

"But I haven't noticed a tail."

"These guys are better than average, and you probably haven't been paying close enough attention—I wasn't either, until it was almost too late." Ezpeleta replied briskly. "Take a nice slow drive towards the airport there, to make sure the tail is following you. The rendezvous point with the GEO team will be inside the Church of St. Andrew the Apostle, about a kilometer west of the airport. Their team leader will be calling you shortly to link up."

"Got it. What about *Ikuste Bat*—was there an AN team after him too?"

"He's out of the country. We think the team that was looking for him has slipped through the net and out of the country. But don't worry about that now—after the operation there with GEO you need to get back to Madrid."

"Why?"

"*Ikuste Bat* got a tip from the French security services about a high-ranking rat in the government here. And we've confirmed that this rat has been communicating with the little mole in the National Police that tried to sell us out."

"How high-ranking are we talking about?"

"Ministerial," Ezpeleta replied flatly.

"*Joder*—you must be joking."

"I'm dead serious. Which is why you need to get to Madrid and join the interagency team that's working this. They're having a sealed meeting with one of the *Audiencia Nacional*[1] in a few days to discuss the basis for a surveillance warrant. I'll try to meet you there soon."

"Where are you going now?"

"I want to see if I can find some more clues about the AN team that got away and where we might be able to pick up their trail. I'll be in touch," Ezpeleta finished and then hung up.

---

[1] *Audiencia Nacional* – A centralized court in Spain, just below the Supreme Court, with jurisdictions that include criminal cases pertaining to crimes against the Spanish Crown, terrorism, organized crime, and cross-jurisdictional crimes, as well as specialized courts dealing with criminal inquiries and surveillance.

The next call Ezpeleta made was to Vano Amaya, who answered using the agreed protocol, "*Ikuste Bat—libre.*"

"*Ikuste Hiru—libre,*" Ezpeleta replied and then continued, "Confirming that *Ikuste Bi* will rendezvous with the GEO team in Vitoria-Gasteiz and then head to Madrid after they secure the AN operatives there."

"What about the third team… the one that was trying to find me?"

"It appears they made it to Hondarribia and a speedboat was waiting to take them into French waters. By the time we found out, it was too late to alert the French maritime authorities."

"Sounds like they had help."

"That's what I think," Ezpeleta echoed. The Russian mafia has a footprint in Biarritz, just up the coast in France. My guess is that they got paid to help with the exfiltration out of the Hondarribia marina. I'm going to go see what I can find out before I return to Madrid."

"Okay—keep me posted. And be careful, my friend."

"Always," Ezpeleta replied, finishing the call. The third and final call Ezpeleta then made was to book a flight to San Sebastián Airport, which, despite its name, is located on the outskirts of the city of Hondarribia, where the Spanish-French border meets the Bay of Biscay, about twenty kilometers east of San Sebastián.

Giger was sitting in a luxurious leather armchair on the upper floor of the Maestro Suite of The Dolder Grand hotel and enjoying its sweeping views when he heard the click of Lina Bormann's heels coming up the stairs. The most recent meeting of the Council had finished but he had decided to stay in Zürich for a few days and wait out the late-

November storm that had settled over the region before returning to his chalet in Bürglen. Bormann had three folders tucked underneath her arm but first set down the serving tray she was carrying before handing the folders to Giger. "Good afternoon, Chairman. I thought you might like some coffee and a small snack to accompany your reading," she remarked as she then took a step back and clasped her hands in front of her waist.

Giger looked down at the tray and let slip a rare expression of delight. "Ahh… Basler Leckerli[2]—a very good choice Lina. How did you know that these were a favorite of mine?"

"It's part of my job to know your preferences and anticipate your needs sir, don't you think?" Bormann replied politely, but devoid of any real feeling.

"Yes, I suppose you're right," Giger exhaled in reply, having already turned back to the window with the panoramic view over Lake Zürich, bored now with what Bormann had turned into a clinical exchange.

"Is there anything else I can get for you before you begin with your reading?"

"I'm fine for now. Thank you, Lina."

"Very well," Bormann replied and then added as she turned to walk back towards the stairs, "I'll be back in two hours for your massage." Giger was leaning forward to pick up the first folder and simply nodded in silent acknowledgement as the click of Bormann's heels trailed away out of the room.

---

[2] Basler Leckerli – Swiss spice cookies, somewhat similar to gingerbread cookies. The recipes typically include honey, spices, nuts, candied citrus peel, a splash of liquor and a sugar glaze.

The first folder was labeled *Iberien* ('Iberia') and summarized the status of the various Council-sponsored activities in Spain and Portugal. Activities in Portugal had remained focused on the central government in Lisbon, but subversion in Spain was spread across three targets—the central government in Madrid, the economically strategic northeastern region of Catalonia, and the geographically strategic southern region of Andalusia. Combining control over the chokepoint of the Straits of Gibraltar with a foothold in North Africa along the Moroccan coast via the Spanish enclaves of Ceuta and Melilla, the region had become the next big focus area in Europe after the Council's successes in Hungary. And notwithstanding the noise that Mendez had stirred up with his little Basque imbroglio, there had been some notable successes, the most prominent being the recruitment of a ministerial-level 'ally' in Madrid and the alliance with the AN organization and their formidable network in the south. Spain nevertheless remained a staunch NATO member and maintained close relations with the U.S., and so the report included a discussion of options to target and weaken those ties more aggressively. Giger read this section closely and scribbled notes in the margins that would form the basis of his feedback and further questions on the proposed options.

After finishing his coffee and a few Leckerli cookies, Giger moved on to the second folder, labeled *Amerika*. John Rudel had prepared the more detailed strategy and proposal that Giger had asked for and most of it was in line with the typical approaches that the Council had relied on for years—subversion and corruption of political infrastructure escalating systematically up from local to central authorities and co-opting local (and typically extreme right-wing) movements. However, there was an addendum in the briefing on a problem that the Council had not yet faced at a large scale—large land holdings and self-government by communities of indigenous people. The main problem Rudel faced was working around or through the enormous Navajo Nation that sprawled across parts of the U.S. states of Arizona, New Mexico, and Utah. Roughly the size of (the Republic of) Ireland, the Navajo Nation would be the eleventh largest U.S. state on a standalone basis and sat directly in the path of the north-south corridor that Rudel was planning—his so-called 'spinal axis' for the Council in North America. Rudel described how they would need to employ a more unconventional strategy for this unique territory and summarized the resources he felt he would need to get started. Giger trusted Rudel's judgement and so signed off with his support but, just as he was closing the folder, he thought back to the Spain strategy and scribbled an additional note in the margins "Rudel to additionally bring ideas on weakening the U.S.-Spain relationship to the next Council meeting."

The third folder, labeled *Analyse der in Spanien gefundenen Computerausrüstung* ('Analysis of Computer Equipment found in Spain'), was a faster read for Giger, being only two pages long. The Council's technician in Switzerland described his analysis of the equipment seized from Llúcia Savall in Barcelona and the portable hard drive provided by Inspector Luis Delgado in Madrid and then summarized his conclusions in two sentences: "It is possible that one other copy of the files was either made or transmitted, but we cannot confirm this to greater than a forty-percent probability. The person who built this equipment, broke the encryption, and performed the transfer operations has a level of talent and capabilities such that an effort to recruit is worth consideration."

Giger closed the file, set it on the table in front of him, and picked up the last remaining Leckerli cookie as he stood up to stretch his legs and walk over to the window. And then, as if on cue, the click of Lina Bormann's heels began marching up the stairs.

"Are you ready for your massage, sir?" Bormann asked as she entered the room.

"Yes, but I need to make a brief call first," Giger replied as he pulled out his phone and scrolled through his contact list to the name of Carlos Mendez. A forty-percent probability was too much of a risk to dismiss.

After collecting the weapons cache that had been prepared for him, Achille de Saint Marc had met for several hours with Sára Weisz and Vano to review the building plans of the target facility in Csepel, generally take stock of the situation, and—being wary of human nature—size up the people he would now be working with. He then spent two days and nights surveilling the building in Csepel and its surroundings from different concealed vantage points, using a high-power Zeiss spotting scope fitted with a camera adapter. Once he was satisfied he understood the 'operational environment' as he called it, then a meeting was convened at the apartment of Sára Weisz to discuss a plan of action, and Maria additionally joined them.

"There don't appear to be more than about six people and a few vehicles coming and going from the target location," de Saint Marc explained as he pointed to the selection of pictures he had arranged on his laptop computer screen. "But, given that we should avoid using explosives, I'm not sure I like my odds, even if only two or three of them are armed or have some close-quarter skills."

"What is the concern with explosives?" Maria asked.

"We don't know exactly what kind of materials and chemicals they may have in there. If we trigger secondary explosions or a large fire, then the thing we're looking for might get damaged or destroyed before we can get to it," de Saint Marc answered.

"What if we create a diversion, to draw some of them away and to give you a better chance of slipping in unnoticed?" Vano chimed in.

De Saint Marc turned and nodded. "It's possible, I suppose. But what kind of diversion? After their recent run-in with you, they are no doubt being more careful with their movements."

"I have an idea," Maria said as she stepped up to the table, her loose blouse flowing over her pregnant abdomen and now hovering just above the table's surface. "What if I get a message to Mendez somehow and propose a trade? I'll tell him that the truce that we had agreed to is now off because of the little genetic time-bomb I discovered he planted in my baby and the raid his associates did in Barcelona to grab Llúcia's computer equipment and the files."

Vano looked skeptical. "That sounds like more of a complaint, or maybe a threat, than a trade. What are you asking for—and what is your leverage—that would get him to leave the facility in Csepel and meet somewhere else?"

"I'll tell him that I want the genetic instructions for reversing the modifications that he made to the HBB gene in my child and that in return I'll hand over to him the extra copy of the files I made as insurance. And I'll tell him that if I don't hear from him in a week that I'll turn the files over to major European media outlets and tell them what I think is going on at his little compound in Csepel. I know it might sound desperate, but it might still make sense. Mendez can't risk calling my bluff because he knows that if he's wrong, it would bring the kind of attention that I am certain he—and whatever this shadowy Council is— does not want."

"But we don't have an extra copy of the files with us." Vano replied skeptically. "And remember the terms of the truce included him and his people staying away from your parents. What if he calls your bluff and refuses the trade… would we really ask Sarfati to release the files, and then what would that mean for the safety of your parents and Llúcia?"

"He doesn't know that we don't have a copy of the files here, and even if he doesn't intend to make the trade, I think he won't be able to resist coming to try to get at me again—and will probably bring someone with him. So then we still accomplish thinning the number of people at the building in Csepel, giving Achille a better chance of getting in and out safely. And I can take a dummy hard drive with me to exchange on the off chance he does bring the instructions with him. If he doesn't agree to meet, then we'll still have a week to come up with a 'plan B' while he's wondering whether we're going to actually release the files."

"Well, based on what we've found out from Sara, that 'plan B' can't involve going to the local police, who have probably been infiltrated. And what if Mendez does come? If he gives you the genetic instructions and takes the dummy hard drive back to Csepel, only to find it's empty and their facility has been raided in the meantime, he and his associates are going to be very unhappy and looking to retaliate in some way."

"It's a gamble, I know. But in that case, I suppose we could try to revert to the original truce agreement, assuming he'll think we might still maintain a copy of the files. I'll plead to being the emotional, desperate mother who simply wanted to save her baby and now just wants to go away be left alone."

"It's risky, but could work," de Saint Marc finally interjected, stroking his chin pensively and eyeing Vano.

Vano was frowning and shaking his head but reluctantly assented. "I won't let you meet with him alone, Maria. I need to arrange somehow to be close by. And it needs to be in an open area with people around, so that he's less likely to try an overt attack.

"I would use the embankment along the river in the center of town, in front of or near the Parliament building," Weisz suggested. "He would be more wary of springing a surprise there, given all the CCTV cameras and extra security presence."

"That still leaves me pretty exposed if I'm completely on my own in Csepel and something goes wrong," de Saint Marc said, shaking his head slightly.

"I'll go with you," Weisz replied. "You'll anyway need a getaway driver that knows the city, in case there's a pursuit. I'll wait in my car nearby and we can communicate with walkie-talkies. If things get hairy for you inside, I'll create a distraction from outside and see what I can do to help."

"What kind of distraction?" de Saint Marc asked.

Weisz slid her chair over by her kitchen cabinets, climbed up on to it, and reached into the narrow space above the cabinets and below the ceiling, pulling down a submachine gun with a long, curved high-capacity magazine. "This kind of distraction."

De Saint Marc smiled approvingly. "A Scorpion[3]—impressive. That will do just fine."

≈

Alain Corbin had returned to Sarfati's office and was pointing to a flashing blue dot on his laptop computer screen that he had positioned in front of Sarfati. "It's still there, somewhere in the Technopark complex that's located in District Five, on the west side of the city, between the train tracks and the river. The locals refer to the area as *Industriequartier* or Zürich-West."

"What do you think they're doing with it there?" Sarfati mused.

"Probably something pretty similar to what we've been doing—examining the files and looking for clues."

"Do you think they've discovered the tracker?"

"It seems unlikely, or they would have disabled it."

"Is it that hard to detect?"

"I spoke to our contact with CNI—it's pretty state-of-the-art technology. It's a passive resonator system embedded in the plastic of the case enclosing the portable hard drive. When it gets hit with an internet-linked signal like Wi-Fi, for example from nearby devices, it can link to those devices and get them to send out a short but specific digital signature that will be picked up over the internet by a signal sweeper tuned to that signature. The beauty of the system is that the resonator system itself doesn't emit a signature, so no one will find it unless they tear apart the plastic housing, in which case the nano-processing

---

[3] Scorpion – The Czech-made Scorpion EVO 3 is a 9mm carbine submachine gun also adopted by the Hungarian military in 2018. Light (6.1 lbs. with a full magazine) and compact (16.1 in. long with the stock folded/26.4 in. unfolded), it has additionally been adopted by law enforcement agencies in several countries.

technology integrated in the resonator will be damaged before it can be analyzed or copied."

"Do we have a capability like this?"

"I've heard our tech lab has been experimenting with embedded resonant systems, but I'm not sure how far they've advanced. Hopefully we can share this information with them soon."

"Not just yet, Alain. I'm still working through the minefield of the names you discovered in those files."

"Maybe we should we try to get some local surveillance in place as a contingency in case the signal goes dark. Should we give the Swiss security services a heads-up?"

"Same answer, for now. I've got an off-the-record private meeting with Mssr. Archambeau tomorrow… to seek his advice."

"The retired Interior Minister?"

"Yes. He's several degrees removed from any of the names on our list, and someone I think we can trust. *Un casse-couille*, but an honest one."

Remarkably, Sára Weisz had been able to source another key piece of information about the facility in Csepel which she had earlier secured the building plans for—the landline telephone number associated with it. Even more remarkably, when Maria called the number it was Mendez's voice that she heard pick up after the second ring. She had been expecting to have to talk her way through someone to get Mendez on the line and had to take a moment to gather herself. In the meantime, Mendez's voice barked insistently, "Hello? Hello? Who is calling?"

Maria realized he was about to hang up and almost blurted out, "Hello, Carlos."

The line was silent for so long that Maria thought Mendez may have hung up, but he finally replied, his tone at once acid and condescending, "Ah… it's you again. How did you get this number? You're taking quite a risk by making contact, Maria. I assume you heard what happened to your CNI friend?"

"He's still alive, Carlos, as am I… and my baby. And we all—including you, I assume—want to stay that way and get on with our lives, which is why I'm calling. I know what you did to my baby."

"What are you talking about?"

"The modification of the HBB gene."

"Oh that." Mendez replied flatly. "Well, if that works at least one problem will take care of itself."

Maria struggled to bite back her rage and the profanity that was coiled at the tip of her tongue, but eventually managed a controlled response. "I want the genetic instructions to reverse the modifications, Carlos. I know you have them with you there… in box number eighteen, no?"

"Hmm… you are lucky to have some of that Basque blood in you, Maria—it seems to have given you a certain acuity that offsets some of the shortcomings of your lesser genetic inheritance. And why would I hand over the instructions to you?"

"Because although you think that the equipment and files that were recently taken from Barcelona and Madrid solved the problem of your potential exposure, I made an extra copy as insurance. I have that copy here with me, and I'm willing to trade it for those genetic instructions."

"And if I don't believe you, or just refuse?" Mendez asked, wavering almost imperceptibly. What Maria could not know was that Giger had called Mendez just a few days before, berating him about the possibility of another copy of the files having been made.

Maria was ready with her reply, her tone clinical and cutting. "Carlos, if I don't have those instructions within one week, I'll assume that means you don't intend to ever give them to me, or don't have them anymore. Either way, if the fate of my child is going to be sealed, then yours will be sealed as well. You must already be embarrassed with what has happened so far and no doubt have disappointed your masters at the Council—imagine how they'll react when I release the files to several major European media outlets and then provide them with a detailed description about a certain building in Budapest, its mysterious occupant, and what is going on in there. But if you give me those instructions, I swear—on the life of my child—that I will give you the files, go away, and keep my mouth shut." She knew she needed to sound like a mother desperate to save her unborn child—and she was. While she waited for Mendez to respond she asked herself whether she was really going to trade the future of a large part of humanity for the life of her child. She convinced herself that someone else—Sarfati, Vano, some security agency somewhere in the world—would figure out a way to deal with the situation so she wouldn't have to… and then Mendez's voice brought her back into the moment.

"What about your CNI friend?"

"Without the files or any sworn statements from me, his hands are pretty much tied legally, as far as I understand it. It's not as if Hungary, or Argentina for that matter, is going to extradite you to Spain or France based only on the unsubstantiated suspicions of a CNI agent."

Mendez's reply was stiff but diminished. "I'll have to think about it."

"Don't think too long," Maria admonished. "I'll meet you next Saturday at two o'clock in the afternoon at the open square at the south end of the Parliament building. Bring the instructions—if you don't show up then I'll know what your answer is." And then she hung up.

≈

A few days after Maria's call with Mendez, Uri Davidov and Ben Vaknin were drinking coffee and playing the Israeli card game Yaniv to pass the time on their three-hour train journey from Bratislava to Budapest. With their quiet manner, graying hair, leathery complexions, and bland clothes, they were as unremarkable to the untrained eye as the rest of the menagerie of passengers on the train. But Davidov and Vaknin were very different—they were retired Mossad agents. Fitter than most men half their age and still in command of lethal skills, they had not hesitated when they heard about the call for help from Guaril Amaya. Theirs was a secretive but deeply fraternal world of comrades, bound together by an immutable code of honor and forged by shared hardships and sacrifice.

Israel's diplomatic relations with Hungary had deteriorated sharply after they had publicly rebuked Hungary's political leaders at the United Nations General Assembly for their unwillingness to condemn or confront the increasing prevalence of brazen antisemitic rhetoric and attacks on synagogues and Jewish-owned businesses. More recently there were reports coming back that Israeli arrivals at Hungarian airports were being harassed and in some cases barred from entering the country. So, as a precaution, Davidov and Vaknin had flown first to Bratislava, in neighboring Slovakia, and picked up forged Slovakian passports that had been prepared for them, as well as a set of Uzi Pro submachine guns and ammunition. Because the suitcases would have to pass through x-ray security machines in the Bratislava train station, their Slovakian contacts had additionally prepared special suitcases that had inner central compartments shielded by a thin layer of lead and which were just big enough to hold the already compact submachine guns and a few magazines of ammunition. They knew they would be able to easily source more of the ubiquitous 9mm ammunition in Budapest, as well as the remainder of the miscellaneous tactical gear they usually worked with— things like knives, rope, zip ties, flashlights, walkie-talkies, and first aid kits. But for now, they allowed themselves to enjoy the swaying of the train, the rounds of Yaniv, and the familiar comfort of each other's company—Budapest would come soon enough.

Meanwhile in Madrid, the meeting between the interagency team that would be looking into the potentially compromised Minister had finished a successful confidential meeting with the *Audiencia Nacional* judge assigned to their case. The requests for surveillance warrants were granted, as well as an arrest warrant for Inspector Luis Delgado. But the team were still waiting for Mattin Ezpeleta to arrive before deciding on a final tactical course of actions and were increasingly concerned that he was not responding to their calls or text messages. Ezpeleta was not responding because he was floating naked, face down, and lifeless between two fishing boats in the marina of Biarritz, his throat slashed open from ear to ear. His clothes and belongings had been deliberately taken to extend the time it would take for the authorities to identify him.

Back in Budapest, Petr Novák was preparing to leave the next day for Keszthely, per his instructions from Franz Eder to check on progress with the facilities there. Across town Sára Weisz had called an impromptu meeting with Vano, Achille, and Maria to inform them that she had found out that Interior Ministry resources had been assigned to hunt for what they called 'a dangerous foreigner, wanted for an attempted attack on a medical research laboratory in Csepel.' "We have to make our move on Saturday as planned and then disappear," Weisz warned. "The net they've thrown across the city is going to get tighter with each passing day." It was the end of November now and the weather in Budapest was turning decidedly cold, damp, and ominous.

Chapter 15: Cold Weather Blues

DURING THE WINTER OF 1944–1945, with Soviet forces advancing across the border into German-occupied Hungary, the militiamen of the local Nazi-aligned Arrow Cross Party began a reign of terror against Jews in Budapest. They murdered thousands. Shooting them at the banks of the Danube River became a common practice, as the river would 'conveniently' carry the bodies away. Shoes in good condition were, however, a valuable commodity during the war and so the Arrow Cross militiamen would have their victims first step out of their shoes before they were shot and fell into the river. During those days of horror, the Danube's waters flowing through Budapest became known as 'the Jewish Cemetery.'

If you visit Budapest today, on the banks of the Danube close to where it passes in front of the Hungarian Parliament building you might be surprised to come across sixty pairs of shoes in the styles that were common in the 1940s. There are men's, women's, and children's shoes and they sit scattered near the edge of the water, as if their owners had just stepped out of them and left. When you look more closely however, you will see that the shoes are made out of iron and fixed to the concrete of the embankment. These sixty iron shoes are a permanent monument and memorial[1]—known as 'The Shoes on the Danube Promenade'—to the Hungarian Jews who were murdered by the Arrow Cross militia in that last, terrible winter of the war.

≈

Sarfati had just returned from his meeting with ex-Minister Archambeau and called Alain Corbin. Before Corbin could even say hello, Sarfati started talking, a hint of frisson in his voice, "Alain, we need to detail some technical plans for a potential 'unofficial' surveillance and interdiction operation at that facility in Zürich."

There was a long pause and then Corbin replied, "That's out of our jurisdiction. And what do you mean by 'unofficial'?"

"Let me worry about all that. Meet me in an hour in my office."

"I take it your meeting with Archambeau went well. But he is an *ex-Minister*, no?"

"Yes, but there are no expiration dates on his friendship with the President and personal influence with key leaders in Parliament. And he has long-standing relationships with the Interior Ministers in Switzerland and Spain that his successor has not yet grown into."

"What does Spain have to do with it?"

"CNI has a stake in this, and one of their agents was recently found dead—murdered on French soil—in Biarritz. We're going to be working more closely with them going forward. I have to hang up now, my car is here. I'll see you in the office." The line closed before Corbin could even say goodbye—Sarfati was clearly in a hurry.

---

[1] The Shoes on the Danube Promenade – memorial and monument conceptualized by film director Can Togay, created by Togay together with sculptor Gyula Pauer, and installed in 2005.

On Thursday, Vano received a message from his father about the arrival of Uri Davidov and Ben Vaknin in Budapest—he had waited to send the message until they were safely in the country—and that they were ready to meet with him. Vano's initial surprise was quickly overtaken by relief at having some back-up, given his injury and Maria's advanced stage of pregnancy. After stopping at a sporting goods and hardware store to pick up some additional equipment on Friday morning, Davidov and Vaknin joined the rest of the group at Sára Weisz's apartment to iron out final plans for the next day. After debating various options, the group finally agreed that Vano and Ben Vaknin would shadow Maria's meeting with Mendez by the river, and Achille de Saint Marc, Sára Weisz, and Uri Davidov would go to the facility in Csepel. The logic was that a serious 'kinetic reaction' was more likely to be encountered in breaching the facility in Csepel but couldn't be completely discounted at the meeting by the river. Also, Davidov and Vaknin had satellite phones and so would be able to efficiently coordinate timing and movements between the two teams without the risk of a cellular signal interruption. Satisfied that they had worked out as much detail as was realistic, they shared a hearty dinner together and went their separate ways to try and get some rest before what they knew would be a fateful day ahead.

Budapest was cold, wet, and grey on that early-December Saturday morning. Across the city, some were bundling up to go out for work, or Christmas shopping, or to meet with friends and family. Others had more unusual business to attend to. In the windowless building in Csepel, Dr. Carlos Mendez was in a storage room, going through the contents of box number eighteen. Down the hallway, he could hear Rózsa the cleaning lady pushing her wheeled mop bucket towards the bathrooms. Rózsa was a Romanian of Hungarian ethnicity, but her education had ended after elementary school due to family disruptions and hardship. She had some extended family connections in Budapest, but she did not have a work permit for Hungary, and so did not ask any questions and was careful not to talk to anyone about her job. Being barely literate, she anyway had no idea what was going on in the facility. All of this of course made Rózsa an ideal employee in the eyes of Mendez and Franz Eder. Petr Novák had already left Csepel for Keszthely, while Franz Eder and Stefan Lang had stayed behind to continue coordinating with their contact at the Interior Ministry and to monitor Mendez's progress—they knew Giger and the Council were getting impatient and wanting to see tangible evidence of progress. Eder had been pacing around the administrative office when Lang called him over to look at the facility's checkerboard of video feeds that were displayed on a desktop computer screen. "What do you think he's doing?" Lang asked as he pointed to Mendez's image on the screen.

Eder leaned forward and squinted at the image. "I don't know, but it looks suspicious."

"He took something out of a box in the storage room and… look now… he's heading for the back exit."

Eder stood up and smiled thinly. "Well, well, Dr. Mendez. What little adventure are you off to?" He then turned and went to pick up his rifle and put on his overcoat that was hanging near it, adding, "Keep an eye on things here—I'm going to keep an eye on him. I'll call you if we need assistance from our local friends."

"Why are you taking that?" Lang asked, looking at the rifle.

"In case our little Spanish gazelle shows up at wherever the good doctor is going. I won't miss this time."

Meanwhile, in the apartment of Sára Weisz, Maria Guevara was finishing up getting dressed. She hadn't slept well. The cold, damp weather was aggravating her now-persistent back pain and her feet were more swollen than usual. "The joys of motherhood," she sighed as she put on and buttoned up an insulated parka with a fur-lined hood that Weisz had loaned her. Underneath the parka she had a wool sweater and a thick scarf; in the inner pocket of the parka was the dummy hard drive she would use in case an exchange came to fruition that afternoon with Mendez. She could hear Vano and Ben Vaknin talking in the next room and knew that they were waiting for her. Carrying several packed duffle bags, Achille de Saint Marc and Uri Davidov had gone down with Sára Weisz to her car, where they would load up and conduct some final coordination and communication checks before heading out towards Csepel.

"How is she doing, Sára… do you think she'll be up to it?" Davidov asked Weisz as he opened the trunk of the car and began loading the bags.

"We've had some time to talk while she's been staying with me. She's nervous of course, and still a little disoriented by everything that's happened to her. And she's more in love with Vano than I think he realizes—she let slip that she even hopes he might even be able to be a kind of father figure for the child. Right now, though, I have no doubt that she's determined to do whatever it takes to protect her child and to stop Mendez. The woman has some steel in her backbone—don't worry, we can count on her."

It was now almost noon and rain had begun to fall. De Saint Marc looked up and then over to Davidov and Weisz with a grin as they all got into the car. "Good infantry weather my friends… easier to sneak up on the enemy."

Stefan Lang and Rózsa were the only ones left inside the windowless building in Csepel when Uri Davidov received the 'greenlight' call from Ben Vaknin. Sára Weisz had parked several blocks away and was listening to her homemade scanner that monitored the frequencies that she knew were used by the Budapest police while Achille de Saint Marc and Uri Davidov were setting up two drones and attaching a payload on each. A few days earlier, Vano had asked László Kolompár if he knew where to get some fireworks, even though they were now strictly controlled. Kolompár had replied with his usual bravado, "Impossible—for most people. But don't worry my friend… I am not most people. I have a cousin in Szeged, down south and very close to the border with Romania and Serbia. It's a smugglers paradise—everything is available, for a price." And so it was that a few days later de Saint Marc and Davidov were attaching fireworks to drones in Csepel.

According to the building plans that Sára Weisz had secured, the best way to get into the building with at least some element of surprise would be through a fire escape access panel in the roof of the one-story building. There were no windows to crash through and the front and back doors were likely reinforced and would potentially have to be fought through in the case of attempting a direct breach. Having finished with the drones, Davidov and de Saint Marc signaled Weisz and moved closer to the building so that they would have an unobstructed view of the flight path. And then they lit the extended fuses that they had fashioned earlier and sent the drones on their way. Once the drones were over the outer wall and near the front door of building, they hit a release switch on their control panel and the fireworks fell to the ground. Everything remained silent for about ten seconds. Then the fireworks started going off, and de Saint Marc and Davidov sprinted towards the back wall of the building. The fireworks were a diversion. The hope was that whoever might be inside monitoring the security cameras would be distracted by them while de Saint Marc and Davidov scrambled over the outer wall and then did a push-pull with one another onto the main building's roof.

Stefan Lang almost dropped his coffee cup when the fireworks first went off. He had been in the facility's small kitchen area and raced to the main office where the camera feeds were displayed. When he saw the fireworks, he reached into the pocket of his coat that was on the coat rack, pulled out his pistol, and then ran first to the front door and then the back door to make sure they were locked. On the way back, he came across Rózsa, who—between the sound of the fireworks and the sight of the pistol in Lang's hand—was clearly terrified. Lang motioned for her to go and hide in the small storage closet where her cleaning supplies and some miscellaneous laboratory chemicals were kept. She did as instructed, went in and locked the door from the inside, piling up some buckets and boxes against it for good measure.

Back in the main office, Stefan Lang was trying to call Franz Eder, but there was no answer. Lang then started scrolling through his phone's contact list to find the number of his local liaison in the Interior Ministry when he heard movement behind him. It was Uri Davidov, but it was too late—Lang only caught a fleeting glimpse of an aging, scowling visage before a hail of 9mm rounds from Davidov's Uzi Pro shredded through him, and he fell to the ground like a rag doll. Davidov spit on the ground, staring at Lang's lifeless body, and muttered sarcastically under his breath, "How disappointing—I really expected more from the 'master race.'" He then turned to rejoin de Saint Marc.

Achille de Saint Marc had located the main storage room and box eighteen and was emptying its contents into his backpack when Davidov found him. "I heard gunfire—everything okay?" de Saint Marc asked without looking up.

"Yes—there was only one," Davidov nodded and then added, "Did you find what we came here for?"

"All secure," de Saint Marc replied, patting his backpack.

Just then the voice of Sára Weisz came over their walkie-talkies. "One of those fireworks has started a fire on the roof at the front part of the building, and I'm hearing over the scanner that someone in the neighborhood has called the fire department. The police sometimes follow behind, so we need to get out of here—now."

"We're on our way," de Saint Marc replied into the walkie-talkie. When he turned around he saw Davidov had his cigarette lighter out and was setting fire to a few of the remaining cardboard boxes. "What are you doing?"

"Hoping that this whole place goes up in smoke," Davidov replied. He then stuffed the lighter back in his pocket before they scrambled out of the building, over the outer wall, and back to Sára Weisz's car.

Meanwhile, back inside the building, Rózsa was paralyzed with fear. She had heard the gunfire from Davidov's weapon and the muffled voices of the two men talking. Even when she started to smell smoke, she was too afraid to leave the closet, for fear the intruders would be there waiting for her.

≈

Mendez had decided to arrive early for the meeting with Maria. After parking his car a few blocks away, he grabbed his umbrella and walked briskly to Kossuth Square,[2] the large open area that opened up at the south end of the Hungarian Parliament building. It was a good place to scan the general surroundings ahead of the planned two o'clock meeting. Satisfied that the square was only populated with harmless-looking tourists and locals going about their way, as well as a few senior citizens—including one in a wheelchair—feeding pigeons, Mendez positioned himself next to the sculpture commemorating the Hungarian poet Attila József. József was captured for posterity seated at the top of several steps with his hat in his hand, gazing pensively over the Danube, and Mendez was standing below him looking north towards the Parliament building, expecting to see Maria coming soon from that direction. But Mendez was not the only one watching the square and waiting. Ben Vaknin had set up in an overwatch position on the roof at the northwest corner of the building housing the 'Anabelle Bed and Breakfast.' From that position there was a sweeping ninety-degree view

---

[2] Kossuth Square – named in honor of Lajos Kossuth, the 19th century political reformer who inspired and led Hungary's struggle for independence from Habsburg Austria. Also the site of the 'Bloody Thursday' Kossuth Square Massacre, where on October 25th, 1956, an estimated 1000 unarmed civilians protesting Soviet rule were shot from vantage points in various nearby buildings.

of the entire square. The 650-foot effective range of his Uzi Pro could cover all of it.

When the ferry coming across the river from Batthyány Square terminal—which was across and slightly upriver from its destination at the Kossuth Square ferry terminal—slowly sidled up at precisely two o'clock, Mendez realized Maria was almost certainly on it. Once it was secured in place, the passengers began to spill out onto the gangway that led up to Kossuth Square. Maria was indeed among the passengers and had the hood of her parka pulled up against the light rain as she stepped off the gangway and onto the promenade that ran along the river. Mendez was about two hundred feet away, so at first couldn't make out any faces among the crowd. But as Maria wandered into the square, obviously looking for him, Mendez spotted her and raised his hand to wave her over. When Ben Vaknin saw this, he made the quick call on his satellite radio to Uri Davidov to confirm that Mendez was present and to greenlight the other team's move on the Csepel facility.

Maria finally spotted Mendez when she turned to look south and took a moment to steel herself. She was tired, her body ached, and her stomach was twisted with a combination of revulsion and fear, but she finally clenched her jaw and walked slowly towards Mendez, looking around warily. She saw the same things Mendez had seen—the locals and tourists milling around the square and a few senior citizens—including the one in the wheelchair now positioned behind the sculpture of Attila József and with a heavy blanket over his lap—feeding pigeons. At almost precisely that same moment, Franz Eder was reattaching the custom-made detachable stock to his rifle, bringing the weapon to its full lethal size. The detachable stock allowed him to break the rifle down to a less conspicuous size and carry it in a medium size tourist's duffel—an ideal option for situations just like this. He was at the uppermost flight of the inner fire escape stairs of the Anabelle Bed & Breakfast, just near where the door opened onto the roof. Eder had followed Mendez from Csepel and had quickly reviewed the area on the 3D map application on his phone once Mendez had parked. Unsurprisingly, this rooftop vantage point was as obvious to him as it had been to Ben Vaknin, who, unbeknownst to Eder, was only about thirty feet away from the other side of the door, already in a prone position and watching Maria approach Mendez through the compact scope mounted on his Uzi Pro.

As Maria approached Mendez and the familiar contours of his face came into focus, she felt her muscles twitch and it began to feel as if things were moving in slow motion and that her vision had narrowed. She realized this was probably a result of adrenaline hitting her system, but there was nothing she could do about it. And then she heard Mendez speak. "It seems we meet again, for better or for worse. I trust you have brought what you promised?"

"Yes," Maria replied, struggling to maintain her composure as the proximity of Mendez and his voice triggered another wave of revulsion, and she felt the sting of bile in her throat. She coughed and then finally added, "And you?"

"Right here," Mendez said as he pulled a large envelope out of his overcoat and added, "Let's get this over with," as he held the envelope out with one hand and held his other out and open to receive the hard drive from Maria. She said nothing as she pulled the hard drive out of her coat's inner pocket, placed it in Mendez's hand, and simultaneously pulled the envelope from his other hand.

Ben Vaknin was watching with intense concentration from his vantage point and had his finger on the trigger of his weapon—he knew that this was the point of maximum danger for Maria. But it was precisely Vaknin's intense concentration on Mendez and Maria, along with his deteriorated hearing due to advancing age and a lifetime of too much gunfire, coupled with the formidable skills of Franz Eder, that caused Vaknin's death in that pregnant moment. Eder had noticed the door to the roof had been deliberately propped slightly ajar and then had spotted Vaknin as he surveyed the roof from around the corner of the door using the camera on his phone. He approached as closely as he dared from behind and then leapt onto Vaknin's back, pinning him with the weight of his body, and with both hands drove the six-inch blade of his Austrian-made Böhler hunting knife up under the back of Vaknin's skull and into his brain stem. Without hesitation he then rolled Vaknin's body aside and took up the overwatch position with his Steyr rifle, zeroing in once he spotted Maria and Mendez.

There was a strange and still atmosphere of desperation-driven trust and a kind of weird serendipity of the moment between the two when Maria made the exchange with Mendez and began to turn toward the ferry terminal again. But as she started to walk away Mendez spoke from behind her, his voice menacing. "There had better not be any more copies or tricks, Maria."

Maria turned, somehow no longer afraid, and met his furious eyes with an icy gaze, a smile, and the kind of cutting tone a woman knows how to use when she wants to slice into a man. "You know, I've been threatened a lot in the last few months, Carlos—I guess we'll just have to see what happens. But I will never let this child become what you hoped he would be. Good luck to you—you'll probably need some." And then she instantly regretted her display of bravado when she saw Mendez start to shake uncontrollably with rage and begin to lunge at her. But before he reached her a shot rang out and his body was jerked to the side.

Standing now in front of the sculpture of Attila József and one step down from it was the man who had been sitting in the wheelchair feeding pigeons. He had thrown off the blanket on his lap to reveal a pistol and shot Mendez, who was now swaying in place for a moment, a look of shock on his face. Although the bullet had passed into his abdomen he was still standing and finally turned and staggered toward the promenade, angling south. Maria was trying to make sense of the jumble of scenes around her when she noticed the man with the gun had one arm in a sling. It was Vano, who had been in disguise.

Vano began to give chase to Mendez and jogged forward away from the sculpture. But he was now no longer protected by it—the sculpture had been the barrier in the line of sight between Franz Eder and Vano when Vano had shot Mendez. Now Eder had a clear shot, exhaled slowly and led his aim very slightly to account for Vano's movement. Vano was at the promenade when the shot rang out and this time Eder hit his target—the round hit Vano in the chest, and he was sent reeling into the river. Maria would have been Eder's next victim, but by this time police sirens were already nearby, and Eder realized he had to leave.

Maria screamed and ran to the edge of the embankment, where she saw Vano's body slowly floating away, face down. She fell to her knees, looking from side to side. "Somebody help him, please!" But she knew it was too late and a silent, black emptiness washed over her. After what seemed like an eternity, she willed herself to stand up and begin walking south on the promenade, not wanting to lose sight of Vano's body. That's when she saw Mendez, further south down the promenade, still clutching his abdomen and staggering forward. He had heard the shot and turned to see Vano fall into the water, but he had also heard the sirens and definitely did not want to have to try and explain to the police why he had a fresh bullet wound. He fumbled for his phone and tried calling Stefan Lang, but there was no answer and, as Mendez tried to put his phone back in his coat pocket, he noticed Vano's body now floating parallel to him. Struck by the sight, and still stumbling forward, his foot unexpectedly caught on something, and he fell face forward onto the ground. His forehead struck something else hard and with an edge. It was the iron shoes—The Shoes on the Danube Promenade—that he had tripped and struck his head on. Writhing in pain and with the blood from his forehead wound now obscuring his vision, he tried to stand again but tripped on yet another iron shoe and finally tumbled into the river, oblivious at the end to the irony of what had just happened to him. His body trailed away in stillness behind Vano's, downriver towards Csepel.

Maria walked up to the point where she had seen Mendez fall in the river and stood for a while, trying to make sense of what had just happened. But the sound of police helicopters and more sirens jolted her back into the moment. She felt inside her coat to ensure the envelope was still there and then walked a block east away from the river where she slipped into the lobby of a small hotel and called for a taxi.

≈

Sára Weisz and Achille de Saint Marc had been on the phone with Sarfati for a long time. In the meantime, Maria and Uri Davidov sat silently drinking tea in the kitchen of Weisz's apartment. What had happened that afternoon hung heavy in the air and still felt almost unreal. But they knew it was true, and they also knew they didn't have the luxury yet of being able to properly mourn their dead—they had to get out of Hungary. Maria had cried until there didn't seem to be any more tears and now just felt hollow. Davidov had retreated inwardly, staring into the distance—Ben Vaknin had been a friend and a comrade-in-arms for more than twenty years.

Finally, Weisz came into the room and joined them, followed by de Saint Marc. Their presence broke the pall as Weisz announced, "I have news. Sarfati has been able to alert the Spanish and Israeli Foreign Ministries and arrangements will be made through diplomatic channels to immediately repatriate the... remains... of Vano and Ben."

"Why would the local authorities be willing to release the bodies so quickly?" Davidov asked incredulously.

"Apparently Sarfati had some names and other information that would be very embarrassing for the Hungarian administration if exposed," Weisz replied. "The Spanish and Israeli ambassadors based here in Budapest will know exactly how to use the information when they make their requests—those little chess games are their bread and butter. Now *you* are our most immediate concern," Weisz added as she looked directly at Maria.

"Why... and what about Uri?" Maria asked.

"Uri's Slovakian documents will get him out of the country and whatever video recordings there may have been of him and Achille at the Csepel building will have been destroyed along with everything else in the fire at the facility there. You, however, were undoubtedly caught on one of the security cameras at Kossuth Square and the police I'm sure are very interested in finding you and bringing you in for questioning."

"I don't want to talk to the police," Maria interjected. "This baby is going to be coming soon—I want to get out of here," she added, looking down at her protruding abdomen to emphasize the point.

"As well you should," Weisz echoed. "There are some compromised officials in the Interior Ministry and whoever killed Ben is still out there—and there's a good chance that there is a connection between the two."

"Maybe I could just go tomorrow and try to get a flight or a train out of the country?"

"Too risky—they'll likely have your name by tomorrow using facial recognition technology. All they would have to do is check the images captured at the square against cameras that are posted at immigration control points—like the airport you arrived at here. Sarfati is arranging for the French embassy in Bratislava to prepare some temporary travel documents for you using a French alias. If the Hungarian authorities put out an Interpol notice they will be looking for someone traveling with Spanish documents, so you need to leave yours here—I'll get rid of them. Achille will use my car to smuggle you across the border into Slovakia—in case they're monitoring the cameras in the train stations—and accompany you to Bratislava."

Davidov had been listening to the conversation intently and suddenly interjected, "I'd like to come along—you two could probably use an extra set of eyes."

"I was hoping you'd say that, Uri," de Saint Marc said as he walked over and put his hand on Davidov's shoulder. "And if you're up for it afterwards, Sarfati has a little job for me in Zürich, but I told him that I'd only do it if I could bring a friend along."

"Thanks for the offer, but after we get Maria to Bratislava I'm going to go hunting for whoever killed Ben," Davidov replied.

"Whoever did it is a professional, otherwise he wouldn't have been able to get the jump on Ben. You know that as well as I do. Which means he'll have gone to ground by now, especially once he discovers what happened in Csepel. It's no use trying to chase the fox through the woods my friend—better to find and root out his den," de Saint Marc added dryly.

Before Davidov could reply, Weisz's phone rang, and she stepped away again back into the other room. When she came back into the room she had an odd expression—somehow at once sad and relieved. "There's been a development," she stated matter-of-factly.

"Well… what is it?" Maria pressed.

"That was one of my 'friends' who works as a reporter for the local newspaper and who went to the scene in Csepel. She said an unidentified female body was found burned beyond recognition at what's left of the building. The investigators there think she was in some kind of storage room that had flammable chemicals inside. As tragic as that is, there may be an upside."

"What are you talking about?" Maria replied, a little horrified at what she had just heard.

"Look, Maria, we need to try and throw these people off your scent and buy you some time. This is an opportunity to do that. I can partially burn your Spanish passport and have my friend find a way to plant it at the scene and then file a story that suggests your name as the likely victim.

Then Sarfati might be able to follow that by filing a fake Interpol report that suggests the same thing—we could even have both of them include something in their write-ups that suggests the victim was pregnant. The police here will be relieved to not have the pressure on them to find you and the rats in the Interior Ministry will be feeling exposed and happy to sweep the whole thing—including the mysterious Carlos Mendez and his connection to the building in Csepel—under the carpet. Case closed, at least long enough for you to get back to Spain safely, have that baby, and figure out what's next for you."

Maria nodded reluctantly. "I suppose you're right." But it was Weisz's last few words that hit Maria the hardest. She knew her life had now changed irrevocably and that she was going to have to figure out what was 'next' for her. Vano was gone, she was going to give birth soon, and would additionally need to fix the baby's ticking mutation. She also faced the possibility that the person who had killed Ben Vaknin might eventually come looking for her.

Chapter 16: At Last

CHRISTMAS WAS AROUND THE corner, but nothing seemed festive about the season at the Amaya household in Arditurri. There were funeral preparations to attend to. Maria and her parents had come to Arditurri to help Vano's parents with finalizing the arrangements as well as dealing with the leftover legal and financial residue that are an inevitable part of the wake we leave in passing through this world. Also, after what had happened in Budapest, Maria didn't feel comfortable surfacing in San Sebastián and so had decided she would give birth in Arditurri, with Vadoma acting as a midwife. In the meantime, Vano's father had been in touch with CNI about arranging a permanent new identity and documents for Maria, but she had no idea how long that might take, or if they would even do it for her. She only knew that she already felt like a different person.

There had been several quiet and sometimes awkward dinners together, but finally, a few days before the funeral, Maria worked up the courage to tell Vano's parents the details of exactly what had happened in Paris and Budapest. While it was partly to give them closure on exactly what had happened and why, it was also a prologue of sorts to what she really wanted to say to them and to her own parents. "I have some things I've been wanting to say, but not at the service… just to the four of you, if that's okay," Maria started, once they had finished cleaning up after dinner and settled in front of the fireplace in the family room.

Maria's parents and Vano's parents all looked at one another quizzically for a moment and then nodded, almost in unison, with Vano's mother Naiara adding, "Go ahead, Maria, we're listening. We know you've been through a lot."

"Thank you, Sra. Amaya. I feel that I need to start by saying that Vano and I fell in love. I did not understand him at first, but I now realize that I also didn't completely understand myself before all of this happened. He made me proud to say that I have Romani heritage, and he showed me that I needed to open my mind and my heart to things beyond what I thought I was or tried to make myself into. And he made me realize that we have to be careful with what science can create, because there is more to the universe that what our minds and our science can comprehend or control. In his honor, I hope to go see Sara-la-Kâli[1] for the festival in May and have the baby baptized there." She then shifted in her seat self-consciously, realizing that she was also hoping, despite all of her scientific training and previous skepticism about the supernatural, that the baptism would give some extra protection to her child against

---

[1] Sara-la-Kâli – patron saint of the Romani people. An enormous Romani festival is held in her honor every May in Saintes-Maries-de-la-Mer in the south of France, where her statue is carried down from her crypt in the 9th century church there to the sea, to re-enact the legend of her arrival in France. To Christian theologians, she is 'Black Sara', an Egyptian handmaiden to Mary Magdalene and other Christians fleeing to France after Jesus' death. Some even believe she was the secret daughter of Jesus, hidden from the patriarchy for her safety. For religious historians, this 'Black Madonna' is a blending of traditions, including the manifestation of the Hindu goddess Kali, a fierce warrior of creation and destruction. In general, the legacy of the influence of Indian deities is observed in multiple Romani proverbs and customs.

the dangerous potential she knew would be part of his genetic makeup. But she was not embarrassed by her hope—she was strengthened by it.

Maria's mother clasped her hands and beamed at this revelation, though couldn't help adding, "I think it was me that first told you to think beyond your science, *alaba*, but in any event I'm glad you have taken it to heart, and I'm so happy that you will finally be going to Saintes-Maries-de-la-Mer."

"Yes, you were right, *ama*," Maria replied. "I guess I've learned that in the end you can't hide from who and what you are and that in this world there really is such a thing as good and evil... and the evil must be confronted. Someone I love... loved... helped me finally understand that."

"Here you are, Maria," Naiara said as she passed a tissue to Maria. It was only then that Maria realized that her eyes were welling up with tears.

"Thank you," Maria replied and wiped her eyes quickly. "I guess I just wanted you to know that part of the legacy that Vano left behind is the impact he had on me... for the better. He didn't leave an heir for the Amaya name, but he also made sure Mendez wouldn't either. So maybe in some sense, the other part of his legacy is that he closed the circle of the story of the two families and helped to reveal the threat posed by the Council." She paused for a moment and then finished, "Thank you for letting me open up to you and thank you for the bond that has remained between our families. I will try to be worthy of it."

An enormous and elegantly-decorated Christmas tree graced the lobby of The Dolder Grand hotel, and its halls were even decked with boughs of Holly.[2] Nevertheless, the Council had still come to meet—there was business to attend to, especially in the aftermath of the events in Budapest. Operations in most of the regions were progressing well, but when the time came to discuss Europe, the room went more still than usual. Giger cleared his throat and began. "Some of you will have already heard of our recent setbacks in Europe. The incidents in France, the compromise of some of our network in Spain, and the unfortunate imbroglio in Budapest—all I'm afraid a result of the poor judgement of the now-deceased Dr. Mendez. But we've dealt with setbacks before, and we'll soon have this one behind us as well."

There was a brief pause and then Arman Petrosian, leader of the Council's Orthodox Eurasia realm, leaned slightly forward and broke the silence. "With Mendez dead and the laboratory in Budapest destroyed, can anything be done to salvage the genetics project?"

Giger smiled inwardly—Petrosian had convincingly delivered the lines of the little performance they had together choreographed in preparation for the meeting. "The Czech protégé we assigned to Mendez—Petr Novák—is safe in a secondary facility that was already under development southwest of Budapest. He has all of the necessary technical and project particulars on his computer and Franz Eder is with him now helping to update the construction plans there to include an adjacent underground laboratory complex and enhanced security measures. So, overall, it appears we've only lost about six to nine months on our schedule. It would have been much more if I had not told Mendez

---

[2] Boughs of Holly – hanging branches, or 'boughs', from a Holly tree was believed by the Druids to bring good luck and protection and it was believed that the sharp-edged leaves would fend off evil spirits and witches when hung on doors and windows.

he had to share everything with Novák and had Franz follow up to ensure it happened."

Petrosian nodded approvingly. "That sounds encouraging. But should we be worried about potential blowback from the French and Spanish authorities?"

"Possibly. Perhaps even likely. In which case, the risk is that it becomes too much of a distraction for me at precisely the wrong time— when Franz and I need to be spending more time on the bigger picture, particularly around the prize of achieving the tipping point in North America. And so that's why I'd like you to take over operational activities in Europe for the time being Arman, in addition to your regional leadership of Orthodox Eurasia. Do you see any problem with that?"

"Of course not. Things are anyway already well in hand in my region."

"Excellent. Thank you, Arman," Giger finished. He then nodded toward Lina Bormann, and she began passing around folders that contained pro forma budget overviews for the new year. It was the last item on their agenda and most of them were looking forward to getting through it quickly so they could get back to their families in time for holiday festivities.

Just a few miles down the road from Arditurri, in the small town of Oiartzun, a group of people were entering the 17th-century *Parroquia De San Esteban* ('Parish of St. Stephen') church. From the outside, the enormous stone building looked more like a block-and-mortar medieval fortress or castle than a church. But once inside, visitors were usually overwhelmed by the towering and intricately-decorated golden altarpiece that rose more than three stories behind and above the main altar. The visitors today though, all dressed in black, were somber and their spirits were heavy. In fact, they didn't seem to take notice at all of their inspiring surroundings or the unseasonably—for early January—sunny weather outside. After their procession into the church behind the priest and Vano Amaya's casket, the visitors that day simply filed into the pews, sat, and quietly waited for the service to begin.

Naomie and Ander Guevara had joined Naiara and Guaril Amaya in the front row and clasped arms with them to try and comfort the grieving parents that were attending the funeral of their only child. Although advised against it for security reasons, Maria had been adamant that she would attend, and so had been brought in through a back entrance wearing an almost opaque black veil and a loosely fitting black dress. A few weeks from giving birth, she was so obviously pregnant though that it was hardly a disguise and so was ushered up a back staircase to a balcony seat recessed behind a latticed wooden screen. It felt to her almost like sitting in a big confessional suspended above the main hall. But instead of a priest adjacent to her, she was accompanied by one of the security detail that had accompanied Aurora Alba—the Director of CNI. Maria had met Alba earlier at the vigil and had been impressed by the woman's dignified gravitas and grace. And Maria knew that the fact that she had personally traveled from Madrid to honor Vano in this way was a symbol in and of itself of the esteem with which the Amaya family was held by the few who knew their true history.

Now seated discreetly several rows back from Vano's family, Alba had large men seated on either side of her. One was her personal bodyguard. The other was Jean-Luc Sarfati, who had come from Paris to pay his respects and also to have a private meeting with Alba after the service. There was the immediate business of course of the need to arrange an impenetrable new identity and 'life' for Maria, likely outside Europe, as well as the broader matter of planning increased cooperation between their agencies.

The service followed the traditional sequence—songs, prayers, Bible readings, Communion, more prayers, and then there was a pause as the casket was being prepared to be walked back down the center aisle and outside where the hearse was waiting. At that moment, Ander Guevara suddenly stood and cleared his throat. It was a minor departure from decorum, but no one seemed to care. Fighting the urge to look up towards Maria, he turned to Vano's parents, and, with his hand over his heart, said, "Guaril, Naiara—please forgive my interruption, but as a father, I must say this. I must declare it, here and now. Your son was a brave and a good and a kind man, and he died trying to protect my daughter. I will honor his name to my last breath… in this holy place and in front of these people, I swear this to you." Until that moment, Maria had been holding on to her emotions, but when she saw the tears streaming down her father's cheeks she dropped her head and began quietly sobbing. The CNI security agent next to her then gently put her arm through his, helped her to her feet, and carefully walked her down the stairs to the back exit of the church.

After having safely escorted Maria from Budapest to Bratislava and ensuring she had boarded and taken off on a non-stop flight back to Spain, Achille de Saint Marc and Uri Davidov had decided to take the train onwards to Zürich. They were looking forward to taking some time to decompress, get to know each other better, and chew over options for executing the mission summary Sarfati had provided. During breaks from the more serious discussions, Davidov was teaching de Saint Marc how to play Yaniv and, as they neared Salzburg, looked up and asked pensively, "Do you think Sára will be okay?"

De Saint Marc nodded confidently. "She'll be fine—she's smart, doesn't scare easily, and she's a fighter who punches above her weight. I would have liked to bring her along with me, but Sarfati said she wanted to stay and continue her work building an underground resistance organization in Hungary. They both think it's going to get worse there before it gets better."

Davidov looked up with a faux pained expression. "I thought it was me that you wanted to bring along for this little job?"

De Saint Marc triumphantly threw a winning card down and then replied teasingly, in the way that men often do with one another, "Well, you're older and definitely less attractive, but you'll have to do. But you need to make sure to focus on the game in front of you, my friend."

Davidov laughed and set down his cards in defeat. "*Oy vey*, Achille, weren't you taught to respect your elders?"

Meanwhile in Madrid and Paris, the coordinated arrests of a handful of key Council collaborators had begun, leaving them no time to alert one another. Aurora Alba and Jean-Luc Sarfati knew that this was only one small victory though—they realized now that the infestation of Council influence ran deep and wide and that the outcome of the longer struggle was far from certain.

≈

Although she knew to expect the pain, the reality of it was still more intense than anything Maria had ever experienced. It was near the end of

January, and Maria was finally giving birth, attended by Vadoma who was an experienced midwife. The decision to have a home birth had been made primarily to avoid creating hospital records of the birth and Maria's presence, but now she was glad that it would happen this way. To ensure privacy, they had decided to use a spare bedroom in the Amaya home in Arditurri, even though according to Romani traditions a dwelling was not supposed to be used for giving birth, lest it become 'unclean.' Supported by her husband—and with Vadoma promising to conduct some 'ritual cleansing' afterwards—Naiara Amaya had made the final decision and so had joined Maria's mother Naomie, who was holding Maria's hand with both of hers and coaching her breathing while Vadoma perched on a stool at the end of the bed between Maria's open legs. Although Maria was—like all first-time mothers—anxious, the calm presence of these older women comforted her. She cried out a few times from the waves of pain, but eventually it was over, and her heart leapt when she heard her *txikito* cry out for the first time as his lungs cleared and he took his first breaths. Vadoma was busy tying off and then cutting the umbilical cord as well as dealing with the placenta, so Naiara prepared the swaddling blanket to wrap the baby in while Naomie stroked her daughter's brow and smiled. "He's beautiful and healthy, Maria… congratulations, my *alaba*."

Maria squeezed her mother's hand, feeling closer to her than she could ever remember. "I'm so glad you're here with me, *ama*. I love you."

Once things had been cleaned up, the women allowed Maria's father and Guaril Amaya to come in the room and see Maria and the baby. There was the expected congratulations and small talk, and Ander Guevara even took the opportunity to reveal that he was going to give

Xavier more responsibility in running Guevara Freight so that he could take some time off and begin preparing for retirement. Maria felt a little guilty that she would not be able to help her father but was pleased with his decision. "That's a great idea, *aita*. You can trust Xavier, and Elixane will anyway be around for a while to keep an eye on things as well."

Guaril Amaya had been quietly holding a small cardboard box and finally opened it as he approached Maria. "Vano had bought this for you a few months ago as a surprise and asked us to hold on to it for him. I guess now is as good a time as any to give it to you." Inside was a pair of corduroy baby overalls with red suspenders and a handwritten card that said, 'With Love, from Vano.' He handed it to Maria, his face still heavy with grief from the loss of his son, and kissed her on the cheek, whispering, "I heard that child is special, Maria. Make his life mean something. Make Vano's sacrifice worth it." Maria smiled softly and embraced his hand, whispering in reply, "I will. I promise you." But as she turned and looked again at the baby overalls with red suspenders in the gift box, she was suddenly struck by the memory of the little boy in Le Bon Marché reading a Tintin book and smiling up at her—the little boy who was wearing red suspenders. "So *this* is that 'synchronicity'[3] thing Vano was talking about."

---

[3] Synchronicity – the theory of synchronicity was developed by Carl Jung, a Swiss psychologist who pioneered the concepts of analytical psychology. Synchronicity is a phenomenon when events are meaningfully related not by cause and effect, but by some other principle or mechanism. The Nobel-prize winning physicist Wolfgang Pauli ended up collaborating with Jung on the concept, as it resonated with some of the counter-intuitive results he was discovering in his research into quantum mechanics, like quantum entanglement (which Einstein called 'spooky action at a distance'). Jung's interpretation of Pauli's dreams during their early encounters ultimately led Pauli to the conclusion that the unconscious was a deep and unrecognized source of insights and inspiration.

≈

It was raining that Sunday afternoon in early February and Maria stood silently gazing out the window of the Amaya home in Arditurri, nursing a steaming cup of tea while she watched her baby sleep peacefully. She pulled in a deep breath and exhaled to try and dispel the anxiety she was feeling as she waited for the phone call from the CNI laboratory. She took a sip of tea, smiled at her child, and then sat down silently by his side. Meanwhile, the rain continued to patter against the window.

At 5:00 p.m. the call finally came. Maria picked up her phone and answered immediately. "Hello?"

"Hello, Señora. My name is Joaquín and I'm a forensic pathologist at a government laboratory in Madrid. I'm afraid I can't address you by your name, as it wasn't provided to me—I was only given this phone number to call. I was told you would be expecting this call?"

"Yes," Maria replied. "I've been looking forward to your call"

"I have good news—we have finished the tests and can confirm that the modification that had been introduced into the HBB gene of the subject has been successfully reversed."

"You're sure?"

"Yes. We ran the test three times to be sure."

"Thank you, Joaquín. Thank you so much," Maria replied as she ended the call, tears of relief now spilling from her eyes as she caressed the wisps of sandy blonde hair that swirled at the crown of her son's head.

Several days earlier, Director Alba had arranged for CNI and other laboratory resources to be brought to Maria so that she could perform the genetic reversal procedure using the instructions retrieved in Budapest. Fearing reprisals from the Council if his files were released, Mendez had actually turned over the instructions to Maria on that fateful day by the river, but she still didn't regret the fact that he was dead, or that the hard drive that she had handed over to him in the exchange had been empty. Her only regret was Vano. Once she had executed the genetic modification procedure several days after giving birth, it was then just a matter of Maria providing samples for the laboratory in Madrid to more definitively assess using a protocol of tests that she had already detailed for them.

The next morning, Guaril Amaya knocked lightly on the door. "Are you awake? I have some good news, Maria."

Maria had just finished feeding her baby and pulled her blouse back down over her breasts as she called out, "Yes, please come in, Sr. Amaya."

"CNI has been working with our American friends and arrangements have been made for your new identity. They have found a safe location, very far off the radar screen also in terms of public records linkages."

"Does it have to be outside Europe? America feels so far away."

"It's for the best my dear… for both of you. But don't worry, it won't be until June, so you'll still be able to make it to the festival in Saintes-Maries-de-la-Mer this May—your parents and Naiara and I are also thinking about going with you, to make sure you're safe and to help with the baby."

"Thank you so much for remembering that, Sr. Amaya. Where in America am I going to be hidden away?"

"In the state of New Mexico, but within the autonomous Navajo Nation tribal land there. The name of the small town where you will live is actually also called 'Navajo,' and they have arranged that you will be a science teacher at the high school that serves the region. They will make it look like you are transferring in from another state."

"What will the locals be told about me?"

"They'll be told you were originally a Navajo orphan who was adopted and raised by a White family. Your cover story for moving to the reservation will be that you now want to try and reconnect with and contribute to the Navajo culture and learn the language."

"I assume I won't be able to use my real name?"

"That would be unwise. Our American friends have anyway already started preparing identity documents for you, including a birth certificate. Your Navajo—actually they call themselves *Diné*—name will be Haseya Nakai. Both fairly common names among their tribe—all part of helping you to blend in."

"Does the name mean anything?"

"I looked it up for you—Haseya means 'she rises' and Nakai means 'one who wanders,' so it's somewhat fitting, don't you think?"

"Yes, I suppose," Maria replied and then added, glancing down at her baby, "What about him, can I choose his first name at least?"

"That's why I came to see you—they need a first name to put on the birth certificate that they're preparing for him. I assume you had something more permanent than *txikito* in mind?"

"I did, but I guess I was afraid to say it out loud until I was sure he would survive."

Guaril then began speaking as he was writing. "So then. Male. Born January 27th, 2032. Last name, Nakai. First name?"

Maria reached down and picked up her baby, bringing his face close to hers, and then finally declared as she looked deep into his eyes, "I will call you Immanuel."

— THE END —

About AJ Hooks

After growing up in California and Nevada, some peripatetic college years and a stint in the Army's 82nd Airborne Division in North Carolina, Andrew went on to a career in the energy industry. Eventually he spent 20 years living and working abroad, including in Europe, Africa and Asia, and in 2018 finally returned to the US, where he currently resides with his wife (of 34 years) in Houston. *Eugenesis: Inception* is Andrew's debut novel, inspired by his love of storytelling and the tapestry of cultures and experiences he encountered in his travels. In addition to writing, he is a voracious reader, a mentor in the Big Brothers/Big Sisters of America organization, a lover (and occasional collector) of art, and remains an avid and curious traveler. Andrew is also the proud father of a talented songwriter-singer (Kira) who currently resides in the San Francisco area.